Praise for The Black Swan Files

AWARDS

GLIMMER, Winner
IPPY Gold Medal
Best Young Adult E-book, Independent Publisher Awards

GLISTEN, Winner
Best Young Adult Fiction, Pinnacle Book Achievement
Award
The Write Touch Readers Award

GLISTEN, 2nd Place
Best Young Adult Fiction, eLit Book Awards
Best Young Adult Romance, Book Buyers Best Award
Best Young Adult Paranormal, YARWA Athena Contest

GLISTEN, Finalist
Best Genre Fiction, North Street Book Prize
Best Paranormal, The Daphne du Maurier Award for Excellence in Mystery/Suspense
Best Young Adult, The Maggie Award for Excellence

The Black Swan Files
001: GLIMMER

"*Glimmer* is a thrilling adventure set in the near future and it completely took me by surprise! I highly recommend it!"
~Sarah Palmer, **YA Love Magazine**

"I loved this story. If you love books with telekinesis, secret government agencies, and superhero powers, then this book is for you…*Glimmer* is like James Bond meets X-Men!"
~Benjamin Alderson, **Benjaminoftomes** Booktube Channel

"*Glimmer* was super intense. So fast-paced you did not want to put the book down. A gripping novel…it will keep readers on the edge of their seat. You will not be disappointed!"
~Nicole and Marija, **Let's Talk Books** Booktube Channel

"HOLY FREAKING MOTHER OF GOD! IT WAS AWE-SOME. Spy story + Prison break + Science Fiction = Best combo ever!"
~Uma Shankari, **Books.Bags.Burgers.**

"Great, innovative storyline with edge-of-seat action while still managing to tug on the heartstrings. A dystopian gem!"
~ **USA TODAY Bestselling Author**, Lynne Marshall

"Incredible! It will leave you begging for more!"
~Maureen Moyes, **MoMo's Book Diary**

"YA readers will love this book. The plot is full of twists and turns, conspiracy theories, and lots of action. Written with snappy dialogue and thrilling action sequences, *Glimmer* kept me hooked to the very end."
~Melanie Thompson, **Librarian**

The Black Swan Files
002: GLISTEN

"*Glisten* had me laughing out loud and on the verge of tears. It is a hard novel to put down! Just as enjoyable, thrilling and emotional as its predecessor."
~Sarah Palmer, **Confessions of a Lit Addict**

"Fast paced, exciting and emotional! *Glisten* is the perfect sequel to *Glimmer* and will have readers rooting for the brilliantly written characters."
~Uma Shankari, **Books.Bags.Burgers.**

"This fast-paced adventure features a uniquely gifted young woman whose power is enhanced by the bonds of friendship."
~**USA TODAY Bestselling Author**, Maureen A. Miller

"Ms. Cerrone packs action, adventure, and intrigue into the second installment of The Black Swan Files, *Glisten*—balanced by friends, family, and first love—a winning combination."
~ **USA TODAY Bestselling Author**, Lynne Marshall

THE BLACK SWAN FILES

002: GLISTEN

TRICIA CERRONE

Published by Mystic Butterfly, Inc.

The Black Swan Files is an official Trademark.

ISBN: 978-1-938258-15-2 (trade paperback)

ISBN: 978-1-938258-16-9 (ebook)

Cover design by Mark Harris, Harris Graphic Services

DEDICATION

For Andrew

ACKNOWLEDGMENTS

It seems like the right people always appear in my life to help each book come to fruition. I would like to thank my trusted story editor, Janet Maarschalk—who found the time to edit, miraculously, in between her deliverables as Lynne Marshall, and as always gave insightful comments that made my book better. Many thanks to my early reviewers: Maureen A. Miller, Sarah Palmer, and Uma Shankari. Special thanks to my Beta Reader and early adopter, David Katzman.

I especially want to thank all the readers who support this series, and the many who have taken the time to post positive reviews. Enjoy!

WHO'S WHO IN THE BLACK SWAN FILES

Jocelyn Esperanza Albrecht (Marques): a.k.a. Sunnie Cashus, a.k.a. Project Sunday, a.k.a. The Black Swan—TOP SECRET

Georgie: College freshman, super sleuth, and crusader for justice

Brittany: Georgie's best friend, expert "maker" and sustainable fashion designer

Lena: Passionate cryptologist, budding hacktivist, and pie connoisseur

Graeme: Software entrepreneur, softhearted protector, and tenacious truth-seeker

Seth: Social outcast, smooth-talking survivor, and a former experiment at Camp Holliwell

Alastair: Georgie's cousin, former Army Ranger, and general badass

Richie: Al's Army buddy, mechanical genius, and Holliwell survivor

Medina: Jocelyn's former military handler, fierce rule-keeper, and tortured soldier

Morgan: Graeme's foster sister, entitled heiress, and Jocelyn's real sister

Benny: Graeme's foster brother, Jocelyn's real brother, and unabashed charmer

John: Dedicated cop, devoted dad, and silent gun collector

Kymber: Head nurse, protective mom, and anxious muncher of sweets

Sabrina: Medical doctor, determined researcher, Benny's aunt and last hope

Laurence Cashus: Jocelyn's former guardian, neuropsychiatrist, and lead scientist on the now closed file—Project Sunday

Jerry Ramstein: The President's top advisor and Secretary of Information of the United States of America, or SOI

Camp Holliwell: Camp Holliwell is a United States Government, Science and Military facility located in the Virginian mountains, specializing in solutions to humankind's greatest issues. The New York Times Square Office is an East Coast branch and secret location. Holliwell's motto: *Science, Technology, Service.*

TABLE OF CONTENTS

002: GLISTEN

CHAPTER ONE

$\mathcal{F}$amily.

Just the word made her throat constrict and her chest tighten. It wasn't a bad feeling—just one filled with longing and anticipation…and perhaps a little anxiousness. She shrugged her shoulders to loosen up. She would deal with the anxiety later.

Right now she was an hour from civilization on the Appalachian Trail. With every step she slowly got closer to New York, closer to her family, and closer to the future that she dreamed was now possible.

Jocelyn had been off the grid for the last two months after leaving Texas and her friend Seth. She followed all his rules for anonymity and had been careful not to be seen or heard while she planned her next moves—until she encountered *them*.

They were a family—mom, dad, daughter, son. Their voices carried through the thick greenery of trees and brush and rock. She recognized from a distant part of her childhood the familiar sounds of parental affection as the boy asked endless questions and they answered patiently, a smile in their voices. The sister added her occasional expertise, albeit with an impatient sigh when it led to yet another question.

Jocelyn caught glimpses of them at points in the trail. The dad was bald, lean and tough looking. The mom was Asian

American and fell on the petite side. The kids were a cute mix of both parents. The boy sounded young, maybe six. The older sister had talked about what she wanted for her twelfth birthday so she was eleven—just a year older than Jocelyn's little brother, Benjamin.

It didn't require extra-sensory abilities to detect the warmth between them or know why she was so curious about them. They represented everything she had lost.

And right now, they were the one thing between her and getting it back.

The sound of the girl's whimper made Jocelyn bite her lip hard. Safety meant not getting involved. It wasn't her fault the girl tripped and broke her ankle.

She assessed the evening sky. They had an hour more of sunlight. Closing her eyes, she took a slow breath and listened—not to the family, but to the three men behind her. They treaded steadily, with no interest in stopping for the night, and had been slowly gaining on the family all afternoon.

She pulled out the Wanted poster she'd taken at the hiking post six days ago and studied it. A lot of people had been deterred from venturing too far into the mountains. The man at the ranger station had been explicit about the danger and how these men tortured their victims. A chill went down her spine at the memory.

She studied the warning with the pictures of the three men side by side, trying to decide if the Butcher, Weasel, and Rabbit were really on a killing rampage, or if they would just hike past the family and not be bothered.

She folded the poster and shoved it in her pack.

They liked girls.

Alone she could easily outdistance them. The family traveled at a slower pace, and now they were stopped.

Therein lies the dilemma.

She knew the difference between good people and bad people. But then there were evil people. The Butcher would not leave the family alone.

The question—what was she going to do about it?

It would be better to get through this part of the country without being seen.

She took note of her surroundings and options. The three men would be upon her soon. She hiked as close as she could to the family without alerting them to her presence, then set off from the trail into the woods. Covering her small pack under some brush, she watched and waited.

Finally, they arrived.

"Shush." The Butcher held up a hand, offering his friends a twisted grin. Motioning for them to wait, he crept up the trail with surprising silence for a giant his size. Jocelyn didn't move and hardly breathed as she watched and waited. He returned with the report in minutes. "One for each of us. Just need to take out the alpha."

The alpha meant the dad. She didn't want to contemplate what he meant when he said there was one for each of them. Descriptions of how the Butcher got his name had given her nightmares on the trail and made her extra diligent.

She took a slow breath. With any luck she could stop them before they struck.

The Butcher sent Rabbit into the woods behind her to track them from the side. Weasel would take up the rear while the Butcher walked right past the family to the front, blocking them on all sides. Jocelyn appreciated the plan. And divided, she had a much better chance to make them fall.

Rabbit scurried through the woods not nearly as silent as his comrades. He wasn't expecting anyone to be there so he didn't notice her hidden behind a tree, her green and brown, trail-worn clothing blending in with her surroundings.

He walked right by her.

She took one step forward before the meat of her hand chopped him hard on the back of the neck and sent him forward. She let him fall.

Searching his pockets she found zip ties. She quickly bound one hand to each foot and stretched his body around the nearest tree before connecting the limbs with another zip tie, to keep him from crawling away. Pulling a nasty bandana from his pocket, she pinched his nose and pulled back, shoving the material into his mouth. The ickiness of touching him made her shiver a little despite the heat.

The Butcher's voice got her attention. He had reached the family.

"Hey, purty gurl. You look hurt." He offered to help.

Jocelyn swallowed a breath. The father sounded suspicious but answered nonchalantly.

"We're good, thanks. An ambulance is going to meet us at the end of the trail."

"Really?" the Butcher said. "That's some reception you have. No one ever gets anything out here. Mighty lucky for you."

The father didn't miss a beat. "Yep."

"Well, I think I'll take a breather myself. Nice place for a stop."

Jocelyn didn't hear a response. Calming her own nerves, she listened, smelled, and searched. She needed to locate Weasel.

Heartbeats raced. The parents, she thought. They didn't trust the Butcher. Breathing deeply she picked up the scent of Weasel—musky, overheated, sour, and just ahead.

She slowly made her way to the trail.

That's when she saw them.

Weasel holding a little boy, his feet dangling as he tried to kick free, his mouth covered.

Outstanding. When did that happen? Had the boy wandered off?

The mother let out a surprised cry getting her husband's attention and fury. He made a move toward his son, then froze when the Butcher snatched his wife and held a knife to her throat—a giant butcher knife. Jocelyn mentally cursed. His signature weapon.

Jocelyn couldn't see the girl but heard her outraged gasp mixed with fear.

New plan.

Jocelyn pulled her beanie tighter over the blond wig and jumped out from the trees and onto the trail. Nothing like the element of surprise.

"Hi!" she said. Weasel and Butcher blinked. She stepped right up to Weasel and put her hand over the bare forearm holding the boy in place. She met the boy's eyes for a brief moment. He was wide-eyed with confusion and terror.

Weasel stepped back holding his prize tighter, just as confused as the boy for a moment.

"He looks a little uncomfortable," Jocelyn said. "How about letting him go?"

Weasel recovered from the shock and gave her a look-over. "Where'd—?"

Jocelyn didn't let him finish. She sent a shot of focused heat through her hand onto his arm. In a split second he jolted in pain and dropped the boy. She caught the kid and swung him backward, off to the side of the trail with an order. "Stay down!"

Weasel reached. She punched hard, twice to the head, then kicked low and fierce to the kneecap. His knee crunched just before he wailed and fell forward into her fist.

The click of a trigger alerted her. She spun as the father pulled a gun and aimed at Weasel. The Butcher pulled the woman into a choke with one arm and launched his knife at the alpha just as the gun exploded three times.

The girl screamed.

Jocelyn threw her hand up instinctively and shot a field of energy toward the father.

The large blade deflected seconds from impact and flew off course sideways. She turned her attention to Butcher. Overcoming his temporary surprise, he went on the attack, reaching for a weapon at his ankle. Hindered by the woman's struggles, he finally tossed her hard to the ground and claimed his gun.

Not gonna happen.

She sped down the narrow trail, leapt the prone girl, and with one strong push launched off a stone and straight at the Butcher.

He pulled the trigger.

Dust swirled around her and trees whipped restlessly at the sudden rush of wind. She led with a defensive blast of energy that knocked him back. The bullet flew askew, and the gun shot into the air as her fist landed in his throat.

He flew backward from the impact, landing headfirst down the steps in the trail. Flying with him, she landed hands first, pushed off the ground, and somersaulted to her feet further past him. Gaining her balance, she spun back around with a heel kick to his temple as he tried to sit up. Before he could lift his head again, she did it for him and slammed it down twice, on solid rock.

It wasn't enough.

He was strong and powered with adrenaline. She under-estimated that.

Using the angle, he rolled his feet backward over his head and kicked her in the cheek, mostly from dumb luck. The gun had fallen from his grip, but now he had another knife—this one a sharp six-inch blade. She grabbed his wrist, using both hands to force him to release the knife. His wrist was thick and seemed as invulnerable as the rest of him.

Giving it everything she had, she sent a hot streak to pierce his hold. It didn't affect him immediately. In fact, it seemed to make him angry. His opposite knee lifted to her ribs and she turned to avoid it. He grabbed at her head and tore off her beanie and wig in one swipe. His moment of surprise gave her the second she needed.

She maneuvered to grip his index finger and broke it as he in turn used his weight to wrestle her to the ground. She rolled with the force coming at her, kicked a leg up into his stomach, and with all her formidable strength, launched him over her head, through the air, and onto his back about thirty feet down the path.

She ran over to him. *Finally enough.* He was temporarily unconscious.

She didn't waste time but patted him down, removing everything from his pockets. He had more knives and a dozen zip ties. She debated the best options, looking for a tree to secure him. It was then that she saw the father on the steps above her, gun still in hand. He looked ready to kill.

"How did you—"

"He's out. Likely only for a moment," she interrupted.

The man studied her, not trusting right away. She guessed she appeared as frightening as their attackers with her bald head and weeks of traveling in the forest. Then there was the possibility that her eyes and skin had turned a little blue after using her powers. She could bio-transmit the energy around her, but it came at a cost comparable to the energy expended. She hoped what her friend Seth had teasingly called "alien face," was in check. She looked for her wig and beanie. Nowhere in sight. She'd find them in a minute.

The Butcher moved his head. That's when the man came closer and with the butt of his gun beat the Butcher in the skull until he was out again. Jocelyn watched as he flipped the gun back in his hand and aimed it at the unconscious man.

"These are the ones you kill," he said.

Jocelyn wasn't sure she understood. She waited to see what he would do. Finally, he holstered the gun under his flannel shirt.

She held up the zip ties.

"Geez," he muttered. "I don't want to think what would have happened." He rubbed his face with a hand.

"John!" the woman called.

"Kymber! Stay with the kids. I'm okay. Be right there!"

"Okay. We're fine. We're all fine."

Jocelyn thought Kymber sounded anything but fine.

"Help me drag him to this tree," Jocelyn said. She lifted the Butcher's feet while the man grabbed under the shoulders, grunting at the Butcher's weight. They made quick work of sitting him so his legs and arms hugged the tree, then used every single zip tie in various formations to make sure he couldn't get loose. She'd never come across a man this big, except maybe her old guard at Camp Holliwell. She hoped the ties would suffice.

Finally satisfied, the man turned to her. "Are you okay?"

She nodded, touching her scalp self-consciously. Convinced, he ran back to his family. She followed, recovered her wig and beanie on the way, and hurriedly put them back in place before joining the foursome. The mother gripped her children close, not letting them see the body of Weasel.

He was dead from what she could tell.

The husband encircled his little family and didn't let go. At her footsteps, he released them. He was forty at the most, she guessed. And in the military or something. She could always pick that out.

Kymber was slim, pretty, and kind looking—if a bit upset at the moment. The kids peeked up at her as she passed.

She kept walking, letting them have a moment of privacy.

She tried not to look at Weasel as she continued up the trail and off the path.

"Where are you going?" the father asked.

She turned to him. "I left one up here. Near my pack."

"Oh my God." The mother wiped her tears, fearing it wasn't over.

"Geezus." The father leapt to his feet, joining her. "Who are you?"

"I overheard them," she explained, deflecting his question. "I knew you weren't safe." She didn't say any more, just turned into the woods. He followed her and they found Rabbit trying to get loose. John punched him senseless with new fury then helped her drag Rabbit out to the trail. They zip tied Rabbit to Weasel with a tree between them. Rabbit would have a shock when he woke up.

Jocelyn grabbed her pack and searched out the Wanted poster. "I saw this. I knew who they were." She unfolded the paper, put it by Rabbit, and stuck a big rock on top to hold it in place in case any random hikers thought to help him escape.

She saw the father's hand go to his gun. The man stared at the poster a long time. They were serial killers. Wanted dead or alive.

She thought the dead part tempted him.

Instead, he took out his phone and took pictures with his camera. "Evidence," he explained.

Finally he put his camera away and reached out a hand to her. "I don't know where you came from, but we owe you a world of thanks. I'm John Morrow."

Jocelyn hesitated. She'd been hiding from the military, the police, the government, and a collection of psychotic scientists since she'd escaped Camp Holliwell. This man was definitely one of the above. He had a sense of authority and toughness. He was also in protection mode. Not what Jocelyn needed.

Stumbling a little, she accepted the hand. "Uh, hi."

He kept hold, his grip strong as he prompted, "You got a name?"

"Uh—" She said the first name she could think of. "I'm, uh—Georgie."

His head tilted and his eyes narrowed. She pulled her hand away and went to her pack, breaking eye contact.

"Georgie?"

"Uh-huh."

"Got a last name?"

"Are you in the military?"

"Used to be. Now I'm NYPD."

"NYPD?"

"New York Police Department."

"Oh." *Not good.* She pulled her beanie lower over her face. She was headed to New York. What if he found out about her and then tried to track her? She bit her lip, anxious again.

"Yeah. So I'm pretty good at detecting lies."

"Is that a police thing?"

"Yeah. And a dad thing."

She took that under consideration. "It's an hour-long hike and it's getting dark."

He nodded slowly, still staring at her. "Okay, Georgie it is." He led her back to the others. "Come meet the family."

CHAPTER TWO

*J*ohn wanted to ask a dozen questions but held back. The girl was skittish, but she had saved his life and his family's so he cut her some slack. Besides, he knew his kids would probably ask most of the questions for him once they recovered from their state of shock.

Kymber gained her composure enough to check the girl's temple where she'd been hit and gave her a baby wipe to clean it. Max unabashedly hugged the girl around her legs so she couldn't move. She looked down at him in surprise, then patiently, if awkwardly, patted his head.

John reloaded his gun and holstered it under his flannel.

Maddie, who had been watching everything and probably saw more than he would have liked, seemed the least upset. "You saved us! How did you do that? That knife almost hit my dad, then it didn't and you totally took that creeper down. Do you take martial arts?"

The girl stared at Maddie. "Uh…yes. Is your ankle okay?"

"It's broken. It hurts really bad. But I'm so freaked out right now, I can barely feel it!" She continued, undeterred. "Which one?"

"Which what?" The girl scavenged in her worn backpack for something, then pulled out a bag of fresh-smelling jerky.

"Which martial art?" Maddie asked.

"Oh. Uh, all of them."

"Like karate?"

"Uh-huh."

"And like Muay Thai?" His daughter liked details.

"Uh-huh."

"And like tae kwon do and jiujitsu?"

"Yes and yes. But never let someone take you down to where you need jiujitsu."

Maddie's mouth shaped into a frozen "Oh." She raised her brows to him as if to say she wasn't so sure about this one. "That explains it then."

The girl, Georgie, if that really was her name, went to the biggest pack, tied hers onto it, then hoisted. "We should get moving. Can you carry Maddie?"

"Yes." She was focused. And she was right. None of them would breathe easy until they were back in civilization and the police had these killers locked up.

Kymber and Max took her cue and put their packs on.

John helped Maddie up and carried her on his back. He took up the rear but stayed close.

Max hurried to keep up with their new companion. "Is that a rabbit skin on your pack?" Max asked. He reached out to touch it.

"Yes."

"Did you kill it?" Maddie asked, sounding a little horrified.

"Yes."

"Why?" she asked.

"I was hungry and it tastes better than squirrel."

"OMG," Maddie whispered loudly in John's ear. "Dad!" He smiled a little. His nerves were shot, his stomach still clenched ready to kill, and his kids had moved on. He should be grateful they were easily distracted.

"Have you eaten squirrel lately?" Maddie called out.

"Not this trip. Lots of rabbits out here."

Max looked backward in awe and nearly tripped. The girl, alert, caught him by the top of his small pack and righted him. "Don't worry. I only eat the ugly ones."

Max nodded as if that was okay with him. He kept glancing up at the girl like she was a new being from outer space. "Are you hiking all alone?" he asked.

"Yes."

"My dad says that's not safe. You should always have a hiking buddy."

"That makes sense."

"How come you don't?"

"Uh…I like the peace and quiet. No one talking all the time." She saw her opportunity and added, "Or asking lots of questions."

Max shook his head. "Sounds boring."

"Max," Kymber's voice chided.

"Sorry. I don't think you're boring. Do your mom and dad know you're hiking alone? Do you have to call them and check in? That would be safer."

Silence.

No one said anything. His family seemed to sense Max had hit on something. They walked on for ten more minutes before Maddie finally ventured, "Are your mom and dad alive?"

The girl hoisted the heavy pack to reposition it a little before answering, "No."

"Let's take a water break," John said.

They stopped and Kymber pulled out some quick snacks. They were all still in shock, tired from the long day, and needed a pick-me-up. They shared the last two peanut butter and jelly sandwiches, giving the girl a half, which she devoured.

"That was good."

"Are you hungry?" Kymber asked.

She nodded.

"You can have the last of the cookies. A little sugar will help. I have some apples too. It will lighten my load if you eat them."

Georgie studied the cookies hesitantly before taking one. She bit into it and her eyes went wide. "That's really good."

Max grabbed the last one and shoved it into his mouth. "I know, right?" Crumbs flew from his mouth. "Homemade."

"I never had anything like this. Not that I remember." She seemed about to say more, then stopped.

John pulled out his phone and tested. "I got reception."

"Thank God!" Kymber rejoiced.

John walked down the path away from the group to make the call. He didn't want his family to relive what they had been through. He quickly got the police mobilized. They were sending the FBI too, since the crimes spanned more than one state, and an ambulance would be waiting for Maddie. He felt one step closer to safety. It would take thirty to forty minutes for emergency personnel to reach them so they needed to keep going. He wouldn't rest tonight until the Butcher was in custody, and his family ensconced in a hotel with protection.

When he returned to the group, he told Kymber the news and Georgie looked even more skittish. Interesting. What was she hiding from?

They set off with renewed energy. Max made it about ten more minutes before he stumbled again, this time from tiredness. Before he could hit the ground he was scooped up into the girl's arms. Quietly she carried him the rest of the way while Max made himself comfortable, resting his head in her neck to avoid the bouncing pack. John knew his pack was heavy, but she didn't complain once. And now she carried his son.

They finally reached the spot where the path widened. It was flat the rest of the way. John and Kymber joined them to walk side by side.

"When did your parents die, Georgie?" Max asked. His son was up for conversation again now that he had a ride.

"About ten years ago."

"Do you miss them?"

"Yes."

"I'm sorry they died." Max gave her a squeeze around the neck.

"Thank you."

His son continued, clearly concerned about her being alone. "Do you have any brothers or sisters?"

"Yes, one of each. I'm going to see them soon…I hope."

"You do? That's good," Max said.

"Maybe. They're younger. They were put with a family after my parents died and I haven't seen them since." She paused. "So I'm not sure they'll want to see me. Maybe they won't."

Kymber jumped in. "I'm sure they will!"

"I would want to see you," Maddie stated, adamant.

"It will be a lot to take in so you might have to give them space to get to know you," Kymber advised. "But in time, you'll see."

John kept silent, still cautious. His whole family rooted for her. It was hard not to. She was alone and she had just saved their lives. It made her interesting to them, something John was very careful not to get caught up in.

They hadn't seen her face, witnessed the odd blue in her eyes, or seen the barren scalp that made her look part cancer victim, part alien avenger. He shook his head. Someone with martial arts training could have done what she did. And maybe his angle on the path created an optical illusion. That made more sense. She couldn't have possibly jumped the distance he thought she did. He'd been caught up in the adrenaline. It distorted one's perspective. As a cop, he knew that.

He glanced at the girl again to see her face. She watched the path, thoughtful, still holding his son who had his arms around her neck like he planned on keeping her.

The evening crickets began to chirp and the night was silent when her head popped up.

"Sirens," she said. "Just a couple more minutes."

John didn't hear anything. Minutes later he did.

An ambulance with a bunch of police cars made their way down the narrow dirt road. He took a slow breath, still not relieved, but maintaining his calm.

"Hallelujah!" Maddie said. "I need pain medication!"

His wife agreed wearily. "I think we all do."

"Kymber, take everyone with you to the hospital. Call me with the address and I'll meet you there. The wrap-up might take a while," he said, referring to the earlier attack.

"Georgie, are you coming with us?" Max asked.

"Um."

His wife intervened. "The police probably need to talk with her, honey."

The girl's eyes brightened in panic when she turned to him in question. He didn't need to be a cop or a dad to see she was ready to bolt.

"Kymber, why don't you take Georgie with you. She's had enough for one day. Plenty of time to deal with all that later."

Relief washed over her face. Kymber saw it as well.

"Of course. We'll treat you to a good meal tonight. It's the least we can do."

The chain of cars grew. Whatever she was afraid of, John wasn't about to throw her to the wolves. "Go with Kymber. There's going to be a lot of questions."

She nodded. "Thank you."

We'll talk at dinner, he promised himself.

In no time his family and the girl were loaded into the emergency vehicle, despite the EMT's reluctance about crowding. Police and FBI flooded the area.

It was many hours later, sitting in a small office with bad coffee and trying to extricate himself from the local Chief of Police and a growing media circus, that he saw the Missing poster. His hunch had been right. Her name wasn't Georgie.

Yet another FBI Special Agent needed his statement, only this one wanted to know more about the hiker who had helped them. The hairs on his neck stood alert as the man scrolled through photos of missing girls.

It said Sunday Cashus, aka Sunnie. Might also be going by Jocelyn. Do not approach. Five hundred thousand reward to anyone with information leading to her recovery.

Do not approach?

He crushed the agent's business card in his hand. Something was not right about that. Sure, she might have commando instincts, but she hadn't seemed threatening, just afraid of being seen—especially by the authorities. She'd been jittery for that very reason, but she'd helped his family anyway. She'd carried his son for an hour like he was her own child. She could have left them all for dead.

Who could possibly want her back so badly that they had a half a million-dollar reward for information? And more concerning, why was she so afraid of being found?

"How old did you say?" Special Agent Newell was persistent.

John shook his head. Something about this man made him not want to be helpful. His cop instincts said the girl was the one who needed protection. "Twenty to twenty-five, maybe." Okay, a stretch, but possible.

"And blond?"

"That's right. Short blond hair." John wanted to get this over and get to his family. He knew the routine, he just didn't like being on the other end of it. This agent was like a dog with a bone. John added with a false, helpful tone, "And short, about your height."

The man smiled at the passive aggressive insult. "You said in your earlier statement she jumped out from the trees?"

"From the side of the path."

"Hmm. That's right. You said she came from off the side of the path. And hit him in the face?"

"That's what I recall. My eyes were on my wife. When I turned she was there."

"Interesting. She must have been strong to disarm him."

"I didn't see it all."

"Real lucky to have a Good Samaritan who knew what she was doing. A girl too. She went to the hospital, how long ago?"

John's protective instincts flared, but he kept his voice low and even. "I said a woman, about twenty to twenty-five. She'd just been in a nasty, terrifying fight. She was in as much shock as my family. If you have anything else, you can reach her at the hospital."

"If I could find her, I would."

John stopped. "What do you mean?"

"We sent people to the hospital, but your wife said she already left. Perhaps her injuries weren't so bad after all."

John got up, resisting the urge to check his phone for messages. "Not really my business."

"A lone, female hiker. Have another look." He held up the device with the photo of the attractive teenager.

John examined the picture again and shook his head. "The woman who helped us was not a missing person, and I can honestly say looked nothing like that."

Special Agent Newell eyed him critically. "I wouldn't want to have to arrest one of New York's finest for lying to a federal officer, Lieutenant Morrow. It is Lieutenant, isn't it? Working your way up the ranks?"

John got up. "Threats generally don't work with me. If you need more information you can call me tomorrow."

"I'll want to talk to your family."

"My kids are off limits. You can talk to my wife after she's had a good night's sleep."

"I'll look forward to meeting Nurse Kymber," he said.

John's creep factor went up a notch. The agent deliberately goaded him by letting John know he already had a fact sheet on his wife.

He left without so much as a nod and made some quick rounds before checking out.

The chief entertained the press outside, answering questions. The Butcher was behind bars, and John's family needed him. Everything else could wait. He headed to the small police lot out back and checked his phone once inside his rental SUV. Other than the earlier text update on Maddie's cast, there was only a voicemail from Kymber to call when he could.

He took a breath. Half a million dollars. For a girl who wasn't missing. Hiding maybe, but definitely not missing.

He called his wife, comforted by the calm sound of her voice.

"Hey, baby," she greeted. "There's a diner at the hotel. We're headed there now. Are you done?"

"For tonight," John said. "I'll meet you there. What happened to the girl?"

Kymber sighed. "She was here one minute then gone the next. There were a lot of cops here for our protection—professional courtesy and all. Plus some media tried to find us. I think it freaked her out. The kids are a little upset about it. I told them she could take care of herself. But—"

"I know," John said.

"I wish she'd let us help her. She saved our lives today, John. I saw photos on the news of other victims." Her voice trembled. "I can't—"

"I know. Don't think about it right now. Get some food and I'll fill you in later. I'll be with you soon. I promise."

John put his phone away, more than a little unsettled. The picture of the girl had shown a young beauty with long, dark hair and innocent, bright blue eyes. His hiker had seen better days, but there was no mistaking the eyes. Whatever she was running from, she didn't want to be found, and those eyes had lost some of the innocence. Anyone offering that much money for someone who didn't want to be found could not be up to anything good.

But half a million dollars…it wouldn't be long before someone made the connection.

CHAPTER THREE

ocelyn adjusted her pack and hustled to keep up with the crowd scurrying off the train at their final stop—New York City. She took a breath, walking along the train platform into the terminal.

Once inside, everything changed.

Instead of the scent of oil, grease, and train tracks there was coffee, sweets, and something she thought might be pizza. She hadn't had enough pizza yet to be sure, but it made her mouth water and her stomach grumble.

The hallway from the tracks into the building shined with warm golden tile. There were plaques on the walls with names of people on them, interesting rectangular wall lamps, and gigantic chandeliers. Her head rubbernecked as she tried to take it all in. She would need to learn what they called this style. Awesome or outstanding seemed appropriate. Whatever it was, it made her smile.

She'd arrived.

She kept walking, following an older woman who strode with confidence.

The crowded hall opened into an enormous, truly grand space, and sound flooded her being like the cacophony of an orchestra tuning instruments. A giant American flag hung from the center, and three humongous windows let in light at the opposite end. Everything was super-sized.

Wow. This must be why it was called Grand Central Station.

It was definitely as big, or bigger, than the open-air entrance to the biology building or the lobby of the optics building at Camp Holliwell. But any similarity ended there.

Where the buildings at Camp Holliwell were about clean lines, cold emotions, and frightening research—this felt human. Hundreds of people—all different in dress, hair, color, attitude, even language—rushed to their next destination, crisscrossing chaotically without ever running into each other.

Jocelyn took a breath and rushed in as well. It was exhilarating!

She was nearly to the Information Booth in the center when she heard a single voice in the crowd begin to sing.

Jocelyn searched, curious, and realized other people heard it too. She stopped not far from the sound and turned as another voice on the stairs by the wall began to sing, and five young people dressed in regular clothes stepped in synchronicity behind the girl, singing in harmony with her. It sounded beautiful and melancholic, and suddenly people cleared a path allowing the singers to meet each other.

Jocelyn watched in awe with the rest of the crowd at this surprise event. Just as surprising were the twenty dancers that jumped in from behind everyone and began spinning and flipping and shaking to a version of the music that was now more hip-hop than orchestrated. It seemed like the two sides were competing, but then they sang together—perfectly in their own styles. It was so beautiful and hopeful, and they sang so much of what was in Jocelyn's heart that she thought it must be a sign that she was meant to be here, and her struggles were over, and maybe her family would be happy to see her and welcome her home.

Her eyes burned with the memories that haunted her since she escaped Camp Holliwell. She wouldn't be here today without Medina's help. She didn't know if her handler and fellow super-soldier got away or got caught. She probably never would. Some sacrifices were complete. She wouldn't waste the time he'd given her. She knew him well enough to know that would *really* piss him off.

Thankfully, in her one communication from Georgie, she knew everyone else was okay. It had been her only comfort during more difficult nights.

Things were better now. Jocelyn took a deep breath. The music built to a frenzied finale, filling her with excitement, hope, and energy. *This is a good sign.*

Then a voice announced that if you liked what you heard, tickets were on sale for a new and modern revival off Broadway.

Jocelyn felt dazed as she took a flyer, aching to hear the music again. She needed to find "Off Broadway."

Reality hit when everyone went back to rushing, and in addition to being lost, she also felt a little like she didn't fit in with her dirty hiking shorts, T-shirt, and pack. Fortunately, she'd tossed the animal skins at the last stop. One good thing was that she was pretty unrecognizable with her blond wig and Longhorns ball cap.

She found a map of the city at the information booth and, after more than a few wrong turns, made it outside to the street.

A whole new sound and smell assaulted her there. Sewer stench wafted around her. White bags of trash lined the street up to nine feet high. A subway train made the ground below her tremble as hot air shot up. The noise of traffic and the voices of a million or more people were denser and more deafening than anything she could have expected or imagined. Her initial excitement turned to panic. This was the biggest city she'd ever been to—at least where she'd been allowed to walk freely. She could turn and go anywhere. Instead, she froze next to a tower of trash.

Jocelyn took another deep breath and regretted it. "Phew!" She waved a hand in front of her nose, planted her feet, and straightened her spine.

She already knew if she didn't manage her senses she would get overwhelmed. Fortunately, years of meditation had taught her a level of self-control that helped.

She breathed in slowly, blocking layers of distant sound. She concentrated on the steps of people going by and blocked another layer. In a shop window the rhythmic tick of a pink princess clock sounded. She pulled her focus even closer. The whistle of a uniformed man at a taxi stand calling cars seemed to vibrate through her and she connected to the moment. Her focus returned, panic receded, her breathing steadied, and her world became manageable.

She took in the space of the block. It was hot and muggy from afternoon rain. No matter.

She smiled.

Today, she would see her family.

The traffic light clicked and the cars moved forward in sync. She stopped to wait just as the first line of cars raced through standing water by the curb and splashed a chest-high wave of dark water on her.

"Oh!"

She stepped back against the building, unable to get any further away as the cars kept coming and the wave kept splashing. Finally the light turned red. She wiped her cheek. Her entire body was wet with muddy water.

The taxi attendant on the corner looked at her, pointed to the curb near the big puddle and said, "Don't stand there."

She nodded, still stunned. The man tried to hold back a smile. It was hard not to see the humor of the situation. She laughed. "I'm new in town."

He nodded with a look that said he'd figured that out.

"Which way is Fourteenth Street?"

He swung a thumb in the opposite direction she expected. "That way."

She hitched her pack. "Thanks."

"Welcome to New York."

"Thank you!" She grinned before taking off. She needed food, shelter, and something clean to wear. Today might be a little ambitious for a family visit.

Rachel Winslow Rochester forced her march to a relaxed stroll as she neared her son's suite of rooms. There were a few things on her mind—her youngest son's declining health, the election coming up, their annual charity ball this weekend, and Graeme.

Of all those issues, her son Graeme was the most troubling. He'd not been himself for the last few months. She knew his older brother, Rex, had covered for him after some kind of fight—over a girl from what she could ascertain—but that had been over three months ago. Unfortunately, a summer of training in the gym, honing his martial arts, and taking his pent-up frustrations out on a bag hadn't lightened his bearing. And of course he never wanted to talk about it.

He probably assumed she had her spies covering it, but she did try to give her kids a semblance of privacy and normalcy—so she'd waited for Graeme to come to her.

Only he didn't.

And he didn't go to his dad. It was damn frustrating.

Her husband assured her it was normal for men to be thinking about their next steps after graduation and that was all it was. If it hadn't been for the synchronicity of other things, she might not have worried. But she did.

She stopped outside his door. Her success in all things was largely due to her laser focus on one item at a time. This moment it was on Graeme.

Before she could knock, she heard him call out.

"It's open."

Graeme glanced up at her with a quick greeting as she entered. "I heard you marching. What's up?"

Her children had joked growing up that the marching meant she wanted something done immediately. Sometimes there was no hiding it. She had a long list of to-dos.

Sighing, she moved a box of computer parts off the nearest chair, hitched her pants, and sat forward, resting her elbows on her knees.

Graeme had converted his outer room into a workshop of sorts. Gone were the leather sofa and coffee table. In their place stood three long, industrial wood-and-metal tables put in a U-shape and covered in electronics and computers. Graeme sat in the middle with three keyboards within reach, a laptop in front of him, long legs stretched out, and head bent in focus.

She watched an animation render on one of the screens. "Are you working on a new game?"

"Yeah." He hit enter and pushed back a flop of hair as he turned to her. "Last one for Windows on the World. The college kids are taking over after this."

She smiled with humor. "You were one of those kids a few months ago."

He returned the smile, snapping his laptop closed. "I feel older." He put the computer in his backpack. "And wiser."

Wiser—and a little harder. "Rex said there was a girl."

Graeme scowled. "Rex has a big mouth."

Still a sensitive topic. Hmmm. "Is that why you're not bringing anyone to the ball? There's still time."

"I didn't say I was even going."

"Of course you are. It's the family foundation."

He shoved a few more things into his pack without commenting.

"Do you still have the guest invitation?"

He opened a zipper pocket and pulled out the elegant black and white invite. It had clearly been in there a while. She saw a glimpse of what remained of his boyish side when he brushed off some gunk, straightened a corner, and held it up for proof before putting it back. It didn't look like he planned on using it.

"Do you want to talk about anything? Maybe I can help."

Graeme grimaced like she'd lost her mind. She hated this age. You couldn't mother them and you couldn't "friend" them.

"I know a lot about relationships."

"Mom." He held up a hand of resistance and shuddered comically. "Please."

She pushed on. "Well, any girl that could turn you down must be crazy." Her sons were all handsome. Her concern had been *they* wouldn't turn down the girls.

"She's not any girl."

Ah hah! Who was she? Okay, best not to press. Especially with Graeme eyeing the door like it was a lifeline.

"And don't start trying to research this either, or I won't be doing the required campaign stops."

"What?" she asked innocently. The timing to step back officially into public office presented itself earlier than planned, but she hadn't discussed the special election with the kids yet.

Graeme flipped over the paper on his desk. "You made the front page. 'U.S. Senate Spot Open.' Should be a shoo-in."

"I like to think so." She linked her arm through his as they left the room. "Of course it wouldn't be necessary if our politicians could keep their pants on."

"It's more than that these days. The corruption is deep, Mom."

She didn't respond right away. The corruption wasn't just deep. It was dangerous. But it had to be stopped. "I'm careful, Graeme."

"I won't be on the trail again."

"I don't need you for this," she assured.

"I mean in the future."

She stopped. "Why not?"

"I don't think I'll be an asset." He seemed to search for the words to explain. "I have a feeling my destiny is going to be out of my hands."

A chill went up her arms. "We all control our own destinies."

"Maybe. But if that's true, you and I will be on opposite sides. I don't trust the government, and I don't think one person can stop them." He kissed her cheek goodbye. "But I love you for trying."

She accepted his words with a nod. Something had happened to Graeme. The government had become institutionally corrupt over the last twenty-five years. Liberty was a con put over on the American people. But what did her son know about it?

And where did this girl fit into the equation?

CHAPTER FOUR

*G*raeme hadn't meant to be curt with his mom. He just didn't want to talk about everything with her—not his trip to Charlottesville, not the wrecked Porsche, not the laser scars on his body that were still fading, and certainly not *her*.

Sunnie.

Where are you? Are you safe? Did they find you? What did they do to you? What right did the government have to hunt you like they did?

Graeme knew he'd been identified the night of Sunnie's escape. What he didn't know was why officials hadn't approached him or his family yet. He could only assume they were waiting for an opportune time to use it against his mom or someone else in the family. If their manhunt had been legitimate, they would have questioned him immediately. Instead, there had been radio silence.

He sighed. He tried daily to track Sunnie himself. He kept tabs on any unusual news reports, searched records, spied on her friends—okay, not proud of that—but all with no luck. Hopefully that meant the government hadn't found her either.

Georgie and Brittany, presumably her friends, were his best shot at tracking Sunnie. Both had moved to New York. Coincidence? He might have to confront Georgie and find out. Somehow she had known his sister had unique skills. Morgan didn't use them. Their parents had made sure of that, for her safety. They didn't want anyone testing on his foster sister, but the government could do that if it was for national security or to advance science that supported any new initiative they determined was important. Morgan must be on a list at Holliwell and Sunnie was the link.

He only hoped, as he did every day, that if Sunnie needed help, she'd go to them. Then he would see her again. The question was, when?

Special Agent Newell didn't like the look or smell of Clarence Cooke, also known as the Butcher. What he did like were answers and Cooke had them.

He showed him the picture of Sunday Cashus. "Are you sure this is the same girl?"

The Butcher looked at the image, then leaned back. "I already said it was."

"What can you tell me about her?"

"What's in it for me?"

Newell had been authorized to negotiate. "There's a five hundred thousand-dollar reward for information leading to her. And I can have you moved to a federal penitentiary. Private rooms. Cushy beds.

The left side of the Butcher's lips curled up. "She's strong. What makes you think you can get her?"

"How do you mean?"

He eyed the cigarettes and Newell nodded to go ahead. Cooke slowly lit one and blew in Newell's face.

Newell breathed in smoke, unfazed. He'd dealt with smarter criminals than the Butcher.

Finally he spoke. "She's strong in a way that's not normal. But yeah, that's the girl. Same eyes. She's wearing a blond wig. She's bald or something now. But nice body. Soft young skin. So soft. Very warm. When I get out, I'm going to hunt her, hold her close, and skin her. Going to be better than a newborn doe." He blew out smoke, and his voice dropped as his eyelids closed. "So soft."

Newell snapped his digital tablet closed and slid some papers across the table.

"If you sign these now, you will become a volunteer of the U.S. Government and be moved under their protection. No trial."

"For how long?"

"There is evidence that will get you the death penalty, Mr. Cooke. At best, multiple life sentences. This is a gift."

Cooke glanced at the papers. "What kind of volunteer?"

"We need your help to find her. Someone with your skills could be useful."

"My skills?" The Butcher raised an interested brow. "My skills might cost you."

"I'm authorized to deposit one hundred thousand of the reward money into your account. The rest will be contingent on how successful you are helping us."

The Butcher gave a full-toothed smile, showing Newell for the first time that he had a silver tooth where one of his incisors had been. The Butcher flipped through the three-page document, then held his hand out for a pen.

Newell watched him sign and slide the papers back. "I'll need the pen too."

The Butcher slowly put the pen on the table. Newell didn't risk retrieving it while still in the Butcher's reach. "Don't do anything to upset the guards. We'll send a car for you tomorrow."

The Butcher was escorted out and Newell took the papers and folded them precisely before stashing them away. He truly hoped the government wasn't planning on releasing the Butcher, but it wasn't his choice to make. Sunday Cashus had destroyed hundreds of millions in military property, stolen government secrets, and killed and injured government workers in her escape. Murder was bad, but treason was worse. She deserved everything that was coming to her. And Newell would be happy to make sure she got it.

Georgie Washington patted her newly shortened brown curls and took one last selfie with her parents before nudging them into the black SUV and waving as they left Manhattan. Her best friend since childhood, Brittany, stood beside her, waving to her own mom in the back seat.

The goodbye part had taken twenty minutes.

Their parents had hoped they'd go to college in Virginia. Not that they weren't proud of them, just protective. And maybe a little terrified, her mother had implied. No parent wanted to leave his or her eighteen-year-old daughter in New York City to "fend for herself."

After being reminded that her cousin Alastair would be here in a week "to check on things," in case they "needed anything" the girls were able to usher their parents off. To be fair, there had been a few moments in the past year when she and Brittany had given them cause for concern, but Georgie was fairly certain her parents didn't know they had been helping someone escape from the science and military freak show that was Camp Holliwell. That would have gotten them grounded for life, even if she argued it was a natural continuation of their family's great abolitionist history.

"Geez, I need a latte after that," Brittany said, shaking out her long, dark, wild hair, and putting on some bright lipstick to match her new Brittany original—an orange-and-pink blouse made from a biodegradable fabric that used recycled truck tarps. Surprisingly, it didn't smell funky.

"Not in our budgets. How about cheap coffee with sugar and lots of milk?"

"College life it is. Let me text my mom. I think she started crying in the car."

"At least they have each other," Georgie said.

"That's probably what they're saying about us right now."

The two of them grinned, excited. It felt like the start of their lives. Brittany had received a partial scholarship to her dream college, Parsons School of Design. She was pursuing her studies in sustainable fashion design. Georgie had gotten a scholarship to Barnard College at Columbia University and was undeclared. She thought she might go into law eventually. She wanted to do something to help people—people like Jocelyn who didn't have anyone to help them. Her throat tightened a bit and she checked her phone for the millionth time. She hadn't seen or heard from Jocelyn except for their one communication. She could be dead or captured, for all Georgie knew.

Georgie, Brittany, and their newer friend, Lena, all suspected they were being watched by the government after that night. Lena, affectionately known as Milk for her pale features, was a super hacker and coding genius. Her summer FBI Internship had been revoked without explanation. Brittany constantly swore she heard clicking sounds on her phone. And

Georgie was certain her home and the movie theater where she and Brittany used to work had been bugged.

It was a relief to be away from all of it and just focus on the future. But Georgie knew Jocelyn's family was in New York. Georgie had found them for her. If Jocelyn wasn't here already, she would be. And she would need help. She only hoped Jocelyn took her advice and didn't go knocking on their front door without thinking it through.

Jocelyn's stomach grumbled with hunger and nerves. She'd barely been able to sleep last night at the hostel thinking about the moment when she would see her brother and sister in person after ten years. She'd spent most of yesterday walking their old neighborhood, staring at the building that had been their home, and wondering why she couldn't remember it.

If she couldn't even remember her old home, there was a good chance her own siblings wouldn't remember her, which did nothing to help the butterflies in her stomach.

Morgan was a year younger. And well, Benny of course wouldn't know her at all. He'd been a baby. All her hopes hung on Morgan.

She'd thought she had imagined every version of how their first meeting might go. Standing in front of their home, she realized her imagination needed work.

It was a mansion—a really big mansion. A really big, unapproachable mansion. In fact, more like a converted fortress than what she imagined a home would be like. She put a hand over her stomach to self-comfort. There weren't many front yards in New York, but this one had a small garden between the guard gate and front door. She'd watched for a while, studying the people who came and went. They went to the guardhouse first, showed some kind of ID, then were admitted through the front gate. Delivery people were sent around the block to another entrance.

She took a nervous breath, making note of where the public and private surveillance cameras were placed. There wasn't a way to the guard gate without being seen—another reason why Seth was against her coming here. She wondered if he might have been right.

Seth did know the world a lot better than Jocelyn, but her friend also didn't trust anyone…or really like anyone. She couldn't live her life like that. She didn't have enough time to live like that.

Jocelyn contemplated her reception dressed in her only pair of jeans, a clean white T-shirt that she had ironed in the common room at the hostel, and a used but decent pair of flat pink sandals she'd gotten for fifty cents at a thrift store in Texas. Not exactly high fashion, or current fashion—she swallowed hard—or any fashion, but it would have to do. She ran her hands over her T-shirt, anxiously flattening the material again.

The delivery people were better dressed.

And what about her wig? She combed her fingers through the short, blond strands. It wasn't looking very good these days. She'd been tempted to wear her beanie over it but knew that wasn't good manners.

She took a fortifying breath and crossed the street. No time like the present. The guard in the booth stepped out before she reached him. His expression was cold and assessing.

"Hi." She smiled.

He stared back, silent.

"I'm here to see Morgan and Benjamin Albrecht."

He lifted a brow. "ID?"

This time she stared at him, silent.

"I take it you don't have a pre-screened ID."

"Uh. No." No idea what that was.

"Driver's license?"

"Um. No."

"If you're not in the system, you'll need to go around the corner, cross the street, and get an identification badge from security. Then come back. It's the unmarked gray door. There's only one. Can't miss it. Ring the bell."

"Great. Thank you." She smiled again.

He nodded and stepped back into his booth.

Thank you, Mr. Unfriendly. Jocelyn walked around the block and looked for the gray door. Easy. She rang the bell and explained to the voice over the intercom that she was there to get an ID badge to see Morgan and Ben Albrecht.

The buzzer allowed her to enter a small square room with a reception counter and thick glass between herself and two guards at desks behind it.

"Fill this out." A security guard got up and slid a two-page document under the hole between glass and counter. "I'll need a New York Identification card, driver's license, or some form of ID."

Before she could tell him she didn't have any ID, he pointed to the small flat screen embedded in the counter to her right. "Place your right hand on the scanner."

She obeyed and watched as a green line quickly scanned up, then down.

"Left hand."

She put her left hand down and the same thing happened.

"Can I have a pen?" she asked while the guard continued to stare at something on his side of the wall.

"Can you put your right hand down again?"

"Yes." She repeated the action on the scanner.

The guard seemed confused. "Hey, Joe, I think this scanner is acting up. I'm not getting any prints."

The hairs on Jocelyn's arms triggered. The man named Joe came over and looked at the monitor on their side and told her to put her right hand down again.

She did it again, watching the expressions on their faces.

"Can you try the left?" Joe said.

She did, her throat getting tighter with worry. A flashback to her former guardian and his punishments made her uneasy. It had been her first month with him and his discipline had been harsh. Harsh and deliberate. He had destroyed her future before she could even hope for one.

She had no fingerprints. And no way to prove who she was.

CHAPTER FIVE

*J*ocelyn had been punished a lot that first year, but the most during the first month. Her throat filled with bile as the memories suddenly made sense. Each question and infraction against Uncle Laurence's rules—known or unknown—was an excuse for the acid torture on her fingers. One finger for each infraction and another if she cried. She only cried once.

Now she understood his plan more fully.

He had removed her fingerprints. She could see for herself nothing showed up on the scanner. She removed her hands, touching her smooth fingertips nervously.

She felt faint. How could she prove who she was? Not even her dental records would help. She'd only had baby teeth when Cashus had been awarded guardianship. And her DNA? She didn't know if that would help. Her DNA was most definitely very different.

Panic filled her, sending a charge through her body and out her fingertips.

After all she had done to reach her family—and she was so close. What if they didn't recognize her or believe her? The hair on her arms stood as she fought to maintain her smiling, relaxed demeanor. She must stay calm.

She failed.

The light in the ceiling above her sparked loudly and went out as glass shattered around her.

"Oh!" She cried out, not realizing she'd been sending panicked energy outward. Jocelyn breathed slowly.

"Are you okay?" the first guard asked.

She nodded, not really sure.

Joe motioned to a door and hit a buzzer. Come have a seat. We'll have to fix that light."

They were a little friendlier and Joe brushed some glass off her shirt. She moved defensively when he touched her wig.

"I can get it," she said.

"There's a bathroom down the hall."

"Thanks." She walked to the bathroom but only got halfway. If she was panicked before, now she was shocked. She followed the progression of the photos. They covered the walls and continued past the women's restroom.

"That's the Jocelyn wall." Joe joined her. "There's another wall for the parents, but we don't get as many people claiming to be them."

Jocelyn stared at the photos ranging from girls eight to seventeen. The most recent—six months ago. Every photo was a girl with dark hair and blue eyes. On the photo was the date they were photographed followed by Jocelyn Albrecht, real name: Claire Longstreet, Sarah Williams, Francine Patterson. And it repeated over and over again.

"Why would they lie?"

"They want to be famous, or get money from the Rochesters, or they're just crazy."

"But what happens when the real Jocelyn comes here?"

"Well, the real one is dead. This is just for our amusement." The guard pointed to the restroom. "Sorry about that light. Take your time. We'll do the fingerprints the old school way when you come out. It looks like the monitor needs to be re-calibrated."

"Okay. Thank you." She clutched the papers that needed to be filled out, and entered the restroom, locking the door and trying to catch her breath. "Oh, God." She leaned over the sink not sure if she would be sick. Her eyes burned and she quickly splashed cold water on her face. Cashus knew this. He knew she would never be able to prove who she was. He'd won.

Shaking with anger, she took off her wig and shook out the glass before replacing it and pulling her beanie from her pack, tugging it low around her face. She wouldn't be seeing anyone today. That was clear. She pushed the disappointment down, swallowed the lump in her throat, and straightened her shoulders.

There had to be another way.

Jocelyn opened the door and paused when mention of Benny's name caught her attention. She left the restroom, walking slowly down the hall, listening to the conversation between Joe and the original guard at the front gate. He wanted to know if the girl with the blond hair had shown up. Joe replied affirmative.

"I called up to the house and Morgan was at theater practice and Benny's with Graeme at the Windows on the World project in Harlem. Neither is expected back until later tonight. Seemed a little weird."

"Okay. I'll check it out," Joe said and hung up.

Graeme? Jocelyn's heart skipped a beat. She wanted to see him, but…it was complicated. He might not even recognize her.

Jocelyn reentered the office area and smiled broadly. "I just realized I left my ID in my other bag. Can I fill these out and bring them back? Maybe the fingerprint scanner will be working by then too."

"Sure," Joe said. "I didn't catch your name."

"Lyn," Jocelyn said. She didn't want to lie. That was close enough.

"Just need you to sign in that you were here."

"Sure." Jocelyn filled out the line on the sign-in sheet, scribbling an unrecognizable signature, adding the time and skipping the rest. "I'll see you soon. Thanks!"

She was out the door and down the street, away from the Rochester home as fast as she could reasonably walk without it looking like a run. She should have listened to Georgie and Seth. The Rochesters weren't going to let her see Morgan and Benny. At this rate, they wouldn't let her see anyone.

But at least she knew where Graeme and Benny were right now. She smiled thinking of Graeme. It had confused matters when she'd discovered he was Benny's foster brother, but he must have known something was going on at Holliwell or he wouldn't have been down there.

And he'd saved her life.

She hadn't mentioned that part to Seth. Or anything about Graeme. It would have sounded too stupid. Her connection to him had been immediate—and at the time, impossible.

But he might be the "in" she needed to reach her brother and sister.

Her pace picked up. And, yeah, she really wanted to see him too.

Graeme paced the 110-foot art installation of Windows on the World. It was a giant game display at the pedestrian street College Walk at Columbia University, linked with two other displays in the city—one at The World Trade Center and another in Times Square. Each location had a display with a different shape that fit the environment and acted as public art in addition to being interactive art—the kind he hoped would bring people together.

Every half hour a different game would activate and groups on both sides of each display would be connected to people in other parts of the city to play together. Graeme had received a grant from the city in partnership with Columbia and NYU, who would maintain the art, sponsor new games and programs, and work with the city for special events and celebrations. After a couple years of planning and pitching, it had all come together, and soon he would pass on the operations and move to the next project.

Graeme watched from the side as the two groups of people in Times Square and the Columbia University location worked together to create a bridge for the animated figures of a boy and girl to cross and reach each other. Everything was functioning. Flying saucers, not unlike drones, came from the sky and soon the teams had to shoot them down and preserve the bridge in tandem to protect the young couple.

The game ended and some of the players wandered off while others continued to free play with partners at other locations. A curious girl, walking up to the display, got his attention—she was in the Harlem location. He'd been there earlier. Now he was testing in Times Square. She held her hand to the screen and jumped back when she experienced the haptic response of the screen that allowed her to feel hot and cold temperatures, textures, and more compelling—a person's hand on the other side. She watched the animation of stars appear then dissipate as she touched again, then a third time drawing a wiggle.

He loved watching reactions like this and walked closer. She was tall and slender and wore a beanie over straw-colored hair. That beanie was familiar.

So is that smile.

His heart did a triple beat, this time his feet moving faster. He heard Benny call out to him but didn't risk looking away as he rushed forward nearly slamming into the screen, his hand reaching out and his palm planting on top of hers.

She jumped away at the contact.

Then lifted her gaze.

Brilliant blue eyes stared back at him, first in surprise, then awe as she slowly put her hand back up to the screen against his. He felt her careful touch press against the textured surface and slowly their fingers melted into the flexible surface and entwined. He put his other hand up and she matched it, smiling wondrously, before she mouthed, "Hello, Graeme."

His heart raced faster. "Sunnie."

He knew she couldn't hear him. The installation didn't have an audio connection.

He needed to get to her.

Motioning for her not to move, he quickly calculated how long it would take his driver, Henry, to get them back to Harlem this time of day. He pulled out his phone, typing in a message for her and held it up. "Stay there!"

She nodded.

He typed again. "I'll be there in fifteen minutes. Twenty max!"

She nodded again.

"Stay there." He held up his hand again to touch hers through the haptic glass, before reluctantly tearing himself away.

He spotted Benny and Poem at the other end of the wall and ran to them, calling out that they needed to get to the car. Benny saw his urgency and hurried, his gait only slightly faster than his walk, but focused.

Poem frowned, worried, as she hurried into the car. "What is it?"

"Nothing. We just need to get to the Harlem location ASAP."

"Oh," Benny said. "I thought we were under attack or something. You scared me!"

"Sorry." Graeme reached to the back seat and ruffled his little brother's hair, reassuring. Spinning back around, he focused on Henry and gave him directions wanting to find the quickest route. "Take Broadway, Henry."

"I know how to get there, young Graeme." Henry only used "young Graeme" to remind him he'd been driving in New York longer than Graeme had been alive and didn't need directions.

"I know, but this is important." Graeme checked the GPS on his phone and advised Henry again, earning a raised brow.

He tapped his fingers trying to ignore the fact that everyone was staring at him. She might not wait. Or might not be able to wait. "Can we get there in fifteen?"

"If you let me drive," Henry said. "What's the emergency?"

"A girl."

"A girl?"

Graeme nodded.

"Should have said so." Henry picked up the speed with a grin. He whipped the car around the corner, sending Poem and

Benny into a strong lean to the right, and zoomed up Broadway, just making the yellow light.

Graeme tried not to think that she wouldn't be there. At least she was alive. That was good news. And in New York. He knew there'd been a connection between her and Georgie and Brittany. Graeme checked his watch again. Almost there. Henry took another right and pulled up to the corner. Graeme bolted from the car before it was even parked.

"I'll be back," he called to Benny.

Graeme ran across College Walk to the installation and looked around. Nothing. Students crisscrossed as he searched her out in the crowd. His stomach clenched.

No! Come on, Sunnie. *Where are you?*

He stood there waiting, searching. *Where did you go?* He scanned the buildings guessing where she might wait. She wasn't there.

Disappointment filled the pit of his stomach. He took a breath to recover.

Then someone moved from the shadow of a building.

She had a small pack on her shoulder, and beanie down tight despite the heat.

Sunnie.

She paused when he spotted her, lifting a hand to her shoulder and giving a little wave. He weaved through the crowd as she slowly walked to him, looking around as if to see if it was safe.

He stopped short of her, breathless, heart on fire. He wanted to spin her in the air. Instead, he took her hand, needing to feel that she was okay.

"I'm so glad you're alive."

"Me too." She grinned widely.

"Where have you been?"

"Here and there. Just recently in New York."

"Did you know I was here?"

"I figured it out."

"I hoped I would see you again."

She smiled directly at him, completely open. "Me too."

Graeme took that as enough permission and slowly pulled her to him for a hug. She felt perfect. Tentative, she put one arm around him, then another, tucking her head under his chin. He felt the moment when she relaxed with relief. He closed his eyes only a moment to enjoy it, then pulled away. Something sparkled in her hair and he reached to brush it off.

"Ouch." Blood pricked his thumb. "Glass."

"Oh! I'm so sorry. I had an accident. I thought it was all out."

He shook his head, amused. "Are you always going to draw blood when we meet?" She didn't smile at the joke.

"I'm sorry about your car."

"It's okay," he assured. "It's being upgraded. And I'm helping the economy. I'll take you for a spin when I get it back next week."

"You weren't hurt?" she asked.

"A few laser burns."

"Oh, no. I'm so sorry. Where?"

He held out his hand for her to examine, milking the attention as she fretted over the scar. "The other places would require me to take off my clothes, so I'll save that."

Her cheeks went red hot before she hugged him tightly again, whispering into his chest. "Thank you. For helping me."

They were still embracing when the sound of someone clearing their throat got his attention. He looked down to see Benny and Poem standing next to them pretending to be impatient. Poem had her arms folded over her chest, and Benny had hands on his hips with an arched brow of curiosity.

Graeme released Sunnie reluctantly but kept hold of her hand while making the introductions. "Sunnie—"

"Actually—it's Jocelyn. Sunnie was like a nickname."

"Oh. Jocelyn." He liked it. Elegant. Strong. "Jocelyn—" He waited for a last name.

She nodded. "Just Jocelyn."

Benny and Poem looked from him to Jocelyn and back again.

"Okay. Jocelyn, this is Poem Rong. And the kid with the funny expression is my little brother, Benny."

CHAPTER SIX

*B*enny.

The air sucked from Jocelyn's body. She reached out to shake, but it felt like slow motion.

He had brown hair, tanned skin, and big dark eyes. He took after their mother in his coloring, but she recognized herself in him—and their father. They both had the angular jaws, where Morgan's was softer and more oval. She also thought that, other than the color, their eyes were similar.

Family.

Emotion overwhelmed her, and an unexpected rush of heat surged outward from her heart, making her eyes burn a moment before she regained control.

His small hand was much cooler than hers, and it was only when he reached out that she realized something was wrong with him. He had a manmade exo-skeleton on his arm peeking out from his long-sleeved T-shirt. She assessed quickly—it was on his whole body.

What's wrong with him?

Georgie hadn't told her anything about this. Her joy at seeing him was replaced with concern. She tried to hide it but failed. Poem's expression let her know it. The Chinese girl stepped forward protectively, moving a little in front of Benny. The action endeared her permanently to Jocelyn.

"Your hands are really warm." Benny eyed her curiously.

"Yes. I'm very warm-blooded."

She touched his exo-skeleton, deciding not to ignore it. "Is this for super-strength?"

"Yep. Helps me kick Graeme's butt in pretty much everything."

"I could see that." She accepted the answer for now and turned to Poem. "Hello, Poem."

"Hello." The girl politely took her hand, clearly not sure about her yet. The sound of Jocelyn's stomach growling interrupted anything Poem might be thinking. The girl's eyes went wide at the noise.

"Sorry." Jocelyn put a hand over her stomach.

"Hungry?" Graeme asked.

"A little."

"Sounds like a lot." Benny grinned.

"There's a place down the street we can walk to. Burgers and ice cream," Graeme said. "You two want some ice cream?"

Benny and Poem nodded vigorously and the four of them started off—as if Jocelyn joining them for burgers and ice cream were the most normal thing in the world! She grinned broadly, filled with a sense of lightness and ease she'd never had, even with Seth.

The walk allowed her time for a steady stream of questions that Benny and Poem willingly answered. Poem's family lived in Shanghai. Poem closed-up a little when her parents came up. They were scientists, which was how they met Benny's foster father, Ford Rochester. Poem lived with her aunt, who was married to the Chinese Consul General, and went to school with Benny and apparently a lot of other kids with rich high-profile parents. Something about the school's security being the best. The two had been friends since first grade and best friends since second grade, which to them was pretty much forever.

When they got their seats Benny and Poem went to survey the ice cream selection. Jocelyn took the moment to quiz Graeme.

"What's wrong with Benny?"

Graeme's expression changed a little, serious but guarded.

"He's had a rare form of pediatric ALS since birth."

"ALS?" she would have to research that.

"The neurons in his brain aren't sending the right messages and his muscles aren't getting the nourishment they need to function. The exo-skeleton is a temporary fix to support the muscle strength he does have. He's doing well at the moment."

Jocelyn's brain went into overdrive. If the brain didn't send messages correctly, he would eventually have trouble eating, maybe even breathing without machines. She thought through the process, her throat constricting.

"He's going to die?" The emotion in Graeme's green eyes confirmed it. She'd just found him. He couldn't die. He was only ten!

"We don't know how long he has, but we are doing everything possible to extend his quality of life."

"There's no cure?" If there were a cure they would have given it to him. She could see that. Graeme cared about Benny. The two had an obvious bond. The kids joined them again, and everyone acted normal. It was easier than she thought. Poem and Benny made it easy. They just seemed to enjoy everything and had an endless stream of patter between them.

A waitress came to take their order.

"I'm treating," Graeme said.

"Thank you." Gratitude didn't express the half of it. She didn't have enough money to splurge on a sixteen-dollar burger, her head had been aching the last hour from hunger, and her stomach grumbled three more times before the food arrived.

Jocelyn ate, grateful for the burger, the fries, and the company. Graeme insisted she have ice cream as well, and they walked the line of choices, few of which Jocelyn had ever tried. When she stayed with Seth they had ice cream once in a while but nothing like this.

"What did Benny order?" she asked.

"He can only have the gluten-free ones."

"I have celiac," Benny chimed in.

"What's that?"

"A disease that damages my small intestine, and I get headaches and muscle pain if I eat it accidentally."

Jocelyn's mouth dropped. "That's not fair!"

"I know!" Benny said holding his palms up with humor.

She hugged him impulsively. "Stupid celiac. I'm not going to eat gluten either. In protest." Her brain spun in turmoil. She had super strength and her little brother had suffering. And they were both going to die sooner rather than later. She forced her eyes to stop burning. Blue tears right now would not be welcome by anyone. "I'll have the vanilla, please."

"It's good with the chocolate syrup," Benny suggested.

Jocelyn took his advice and proceeded to eat every bite of ice cream.

"When did you last eat?" Graeme asked.

Jocelyn shrugged off the question. "Breakfast, I think."

"What did you have, Top Ramen?"

She froze before reluctantly admitting it. "How did you know?"

Graeme's expression changed. "Where are you staying?"

"I have a place. Don't worry."

"Can I call you?"

"I don't have a phone."

"You don't have a phone?" Poem burst out loudly. "What do you do? Do you have something else?"

Jocelyn shook her head, conscious of others nearby looking at her.

Benny came back from the restroom and put his arm around Graeme, leaning into him, the top of his head barely as tall as his brother was sitting down. She noticed they had similar haircuts. Short but with a floppier long bit pushed to the side.

"Benny," Graeme said. "Why don't you and Poem go next door to the toy shop? We'll be out in a minute."

Benny nodded immediately, giving them privacy. It made Jocelyn even more uncomfortable. She heard Poem whisper about her not having a phone.

She knew she didn't have much. She didn't need pity. And she was already well aware that her fifty-cent sandals weren't going to survive the walk back to the hostel.

"Thank you for lunch." Her voice was stiff, but she couldn't help it.

"And?" He rapped his fingers on the table.

"And?" she repeated.

"And you're just going to get up and leave and never see me again?"

"I—no."

"So, you don't have a phone. How can I reach you?"

"I can meet you somewhere."

"Interesting." Graeme stared at her. "Very old school. I'm going to need your address and where you're staying if we're doing it that way."

"I can't do that. And I move around a lot. I'm not sure how safe it is here. I've been very careful, but the city is full of cameras and surveillance and cops.”

“What if you need help? You have no way to reach me.”

“I can find you.”

“Okay, how about tomorrow?”

“I have to work.”

“You have a job?”

“I do work and they pay me.” She ended that topic. “I would like to see you again. And Benny too. He’s adorable.”

“What are you doing Saturday night?”

“Saturday night? Nothing.”

Graeme reached into his pack and searched for something. It was a little bent but seemed to have survived the technology he had stuffed in his backpack. He wiped off some dirt and fixed the bent edge.

“Would you be my date to the Black and White Ball?”

“A ball?”

“Yes. It’s a charity event my mom and dad throw every year. There isn’t anyone else I’d rather dance with.”

“I—” She wanted to say yes. She wanted to be normal. There was just too much going against her. “Does your whole family go?”

“Yes, but I could keep you away from them, if you’d rather not do the introductions.” He grinned.

“Even Benny?”

“And Poem. Everyone gets to bring a friend or date. It would be intolerable otherwise.”

Benny and Morgan would be there. “Can I think about it and let you know?”

“You’ll call me?”

“Yes.”

He wrote his number on the envelope to the invitation. “Let me know tomorrow?”

"Okay."

"I have to get Poem home. Can we give you a ride?"

"No, I have things to do up here."

"You're not going to disappear, are you?"

"I hope not."

"I'll send a car to pick you up on Saturday."

She nodded.

He paused again. "Look, Jocelyn. Do you need…"

She stopped him. "I don't need money. I'm fine."

"Okay." He gave her a hug when they got outside. She leaned into him again, feeling the hardness of his chest and the strength of his arms. It was comforting and stimulating. Just like the first hug. She really, really wanted to stay just like that for another hour.

When he released her, one hand slowly caressed down her shoulder to her hand, leaving a trail of goose bumps. He held her fingers gently, then squeezed before releasing. She thought maybe he didn't want to let go either. "Call me tomorrow."

"I will."

Right after she figured out how she would pass the fingerprint test, cure her brother, find something to wear, and come up with a new last name.

First things first. She needed help.

CHAPTER SEVEN

Georgie smiled as Brittany excitedly scribbled designs on a napkin in the coffee shop as she talked. Doodling ideas was part of her friend's thought process and when the doodling got faster she was usually close to a solution. "So my first assignment is to design a clothing item from the past with a material from the present that gives the item a new purpose."

"Like, what's an example?" Georgie asked.

"Fire retardant riding boots. Or sun-blocking wedding veils. Only those have been done." Brittany sighed. "A lot of things have already been done."

"It doesn't mean you can't do them better."

"Yes, but..."

Georgie understood. It wasn't Brittany's style. She strived for original if nothing else.

The bell to the coffee shop rang and Georgie glanced up to see another female student with a backpack enter and look around for a seat. It had become second nature to be ultra-aware of her surroundings. Reassured, she turned back to Brit.

Until the student came by their booth and stopped.

Then she slid in next to Brittany, surprising them both and causing Brittany to give an annoyed, "Hey!"

It took Georgie only a second longer to register the blond wig and beanie before the girl slowly took off her sunglasses and smiled.

"Hello Georgie of the RCC," Jocelyn Albrecht said very softly. "I almost didn't recognize you without your long braids." She turned to Brittany. "Hello, Brittany."

Brittany's heavy mane swung like a weapon, green eyes widened, and mouth dropped. "Ohmigosh." She gulped. "You're here!"

"Shhh!" Georgie warned, happy but in shock.

"You're alive! Here," Brittany repeated with a hush. "Are you being followed?"

"They're still looking for me. But they know I was headed here so it's only a matter of time. I just have to be a little faster than they are."

"That doesn't sound like a good plan," Brittany said.

Jocelyn looked at Georgie. "I met my brother. I spoke with him. We had ice cream."

"What!" Now it was Georgie's turn to squeak loudly.

Jocelyn grinned widely.

"You have a brother?" Brittany's eyes narrowed at this information.

"Yes. A brother and a sister. They were raised by foster parents. They don't know I'm alive."

"Well, now they do," Brittany deduced.

Jocelyn shook her head. "I went to their house. It was sort of a disaster."

"Oh, no," Georgie said. "I told you!"

"I know." Jocelyn explained to Brittany. "The foster family is sort of really, really rich, and you have to have a security badge just to be a guest."

"That's a little paranoid." Brittany's snarkiness came out in her tone.

"So I go to the front gate—"

"You walked right up to the front gate?" Georgie winced. "I told you!" she repeated.

"I know," Jocelyn said again, covering her face, laughing. "It was—humiliating." She put her hands down and explained. "I was sent to this guard office where they take your picture and fingerprints and you have to give them your ID—which I don't have. And worse, you are not going to believe this—"

"What?" Georgie waited, her stomach tensing as Jocelyn held out her palms.

"I don't have fingerprints."

"What!" Brittany cried, grabbing her hands to examine. She touched the smooth tips. "Huh. That's a little creepy."

Jocelyn pulled her hands away.

"What happened to them?" Georgie asked, not sure she wanted to know.

"My uncle—" Jocelyn stopped and reframed his title and the story. "My psychotic guardian, Laurence Cashus, used to punish me for not obeying. It was when I first lived with him. Each time I made a mistake he would put a finger in acid. I thought it was normal punishment for bad children, but now I realize…"

"He was trying to eliminate your ability to prove who you are and also use the torture to manipulate and control you." Georgie got it.

Jocelyn nodded and put her hands over her face again, taking a breath.

"Bastard," Brittany said.

Georgie called to the waitress and ordered chocolate milk for Jocelyn. "It's on me."

"Thank you." Jocelyn continued in a hushed tone. "So I'm in this security room and they think the fingerprint machine is broken, and I ask to use the restroom while they check it out because I just figured out the problem myself and was not feeling so well, and when I go behind the desk, down the hall to the restrooms—"

She paused and shook her head.

"What?" Brittany demanded.

"The hallway was lined with all these pictures of girls at different ages over the years with blue eyes and brown hair."

"I don't get it," Brittany said.

"They were pictures of all the people who came there claiming to be me."

Georgie felt sadness and pity at the desperation in Jocelyn's voice.

"I have no way to prove who I am, and even if I tried, they would just think I was another crazy person or liar like the hundreds on the walls. There were even some people who claimed they were my parents."

The chocolate milk arrived and the table was silent. Georgie wasn't sure how to comfort Jocelyn. She'd come so far to find her family.

"How did you see Benny?" Georgie asked.

"I heard the men talking about it on the phone and found them at Windows on the World. Graeme is working on it and Benny was with him."

"Graeme?"

"Porsche guy," Georgie said.

"Okay, but why is he with—" Brit put the pieces together. "How do you not tell me things like this? Porsche guy is his uncle, brother, friend?"

"Foster brother."

"I think Graeme came down to Charlottesville to investigate after I called," Georgie said. "It's the only connection. He's supposedly some super software genius. He might have as many resources as the government. He knew to be at the pick-up location the night of your escape, so he was definitely monitoring us. I don't know if you can trust him."

"He saved my life."

"Maybe."

"He's really nice, Georgie. And he's wise and thoughtful."

"You got all that from a car chase?" Georgie didn't have such a high opinion.

"Wait." Brittany pulled out a *Campus Today* magazine with the Windows on the World article and held it up. "Graeme *Rochester*?"

Georgie and Jocelyn nodded.

"Are you two freakin' kiddin' me?" Brittany looked between them, dumbfounded. "This is the project Milk is working on."

"I know." Georgie turned to Jocelyn. "She's going to be here this weekend. Maybe she can help get you an ID."

"That would be outstanding. How is Lena? And Al?"

"Both good," Georgie said. "Al is visiting next week with his buddy, Richie. Richie fixed the Porsche and has been working for Graeme. They're delivering the car, then vacationing."

"Does Graeme know Al is your cousin?" Jocelyn asked.

"Yeah. I'm guessing he figured all that out," Georgie said.

"I can't believe the Porsche is fixed." Jocelyn smiled. "It makes me feel a little better."

Brittney interrupted. "Look, I hate to be the one to bring this up, but goody-goody Graeme's family is very powerful. How do you know they aren't the ones who put you in Holliwell?"

"If they did, Graeme doesn't know anything about it," Jocelyn said, defending him. "He's not like that."

"Kind and brave and hot, blaa, blaa, blaa. I got it." Brittany scowled, unhappy with both of them.

"I didn't think it was my place to tell you who her family was, Brit."

"Makes sense." Her friend's voice was hard.

There was an awkward silence at the table. Georgie knew she was going to get heat from Brittany for holding back. Finally, she asked Jocelyn, "Why didn't you call?"

"My friend Seth was afraid your phone would be tapped so I destroyed it after you texted your New York location. It was easy to find you today. I came to your college and listened until I heard you!"

Jocelyn seemed to sense Brittany was hurt from being excluded. She turned to her and explained. "When I was at Camp Holliwell there was a guy there, Seth. He was transferred to another facility in Colorado but escaped. I've been with him up until a month ago. He's also really strong. Another scientist experimented on him and found a way to replicate me. Or at least most of my abilities. The others in his group all died, but he lived and was really valuable."

"I suppose he's really hot too."

Jocelyn was taken aback. "I don't know."

"Have you kissed him?"

Jocelyn blushed, embarrassed.

"Jocelyn?" Georgie asked. "You've been holding back."

"Well, it's not like we've had a lot of time to talk. I didn't even know if you guys would want to see me again."

Brittany gave her a skeptical look. "Don't change the subject, girlfriend. I want to hear about Seth."

Jocelyn stammered a little. "We're friends. That's all. He wanted me to go to Mexico with him, but the whole reason I escaped was to find my family. And he's so cynical he doesn't think they will even care. He says they've moved on and I'm just torturing myself. But he didn't know Benny was really sick. I have to figure out how to help him. With all the science at Holliwell, I can't believe there isn't something to save him."

"The Rochesters would be able to find a cure if there was one, Jocelyn," Georgie said, her tone encouraging. "I'm sure they're still trying."

Jocelyn gave a nod of agreement, but Georgie could see her still thinking.

"Okay, so," Brittany continued, "When did you kiss Seth?"

"At Camp Holliwell, and mostly when I thought I would never see him again. And then recently, but that was more friend kissing."

Brittany bit her lip to suppress a smile. "You're such an innocent. But we'll go with the friend kissing for now. And how about Graeme? Have you kissed him yet?"

"No." Jocelyn turned pink again and Georgie saw danger coming a mile away. Jocelyn already had a thing for him.

"But you want to," Georgie said. "Jocelyn, that's not a good idea."

"I told him I would call him tomorrow. That's why I need your help."

"If it involves laser-shooting drones, exploding trucks, or armed militia"—Brittany stared pointedly at her—"I'm out." She held open her hand. "Look at this."

Jocelyn looked dutifully.

"Here," Brittany insisted when there was no response.

"It looks like a wrinkle."

Brittany examined. "Well, that is." She pointed again. "Here."

Jocelyn and Georgie looked again, then at each other, and shrugged.

Finally Brittany admitted, "The vitamin E worked well. Otherwise there'd be a scar."

"I'm sorry," Jocelyn said. She took out an envelope from her backpack and Brittany grabbed it without asking.

"Ohmigosh!" Brit didn't ask permission before carefully taking out the inside envelope and opening it to reveal the elegant black and white invitation. She held it like a precious gem. "Oh. My. Gosh. Where did you get this?"

"Graeme asked me to be his date."

"Oh, no." Georgie worried. "What is it?"

"The Black and White Ball. They raise money for literacy and education." Brittany stared at them. "The tickets are a hundred thousand a piece."

"What!" Jocelyn turned white.

"Don't worry, you don't have to pay. This is the invite." Brittany held the velvet-encased invitation to her cheek and murmured softly to it. "This is a ticket to a designer's dreams."

"He said he would send a car for me." Jocelyn spoke, dazed. "My whole family will be there."

Brittany's head popped up, alert. "And you haven't a thing to wear?"

Jocelyn shook her head.

Georgie tried to stop the train wreck in motion but was already outpaced.

"*This*," Brittany lifted the invitation triumphantly. "*This* The Fabulous Brittany Walsh can help you with! That's with a capital 'T' if anyone asks."

Jocelyn smiled brilliantly while Georgie suppressed the feeling of alarm slowly rising in the pit of her stomach.

This was not a good idea. With a capital 'T'.

Jerry Ramstein ran the White House, and as Secretary of Information, he often felt like he ruled the world. He'd done what was necessary to win the last three elections and had handpicked the current Executive Staff, including the President and Vice President. Under him, the NSA, CIA, FBI, Homeland Security, and Special Projects operated. He knew the dirt on everyone and had his fingers on the money—sometimes because of shared interests and sometimes because he had the dirt.

The world mostly ran according to his plan, and the worst problem he had with the current "leader of the free world" was that he was simple and vain.

"The election is close, Jerry. Can't we flip Florida and Virginia?"

"Mr. President…" Jerry took a sustaining breath for patience, explaining again. "We don't need them. We have three other swing states. It would look suspicious if we pushed too hard in states where you're behind."

"I really want them."

Jerry stood up to go. "They don't matter."

"Don't go." The president pouted. "People are threatening not to use the voting machines because politicians have ownership in the company."

"There's nothing they can do before the next election. It's too close. And we've been using the machines for years. Everyone knows that politicians have invested in the company.

Nobody cares. Only outliers and conspiracy theorists believe anyone would rig an election. And the algorithms are perfect. There's a diverse variance in every county to make sure you carry the key states. The next election is over. Focus on something else."

"Okay."

"I'll see you tomorrow." The president still sat, but Jerry had things to do. He exited and his new assistant, Mercer, followed, keeping a half step behind.

"Iran is testing another nuclear bomb on Friday."

"Make sure they don't do it over an oil field this time and send someone to monitor it. Let's also inspire the International Climate Control Organization to put some pressure on them so it doesn't have to come from us."

Mercer made a note. "The Federal Reserve wants to know how many treasury bonds we'll issue next quarter."

"We told them the total was one trillion per quarter and we're taking seventy-five percent of what they print." He smiled at Mercer. "Free education costs money."

Mercer wrote but didn't question. That was a good sign. She'd been deeply vetted and was a proven party soldier—the kind he had around the president, who knew their job was to follow orders and take the fall when situations arose.

"What's our current national debt?"

She didn't hesitate. "42.653 trillion."

Exacting. A good sign. "Anything else?"

She handed him a note with a phone number. "An NSA tracker spotted a missing asset. No other details. I asked them to send the information to your office via the secure line."

A rare thrill of excitement sent a tingle up his arm. She took the hint not to enter his office and he closed the door.

He sank into his large leather chair and clicked on the link.

Graeme Rochester was identified with an arrow on the video. He waited. Finally, a girl came out. The two hugged. The girl looked up at the Rochester kid. The video froze and zoomed in on the face.

Jocelyn Albrecht—Project Sunday.

He smiled and leaned back in his chair. "Well, aren't you a bright spot in my day."

He pressed his intercom. "Mercer, connect me with Camp Holliwell."

CHAPTER EIGHT

"Dr. Cashus? Phone call."

Laurence Cashus was in a surgical room observing and overseeing the eye transplant firsthand. This experiment was particularly near and dear to him, since the subject was Medina—the man who helped Project Sunday escape.

Now *Medina* was an experiment.

Everything Laurence didn't get to do to Jocelyn he now did to Medina. It was perhaps stretching it to say he enjoyed the work, but it did give him immense satisfaction and buoyed his confidence.

"No one disturbs me during a procedure, Nurse."

"It's the SOI. I thought you'd want to take the call."

Cashus stepped away from the table and walked outside the surgery. "Patch him in." His life depended on the Secretary of Information. Jerry Ramstein was the one phone call everyone at Holliwell always accepted.

The symbol of the Office of the President displayed on the digital intercom followed by the face of the Secretary.

"Mr. Secretary."

"Dr. Cashus, I need you in New York."

Laurence froze. "You found her?"

"We have someone who identified her. I want you to help him deal with her."

"Help him how?"

"Give him a little boost. Extra strength."

Laurence clenched his fist, frustrated. "Why don't we just bring her in?"

"That would require a military effort, and those methods have proven unsuccessful with Project Sunday, if you recall."

A mug shot slid onto the screen.

"The Butcher?"

"He identified her on the Appalachian Trail. She took him down. Now he wants revenge. It's an easy story to manage in the press."

The SOI came back on the screen and gazed past him. "How's Project Monday?"

"Obedient despite himself. The mind drugs are working well. I'd like to try the chip next time. The optics team is doing their next generation ocular replacement. It allows us to see and record his movements. It's a superb tool for future soldiers, and the upgrades can be done through regular WiFi."

"Excellent."

That was high praise from the SOI, but then Laurence had a long way to go before he'd earn their leader's full support again. Project Sunday had assured that.

"Bring him with you," the SOI said. "We can run some field tests."

"Of course, sir." He wouldn't argue. Medina wasn't ready for prime time, but there might be some limited opportunities to test him out.

"I've sent through the orders. You should have them later today."

"Yes, sir. Goodbye." The screen had already returned to the Presidential logo.

"Dr. Cashus?" One of the surgeons wanted his attention. "Did you want to go through with the second eye?"

Medina looked up at him with his one original eye, paralyzed with fear. Cashus leaned over him and smiled. "Take one last look, Project Monday," he whispered in his ear. "Tomorrow, everything you see will be what I choose it to be." He stood up. "Remove the second eye. The research opportunity will be invaluable."

The surgeon nodded and they brought over the other artificial eye for replacement.

"Goodbye, Medina." Cashus watched the surgery a few minutes more before departing.

This time Medina would be working for him. And little Jocelyn would get a taste of everything she deserved.

The girls landed in Georgie's dorm room, which was a lot like the youth hostel, only better mattresses and more secure.

Jocelyn stood obediently while Brittany moved her measuring tape every which way around Jocelyn's body. It seemed like Brittany carried everything in her purse from a hot glue gun to needle and thread, plus a little bag of weird and miscellaneous items like an X-Acto knife, erasers, two-sided tape, silicon packs, hairspray, and several objects that Jocelyn couldn't identify.

"What *is* this?" Brittany snapped the shoulder strap of the sports bra under her T-shirt.

"My bra."

Brittany inspected then pulled off Jocelyn's shirt. "Oh my." She shook her head in horror and snapped the elastic shoulder again. "This is not a bra." Snap. She swirled her index finger in front of it in horror. "It's a weapon of mass obstruction. The mass being your boobs in this case. What size are you?"

"What do you mean?" Jocelyn looked down at the offending undergarment. "I'm this size. It's medium."

"I mean your bra size."

Jocelyn turned to Georgie for help.

"Don't look at me." Georgie shrugged. "You look like—maybe a B cup?"

"Cup?"

Brittany and Georgie stared at her.

"Oh," Georgie said.

"Oh, what?"

"Nothing." Georgie then explained about bras and bra sizes, and had Jocelyn try on one of her roommate's bras of similar size. It made her breasts look very different.

Brittany clapped her hands and sung a halleluiah. "She has boobs. I can't believe they survived. The dress I'm making has a low back, so no bra, but I'm building it into the dress, so don't worry."

"Nothing slutty, though, right?" Georgie said. "She's seventeen."

Brittany glared at her friend. "You question my art?"

"No, just your judgment."

"You may leave now."

"It's my dorm room."

"Well, get us some sodas or something. I saw a vending machine."

"Fine." Georgie left the room.

Brittany finished her work and Jocelyn changed back into her clothes and sat on the bed. Brittany opened her large notepad and sat next to her, drawing while she talked. "This is what I'm thinking. I have a bunch of material I ordered last spring and was waiting for the right project. It's perfect for you. White. Soft. Flowing." She sketched a long sleeveless dress that fell into soft folds. The edges had little bits that looked something like feathers.

"When you move, it will look like you're floating," she explained. "Faux feathers." Without glancing at Jocelyn she asked, "What's that scar on your shoulder from?"

Jocelyn touched her shoulder self-consciously, even though the spot was now covered. "Nothing."

"I don't know a lot about these things, but it looks like a bullet or something. Only it didn't go out the other side."

"It's healed a lot. It might disappear in time."

"I was going to do bare shoulders, but I can make a translucent white top. It will still be appropriately sexy but cover it."

"Thank you."

"So…you really like Graeme Rochester?"

Jocelyn smiled at the question. She smiled whenever she thought of Graeme. "Yes."

"What happens when he finds out you're just using him to be with your family?"

"I'm not! I really like him."

"He might not see it that way."

Jocelyn hadn't thought about that. She liked being near him. It didn't have anything to do with her family.

"Maybe I shouldn't go." Just saying the words made her sad.

"Oh, no! You're going. And you'll tell everyone that The Fabulous Brittany Walsh personally designed your dress."

Jocelyn smiled.

"I just think you need to be careful. Withholding information from people who care about you is never a good idea."

"I guess." Jocelyn didn't know whether it was or not. "Is everything okay with you and Georgie?"

"Yeah. We're family. We always get through."

"You're related?"

"Not by blood," Brittany said. "Sometimes the people you call your family aren't always related."

Jocelyn thought about that. She was starting from scratch. And she had such a deep longing to connect to her siblings. Morgan might be able to share memories of their parents. The world was lonely if you didn't belong anywhere.

"I like Graeme. I just feel like I want to be near him. And he sees me. In Charlottesville, the day we met. It was like somebody saw me for the first time. He knew what I was feeling. I was almost afraid other people might as well, but they didn't. Otherwise, I wouldn't have been able to escape."

"But he doesn't know *who* you really are?"

"No."

"Are you going to tell him?"

Jocelyn didn't know. Not right away. Would he believe her? It was all getting so complicated.

"I don't know. I just need to see everything that's going on first. Maybe if Morgan and Benny are really okay..." Jocelyn swallowed painfully. "Maybe they don't ever need to know about me."

Brittany stopped and looked at her. "They'll *know* you," she comforted. Then she held up the pad. "And in this dress, no one will *ever* forget you."

Jocelyn gasped. "It's beautiful!"

Brittany agreed with a knowing grin that made Jocelyn laugh. "You'll look like a white swan."

Jocelyn touched the drawing, struggling to imagine herself in such a dress.

Georgie heard Brittany as she walked back in, arms full of sodas and chips. "But what if someone recognizes her? And there will be publicity photographers everywhere." Georgie dumped her treasure on the bed. "I was thinking about it. I'm not sure this is a good idea."

Jocelyn and Brittany stared at her in horrified silence. Then Brittany held up the drawing, pointedly. Jocelyn nodded vigorously in silent agreement.

She needed to wear that dress! Even if it scared her a little.

"Okay, okay. But we need to be prepared."

"I already figured it out." Brittany turned to Jocelyn. "Tell them you're under eighteen and your parents won't allow you to be photographed, but they can photograph the dress and block out your face. They do it all the time in magazines."

"Got it." She turned to Georgie. "That will work, right?"

"It's completely naïve." Georgie sighed. "What about her hair? And"—she lifted Jocelyn's hand—"no offense, Joss, but blue nails. We need to test nail polish and make sure they don't glow in the dark or something."

"They don't. I would know by now." Jocelyn lifted her worn-out sandals. "But these won't last until Saturday."

Brittany swirled a hand dismissively over them. "They're an abomination." She shuddered, then moved on. "I measured her head. We'll get her a wig. A good one. You're due anyway. Blond never suited you and this one has seen better days."

They spent another hour strategizing what to do with Jocelyn's blue nails, bald head, and lack of makeup. The details made her head spin but sitting and talking with Georgie and Brittany was so much fun she didn't want to leave. She felt like a regular girl. And she was learning a lot about boys, makeup, flirting, and college.

Walking back to the hostel that night, the thought crossed her mind that maybe someday Georgie and Brittany would think of her as family.

Special Agent Newell watched the surgery on the Butcher, Clarence Cooke, from the observation room of one of the state-of-the-art chambers of Holliwell-New York. He hadn't known this place existed. It was huge building and expanding into another block. The alley between the buildings was already sealed for construction. Apparently Holliwell had more than a few locations and none of them had citizen oversight. The politicians in Washington didn't know what was really going on, but thankfully the President was apprised on an "as needed" basis. That was something. The President wouldn't let things get out of hand and it was thrilling to see the government actually innovate and advance science.

The interior of the New York office was impressive. Once past the fake shops, restaurants and security, the lobby was more like a space he'd seen in Silicon Valley—friendly, open, and filled with young people working on laptops, drinking the free coffee.

The building had forty-four levels of scientific activity, all of which were completely beyond his comprehension.

The plan to send the Butcher after Project Sunday seemed one of the more extraordinary plans, but the White House wanted Sunday Cashus to be a citizen casualty—a tragic runaway, and a statistic that would be forgotten the minute after it was read about.

The Sunday drug that had been developed from Project Sunday's blood was administered to the Butcher. They installed a tracking device in his arm and surgically put an obedience device in his ear. None of those things reassured Newell. For one, this Sunday drug would supposedly give the Butcher super-strength. The tracking device could be removed if discovered. And the obedience thing…yeah, maybe that would work. Every day they could adjust the Butcher's parameters, and if he went beyond the borders established, his hearing would explode from high frequency torture that only stopped when he moved back within his borders. That didn't mean he couldn't do a lot of damage in the interim.

Laurence Cashus, responsible for the Sunday drug, made a comment to one of the surgeons and nodded approvingly before exiting. The man had arrived an hour before the surgery and didn't seem the least upset at his niece's pre-determined death. Newell had to remind himself that she'd tricked the man, killed her trainer, and single-handedly caused over three hundred million in losses. She was devious and cunning.

But in three days, they would be letting a super-charged Butcher loose on the world, bent on revenge and thirsty for blood. Newell wasn't squeamish, but what would be the collateral damage before they achieved their goals?

CHAPTER NINE

*J*ocelyn lifted another package from the delivery truck and carried it into the store. It had taken over fifteen attempts to find work in Chinatown, but it helped that she spoke Cantonese and Putonghua. It garnered more trust with the storeowners. She also realized that the oldest and most feeble owners valued her service.

She knew she was being watched but refrained from looking back. It could have been coming from anywhere—a camera, binoculars, satellite. It didn't matter. What mattered was she could feel it. The days of her freedom were over. She just needed to make sure no one around her was hurt because of it.

She finished the job and collected twenty dollars from the storeowner.

There were three store deliveries today, but nothing tomorrow. She'd need to find something else. Then Saturday she would help one of the families do store inventory and that would be something else she could add to her skills.

Overall, she could get twenty to sixty dollars a day. Her dorm bed at the hostel was thirty dollars a day, so with sixty she felt rich. She could get food for the day. Soon she would have enough for another set of clothes. She needed to have a few basic items to survive and look respectable. It was exciting to be able to choose her own clothes and wear something other than Army-issued gear, but her budget didn't give her a lot of options.

Until she could depend on regular work every day, she needed to save for her room first. Her next goal was to afford to pay weekly. And then…maybe monthly. It seemed like a big goal. A lot had to fall into place for that to happen.

Mrs. Wong invited her in when she finished unloading her last job. She and her husband had recommended her to two other shops. The old woman waved to a small folding table in the corner of the storage room. Mr. Wong nodded to an extra folding chair, and she saw the food on the table. Her stomach grumbled in instant response and gratitude. Mrs. Wong brought in tea, and Jocelyn thanked them profusely, trying not to gorge on rice.

They chatted about the shop and neighborhood, then politics in China. Jocelyn listened and asked questions. She was still learning about the world. It wasn't at all as she had been led to believe by the leaders at Holliwell and sorting through the facts and opinions was confusing.

When she left, Mrs. Wong gave her a plastic container with lunch and Mr. Wong slipped her an extra five-dollar bill with a wink and an awkward pat on the shoulder. She hugged him impulsively and promised to be there Saturday.

Sixty-five dollars! The money made her hands tingle. It meant freedom. And she had earned it on her own.

The tingle in her hands moved to her neck as she glanced down the alley. She kept moving, occasionally looking back. Whoever watched was invisible. Heck, knowing the work at Holliwell, they might be able to make someone invisible.

It was almost 8:00 a.m. The traffic buzzed along Canal Street, and construction teams rumbled high above on cranes.

There seemed to be a lot of new construction over old buildings. She let her hearing drift a bit to the workers in the sky. They talked about a sporting event one man had taken his son to the night before.

She smiled, loving the different New York accents.

A loud creaking sound got her attention and Jocelyn glanced up curiously. From what she had learned of the city so far, that was not a construction sound.

She crossed the street just as a crane swung around dangerously with a man hanging from it. Someone cried a warning seconds before a large piece of equipment fell off the building and shot to the ground.

"Watch out!" Jocelyn saw the object falling in slow motion. People ran and scattered, but a worker with headphones on didn't understand the danger.

She ran and knocked him out of the way as a metal generator exploded on the concrete near them, crushing a massive hole into the sidewalk.

Commuters cried in panic, then screamed as an even louder scratching sound echoed between the buildings. People scattered in panic.

Jocelyn rolled off the construction worker onto her back. Every nerve ending in her body fired.

The crane was coming down.

Acting without thinking, she forced energy through her body and directed it at the rapidly approaching steel. She wasn't stupid. She pushed it against the nearest building in the hopes people would think the building slowed it. Partially obscured by a truck and the fallen generator, she was safe. Everyone else had run for cover. The challenge was lowering the heavy object so the man hanging from his safety harness wasn't jolted to the point of losing circulation—if he hadn't already.

The crane stopped miraculously when the man's feet touched the ground. A more alert co-worker snapped the man free and called for first aid while others yelled to stay clear. When the man was safe, she let the crane drop the remaining distance with a crash.

Her hands fell to her sides and she took a slow breath, recovering for a few seconds before rolling to her feet.

She spun to go and turned right into the first construction worker she had knocked over. He stared at her dazedly.

"Excuse me." Jocelyn ran back to the corner. She'd dropped her lunch somewhere.

"Miss!"

She ignored the call and ran faster, spotting her knotted plastic bag in the gutter. She quickly rescued it and pushed her way through the crowd of bystanders. Her pace became a run. She didn't stop until she reached Union Square.

Her heart raced with fear rather than exertion. Breathing slowly she assessed her surroundings and decided that no one followed. Not even the invisible man. The only problem appeared to be a gash on her arm and the dirt and oil all over her clothes. She hadn't noticed it in the chaos. Crud. She needed to take care of this. And some of her earnings would need to go to another set of clothes.

She clutched her lunch. At least she had one meal covered. Maybe she could convince another shop owner to let her help them today. She just needed a little extra to get by.

Lieutenant John Morrow flipped through the reports from the night before. Nothing good, but nothing out of the ordinary.

One of his young detectives popped his head in. "Boss? I think I got something. You hear about the crane incident this morning?"

"Yes. A crane crashed down in Chinatown. No one was hurt, right?"

"No. Kind of a miracle too. One of the workers said a girl saved him. Knocked him out of the way, then did this." He put his hands up at the sky. "And the crane safely landed."

"Sounds like an instinctive action. It slid against the building. That likely diminished the velocity."

"Only surface damage to the buildings though." The officer tilted his head. "Strange. Right?"

"Not sure," John said, ignoring the chill going up his arm.

"All right, let's say it's nothing." He put down a short stack of reports on John's desk. "Purse snatching in Union Square."

"Not our precinct."

"Purse recovered by bystander, a girl with blond hair. Petty theft from store in Chinatown."

"Also, not our precinct."

"Goods recovered by bystander. Also a girl with short blond hair, this time wearing a black beanie." He kept going. "Child snatched from the street just before a taxi careened into a light post. Woman saved from assault. Purse-snatcher caught. Starbucks computer stolen and thief knocked out on the street when trying to escape—our precinct. He tripped or something and a blond girl returned the computer. They run mostly in the Chinatown area, but I wonder if I contacted the other precincts what might turn up."

John stared at the detective—for a long, meaningful, time. "You realize our job is to find and arrest criminals."

"Yes, sir."

"Well, I'm not sure what you want me to do here. Hunt down a Good Samaritan and tell her to stop?" He rubbed his jaw. "It could be a sorority of blonds doing community service."

"But don't you think it's strange?"

"Did she or they commit a crime?"

"No."

"So?" John extended a hand. "We're done?"

"Why didn't she stay at the scene? Not even to get credit or give a statement. It's suspicious."

"Hate to break it to you. People don't love cops. Even New York's finest. And not everyone wants to be a celebrity."

"She might be on a wanted list."

"For doing good deeds?"

"Okay, that doesn't make sense, but I'm just sayin'."

"Please stop sayin'." He took the reports. "I'll look through these since you did such a thorough job. But go catch some bad guys now, okay?"

"Sure boss. Thanks."

John pulled the pile of reports toward him. Not ordinary. Not ordinary at all. He looked at the first report. But at least she was safe.

For now.

The Butcher walked out of the building and onto the streets of New York. He could feel the power coursing through his muscles. He'd always been strong. He cracked his neck. Now he felt invincible.

He rolled the cash in his pocket. Unbeatable and unstoppable.

The test drug they had given him hurt but was worth the pain. Every sense was heightened…along with every desire. He was hungry for flesh and thirsty for blood. But not just any blood. He wanted hers—the witch that brought him here. He would thank her before he killed her.

He ran a hand over his smooth scalp. First things first. A nice room, a hot shower, new tools, then—he looked at the address provided—then he would get to work.

Another man walked out of the building. He gave the soldier a sneer. He didn't need Medina's backup. Rabbit had been released the day before, and he knew just where to find him.

The other man seemed to agree. With one glance, he turned and walked away. They both had hunting to do.

CHAPTER TEN

They had thirty minutes to get Jocelyn into supermodel mode and decide what name she should use. Georgie knew that if Graeme introduced her to his former governor mom, she'd want details. Any mom would. A last name was basic, and they all agreed Albrecht would be an issue. They just hadn't discussed it with Jocelyn yet. She had enough on her mind with wanting to impress her family, not embarrass Graeme, memorizing dances from YouTube videos, and practicing walking in heels. They were only two inches, but she'd never worn strappy, spike-heeled sandals before.

Lena had arrived from MIT the night before, and with her usual intensity, the petite programmer worked on her laptop, head bent over, pale blond hair swinging with the persistent rhythm of her typing, while concealing most of her paper-white skin. She'd been assigned to getting Jocelyn an identity.

Brittany had the hard job—getting Jocelyn to be still for makeup. She'd already designed a stunning dress, and the bags under her eyes showed the effort it had taken to do it in less than five days.

Meanwhile, Georgie fanned Brittany, occasionally offering unwanted directorial advice. Brittany's two-person student suite in the Greenwich residence hall was just big enough for them. Brit's roommate was gone for the weekend so all four girls were camping out. Everyone wanted the post-party story firsthand.

Jocelyn sat obediently in Brittany's tropical fruit-colored robe as Brittany did her makeup. Her bald head had a few wisps of bluish peach fuzz growing that made her look vulnerable and very young. They were all feeling a little protective.

Jocelyn's toenails and fingernails were painted light blue. It was better not to fight their natural color. The dress and wig hung nearby. Brittany wouldn't let anyone touch them.

Brit glared at Jocelyn whose feet had started to jitter again. "I know you're excited, but don't move. I'm doing your eyes. They are the pièce de résistance of your makeup."

"*Oui*," Jocelyn said. Then she added something else in French.

"I only speak fashion French," Brittany replied.

Jocelyn laughed, forcing Brittany to take a break. "I said tonight I am your canvas."

Brittany smiled. "That you are."

Georgie took a moment from fanning Brittany to fan herself then Jocelyn and Brittany again.

"So, I have something interesting," Lena said, then typed for a while in silence.

Brittany stopped with the makeup and sighed loudly with pointed frustration. "Are you going to share?"

"Oh." Lena stopped. "Okay. I did a lot of research since you called."

"By research you mean illegal hacking?" Brittany asked.

"Um, well."

"It's okay, Lena. Whadda you got?" Georgie asked.

"Okay. So, Jocelyn. I don't say these things to bring you pain in any way."

Jocelyn turned her head causing a black streak of mascara from the brush in Brittany's hand to whip across her check.

"Ahhh!" Brittany cried out. "Never do that again."

Everyone apologized.

"What is it, Lena?" Jocelyn looked worried.

"I found the death certificates for your mom and dad, Illeana Marques Albrecht and Grayson Albrecht. Everything seems in order. And interestingly, I also found the birth certificate for Sunday Cashus, and—"

"And?" Brit had no patience.

"The death certificate for Sunday Cashus."

"Looks like they wanted you dead one way or the other," Brittany said.

"Likely the project was terminated," Lena explained. "The FBI and CIA do things like that. Usually to protect someone." Her dad was FBI, and Lena's voice held a little bit of defensiveness on his behalf.

Georgie encouraged her to finish.

"Okay." She looked at Jocelyn. "The strange or really lucky thing is, I can't find a death certificate for Jocelyn Esperanza Albrecht."

"Because I'm alive."

"Yes, but when the government took you, they didn't wipe you clean. I wonder why. There are papers filed in Virginia by Laurence Cashus. He really did make you his ward. So he had no control over Sunday Cashus, but if he wants control over you, he would have to admit you were you."

Three voices spoke at once in confusion.

Lena held up a hand. "Maybe he wanted to secure you as his personal asset, and in doing that could better negotiate with the government for his grants. You would have still been in a coma when these papers made him your guardian."

"How could he do that, when my parents left the Rochesters as our guardians?"

"I'm assuming they didn't know. He probably told them you died. The whole explosion had people worried about contamination and stuff. The EPA had the site quarantined for months. He's a doctor. Maybe he gave them a death certificate, or the government made a fake one. I'm just saying there isn't an *official* one filed."

Jocelyn's relief was palpable. "So I can use my identity."

"Umm." Lena looked back down at her computer.

Brittany glanced at Georgie, then started to urgently scavenge in her makeup bag.

Silence.

Jocelyn turned to Georgie for help.

"Joss, I don't think you should use your last name. It's a little too obvious, you know. They will question it. And…"

"Okay stop." Jocelyn pushed away from Brittany's makeup station and stood. "Stop, stop, stop." There was nowhere to go in the room. Jocelyn pulled the robe tightly around her and faced the corner. Her head shook as if refusing to accept it.

"Jocelyn," Lena said. "I know it sounds hard, but even with this, we can't prove you are you. But we can use your identity and social security number to change your name and get you identification."

Georgie chimed in. "And that means a bank account and job opportunities. Those are your biggest problems…other than being hunted by the government. But you know, your more immediate concerns."

"And you think they won't track this?" Jocelyn asked.

Lena was optimistic. "Anyone looking for you from Camp Holliwell already knows you were going to come to New York. It's a given. And you would likely be using the Cashus name or

Albrecht name. Even when they do find this paperwork, it will be months. The bureaucracy is insane. But regular people won't know unless they were looking for it. It gives you a start and a little time until we can figure out something else."

Jocelyn shook her head again, not turning around. "Everything…everything I did. And I still don't get my name…or my family." She couldn't continue.

Brittany jumped in quickly. "Jocelyn, if you cry, you'll ruin my last hour of hard work and we are seriously on a schedule."

Jocelyn shook a little. Georgie hoped it was a laugh. Instead her friend tilted her head up, a sure sign of holding back tears.

"Jocelyn," Lena explained, "I know it's not perfect, but the beauty of it is, you can do this and it's legal. It's not a lie. You can legally change your name and not feel like you are lying or hiding."

"Well, it's sort of hiding," Brittany chimed. "Come back and sit down. The ball is happening whether you have a last name or not." Brittany stood up and shoved a tissue in Jocelyn's hand. "One problem at a time."

Jocelyn obeyed, dabbing at the corners of her eyes. She blinked a little and steeled herself. "Continue your torture."

"The price of beauty, my friend. The price of beauty."

"What about if you simply make your name Marques," Georgie suggested. "Probably no one remembers your mom's last name."

Jocelyn seemed to warm up a little.

"It's a pretty common name," Lena agreed.

"The reality is, that the new name will give you access to your family and that's the main goal," Georgie insisted. "You'll be able to get to know them."

"I guess."

"A lot of people who are family don't even talk to each other, so it's not about the name," Brittany said.

"I haven't talked to my mom in three years," Lena piped in helpfully.

"What?" Jocelyn's head shot around, mascara swiped, and Brittany took a very slow controlling breath.

"Sorry." Jocelyn smiled a little. "Really."

"Milk. You're killing me." Brittany blamed Lena completely. "And why the hell haven't you talked to your mom?"

"She's busy with work. There's always some world crisis with her job. She's a disease specialist in Geneva. I don't think she wanted kids. But my dad is the best and he makes up for it. She just never cared. I barely remember her being around as a kid, to be honest."

Georgie thought that was incredibly sad. She had a feeling Lena did too. Lena was just used to it.

"Phew!" Brittany stood up. "The creative energy just got sucked from this room." She turned to Georgie and Lena. "Lena, can you get us some sodas from the vending machine? Georgie, there's grapes and cheese in my mini-fridge. Make us a snack. I just need five minutes with no interruptions, please."

Everyone obeyed, and finally Brittany wrapped up her makeup. "I'll put the lipstick on after the dress and hair are complete. Show Georgie."

Jocelyn turned to Georgie for approval. "You look really beautiful, Jocelyn. Even without hair."

"I think Jocelyn Marques sounds exotic," Brittany said. "And it rolls off the tongue. Albrecht is very strong and German sounding. Like I'm gonna 'brecht' your neck."

Georgie watched. Jocelyn smiled.

Progress.

Rachel sat patiently while her husband attached the diamond necklace at her nape. He leaned forward and kissed her softly in the same spot then growled playfully in her ear. She knew he did it to relax her and she loved him for it.

Their eyes met in the mirror. "Remember when we were poor?" he asked.

She turned around and leaned into him. "We had our brains and we had each other. I never thought we were poor."

"That's sweet, but I'm pretty sure there were days when you wanted to call your parents."

"Everyone has those." Rachel kissed her husband lightly. "Graeme is bringing someone tonight. I saw it on Henry's assignment sheet. Did he tell you?"

"Yes," Ford answered. "He said she was special and asked that I do my best to keep you occupied and not let you ask a lot of questions." Ford smiled. "As if that would work."

Rachel's mouth dropped. "I'm his mother. How could he say that?" Rachel dabbed her lipstick in the mirror before adding, a little hurt, "I'm very friendly. And most people agree that my relationship-building skills are unequaled."

"For a politician."

"I hate that word."

"You're a former governor and soon to be senator. He might just want to give her time to get used to the idea."

Rachel thought it over. "Yes. Maybe. Did you get a name?"

"Jocelyn."

Rachel startled a moment, then stood and grabbed her phone. "A last name? I might have time to search for her."

"No last name. I think that was deliberate." Ford spanked her playfully to move along. "Let's go. The receiving line awaits."

"Remind me to tell you something later. A funny email I got a few months ago."

"Later. Email. Few months ago. Got it."

"You're all charm, Ford Rochester."

"I know." He winked. "That's why you married me. And I look sexy as hell in a tux."

Rachel smiled and took his hand, hiding her unease for now. *Jocelyn?* It had to be a coincidence.

CHAPTER ELEVEN

Georgie's phone rang. "Oh-mi-gosh. The driver is here."

"I'm not ready!" Jocelyn squeaked.

"Of course not," Brittany said. "You're supposed to be late."

"I am? Why? I'm never late. At least I didn't used to be, now I do seem to have a lot of interruptions." She bit her lip. Being late had always come with a punishment. She couldn't shake that feeling now, no matter what Brittany said. She began to fidget.

"Stay still, please." Brittany carefully adjusted the wig. "Tell him it will be fifteen minutes."

"It will be just fifteen minutes," Georgie repeated into the phone.

"Everyone stay calm and stick to the plan."

The room went silent. Brittany made some adjustments with the curling iron. "All right. Everyone outside." Brittany spoke softly but took a slow deep breath. Jocelyn thought she might be a little nervous. Maybe Jocelyn wasn't fixable. Her stomach flipped and her hands felt clammy. Nobody moved.

Brittany pointed to the door with the hot iron. "Out!"

"Okay, okay!" Georgie agreed.

"Sticking to the plan," Lena added.

Georgie gave Jocelyn the okay sign and left.

Brittany finished with the wig, then helped Jocelyn into the gown and sandals, and adjusted her hair again.

"It's almost the same color as my real hair," Jocelyn told her.

"That's what I was going for. It's actually real hair too. I doubt anyone will know the difference. That blond thing is done." Brittany shuddered.

Jocelyn laughed. "I know. Could I…could I keep this?"

"Uh…"

"It's okay if I can't," Jocelyn added hurriedly.

"No, no. It just, um, it's on a payment plan."

"My hair is on a payment plan?"

"It's really good hair," Brittany started to explain.

"No, no. I just thought it sounded funny."

"Oh." Brittany relaxed. "Yeah. It does, kinda." She smoothed the material at Jocelyn's shoulder. "It's sheer but it completely hides the scar."

Jocelyn nodded, grateful. "It was a bullet. I stopped it, so it didn't go through, but—"

"You can stop bullets?"

"Only if I see them coming."

"That's unfortunate."

"Yes."

"He shot Seth too, but Seth was wearing Kevlar. It was kind of a test."

"I miss spelling bees," Brittany quipped.

"You're sure I don't need a bra?" She felt very daring with the low back, even though the girls said it was safe.

"The corset is built in. I can't believe how small your waist looks. And you actually have a figure. I think I might be a genius."

"You are."

"Why weren't you wearing a bulletproof vest?"

"That was the test."

"Oh." Brittany frowned. "To see if you were bulletproof?"

"Yeah, sort of. Anyway, I don't like Kevlar. It never fits women well. It feels a little bit like this corset actually. But not as comfortable or attractive. Someone should design decent gear for women."

Brittany stared at her. "A bulletproof corset."

"Sure. Not everyone has superpowers."

"No, I mean that's what I'll make! You're a genius!"

"I thought we agreed you were," Jocelyn teased. Their banter helped her relax.

"Oh, I am! Wait until you see…" Brittany opened her closet door for Jocelyn to look in the full-length mirror.

Jocelyn gasped. Then stared. Then didn't know what to say. She saw herself but had never imagined herself like this. She was pretty and sort of exotic. Her tall sporty figure seemed graceful in the flowing lines of the white dress. And her hair looked real and natural and beautiful! Brittany had performed a miracle!

"Okay, I'm not liking the silence."

"I don't even look like me!"

"That's the point!" Brittany stressed. "I mean look." She showed the pictures on her phone. "Before. After. Before. After. And on the upside, anyone looking for you won't expect this." She clutched the phone to her chest, an expression of pure panic on her face. "Ohmigosh. You hate it."

Jocelyn laughed. "Brittany! I love it! I didn't know I could look like this. You really are a genius." She spun in the mirror, relishing the soft feel of fabric on her skin, then gave a little hop, her confidence building.

Brittany exhaled dramatically with relief. "Well, I had a good canvas to work from. And you have like a perfect figure. It's disgusting. Too much exercise."

Brittany gave her one more look-over. "Wait here." She went to the door and called out, "Ladies, may I present, wearing a Fabulous Brittany Walsh Original, Miss Jocelyn Marques!"

She motioned for Jocelyn to come out. Squeals followed. Other girls gathered and admired the dress.

"Give us a twirl," Georgie said.

Jocelyn turned and the material floated around her legs, gently swinging. The dress felt incredible. She touched the material again, not believing that she wore something so beautiful. She felt special. Like she could conquer the world. And in a ball gown!

Brittany quickly took photos for her portfolio. "If they take pictures, don't forget my poses."

"I won't," Jocelyn promised.

Georgie handed her a small purse. "My phone is inside if you need us. And there's cash, lipstick, and a compact."

"Okay," Jocelyn said as they took the elevator down to the car.

"Don't forget everything else. You were homeschooled. You're taking a year off."

"Don't worry, I remember everything." Jocelyn felt her excitement grow. It was amazing what a dress could do to her self-esteem.

A black town car waited below and a man in a suit of the same color came up to the bottom of the steps to offer his arm and a warm smile. "Miss Jocelyn?"

"Yes, sir."

"Allow me." He escorted her gently to the car and opened the door with a flourish.

"Wait! One last shot," Brittany begged. "In front of the car."

Jocelyn turned and struck a Brittany-approved pose.

"Don't forget, it's The Fabulous Brittany Walsh."

"With a capital 'T'," Jocelyn affirmed. "Www dot the fab Brittney Walsh dot com."

"You look beautiful," Georgie said again.

"Just have fun," Lena added. "We'll be waiting up!"

Her three friends finally stopped. She put a foot in the car, then froze at the sound of a low whistle. She could have sworn it was aimed at her.

"Everything okay, miss?" The chauffer immediately noticed her concern.

"Yes. Thank you."

Where are you going?

Jocelyn heard the words. She turned around and spotted a figure leaning against a light post, smoking a cigarette, face shadowed by the low brim of a cowboy hat.

Clutching her bag defensively, she pivoted and slid into the protective comfort of leather seats. Graeme was waiting. At least she hoped he was. Nervous doubts assailed her as the door closed.

"It's very close, Miss Jocelyn. Give it ten minutes."

"Thank you, sir."

"It's Henry."

"Thank you, Sir Henry."

"No—"

Jocelyn caught the older man's deep chocolate eyes in the rearview mirror and smiled. "It suits you." He had kind eyes and a dignified bearing.

The man laughed. "All right then."

They were at the Rochester home in no time. A few people still entered.

"Am I late?"

"No, Miss Jocelyn. Just long enough to keep young Graeme guessing."

Jocelyn smiled at that. "Have you known him long?"

"His whole life."

Jocelyn nodded. "Sir Henry, between us, do I look appropriate? No one will notice that I—" A list of things filled her head. That I don't belong. That I have fake hair. That I've never really worn a dress like this.

"You look very appropriate, Miss Jocelyn. And everyone will notice you because you look beautiful and regal."

She relaxed a fraction. "Thank you." Then she saw the security stop before the entrance. It was being managed by the guards she had met earlier that week. Would they recognize her? Panic shot down her arms and her energy heightened.

"Sir Henry, I don't have a security badge. Will you walk me to the door?"

"My honor." Henry walked her slowly to the station, then told her to wait to the side away from the small crowd. He spoke to one of the guards, then came back and brought her the rest of the way.

"All set. At the top of the steps, take a slow breath, enjoy the view, and smile. It's going to be a wonderful night and I'll be here to take you home."

"Thank you. I'll look forward to seeing you later."

He bowed and handed her off to an usher.

There was a lineup of security guards on both sides of Jocelyn as she crossed the short hall to the grand entrance. She straightened her back. If this was the lions' den, she'd be ready for it. But this could also be the opposite. The one place she might be safe. But which was it? The tension and uncertainty set her skin on fire.

One night. Please, God. If you exist, give me one night with Graeme and my family.

Jocelyn opened her eyes and did as Henry told her. She stood at the top of the steps and stared out in wonder. A sea of people mingled, drinks in hand, jewels glittering, music playing.

She was definitely late!

The magnificent hall sparkled with decorations that were black, white, gold, and silver. Excitement and anticipation filled the air. And then she realized there wasn't a single familiar face and she had no idea how she was going to find Graeme in the crowd.

Her energy built until her skin felt so charged it almost hurt. She breathed slowly for control, but it kept building.

And then she saw him.

He was on the opposite side of the room staring at her. Relief and joy filled her. Smiling was easy. She couldn't contain it. The feeling of happiness and contentment surprised her so much that shimmering energy exploded right out of her.

And into the ballroom.

Moments earlier he'd been pacing. Truthfully, he'd been pacing since he arrived in the ballroom. His older brother, Rex, joined him.

"Never seen you this nervous."

"What if she doesn't show up? I don't think she's used to this kind of thing. I should have sent her a dress. I didn't think of it."

"She probably figured it all out before she accepted. And this kind of thing…" He waved a hand encompassing the room. "Natural for women."

Graeme nodded, checking for a message from Henry again, and hoping his brother was right. "No date?"

"Umm. No." His brother took two glasses of champagne from a nearby server and handed him one.

"Sabrina is solo as well."

"Really?"

Graeme smiled. His brother already knew. Sabrina and Rex hadn't been together since Rex blew it. Maybe his brother wanted another chance?

Graeme paced. The floor continued to fill. The orchestra played light background music. A mix of perfumes floated by.

"Holy moly."

Graeme glanced at his brother. "What?"

His brother's gaze drew him back to the entrance.

Graeme sucked air, his heartbeat accelerated, his temperature rose. Then he released a low breath of gratitude. "Thank you, sweet baby Jesus."

Rex laughed. "No doubt."

At the top of the staircase, the grand doors behind her, stood Jocelyn, a slender silhouette in white. He swallowed hard. A silhouette with curves. And long hair falling in soft waves to her shoulders—like when they met.

"If it's not her—"

Graeme nodded affirmative, taking a slug of champagne to wet his dry mouth.

"Well, now I get it," Rex said. "Definitely, thank God. But later. I think she's looking for you."

Graeme didn't take his eyes off her, blindly handing his glass to his brother.

"Yeah, I'll just take that. Not that you even know I'm here right now."

Graeme nodded agreement to whatever his brother said. He didn't want to lose her in the crowd. He willed her to look at him.

Then she did.

And she smiled. Brilliantly.

Just as suddenly, the balloons in the ceiling that were to be saved for the last dance, exploded above her, showering down shiny silver and gold confetti, and surrounding her in a surreal curtain of glittering magic.

His slow smile widened. The ballroom filled with chaos, laughter and surprise, but they held their gaze, slowly moving toward each other, the crowd parting for them while the balloons above continued to pop in a wave across the entire ceiling.

They met in the center, the rain of confetti still floating lightly around them.

"Graeme."

She said his name with the same purr as the other day, only it held more confidence. Her eyes were bluer, and the smoky makeup made them even more mysterious.

"Jocelyn. Wow." He took her hand. "You look incredible." He was about to start blabbing and caught himself. "That dress is perfect for you."

Freaking innocent, but sexy as hell. He felt the sweat build under his shirt.

"Brittany made it."

"She's a genius."

"She knows."

He laughed, relaxing. The dress didn't change the person. The orchestra changed its tune and struck a lively waltz. He caught his parents from the corner of his eye starting the first dance—and coming dangerously close.

He offered his hand. "Will you do me the honor?"

"Is this a waltz?"

"Yes. Or we can get you a drink."

"I can do this," she assured.

"I hope I can."

This time she laughed.

He managed the waltz with confidence, but when they were meant to switch their heads opposite at the turns, their gazes met in the middle and were slow to turn away.

His mother caught his eye and motioned for them to come near. He nodded back, and deliberately steered Jocelyn the other way.

Not falling for that.

Jocelyn just got here. They needed warm-up time before his family barged in. His mother's brow arched meaningfully and he smiled even bigger before guiding them toward the open doors leading to the backyard.

CHAPTER TWELVE

*R*achel sighed. Her son had learned diplomatic evasion from her.

"Don't be mad," Ford said. "You can't blame him for wanting her to himself."

"I don't."

She'd been standing with her husband and another couple watching her sons when she'd seen Graeme transform. A sucker punch in the gut would have felt better. That's when she'd seen the beautiful girl on the steps and realized. This was Jocelyn. *His* Jocelyn.

One word struck her. Radiant. The girl seemed to glow with youth and beauty and freshness.

Then there was the expression on her son's face. It reminded her of Ford's when they first courted, and truthfully, even moments now in their marriage—which was a rare blessing. But she knew that look. Graeme had found his… someone special.

She felt a motherly knot form in her chest.

She wanted that for her children. She just hadn't been ready to lose Graeme in that way, and so unexpectedly. The knowledge that she would never again be the most loved woman in his life, or the most important woman in his life, filled her with bittersweet emotion. And she knew nothing about this girl. What if she broke his heart?

Then all the balloons popped in a wave of some electrical or power surge, sending her event producer, Pierre, and his team into conniptions. Ford quickly cued the orchestra conductor to hit the music hard, and suddenly everyone was laughing, dancing, and the event had begun. A happy accident she told the pale-faced Pierre.

"Let's go left, darling. I could use some fresh air."

"You never get the message," Ford said.

"Persistence is why I'm successful."

"Hello, Mother." Rex danced up to them with Sabrina before she could escape the floor. "May I have this dance?"

"Oh, for crying out loud. Is everyone in on it?" Her son quickly whisked her away and she had to laugh. Very well. She would work on Rex. "Sabrina looks lovely."

"As always."

"Are you two patching things up?"

"No. Just dancing." Rex smiled. "Don't meddle, Mom."

"I'm not."

"Good."

"Fine." She gave in. "Have you met this Jocelyn yet?"

"No. Graeme will introduce me when he's ready." He smiled knowingly. "He might need to catch his breath first."

"It's character that matters."

"Don't worry, Mom. I learned that the hard way."

"Sorry, Rex. I didn't mean anything by that." She looked him in the eyes. Her oldest son had been through so much. She knew parts of him were lost to her, but she believed time could heal him eventually, if he would let it.

"You know you're my number one baby, still."

"At twenty-eight?"

"Yes," she said. "Just embrace it." She glanced at Sabrina and her husband on the dance floor. "What are they talking about?"

"Sabrina got news from Ketevan. Her father was released. He's being guarded in Russia. For their protection, not his."

Rachel's steps faltered. Rex understood and kept her moving. Sergei Baratashvili, Ketevan's father, was a premier geneticist who had worked with Benny's biological mother before she passed away. They had hopes his work would aid them in finding a cure for Benny before his disease advanced further.

"It's good news, Mom."

"I know." It was the best news she'd heard in months. It had been a blow to their entire family when Sergei was kidnapped, presumed dead, and his entire hospital and life's work had been destroyed.

"Can we reach him?"

"Not right away. I think Ketevan waited for the right moment before reaching out. The Russians are only 'friendly-ish.' They want the science as much as everyone else."

"We might not have that much time." Another guest passed by on the dance floor and said hello. Rachel greeted them and smiled as a photographer captured the moment.

"Take me to your father."

Rex nodded and guided them across the floor to Sabrina and Ford.

Sabrina updated Rachel quickly but without further information.

"Rachel." Ford took her hand. "It's going to take time. We didn't even know before if there was anything in his work that would help us."

"But it's hope," Rachel said.

"Yes." Ford agreed with a happy smile. "It's hope."

"That's all I wanted to know." She lifted her head regally. "I see Graeme with his young woman. You may all carry on."

Three voices objected, but there was no stopping her now.

"Already?" Graeme frowned.

Jocelyn caught the anxiety in Graeme's voice.

"What?"

"My mom. And dad. Rex was supposed to run interference."

Jocelyn girded herself. "It's okay." It was better to get it over early, and more respectful.

Graeme guided her to his family. His mom looked intimidating in all black. Her dress had a high collar, low neckline, and was sleeveless. The dark-haired woman was a little taller than Jocelyn and in very good shape. She smiled at Jocelyn as they approached and Jocelyn relaxed a little, enough to look at the other companions.

Her steps faltered.

Graeme caught her. She looked at him in panic.

"What is it?"

"I—nothing. I got nervous."

That wasn't true. She knew them. How was that possible? It took her a moment to remember the incident, but it came back with startling clarity.

Paris.

Mission gone wrong.

The two men and the stunning blond in the elevator. They were standing next to Graeme's mom. Did they recognize her? They were all staring. Then she remembered—she'd been wearing a gas mask. And she spoke in French. She breathed in relief. There was no conceivable way they would know that person had been her. She'd been part of a mission to kidnap international renowned longevity scientist, Sergei Baratashvili, and bring him to Camp Holliwell. She hadn't known that at the time. She rarely knew how her part of the mission fit in with the overall plan. She just obeyed orders. That's how things worked. Only this time, she'd become friends with the target. And then she had betrayed him.

The guilt still haunted her.

But what had the Rochesters been doing in Paris? Her mind raced to connect the dots. They'd been getting off on Sergei's floor. Ford had an international pharmaceutical company. They must have been there for Sergei. But why? A thousand questions burned to be answered. Instead, she was bombarded.

"Jocelyn, this is my mom, my dad, my brother Rex, and our family friend, but mostly family—Sabrina."

Jocelyn smiled and greeted each with a firm handshake.

"Mr. and Mrs. Rochester, thank you so much for having me. Everything is so spectacular. I was telling Graeme how magical it all is. Especially the confetti. That was amazing!"

"Thank you," Mrs. Rochester said. "It's a pleasure to meet you as well."

"I feel like I might have met you before, Jocelyn." Rex eyed her curiously.

"No," Jocelyn answered quickly. "We've never met."

"I had the same feeling," Sabrina said.

Jocelyn looked to Graeme for help. "Jocelyn is very new to New York."

"Just a week," she confirmed.

"Oh." Mrs. Rochester was curious. "How did you two meet?"

Silence. Neither she nor Graeme had prepared an explanation.

Jocelyn jumped in, truthful. "In a movie theater. We actually bumped into each other."

"I knocked her down."

"Flat on my butt. But he helped me up."

Ford Rochester grinned. "I should hope so. Not very smart knocking her on her butt, son."

"Sounds like good manners prevailed." Sabrina saved them.

Jocelyn liked Sabrina instantly. She had a kindhearted smile that reached her bright blue eyes. And Rex *definitely* liked her.

"And then he asked me out." Which was also the truth even if her guardian had given him the shut down.

"And the rest is history," Graeme finished.

Jocelyn could feel a bead of moisture on the back of her neck. As if knowing she was nervous, Graeme took her hand in his. She linked her pinkie through his index finger and middle finger and held tight.

"Where is your family from, Jocelyn?" Rachel Rochester's question was innocent, but Georgie had told her that family was important in these circles.

"New York, ma'am."

"Really? Would I know them?"

And there it was. With any luck the pity card would shut her down. "I doubt it. My parents passed away several years ago."

"Oh!" Graeme's mom gave him a look that said he should have warned her. "I'm so sorry."

"I lived with a distant relative after that but wanted to come back and see New York as an adult. And I have friends here."

"One of them is working with me on the Windows project," Graeme said.

"Yes, Lena. She just started at M.I.T. She's brilliant."

"Actually, she is," Graeme told them. "I'm going to steal Jocelyn away for appetizers. We'll see you later."

"Oh, but—" Mrs. Rochester closed her mouth, then rephrased. "Try the canapés."

Jocelyn and Graeme hurried off.

"I said 'butt' in front of your parents." She put a hand to her forehead in embarrassment.

"I know. It was awesome."

She laughed. "But it was true," Jocelyn said. "And I knew…"

"Yes?"

"Nothing. I just knew when I saw you, there was something about you." Graeme introduced her to canapés and she put one on her small plate. "And then you saved my life!"

"I'm kind of a hero like that. Here, try this." He fed her a mushroom canapé.

The moment his fingers touched her lips another spike of energy shot up her spine, and a whish of air fluttered above them causing the silver fabrics draped dramatically to billow overhead.

Jocelyn bit down on the canapé and joy exploded in her mouth. "Wow. That's really good!" She gazed happily at the spread of food, her mouth watering from the scents—and from being so close to Graeme. He looked amazing in his tux. She had so many things to worry about, but when he smiled at her, everything melted away like it would all be okay.

"Graeme. I have to tell you." Time for the confession.

"Yes?"

"I can eat a lot."

"Really?"

She nodded. "And I'm pretty sure everything here"—she inhaled with joy—"I've never had before."

He solemnly handed her another plate. "You'll have to try everything."

"I really want to."

"There's a full sit-down dinner at ten o'clock."

"If I eat everything now, I can be hungry again by ten."

They laughed and he helped her pile on a diverse collection of canapés. She took the time to learn more about his family.

"Are Sabrina and Rex together?"

"No. They used to be. Then Rex went off to war and wasn't the same when he came back. He lost both his legs up to his knees."

Jocelyn gasped, then suppressed her shock to listen. She would have never guessed Rex had prosthetic limbs.

"He made a lot of mistakes. Pushing Sabrina away was one of them."

"Why did he do that?"

"Don't know. He was angry about a lot of things. He doesn't talk about what happened, so I'm not sure I'll ever know."

"Can't he apologize?"

Graeme hesitated and lifted his shoulders, doubtful. "It's a little more complicated. He slept with another woman, she got pregnant, and now he has a son."

"Oh." Jocelyn hadn't thought about something like that. "Is he married?"

"No. The woman was in our family circles, but a real mercenary, narcissistic psycho. So they share custody. But my nephew is the most adorable thing in the world. Still, it complicates matters. And Sabrina is Ben and Morgan's aunt, so she is real family and Rex can't mess things up any further."

One of Jocelyn's plates tipped over in her shock, spilling canapés at their feet. An instant later two servers were cleaning the mess while Jocelyn apologized. Graeme got her a new plate and filled it up.

Ben and Morgan's aunt? She choked. She had an aunt? Sabrina! She had the same eyes as Jocelyn! They had the same blue eyes. Had anyone else noticed? And they were the same height. She had an aunt! An aunt she only vaguely remembered but she was in their lives. Was that why Sabrina recognized her?

"Are you okay?" Graeme handed her a fresh plate of goodness.

"Yes. I'm just so happy." It was true. She was. She didn't even mind if she had to give up her name for now.

A small hand reached past her to the table and she turned to find Poem and Benny piling up their plates—Poem with only a little more restraint.

Jocelyn turned and said hi.

Benny's eyes went wide with surprise. "Jocelyn. I didn't recognize you! You look—" Benny paused and rethought his words. "Different, but in a really good way."

Poem agreed, staring at her. She touched her dress. "It's so soft."

"It's made from milk. Biodegradable. But not recommended for eating unless you're really desperate."

"Very cool," Poem said. "And your hair is different."

"I was trying out a wig when we met."

"Oh." Benny and Poem thought that over. "This is better," they said in unison.

"And that's why they're best friends," Graeme noted.

"You both look great," Jocelyn said. They looked adorable in complementary tux and dress. Jocelyn noticed they were the only two young people in attendance. They filled their plates, then excused themselves to go eat by the fountain. Jocelyn didn't want Benny to go, but it was still fun to see him. She watched them put their heads together talking and eating animatedly. Another woman joined them, and Jocelyn heard them speaking in Mandarin. Poem pointed to her and Graeme, and the woman came to join them.

Graeme introduced the young woman as Poem's aunt. She in turn introduced an older woman who was the mayor of Shanghai. The Chinese mayor pointed out a woman across the buffet and explained she was a Russian ballet dancer that she would like to meet, but she didn't speak Russian and the dancer didn't speak English or Chinese.

Graeme understood the problem. "My Russian is limited to ordering drinks."

"I could translate," Jocelyn offered. The three looked at her. "Graeme, could you introduce us?"

"I don't really know her either," Graeme said.

"Oh." Jocelyn popped a canapé in her mouth and handed him her plate. "Wait here." Jocelyn walked over to the dancer and introduced herself. She loved that there were so many interesting people here. In minutes, all the women were talking like old friends, taking selfies with the ballerina, and giving Graeme the opportunity to get them all drinks.

Rachel and Ford were making the rounds when they heard the burst of laughter on the patio. Curious, Rachel saw the elegant group of women holding their sides. More curious, was how Natasha Millakova laughed with the Mayor of Shanghai. She released her husband to join them and found Jocelyn chatting animatedly about getting ready for the party—in Chinese and Russian. The ladies burst out laughing again when Jocelyn said, "and my hair is on a payment plan."

Poem's uncle overheard and joined them. "At least you have hair."

The group made room for Rachel, and Jocelyn greeted her with raves about the canapés, claiming to have tried all ten.

Natasha's eyes went wide.

"I know," Jocelyn said in Russian. "If I eat dinner and dessert and midnight snacks, I'll need to run twenty-seven point six miles tomorrow." She repeated in Mandarin. "And I'll need another pair of running shoes."

Rachel joined the conversation, surprised that she enjoyed it, and taking the time to observe Graeme's choice in women. As a mother, she simply could not complain. Jocelyn was charming, authentic, and curious. And apparently well educated.

Natasha's date took her away to dance, so they switched to just Chinese.

"Where did you go to school, Jocelyn?" Rachel asked.

"I was homeschooled."

"Oh." That surprised her. "Very well done. Your languages are excellent."

"Thank you."

"Are you in college now?"

"No, ma'am. I'm taking a year off to travel and think about what I want to do."

Graeme stepped in. "That's a good approach before committing to college. My dad did that. Right, Mom?"

Rachel smiled. Ah, her protective son. "Yes, that's true. A very wise move to take time to *think* about things and *not rush in.*"

The other women nodded agreement. Rachel could have kissed Poem's aunt for asking the question that tempted her.

"How old are you, Jocelyn?"

"Seventeen."

"Oh, you have plenty of time." Rachel swallowed a sip of champagne and gave Graeme a stern eye. Her son knew better. Until Jocelyn was eighteen, this was not a good idea.

"And…time for another dance," Graeme took Jocelyn's hand and excused them.

Rachel sighed but turned back to her guests with a smile. She really shouldn't be so worried about Graeme when it was her daughter, Morgan, who gave her the most trouble. But she could only worry about one child at a time. And Morgan was exhausting at the moment.

CHAPTER THIRTEEN

*G*raeme ducked the security lines and brought Jocelyn into the family side of their home for a tour before dinner. Benny and Poem caught up with them and asked to join. Benny wanted to show off his room, much to Jocelyn's delight. Jocelyn loved it. She got to see a little history of Benny and Morgan in the family photos, but she still hadn't met Morgan. She was pretty sure she hadn't seen her in the ballroom either.

Graeme and Benny toured the house with pride—not because of the grandeur but for the stories and memories in photos and items that filled it. Jocelyn could hear their love for their parents and family in every story. It made her happy and sad. Happy that Morgan and Benny were loved and enjoyed a safe childhood, and sad that they had not only forgotten her, but also their parents. Benny's room didn't have one picture of their parents. Everything was with his new family. It hurt.

They entered Morgan's suite and it was larger than Graeme's with an expansive entry room, the size of her former living room at Holliwell. It was decorated very youthfully with pink and yellow colors, ornate white furniture with striped cushions, large mirrors, art by someone named Lichtenstein, and a very feminine desk. Jocelyn thought she heard voices giggling and shushing, but dismissed them as other partygoers nearby and focused on Benny, who gave a detailed history of Morgan's interior design choices and the drama that went with it.

Morgan's bedroom was similar to the outer room, a little larger, with a big bed, a long dresser, a makeup area that Brittany would have loved, and lots of photos on the wall that Jocelyn would have liked to have more time to view. Strangely, it was a mostly empty corner that got her attention. A simple wood chair stood with a cello bow on the seat posed next to a beautifully polished instrument.

Jocelyn froze at the sight of the cello. She knew it was a cello even though she hadn't seen one in ten years. Something deep within her hummed, her palms tingled, and a memory of playing it drew her. She knew how to play it. She just knew!

Dazed, she walked over and touched it, vaguely hearing Benny's continuous touring banter. Her mother had taught her how to play. She picked up the bow, took the cello off the stand, and sat down with the instrument between her legs. It was only then that she saw the surprised faces of her guides.

"May I try it?" She really wanted to try it.

Benny shrugged and Graeme gave a curious nod. Jocelyn felt her body form to a long- remembered position against the instrument. Tentatively, she touched the bow to a string. It sounded off tune. She touched a few more times and produced a long warm vibration of sound. Her eyes closed at the sensation and memories rushed her. She slowly inhaled as the music came back. The song that had haunted her dreams was meant to be played on a cello. The movement, the notes, the joy—all came to her like it had never left. She had no idea what the music was called, but she played it—a beautiful haunting melody that was suddenly a direct link to her childhood. And then she couldn't remember the rest.

She stopped just as suddenly as she started, eyes popping, her grin wide. "I'm a musician!"

Benny laughed. "Didn't you know it?"

"No!" She shook her head. Then she heard the hushing again and frowned. It wasn't in the hallway. She turned to the closet, then the bed, noticing that the cover was not pristinely flat like in the other rooms. Someone had been on it. She stood quickly, turning to Graeme. "We should leave."

He noticed the bed the same time as her, and something dangerous changed in his expression. He walked over to the closet and yanked open the door.

A girl fell out.

A string from the cello snapped loudly.

The girl glared at Jocelyn with outrage, her black dress in disarray. A tall, square-jawed, bleached-blond man followed from the closet. He looked a little older than Graeme. His bow-tie hung loose and he made a deliberate motion of fixing his belt.

Benny's eyes widened and Poem gasped before covering her mouth and looking at Jocelyn in panic—as if something adult had happened or was about to happen and she didn't want to see it.

Graeme grabbed the man by his collar and looked ready to throw him through a window.

"Graeme!"

Everyone froze. Rachel Winslow Rochester stood on the scene, her body erect. Jocelyn heard Benny breathe, "Uh-oh," as he pivoted from parent to siblings. They waited. It seemed like the blond man knew Graeme couldn't hit him.

Graeme took a breath and gave him a shove instead.

The blond man eyed Mrs. Rochester rudely and saluted. "Governor."

Jocelyn thought the governor might do more damage than Graeme.

"Benny, take Poem back to the party," Mrs. Rochester said.

Benny and Poem scattered.

Despite the sexy gown, ruffled hair, and makeup that gave her the appearance of an exotic Latina, Jocelyn knew with shock and surety that this was her sister. Little sister, she reminded herself, despite the impression.

And their first meeting was not going to go well.

As if from the heightened stress, the other strings on the cello snapped comically.

Morgan's fury and embarrassment shot across the room at Jocelyn and the instrument.

"That was my mother's!"

Jocelyn turned to Mrs. Rochester, not thinking. "It needs to be restrung."

"My REAL mother!" Morgan hissed.

"Morgan!" Graeme's voice held shocked anger and something of a warning.

His mom didn't move, but Jocelyn saw the color drain from her face at the unexpected blow. Torn and confused by the tension between mother and foster daughter, Jocelyn sought to diffuse the situation. She took a breath and smiled at Morgan. "It still needs to be restrung."

Morgan's chin rose, her expression scornful. "Who *are* you?"

"We can save the introduction for later." Mrs. Rochester addressed the man from the closet. "Chandler, my daughter is sixteen, barely. If charges need to be pressed now or in the future, please know that I won't hesitate." She gave a slight nod to the door dismissing him. "Enjoy the ball."

Chandler didn't take the exit offered. He walked right up to the formidable woman, angled his head and said, "I kinda don't think you'd want that kind of publicity."

Jocelyn couldn't believe the guy said that. She watched in awe, as Graeme's mother seemed to get taller, her voice deadlier.

"Don't threaten me, child. If your idea of the big leagues is hitting on high school girls, then I have to wonder what that fat head of yours is compensating for. Now get out of my sight before I have you thrown out."

Chandler left, albeit sullenly.

Jocelyn stood, carefully put the cello and bow back how she found them, and apologized. "Graeme, I'll wait downstairs." Jocelyn went to the hallway and followed Chandler back to the main room. She spotted Rex and lifted a hand. He joined her immediately.

"I think maybe that man needs some encouragement to make it an early night."

Rex scowled. "What happened?"

"Umm." She didn't know what you said in these circumstances. And she didn't want to say anything negative about the sister she only just met. Her stomach twisted. Morgan was nothing like she expected.

The sound of Graeme's steps at the top of the landing saved her. She turned and felt his energy, heard his heartbeat pounding. Rex saw him too and got the message.

"Tell him I'll take care of it."

Jocelyn nodded. "Thank you."

Graeme joined her and she took his hand. "I'm so sorry. I should have never played the cello. We should have left."

"No," Graeme interrupted. "Believe me. I'm glad we were there. My sister is an idiot. And I can't believe she said that to my mom. I want to kill her. And that—"

"Rex took care of him." She clasped his other hand to comfort, and not sure what else to do, leaned up and pecked him on the lips. It was a light kiss, but it took him by surprise. A smile twitched at his mouth. Seeing her opening, she grinned at him, and earned a smile back.

"Okay. Let's find Sabrina and Rex and join them for dinner."

"I would love that! I really wanted to talk to Sabrina more. I heard she was a doctor?"

Graeme slid his arm around her waist and pulled her to him briefly. "Thank you."

She felt brilliant for lightening his mood. It made her worry a little less about Morgan as well. Maybe things were not so bad as she thought.

"So you play the cello?"

Jocelyn nodded. "I didn't even know it! Isn't that outstanding?"

He laughed out loud this time. "Let's go. You've got to be hungry after that."

"I am! How did you know?"

They had made their way across the bustling floor when Jocelyn heard her name. She peeked back to see Morgan and Mrs. Rochester looking down from the second floor. The older woman glided down the steps as if nothing had happened. Morgan obviously didn't feel the same way. Heart sinking, Jocelyn felt the heat of her sister's glare aimed at her.

Morgan blamed her for tonight. And she mouthed the warning right at Jocelyn, across the ballroom, never knowing that the sister who had fought off an army to get to her, would hear the painful declaration.

"Just wait."

Graeme and Jocelyn set out to enjoy the rest of the evening. They danced past midnight, talked with Rex and Sabrina, sampled every dessert offered, and laughed a lot. Jocelyn posed for several pictures, careful to turn her face away or make sure it was blocked, and always making sure they wrote down The Fabulous Brittany Walsh—with a capital 'T'—sustainable fashion designer.

She was sorry when the drive back to Brittany's was over, but happy when Graeme got out of the car with her. She thanked Sir Henry, who had parked discreetly away from the door, and they walked up the steps to the residence hall.

"I wish the night didn't have to end," she said.

"I know. I had a great time. Tell Brittany all her work was worth it."

"I will. Maybe that blogger will post a picture of the dress."

"I'm pretty sure she will." Graeme caught her hands in his, one of his thumbs caressing lightly over her skin.

She had to tilt her head back to make eye contact but was close enough to feel the heat emanating from his body. She put a hand over his heart and he covered it with one of his. His heart pounded as fast as hers.

Please tell me you are not going to kiss that pretty boy.

Jocelyn jumped. The moment disturbed.

"What is it?"

"Uh. Nothing." She said it too quick, spinning her head to peer across the street into the darkness. There was a small park. He must be waiting there. Dang it. He knew she could hear him. Why did he have to show up now? "I should go in."

"Okay." Graeme squeezed her hand and released it.

"I really had the greatest night ever. Thank you so much."

"Of course."

Blaa, blaa, blaa. Get rid of him.

Jocelyn closed her eyes in frustration. Seth had the worst timing. If Graeme was going to kiss her, the moment was gone.

Graeme contemplated her a moment, then smiled softly. "Where's your key?"

"Here."

He took it and opened the door for her. "I'll see you to-morrow at 11:00 a.m. Brunch at Cravings."

"Yes." She beamed. "I can't wait."

"Okay." Graeme pecked her on the head. "Goodnight, Jocelyn."

Graeme got in the front seat of the car and tilted his head back with a groan.

"Why didn't you kiss her?" Henry pulled away from the curb.

"I don't know." Graeme exhaled, his body sinking, hand over his eyes. "I was about to, and something happened, and then all I could hear in my head was my mother's voice saying she's seventeen."

"That's messed up."

"I know!"

"Youth is wasted on the young."

"I know!"

Henry sighed heavily for him. "Well, no harm in waiting. Plenty of time for romance."

Graeme nodded. Comforted a little. It had been a great night. He got to experience the girl of his dreams really being the girl of his dreams. Sure, she had secrets, could kick ass like a marine, and was probably hiding more than she was sharing… but he was crazy about her.

He knew she had felt the same connection as they held hands in the back of the car. And then they got out…

"Pull over a minute." Something had not been right. "Wait for me here. I'll be right back." Graeme hurried back down the street, cutting through the park and stopping short in the darkness to see Jocelyn walk back out the door of the residence hall still in her dress. She waited, then smiled a little as a guy in jeans, black T-shirt, and cowboy hat sauntered up the steps and checked her out. He made a twirling motion with his finger and she spun showing him the dress. Graeme's stomach clenched as the guy stepped forward and put his arms around Jocelyn. She hugged him back and lifted her head for a kiss, giving him her cheek. The guy pulled her arm to bring her down the stairs and she pointed up, like she had to go see the girls. He didn't give up.

Finally she relented and went with him down the street. Graeme scowled at their backs as the cocky bastard slung an arm around Jocelyn's shoulders like he was used to it.

What did that mean? And where did this guy come from?

Graeme Rochester wasn't the only one spying.

Medina watched the scene with regret. Jocelyn and Seth. The two of them together. He had no control of his new eyes and the evidence of Seth's arrival was instantly relayed back to Cashus.

Jocelyn should have stayed underground. Instead she went right where they expected. And Seth had been drawn to her despite knowing better.

She'd be dead inside a week, and Medina didn't want to be the one to do the job. He'd given his life so she could escape. Now he might be the one to take her life. For the first time in his military career he had true fear. He couldn't control himself anymore. Whatever Cashus had done, the man could mess with his mind and puppet Medina's actions. Every ounce of free will he used took extreme effort.

The sound in his ear penetrated his skull painfully.

"Return to the office, Medina."

"Copy." He took a step in the wrong direction and the pain intensified. It wasn't until he made it a block in the right direction that there was some relief. Sound waves—the worst kind of GPS ever invented.

He walked back to the office like an automaton. A rare truth hit him—maybe that's all he'd ever been.

CHAPTER FOURTEEN

*J*ocelyn woke with a start. Brittany was screaming.

The girls scrambled to see what it was. Brittany held her chest trying to breathe.

"Oh-mi-gosh! Are you choking? Hold your arms up, Brit!" Georgie desperately tried to analyze the symptoms while Brittany screamed.

"I don't think she's choking," Lena said, adjusting her glasses.

Finally Brittany sat down. Then she started crying. That made Jocelyn worry.

"What is it?" Jocelyn heard the fear in Georgie's voice. The room went silent. They waited while Brittany hiccupped and gathered herself.

"I'm…I'm…"

Jocelyn thought Georgie might beat it out of her in a minute. Then Brittany turned her laptop around.

"I'm famous."

They stared at the computer and there on the *Vogue* blog was Brittany's dress.

"Seriously?" Lena threw a pillow at her and flopped back down on the bed.

"And they spelled my name with a capital T!"

"Of course," Jocelyn said. She checked the pictures, and the one that had her face was suitably blurred.

"That's great," Georgie said. "But next time, don't give us all heart attacks."

"I'm sorry. But that's not all." Brittany wiped her eyes. "I got an email from my website. Actually a lot of them, and my Twitter has like ten thousand new followers since this morning, and anyway, one of the women who emailed wanted a dress made from the same material. Basically she wants Jocelyn's dress but in a size ten, and I said"—Brittany took a deep breath while they waited—"I said it would be five thousand dollars."

Lena sat up in shock. "Five thousand dollars?"

Brittany nodded, tears forming again. "For the fifty percent down payment."

Lena and Jocelyn gasped.

Georgie laughed.

Brittany nodded some more. "She deposited it into my account this morning."

"What!" Georgie screamed. They all screamed. Then they jumped up and down and screamed more until someone outside yelled to keep it down.

Brittany came over to Jocelyn and held her. And kept holding her. Jocelyn patted her back as the hug extended past awkward, and a little longer.

Finally Brittany released her. "*Vous êtes ma toile.* I learned how to say it last night. And now that I am your designer, you can't take on anyone else."

"Of course not. And that's great news, because I have brunch with Graeme at eleven and not a thing to wear."

"That's an hour away!"

"Yes."

"You never give me any time! You think I can just whip up a miracle every day."

"Yes."

"Maybe I can, but you shouldn't take advantage. Get in the shower, then come back and give us details. You got in so late I had to hear about the party from the Internet. How do you think that makes us feel?"

"That's right," Georgie chimed, smiling. "Terrible."

Brittany ranted a little longer in a loving way. Jocelyn knew she was really too happy to care about anything but the *Vogue* article, the money, and being famous.

"Jocelyn." Lena rubbed her eyes. "We need to go to your childhood church after brunch, so come right back. We have to request your baptismal certificate. I need two forms of identification."

"What's the other going to be?" Jocelyn asked.

"Your birth certificate. We can get that Monday at the government office."

Jocelyn froze. "How?"

"Well, I'm hoping just with your SSN and your baptismal. We can do it online, but it takes longer. We should be able to get it same day if we go in person. I already made an appointment. I'll go with you and catch the train right after."

"Okay." Time to move forward.

"Now tell us about last night," Georgie insisted.

Jocelyn began with, "It was the most amazing night of my life." She didn't tell them about the incident with Morgan, just that she didn't really get to talk to her much. She did tell them about Sabrina, and Georgie researched her while Jocelyn was in the shower. When she came out they had an outfit all ready.

Jocelyn hurried into Cravings, twenty minutes late. Graeme stood immediately. Thankfully Georgie had texted him for her. They hugged, she apologized profusely, they went to the line to order, then waited in a booth for the food. Jocelyn had barely relaxed when she heard someone comment that those shoes looked like Goodwill rejects and realized they were talking about her. She glanced over and saw Morgan with two friends. Jocelyn tucked her shoes under the booth as much as she could. They *were* used but from the Salvation Army store.

"So, did you get enough sleep last night?" Graeme asked.

"Yes. The girls were crashed when I got in so we were catching up this morning. Sorry to be late."

Graeme nodded. The food arrived and they talked about their plans for the day, and Graeme invited her out Thursday night. She agreed readily. She would have liked to see him sooner, but with Seth around, a break was probably a good thing.

"Hey, sweetheart. I didn't know you were going to be here."

Jocelyn froze in panic. As if on cue, Seth slid into the booth next to her, propping his cowboy hat on her head. Graeme raised a brow.

"Probably because I didn't tell you." Jocelyn took off the hat, scowled at him pointedly, and shoved it on Seth's lap. "Um, Graeme, this is Seth. An old friend." She searched for an explanation. "We were homeschooled together."

"Is that right?" Graeme said. Jocelyn saw a look on Graeme's face and knew instantly he didn't like Seth.

"Yes. Homeschooled. That's one way to describe it." Jocelyn felt Seth's gaze on her.

"Seth is visiting for a short while. How short are you here for, Seth?"

"As long as it takes to bring you back home."

Jocelyn choked on her water. What was he talking about?

"I don't think she wants to go with you," Graeme noted.

"We'll see." Seth picked at the fries in front of her. "Can I get you anything, baby? I know you're still hungry."

She was going to kill him. Only she couldn't now because Morgan and her friends were coming over.

"Hi there." Morgan didn't even look at Jocelyn.

"Hello, darlin'." Seth's Texan accent came out a little stronger as he took in Morgan's tight jeans and low-cut T-shirt.

Morgan slid next to her brother and checked out Seth with a smile. Graeme's grip on his soda tightened. Jocelyn thought he might crush the glass in his hands.

"Seth, this is Morgan, Graeme's sister."

"Well, I see who got the looks in the family."

Morgan laughed, delighted. "These are my friends, Meghana and Jenna."

"The sights of New York just keep getting better," Seth said.

Jocelyn recognized the Indian-American girl from last night. She'd worn a stunning black and white sari. Jenna, she didn't know. The blond girl squeezed next to Seth, forcing Jocelyn up against the wall, her leg pressed to Seth's.

"Seth is a friend of Jocelyn's," Graeme said.

"Uh-huh." Morgan continued to make eye contact with Seth.

Jocelyn greeted the other girls, then looked down at her fries. Might as well eat. She dipped a fry in her ketchup and let the train wreck begin.

"Where are you from, Seth?" Morgan asked. "I love your accent."

Jocelyn didn't need to see it to know Seth winked at Morgan while replying. "The great state of Texas. We live large or laugh tryin'."

"It must be great," Jenna teased seductively, "with guys like you there."

"He's actually here right now, not Texas," Jocelyn noted.

No one listened.

Oh man, her sister was flirting with Seth and Seth flirted back. And Graeme wanted none of it. Of course, Seth didn't know Morgan was her sister, so she couldn't really blame him. But Seth was definitely trying to piss off Graeme. Jocelyn looked at the clock on the wall. Maybe her friends would come early and rescue her.

Seth started playing with her hair and she slapped his hand away.

Morgan eyed her curiously—an unfriendly curious.

"Jocelyn, was it?"

She nodded. "I think I saw that shirt at Target. Did you get it on sale?"

Jocelyn wasn't sure what Morgan meant, but the tone warned her. "Actually, I borrowed it."

Morgan gave it a dismissive glance. "It looks cheap."

Jocelyn blinked. Morgan didn't mean that as a compliment. "At least it fits," Jocelyn snapped back.

Graeme smiled a little. "As your brother, I agree—about your top."

Seth jumped in. "I think it's gorgeous and shows off your—"

"No one asked you!" Graeme and Jocelyn spoke at once.

Seth smiled and finished his sentence. "—coloring."

"Seth." Jocelyn took a breath. "Dear friend who is visiting for a very *short* visit. Why don't we catch up later?"

Seth put his arm around her shoulder and kissed her on the forehead. "Are you thinking of another all-nighter?"

Yep. Definitely going to kill him.

"I should get going," Graeme said.

"If you're not doing anything, I could show you around this afternoon," Jenna offered to Seth as she scooted out and tried to give her number.

Morgan's phone rang and she also scooted out to take the call in private. Something on her face made Jocelyn listen in. It was Chandler and he wanted to meet Morgan tonight at a bar. He asked if she had an ID. *What did that mean?* Of course she had an ID.

Everyone moved at once. Jocelyn's head spun a bit as she was separated from Graeme. Finally, she gave up and went outside for air. She shouldn't have antagonized Morgan. And Seth should have *never* followed her here. She shouldn't have told him she had brunch plans. She covered her face. Someone tugged her hair. Seth!

"Go away!"

"Sorry," Graeme said.

"Graeme! Not you. I'm sorry."

"So…not the quiet brunch."

"I'm really sorry. Seth is just…his sense of humor some-times…"

"Can be annoying? Egotistical? Antagonistic? Make you want to bash his face in?"

Jocelyn laughed. "But he's my friend. And—"

"I get it. It's okay." He handed her a phone. "It's a secure line as long as you only use it to call me. I know dating you is not going to be like dating other girls and things are a little more complicated."

"Dating?" Seth asked. "It was only one date last I heard."

Jocelyn put her hand subtly on Seth's hard bicep and zapped him fiercely.

He jumped. "Fine. I can take a hint."

"Thank you," Jocelyn said.

He turned and put an arm around Morgan's shoulders and she slid her arm around his waist. "I'll go where I'm wanted."

"Who's not wanted?" Brittany asked, coming up behind them.

Now they get here. Feeling overwhelmed, Jocelyn quickly made introductions.

Georgie eyed Graeme warily. "So, we officially meet?"

"Yes, and it's a pleasure."

"I'll take my time and think about that," Georgie said.

Lena was friendly with Graeme and Graeme easily won over Brittany despite any suspected spying on her.

Brittany just laughed when she met Seth, giving Jocelyn a raised brow. "You didn't tell us Seth was in town."

"He just got here late last night," Jocelyn explained, aware that Graeme paid attention.

Jocelyn also saw right away that Morgan didn't care for the college girls, probably because they were her friends.

"Brittany is the one who designed my dress," Jocelyn said by way of introduction.

Morgan dismissed her, as if understanding. "I thought it looked homemade."

Lena gasped at the insult, backing away and hugging her computer defensively.

"Read *Vogue*, much?" Brittany didn't miss a beat.

"She's famous," Jocelyn added, upset that her sister would insult one of her friends.

"Morgan." Graeme's tone scolded his sister and she shrugged as if that was her opinion and she should be able to speak the truth. Meanwhile, her friend Meghana looked embarrassed. Jenna was busy with Seth.

"We should go." Jocelyn awkwardly hugged Graeme, pulled Seth away from the younger teens, and reminded him that he was going in the same direction.

The groups separated and they were a block away when Brittany finally burst out. "Your sister's a bitch!"

"And I don't think she likes you," Lena said to Jocelyn.

"What?" Seth froze on the sidewalk. "Who's your sister?" Everyone stared him. Jocelyn scowled.

Brittany stood, firmly unapologetic. "I told you it was bad to keep secrets from people close to you."

"I guess I'm not that close." Seth stared thoughtfully, working it out. "Are you kidding? Morgan?" Seth asked. "Yeah, I can see it."

Jocelyn shrugged.

"Does she know?" he asked.

"No!" everyone chimed.

"Don't yell. You told me you had family to check on. I thought it was an old aunt or something. So what, she was adopted into a filthy rich family?"

"Pretty much," Georgie answered for her. "We don't really know how much they know, or if they put Jocelyn away."

"They didn't put me away. They're really nice," Jocelyn insisted.

"You think everyone is nice," Brittany said.

"She does," Seth agreed.

"She said you were nice," Georgie added.

"Nice. That's all I got? After all we've been through." Seth halted again, forcing them to stop. "Nice?"

Jocelyn sighed. "I said *really* nice!"

"You know she has a thing for Graeme, right?" Brittany told him.

"Yeah. Whatever." He continued to walk. "I thought she had better taste."

"Graeme is hot," Lena defended. "And he's really smart and a good leader. I've worked with him."

Seth smiled. "That's cool. I was just teasing. It's nice that she has such nice friends. Sooo nice."

Jocelyn spun around and dust flew in a whirlwind surrounding them. Everyone paused, expectant. The dust literally settled before Georgie touched her arm.

"It's okay, Jocelyn. It's just friend teasing."

Jocelyn registered the touch first, then her words. "It is?"

Seth apologized. "Sorry. I didn't know she was your sister. I only flirted to piss off *Graaaeme*." He said it in an exaggerated, dreamy voice, emphasizing friend teasing.

She wasn't sure she liked it. "Why did you want to piss off Graeme?"

"Because he likes you." He shrugged like it was obvious. "That's what guys do. We test each other."

Jocelyn looked to the others for confirmation and received several nods.

"It's messed up but true," Lena said.

"Morgan's still a bitch," Brittany said. "The bad egg in your family, I guess. 'Homemade!' She will *rue* the day. I will *never* design anything for her when I'm even more famous than I am now."

"I'm really sorry, Brit. You know your dress was a hit last night. Graeme even said you were a genius without me telling him."

"He did?" Brittany recovered a little. "Okay. He has good taste at least."

"You guys," Lena interrupted. "I know there's a lot happening, but we need to get there by two."

"Where are we going?" Seth asked.

"To hack a church," Lena told him.

"Fun! I like hanging with you girls." Seth moved to put his arm around Jocelyn. "Don't be mad at me. I'm just protecting you. In my way," Seth added after he didn't get a response. "Okay, in my weird, Texas charming way?"

Jocelyn smiled finally.

"It's my job. You were really sheltered."

"Homeschooled. Get the story straight."

"Got it. We were homeschooled together, and I was your first love."

"We'll work on that part."

"Childhood sweetheart?" he negotiated.

Jocelyn put her arm around his waist for a sideways hug. Seth was irrepressible. She kind of liked that about him. She just wasn't sure having him in New York was a good idea. Things were complicated enough.

CHAPTER FIFTEEN

At the church they agreed that only Jocelyn and Brittany would go into the office. None of them would let Georgie, since if they were caught, it was a crime, and of all of them she was one who might be a lawyer or President of the United States some day. Seth insisted that this was his expertise, but the girls thought if there was a nun running the office, she would see right through him.

So Jocelyn and Brittany went in. The plan was simply to tell the truth, and while doing so, attach a small USB, the size of a mini-adapter, to the office computer. Lena would do the rest from the coffee shop down the street.

Jocelyn smiled her sweetest and made her request to Mrs. O'Brien who sat in the office answering phones and listening to church music.

"Dear, the office is closed today. Someone could find your records tomorrow."

"Are you sure? I have an appointment first thing in the morning, and they need a second form of identification."

"I'm sorry, dear."

Brittany pulled a large yearbook off the shelf and rifled through it. "Would you have any more of these?"

"The church album?"

"Yes," Brittany said. "It looks like you do them every year."

"Sometimes there's extra in storage. I'd have to look. They are fifty dollars a piece."

"That's okay. I'll buy it for you, Jocelyn." She opened to a page. "Look."

Jocelyn gasped. "It's my family. It's me! Look!"

"I know, I found it." Brittany grinned and looked at the lady. "Do you have this one?"

Mrs. O'Brien came around the desk, putting on her glasses.

"This was the year her parents died," Brittany said softly.

"And I don't have any pictures of them. Or of our whole family together." Jocelyn didn't have to fake at wiping her eyes, but she certainly didn't want blue tears freaking out Mrs. O'Brien. "This might be one of the last ones taken of us as a..."

"Oh! You poor thing." Mrs. O'Brien looked about to cry herself. She took a key out of the desk. "I don't know what we have in the storage room these days, but any extras would be there."

Jocelyn followed her until Brittany hit her arm and motioned for the USB. Jocelyn passed it to her and went into the closet, full of hope. They looked around for a while before Mrs. O'Brien shook her head and returned to the desk. "There are so many boxes. I'll look through this week and call if I find one."

"Okay," Jocelyn said.

Mrs. O'Brien touched the computer keyboard. "When were you born?"

Jocelyn gave her the information needed.

"Usually a baptism is about two weeks after your birth. You might not have been baptized here but we should have a copy for your school record." Mrs. O'Brien began talking to herself.

"Here we go. Jocelyn Esperanza Albrecht. You were in Miss Logozio's class. She's Mrs. O'Connor now, but I bet she would love to see you. Teachers love when students come back."

"I would love to see her," Jocelyn agreed, excited.

Brittany kicked her shin in warning and smiled.

"Well, this might help. If not, you can get a new one issued." The printer buzzed and paper came out. It was a copy of her original baptismal certificate.

"Thank you so much!" Jocelyn held the precious document, overwhelmed at having a piece of her history.

"We should go," Brittany suggested.

"Yes. Thank you so much."

"Wait. I'm not done with you yet, Miss Albrecht."

Jocelyn swallowed and Brittany's eyes widened with caution. Mrs. O'Brien continued. "We have all the photos digitally." The printer made another whizzing sound and she walked over to catch a piece of paper. "I'll email this, but you can have it for now." She held up a color photo of the Albrecht family. Jocelyn teared up again.

Brittany jumped in. "Here's my info. Jocelyn is still getting settled. I'll make sure she gets it."

"Of course. You two take care and don't be a stranger now that you're back."

"I won't," Jocelyn said. "Thank you again." She held up the photo. "This means so much more than I can ever express." Brittany pulled at her arm. "Thank you."

Brittany hurried Jocelyn along and back toward the coffee shop.

"Ohmigosh!" Jocelyn squealed. "Ohmigosh, ohmigosh! I can't believe I got my baptismal thing and this photo! Brittany, you are like a super spy. I couldn't keep my head together. That's not like me, my hands were tingling. I felt so close to like… my family and my past. And being real again. I know it sounds stupid.”

“It doesn't,” Brittany said. “But you're babbling.”

“I am! Isn't that wonderful. I'm free and I'm babbling and I'm walking around New York City and I have friends!”

“Uh-huh.” Brittany nodded to a passerby who checked them out.

“And look how cute Benny is.” She held up the photo again, staring. “Such a little baby. And my parents—” She choked again.

Brittany stopped her. “Do *not* cry. Your eyes fill up and look a little…unnatural when you do.”

“I know. I never cry. Not even really when I was shot. Now all this happy stuff makes me cry. It's so weird. I'm so happy right now.”

Brittany laughed. “Okay. Let's see what else Milk is able to get. Hopefully even more to be happy about.”

They popped into the café. A small three-piece band played contemporary tunes. She stopped in front of them, listening. The music lightened Jocelyn's spirit even more—and there was a cello player! The vibrations seemed to soothe her all over. She felt like anything might be possible.

Brittany directed her to the others and Jocelyn waved to the musicians, turning with a little spring in her step. She imagined her own little apartment and a chair with a cello like in Morgan's room. She wouldn't need much.

They found the other three in the far corner of the venue, laughing around Lena's computer. Lena spotted the envelope in Jocelyn's hand and snatched it. “I'm already in.” Lena studied them with a smile. “Is this your family?” She passed it to Georgie and Seth. “That's really nice.”

"I discovered it," Brittany said, sharing more on their successful intel-gathering session.

Seth stared at it a long time before turning his head to Jocelyn. "I didn't know. I'm sorry."

She shrugged.

"Really," Seth said. "I never had anything to lose. You had this." He kept staring at the photo. "Picture perfect. You can tell your parents were cool. And they loved you. All of you. It's effed up what Cashus did. You might have had a chance at another family."

Jocelyn gazed at the picture again. Only now the paper was on fire. She squeaked as did the other girls, but Seth held the paper away for the few seconds it needed to be consumed in flames. He put his lighter back in his pocket. "And that's why I'm here."

The girls gasped in horror. Jocelyn nearly yelled, but instead caught herself and sat silently with the others before responding. "I would have been safe."

"Right. Like you were about staying out of sight and off the society page and keeping a low profile? *Vogue* Online? Really?"

Jocelyn defended herself. "Live large or laugh tryin'."

"Don't quote me," Seth snapped. "You know they want to either kill you or slowly destroy you, and you went straight to where they could find you."

Jocelyn decided to change the subject. She gave Brittany a look of hope that she wouldn't mention the digital version of the photo, then turned to Lena.

"So what fun stuff did you find?"

Lena blinked anxiously through her white-rimmed glasses. "Um. Oh, yeah. Tons of stuff! The most fun are the student report cards. Wanna hear?"

Jocelyn nodded.

Recovered, Lena imitated a teacher's voice. "Jocelyn is a bright, thoughtful, well-liked child. She is an outstanding student who is always willing to help others. She is a delight to have in my class."

Seth smirked, shaking his head. "That's exactly like you. Disgusting."

Jocelyn ignored him. "How was Morgan's?"

Lena repressed her smile and took on the teacher voice again. "Morgan is a good student but has trouble sharing."

"Right?" Brittany laughed.

"She enjoys performing in front of the class—sometimes a little too much—but she has a good heart."

The girls laughed.

Jocelyn frowned. "Don't laugh at her."

The girls stopped.

"She's my sister. It hasn't been easy on her."

Brittany raised a brow and Seth tilted his head like he would argue.

"Sorry," Georgie said.

"We used to live in this neighborhood. But the only thing I really remember is that music store we passed. I was thinking after I get my identity, then a full-time job and a place to live I could save up for a cello. I've always liked music. Maybe I could play with an orchestra some day. My mom played the cello."

Everyone stared at her, silent.

"It's good to have goals," Brittany finally said. "I'm making a bulletproof corset. I just need someone to shoot at it to test it out when I'm done—and someone else to wear it."

"Hmm. Tempting," Georgie said. "Let me think about that. Hmm. No."

Jocelyn changed the subject. "Lena, was there anything else useful?"

Lena shoved a bite of coconut cream pie in her mouth and nodded. "Um-hmm. I hit payduh."

"What?"

Jocelyn laughed at Lena's full mouth, regaining her happier mood.

"Pay dirt," Lena said. "I got your social security number and"—she turned her laptop around to show—"your fingerprints. They were part of the school security system."

"What?" Brittany sulked. "That's a bummer."

Everyone looked at her.

"I just designed you some last night with cool hidden messages like 'Brittany is fabulous.'"

"You put 'Brittany is fabulous' on my fingerprints?" Jocelyn laughed.

"Okay, I might have gone too far. But they're really nice prints."

"We'll use these," Georgie said. "But good effort, Brit."

Brittany waved a hand. "I can print these ones, I guess. I ordered the material already. They peel off and apply to your tips. It will be perfect, of course."

Lena nodded. "I don't think we need them until you apply for your identification card."

That reminded Jocelyn of something. "Do you need an ID to get into a bar?"

"Yes," Georgie said. "You can't legally drink alcohol until you're twenty-one."

"But lots of people have fake IDs," Lena said.

"So they can get in and drink?" Jocelyn worried about that. Morgan was sixteen. *Barely sixteen.*

Lena nodded. "Do you want another card that says you're twenty-one? I could do that."

"No. No. I was just wondering." What was Morgan up to? Seth might be mad that she went straight to her family, but as far as Jocelyn was concerned, with Morgan's decision-making and Benny's illness, she was just in time. She only hoped she was wrong about tonight.

Jerry Ramstein surveyed the office at the NSA. The tracker who had spotted Project Sunday had been given a promotion and an upgrade from a cube.

"She's wily at times, usually at night," the tracker explained, sharing some footage of her disappearing into the subway system. "I lost her a few times but can usually pick her up again in key neighborhoods." The tracker spun to his new partner in the office and had her play some live video. "We also tracked Dr. Wicker's asset. He's in New York as well but sticks to neighborhoods where we don't have strong infrastructure."

Jerry gave an approving nod to them both. "Keep up the good work. I have my office wired now for direct links to your system. This mission is highly sensitive."

"Yes, sir."

The lead tracker looked about to say something.

"What is it?" Jerry asked.

"Are we going to be picking them up soon, sir?" He seemed to realize that was a presumptuous and classified question so hastened to add, "Just so we are prepared for backup of all the material if it's an extended surveillance."

Jerry gave a closed-mouth smile. "We have Project Sunday underway, but always prepare for the worst. You don't have to worry much longer about Wicker's asset." The trackers and his assistant waited patiently for his explanation. He loved knowing people waited on his every word. Even more, he loved having the information everyone wanted.

"Let him enjoy the sights." He smiled finally, this time showing teeth. "His expiration date is coming soon."

CHAPTER SIXTEEN

*C*larence chatted up the polite coed outside the resident hall housing. The perky blond girl tried to be helpful but didn't remember anyone named Jocelyn. Another girl came down the street, carrying a package. The girl turned to her.

"Brittany, do you know a Jocelyn who lives here?"

Brittany adjusted her box. "No. Who wants to know?"

"I do." Clarence smiled at her. Even bald, women appreciated his bodybuilder form.

"And you are?"

"A friend."

"Sounds like you were given the wrong address."

"Are you sure?"

"Yes," Brittany asserted. "I know everyone in the building and there's no one with that name."

"Can I show you a picture?"

Brittany adjusted her box, impatient. "I'm pretty busy."

He put the picture in front of her.

"Nope. Doesn't live here."

"I think I've seen her," the blond said. Then she looked at Brittany. "Don't you know her?"

Brittany scrutinized the photo. "No."

"She might have short blond hair now. But not as pretty as yours," Clarence said to the petite blond. The girl smiled.

"Do you have a last name?"

"Cashus."

"No one named Cashus here."

"Maybe I could come in and talk with the manager."

"Absolutely not!" Brittany said. "Students only. Come on, Belinda."

"Aw, really?" Clarence pouted.

"Really." Brittany hurried up the stairs and tried to juggle the box while getting her keys out. He could tell when a woman was rattled. Clarence followed and took her box.

"Please put my box down." She got her keys out.

"Just trying to be hospitable."

"Belinda, are you coming?"

Belinda slipped inside. Brittany took her box back, staring at his hands. All the better to strangle you with, he thought.

"If you have a missing person, you might try the police station. Goodbye."

She closed the door shut and locked it.

Clarence smiled.

He'd come back. Brittany was cute. And feisty. Just how he liked 'em. He flexed his hands, observing his light blue nails. Did Brittany notice?

He nodded to Rabbit at the corner, leaning on a pole and eating a burrito. Jocelyn was probably at the other location. He'd go there first, then come back for Brittany.

Georgie got the urgent text from Brittany but didn't have any way to reach Jocelyn. They weren't meeting until Monday evening after classes. She debated texting Graeme. He'd given

Jocelyn a phone that was supposedly secure. Maybe she was with him?

Shoot.

She took a chance and texted. He called back.

"Hey, she said she had plans tonight. What's up?"

"I'm not sure. A man was looking for her outside Brittany's place. She said he was big and creepy. And…"

"And?" Graeme asked.

"Well, she said it might have been the lighting and all, but that his nails had a distinct blue color that reminded her of Jocelyn's."

Graeme was silent.

"What do you think?" Georgie asked.

"I'll find her."

"Okay. Please let me know. Thank you." She hung up, texted Brittany, and waited. After an hour, Graeme called and said she wasn't answering her phone. He sounded concerned. She'd left Jocelyn with Seth that afternoon and had no idea where to look first. From the sound of it, neither did Graeme. She just hoped Seth was with her.

Seth didn't like spying. It was tedious. But he was with Jocelyn, so that made it better. She entertained him with her views of the world. Everything was fresh to her. That didn't change the fact that they were spying—on one of her family members.

"How do you know she's going to sneak out?"

"I heard her on the phone at Cravings. She was talking to that jerk Chandler."

Seth shrugged, holding his palms up. "Maybe she wants him to be the one."

"What one?"

"You know." He jerked his head at the obvious.

She looked at him blankly so he decided not to go further. He didn't want to explain female virginity to her. In fact, he didn't even want Jocelyn thinking about sex. Unless it was with him—but that was just ego. He respected her too much to think about her that way. *Hell. Maturing sucked.* But she deserved better than him, anyway.

Her thoughts were on the job. "He said eleven so she should be arriving soon. Do you think we missed her?"

As if on cue, a figure in heels and a long trench coat, got out of a cab.

"Is that her?"

Jocelyn jumped. "Yes!"

Morgan took off her coat and wore a short, tight black dress underneath.

"That's trouble," Seth noted as she floated past the bouncer and down the steps into the bar.

"I need to follow her." Jocelyn pulled her black beanie over the nasty blond wig she still owned and looked to him for guidance. "How do I get in?"

Seth saw another guy come up the steps and start to talk with the bouncer.

"Okay." He flexed his fingers and loosened his shoulders. "I'll create a distraction. You walk in."

"Just walk in?"

"Yep." He gave her a wink. "Then smile at the bartender and do what you do, Sunshine."

Jocelyn wasn't sure Seth's plan would work, but sure enough, he created a distraction and she walked right in—trying very hard to ignore the sound of fists smacking behind her.

She spotted Morgan immediately. There weren't many females. Mostly guys drinking beer and playing pool in the back. Jocelyn took a stool at the corner of the bar and asked for a water while she pretended to peruse the drink menu. Morgan had her back to Jocelyn, but she could imagine her smiling up at Chandler the dirtbag. They ordered drinks and she was relieved when she heard Morgan ask for a Diet Coke. Thankfully her sister wasn't totally clueless.

Chandler seemed to know the bartender well and slipped him a bill. Jocelyn noticed it was a hundred. She also noticed the bartender got the change and pocketed a fifty.

That was a big tip for a beer and a soda.

Smiling, Chandler chatted about his weekend in Atlantic City and how great he did at the poker table. He leaned in randomly at one point pressing his cheek against Morgan's, brushing back some hair.

Jocelyn almost missed the bartender dropping some powder into the soda before mixing and serving the drinks. She didn't know if that was part of a special drink or something else. Shoot. Should she warn Morgan?

They finished their drinks and chatted some more before Chandler invited Morgan onto the miniscule dance floor. They were the only ones there. Morgan appeared very relaxed. At one point her head lolled back, and she straightened as if to shake it off. They danced some more, and Morgan's body began to crumble like a noodle. She caught herself again and blinked as if trying to focus. She looked ill and confused.

Morgan still had her small bag over her shoulder and touched it, excusing herself to go to the restroom.

Chandler smirked and kissed her. As she disappeared around a corner, he turned toward a table where two guys were drinking beers. Jocelyn hadn't really noticed them much. Chandler inclined his head and the two followed Morgan.

Jocelyn's nerves went on alert. She got up and followed, barely registering that Chandler had put a loud rock song on the nearby jukebox. Jocelyn went straight to the ladies' room and panicked when Morgan wasn't there.

She hurried out and back to where a muffled cry called out from the men's room. She tried the door. It was locked.

"Get lost!" one of the guys called.

Then she heard the guy say, "Get away, dude. I'm totally going to do—"

Jocelyn yanked on the handle, snapped the lock, and shouldered the door open, forcing it to swing back with a bang.

"What the—?" a guy voiced, irritated.

Jocelyn gaped.

Morgan lay on the filthy floor with one guy straddling her taking pictures with his phone while the other used the urinal and stared at her in open-mouthed surprise.

"Do *what*?" Jocelyn said with deadly fury.

The man standing, recovered, and zipped his pants. "Get the hell out of here unless you want it too, bi—"

Her fist smashed his mouth before he could finish the word. She felt his teeth loosen on her knuckles. He swung in surprise, but her next punch crushed his nose, watered his eyes, and sent him backward, stunned, and landing his butt in the urinal.

The whole scene filled her with disgust. The other guy had gotten to his feet and his long reach almost connected, but she was fast, trained, and filled with primal rage she'd never experienced before. She heard a light moan from Morgan and the sound fueled Jocelyn as she swung in succession, stunning the guy. She grabbed him by his shirt and swung him around, throwing him against the door before he could fall on Morgan.

He struggled to get up and she kneed him repetitively in the face, knocking him out. The jerk sitting in the urinal spit out teeth and pushed to his feet. He fell forward at her and she stepped aside to let him fall into the sink.

He wanted more apparently because he got up, called her some names, kicked out defensively and swung again.

She gave him a left hook strong enough to rattle his brain and keep him down. Quickly, trying to think what to do, she searched for the phone the one guy had used. Finding it, she pressed his finger on the phone to unlock it, like she had seen Morgan do at brunch. She removed the mandatory password and shoved it in her pocket. She opened Morgan's purse and found her phone, quickly swiping to camera mode.

Shaking, she snapped pictures of the two men for evidence. She put Morgan's phone back in her purse, zipped it, grabbed her sister's scattered shoes, then hoisted her to her feet.

Morgan moaned for her mom, trying to fight whatever they'd given her.

"Hey? Guys? All good?" Chandler pushed the restroom door to get in but couldn't with the unconscious lump that blocked it.

Jocelyn used her pent-up energy and put it to good use. With one hand she aimed and blasted. She didn't bother to warn Chandler about the door about to fly off the hinges at him.

He slammed backward, and she buried him between the door and the wall, while she scooted around and back into the bar. He deserved any headache he got.

A few people checked out her and Morgan as she half-carried her sister over to the bar, grabbed Morgan's coat from the stool, and glared at the worried bartender.

"My friend is sick," she said. She was going to say more but thought better of it. Instead, she memorized his face. He would get his, in due time.

Jocelyn dragged her sister up the steps to the street. The bouncer had ice over his eye and sat in a chair, looking annoyed.

"Jocelyn!" Seth called from the corner.

"Get a cab!"

She threw Morgan over her shoulder and hurried to the corner as the cab pulled up.

"Midtown Memorial Hospital."

"There's one closer, miss." He peeked in the rearview mirror at Morgan. "If you need a hospital."

"No, go to that one."

"Will do."

She closed the window between them and the driver. Sabrina said she was doing her residency at Midtown. Jocelyn prayed she was there. She knew already that the Rochesters protected their family privacy and controlled the press very tightly, but she couldn't risk not taking Morgan to a hospital.

"They drugged her," Jocelyn said, her voice shaking. "And then Chandler sent two guys after her and they trapped her in the men's room." She pulled Morgan's trench coat over her front like a blanket and tucked it around her shoulder. "They were taking pictures. They were going to do stuff to her."

Her sister, for all her grown-up dress and makeup, looked very young at this moment. She brushed Morgan's hair into order with her fingers. Her sister moaned. "It's okay, Morgan. You're safe."

Seth reached across Morgan and grabbed Jocelyn's trembling hand. "Are *you* okay?"

"I almost killed them."

"If you didn't, I'll go back and take care of it for you."

Jocelyn exhaled a shaky breath and smiled. "Thank you."

The cab pulled up to the Emergency entrance. Seth paid. They were at the entrance when Seth stopped.

"You go. Drop her off and don't linger." He pulled blond strands more around her face. You don't want to be recognized."

This time, Jocelyn noticed his hand shook. "Seth?"

"I'm-m going to w-wait outside. See you." He took off around the corner in a rush.

Confused, Jocelyn refocused on Morgan. The night attendant stared at her until she asked for Dr. Sabrina Albrecht and said this was her niece. Then things happened. An orderly helped Jocelyn get Morgan into bed in the Emergency room and pulled the curtains around them before going for the nurse. Jocelyn put the blanket over Morgan and put her shoes and trench coat on the chair next to it. She put the dirtbag's phone in the trench coat and this time pressed Morgan's thumb to her phone.

Scrolling the contacts she found "mom" and began to type. "Mom, at Midtown Memorial. A bartender drugged me. Sick. So sorry. Please help me."

Jocelyn wondered if she should name Chandler or not. She pressed send and put the phone in the pocket with the other phone. Her parents would know what to do.

She heard Sabrina coming and grilling people for information. Jocelyn hurried to the furthest end of the beds and ducked to hide. Sabrina was alone with a nurse. "Has any information been filled out?"

"Not yet. Is this your niece?"

Sabrina didn't give an answer. "There's a mark on her thigh. It's going to bruise. Get a compress for her eye and I want to do a full toxicology report. Get me tweezers, a knife, and plastic baggies. I want to see if there's anything under her nails. Just in case."

"Yes, Doctor." The curtain swished as the nurse hurried away.

A phone rang with a music mash-up of Rachel Rochester saying, "This is your Mom."

Jocelyn heard Sabrina wrestle with the coat and answer.

"Rachel? I got her. I got her. Don't worry. She's passed out, but her vitals are stable."

Jocelyn heard the panic in Rachel's voice. "We're running to the copter, there in five minutes. Is she okay? What happened? Was she hurt?"

"Rachel, I don't know, but she is going to be okay. I'll see you in just a bit."

Jocelyn slowly moved from her crouched position and walked casually past the emergency room beds and out the exit. She kept her head down and didn't turn back.

Morgan would be taken care of—by her real family.

Seth pressed the stopwatch button on his watch. Four minutes. That was a leap.

His body felt wrecked.

The last seizure was three minutes, twenty-five seconds. Those extra thirty-five seconds did some damage. He lay still, exhausted, tired, a little drowsy, and not at all sure where he was or how he got there.

Finally, he pushed himself up to sitting position against a wall. A big red and white emergency room sign glowed nearby. Was he going to get help?

His mind raced trying to piece together the last hour. Then he heard his name called. Jocelyn. Relief coursed through him. She was safe. And he was—well, mostly safe.

"Seth! What happened?" She bent over him. "You don't look well."

"That bouncer punched hard. Just recovering."

She helped him up and put an arm around his waist protectively. "I'm so sorry. What do you need? Are you going to be okay?"

"I feel better now." He moved slowly, making sure his feet and legs obeyed. "Let's take a cab."

"Okay. Where to?"

"A little hotel, but very nice. Stay with me tonight." He missed her. Even the great state of Texas wasn't the same without her.

"Of course." He heard the concern in her voice.

He'd be okay. Mostly, he just needed the comfort of her presence. He'd thought about it a lot and he didn't want to be alone when he died. Whatever their relationship, she was all he had.

CHAPTER SEVENTEEN

Rachel knew how to fight tears. She'd done it a lot. Thankfully Ford was by her side, squeezing her hand so hard it took away some of the tension they felt. The helicopter landed, and she was first down the stairs, rushing to her baby girl. Ford, Rex, and their security officer hurried behind.

Rachel froze at the stillness of her daughter lying in the hospital bed. She hated it. "Can we get her a private room?"

"Yes, they are going to move her shortly," Sabrina said.

Rachel studied Sabrina's face for the truth, afraid to ask for details.

"She appears okay. I didn't order a kit," Sabrina said. "I can if you want me to."

"Oh, God." Rex clutched his side as if the possibility was too much to consider. "I will kill whoever did this. I will kill them."

"You'll have to get past me and your mom first," Ford said.

"There's more," Sabrina said. "I found another phone with hers." Sabrina handed over the phone in a plastic bag. "Not sure what's on it, but there are pictures on her phone. She got evidence somehow."

Ford looked through Morgan's phone and scrolled. "Good girl. I'll get security on this. We'll find out whose phone it is."

Rex put on a latex glove, took the other phone from Sabrina, and checked the photos.

"Sonofa—" He took a breath. "We need to download it before he erases it remotely," Rex said.

Rachel glimpsed the photos and choked on her tears. "How could they?"

Ford put his arm around her and held tightly. "Where was she?" he asked.

"She's been unconscious since she arrived, so I have no idea."

"But she texted me that she was here," Rachel said. "How did she get here?"

"Someone brought her. The front clerk said it was a friend. She asked for me. So it was someone who knows I work here. Blue eyes, blond hair wearing jeans and a beanie."

"A girl?" Rachel asked.

"Yes."

"She didn't stay?" Rachel was furious. Probably Jenna.

"We'll get the security footage," Ford assured her. "And we probably owe the person a thanks, even if they did leave."

Rachel didn't answer. She'd get the information and decide later. For now, she wanted to know what her daughter had been drugged with, when she would wake, and how fast before all the offenders were arrested.

John Morrow woke to a 5:00 a.m. call followed immediately by a knock at his door. A patrol car and two unmarked vehicles were parked outside his house.

When his captain said the words—"The Butcher was released"—he hurried to check on his children.

Finding them safe, he asked questions.

"There was a murder last night," the captain said. "The style was unmistakable. A little rushed, but unmistakable. We called the FEDs right away. They reluctantly admitted that Clarence Cooke had been released on some new kind of pilot program the government is running."

John felt his blood pressure spike dangerously. "I hope they realize the program's an effing failure!"

"That's what I told them. I know you're worried. I have your house and family on twenty-four-hour protection."

"Great. What do I tell my kids? The government let a psychotic serial killer out and he's probably gonna come after us? After I reassured them that same man would never hurt anyone again?"

Kymber paused on the stairs, her face turning white. He reached out and pulled her into his arms.

"He'd be crazy to try to attack your home, and that's not his MO. He picks girls who are between sixteen and twenty-six and are generally easy targets."

"So the trail was just bad luck."

"John, I'm sorry. It's messed up beyond belief. Someone will pay, but right now, I want you to know we're going to take care of you. I'm heading downtown to see if I can get more from the FEDs on site. He killed a girl at a Youth Hostel in Chinatown. No parent should get that news."

John's blood went cold. Had the Butcher hunted the girl down?

"I'll meet you there," John said. His captain argued, but John insisted. If he had killed the Butcher when he had the chance, this wouldn't have happened. So much for being a true-blue lawman. Now he had innocent blood on his hands. And he had to make sure it wasn't Jocelyn's.

Jocelyn woke with Seth's arms around her and the air conditioning at sixty degrees. They were both typically warm. Jocelyn a lot more so. Together, they made the place a furnace. Air conditioning felt like a luxury. The hostels had heat but invariably a fan was the normal cooling method.

She used the hotel supplies to brush her teeth and shower, then kept all the extras in a plastic bag for later. Seth said they supplied more every day, which was a super luxury. She sat back on the bed and studied him, her hand naturally taking his pulse and assessing his well-being. They'd started doing that in Texas, making sure they stayed stable, and trying to understand the things that affected both their health and their powers. Something had definitely changed with him.

He'd been drowsy ever since she joined him outside the emergency room. Had he been drinking? She kept her one-day supply of meds on her, but she had two more months worth in her locker at the youth hostel, and a week's supply with all her important documents in a locker at Grand Central Station. Should he be taking the meds as well? Would she get like Seth? She knew she had an expiration date on her life; she just didn't know all the factors that went into that date.

Part of her wished he hadn't come to New York. She preferred having the image of him living his life at the beach in constant sunshine, enjoying the things he'd never had. He was a good worker and apparently a good poker player. He would always have enough money to get by. She just wanted his happiness.

He opened his eyes, as if sensing her thoughts. "It's not too late to run away to Mexico."

She smiled and clutched his hand. "I have to go to work. Then I'll pick up my stuff."

"Stay with me tonight. It's cheaper for you."

She knew that wasn't why he wanted her to stay. "We should switch locations tonight."

"Meet me for lunch and we'll work it out."

They made plans and Jocelyn headed out. Between 5:30 a.m. and 7:30 a.m. most of the deliveries at the Chinatown stores were made. She liked the quiet and cooler temperatures of the morning as she jogged lightly to work with just her shoulder bag. Simple regular things made her happy. She already knew this part of town and some of the people. Other strangers who were up early would give her a wave or nod, recognizing their fellow early risers. There was comfort and community in that, and it fed a part of her need to belong.

Now Jocelyn stood down the street from the Chinatown Youth Hostel clutching the plastic bag that held her rice and chicken from Mrs. Wong. She'd finished her morning work and had picked up a fourth store, thanks to the Wongs. Eager to wash and change, she hurried to the hostel before it locked the doors for the day.

Only the street was blocked with emergency vehicles, police, and from the looks of the clothing on some of the people—the FBI.

This was it. They found her and they were taking her in.

She should have hugged Seth longer and told him how important he was.

She should have stayed the night with Morgan to make sure she was okay.

She should have kissed Graeme the way she dreamed of kissing him.

She should have been smarter about not getting caught.

People in the crowd buzzed with gossip waiting to hear what happened. Other travelers from the hostel were huddled together being interviewed by the police. When no one came after her, she overcame her panic and tuned in, focusing on the conversation, trying to see how bad the situation really was.

Then she heard "Butcher," "girl murdered," and "unidentified."

Jocelyn's heart raced. She didn't even notice she'd squeezed her lunch until someone said her bag was leaking. She tossed her hard-earned meal and wove her way through the crowd. She recognized the young man who ran the hostel's small office, along with other travelers her age who had been at the hostel earlier that week. Then she saw a familiar figure being escorted through the chaos.

John Morrow. She swallowed hard. What was he doing here? Working the case? He went inside and she waited nearly an hour before he came out and was led to an evidence van. Jocelyn scurried through the crowd to the other side of the block to follow.

The FBI woman with him talked through what they had so far. In a plastic bag was her backpack. John held it and didn't move. She listened and waited, but he didn't say anything. Finally, he put it down. "I don't recognize it, but I have to wonder what the FBI screwed up, that led us here today." Then he said a few words that she was pretty sure he wouldn't say in front of his kids. The woman nodded agreeably.

He ended with, "Please keep me in the loop." Then he walked away from the van and off to a side street, ducking under the police blockade. A cop followed him and he held up a hand to give him a moment as he hurried into the nearest coffee spot. She didn't know if she should follow him. She was pretty sure he recognized her pack. But he hadn't said anything. Didn't he trust the FBI? She waited outside the coffee spot. It was just far enough from the crowds, but not far enough away from lingering cops. She walked a little further past the coffee shop and hunkered down on some steps. He came out finally, guzzling a bottle of water. Then he crushed it and tossed it in the trash, hands back on hips, staring at the ground. She stood slowly. Not sure if it was the best time to say hello.

As if seeing movement, he turned toward her.

She went still.

So did he.

She debated running, but something about his behavior didn't strike her as dangerous. He looked sort of relieved. Still uncertain, she gripped the iron rail on the steps until she thought she might crush it.

Finally, he gave a slight nod of his head, acknowledging her. She released the iron rail and gave a little wave from the hip. It made him smile. Another cop called to him and he dismissed the man, letting him know he was going to grab some breakfast and check in with his family. They waved goodbye, and John Morrow walked her way. He didn't look at her as he passed, but simply said, "Follow me."

Shock. Relief. Confusion. John had already had the most stressful morning of his career. He checked in quickly with Kymber. Her parents were on their way and would stay with the kids while they were at work. With police surrounding their house, she felt somewhat safe. He would feel better when the Butcher was captured, preferably dead.

But the girl was alive. That meant they could identify the dead one quickly. None of it made him happy, but regardless, he was grateful to see her. She stood at the entrance of the diner where he stopped and he waved for her to come take a seat.

"Hungry?" he asked.

She nodded.

"I still owe you a meal, have at it."

She tentatively perused the menu, choosing a large orange juice, water, and a steak and eggs breakfast.

"So, Georgie, was it?" Bright blue eyes stared at him. He recognized the skittish energy again.

"Actually, it's Jocelyn."

He nodded. "Nice name."

"Thank you."

"So, you ran away?"

She tilted her head, and her expression hardened. "More like escaped."

He nodded again. *Interesting.* "Mind saying from whom? Or where?"

"Not right now." The orange juice arrived and she took a long drink. "That's really good." She relaxed a bit, revealing a hint of a smile.

"There's a federal agent after you. Special Agent Newell."

The smile disappeared. "I don't know him. Did he say why he was after me?"

"Just that you were missing."

"I'm not missing."

"And there's a five hundred thousand-dollar reward."

She choked on her next drink of orange juice. Her eyes got brighter. "Are you turning me in?"

"Settle down. Do I look like I'm turning you in? I just want to get to the bottom of all this. Let me help you."

"How?"

"I don't know, but if you don't tell me the truth I can't help."

"I won't lie to you, but I can't tell you everything. They might try to kill you too. What happened at the hostel? Why is everyone there? Are they looking for me?"

"The Butcher was set free. I don't know why. It sounds suspicious. But the girl who shared a room with Anna Parks—which I'm assuming is your fake Texas ID—was killed and butchered by the Butcher. The room was a blood bath and I won't go into the details of his work. I saw the backpack and I thought you were dead. I don't know why he was released, but it wasn't a coincidence. Where were you last night?"

Jocelyn's voice became a whisper. "I stayed with a friend last minute."

"Damn lucky." The waitress put her food down and brought his toasted bagel. He wasn't sure he could eat yet, but he took a bite.

"But not for Katie," she said.

Katie was the girl who had been murdered. "No, not for Katie."

Jocelyn sipped some water thoughtfully before speaking. "I understand what you meant now." She cut a piece of steak, then didn't eat it. "When you said, 'these are the ones you kill.'"

John sighed heavily.

"Why didn't you?"

"Have you ever killed anyone?"

She shook her head.

"It's very final. And I took an oath to uphold the law. Believe me, I wanted to kill him. He attacked my family and what he planned was pure evil."

She stared intently at him, listening.

"It was a real test. I just wish passing it hadn't resulted in this. The law failed."

She stabbed the meat on the plate a few times, still not eating. "Or people failed."

"We'll catch him."

She didn't look optimistic. "Can I get my stuff back?"

"I doubt it. There wasn't much left. Shoes, socks, jeans, a shirt."

"My wig?"

"No wig."

She stabbed the plate again. "It wasn't even paid off yet."

"Payment plan?"

"Yeah." She switched back to orange juice. "I can't see my family without a new wig. They met me with…better hair than this."

"So that part was true?"

"The only thing I lied about was my name. I promise I won't lie to you again, but I can't tell you everything. And anyway, it's safer for everyone that way."

"How did it go with your family?"

She sank into her seat and gave up on the food. "My sister hates me and my little brother has a degenerative disease that is going to eventually kill him, maybe in just a couple years. I've researched it a lot at the library."

"That's tough."

"And I think there's something wrong with my other friend."

She stopped talking, and he waited. He could tell there was something else.

"I had two months of medications in my backpack. I'm not sure what will happen if I stop taking them."

John settled his elbows on the table and cupped his chin in his hands. "You gotta lot going on."

"The free world is complicated." She took a breath and sat up straighter. "But I still like it lot." She smiled as if to encourage him.

"No meds were collected. Not that I was told. I'll check though. What were they for?"

She sighed heavily. "Just what they gave me every day."

"They?"

"The doctors and techs. It's a very specific schedule. I knew I would have to figure out a plan eventually, I just needed more time. I have a small stash stored away. Only for a week."

"We'll have Kymber help you. If she doesn't know, she can ask a pharmacist to advise."

"Really?"

"Really." This time he smiled, encouraging. "See, one problem solved."

"Okay." She took a bite of her steak and eggs finally, and he answered his phone.

Then she stopped eating. She stared at him while the cop updated him. Could she hear? There was another murder, a coed named Brittany at a residence hall near Parsons.

The plate and silverware on the table began rattling like a train was going by. John glanced up. Jocelyn's skin paled to a bluish white. Her eyes glowed with fear. She was off and running before he registered her words.

"That's my friend."

CHAPTER EIGHTEEN

Graeme brought Benny to the hospital. His brother had been up since six trying to keep a brave face, but Graeme knew until he saw Morgan in person it didn't matter what anyone told him. At 9:00 a.m. on the dot they entered her room and Benny launched himself at Morgan, putting an arm around her protectively and burying his head in her neck.

She touched his arm. "It's okay, Benny. I'm going to be fine."

He lifted his head. "What were you allergic to?"

"I'm not sure. Something in my drink."

"Did you put your drink down and walk away? You're not supposed to do that. Maybe someone put drugs in it."

Graeme smiled at his mom. "I brought your stuff and some clothes for Morgan."

He dropped the bags on a chair and gave his sister a kiss on the head. "You look good for an allergic reaction. Except for the hives on your face."

She blinked in panic and Benny laughed.

"Jerk."

"Yeah. I'm the jerk. At least *you* had a good night's sleep."

"Sorry."

He forgave her. "I'm just glad you're okay. Hopefully there's no permanent damage."

"What was your name again?" Morgan asked.

This time his mother smiled. Everything would be okay. There was press to deal with, and men to arrest, but just another day at the Rochester house. He put the rail down on Morgan's bed and hoisted Benny. "There. You can share."

Morgan scooted over happily and they began to play with the bed controls. She was still tired, but overall looked okay. His mom used the restroom to freshen up and he checked his phone again for a message from Jocelyn. Nothing. He was about to text Georgie again when she called him.

He answered and heard the fear in her voice bordering on hysteria.

"I can't reach Jocelyn, Lena, or Brittany, and there were three murders of young women last night.

Graeme's skin turned to ice. "Where?"

"One at a youth hostel and two at Brittany's student housing. I just got off the subway. Turn on the news. I'm freaking out. The guy must have come back. Maybe he killed them. They might all be dead. Lena was with Brittany. And the hostel was the one where Jocelyn stayed. I don't know what to do. I'm so scared. Have you heard anything? Please tell me you heard something."

"Not a word."

"I'm on my way to Brittany's dorm."

"I'll meet you there. Stay positive."

He hung up to find Morgan staring at him. She reached for the TV remote. "What's on the news?"

It took two seconds to discover what was being covered on every channel. He caught a glimpse before his mother snatched the remote with a pointed look at Benny.

"Mom, I need to leave. Benny, you should stay with Morgan."

Benny agreed, and Graeme took off before she could argue. He checked his phone as he ran to the car. Henry stood at the ready, phone in hand.

"I've been watching the news. Have you heard from Miss Jocelyn?"

He shook his head.

"The subway will be faster at this hour."

Graeme nodded. He couldn't speak. He didn't trust himself to talk just yet. But he knew Jocelyn was strong and it would take a lot more than a serial killer to take her down.

Jocelyn was the first on site and literally forced her way through the crowds, pushing frantically, listening for a familiar voice or name. Media teams crowded the entrance as the president of the college made a statement. Names would be released after the families were notified.

She felt dizzy. This was her fault. The Butcher was after her, and her friends just happened to be in the way. Hysterical students cried as police tried to usher others from the building, the masses pushed in, and the pressure of human energy made her light-headed. She needed to release the tension. She wanted to run.

There were so many emotions in her body that she hadn't processed before—panic and confusion at the top. She pulled her beanie down on both sides, blocking out the noise for just a moment, trying to gather herself and find someone who could help. John Morrow should be here soon. He would find out.

"Jocelyn!"

She turned at the sound of her name. "Jocelyn!" It was Georgie. She ran to her, tears already forming. Brittany had said they were family. Now Georgie was losing her family because of her. Georgie would hate her.

Instead, Georgie wrapped her arms tightly around her. She did the same.

"I thought you were dead. I didn't know what to think. We couldn't reach you. I haven't heard from Brittany or Lena."

Jocelyn lifted her head and shook it negatively. "They said one of the girls was a Brittany. I didn't hear the other name. But Lena was with her."

Georgie's eyes filled, shock and torment covered her face before she took a breath. "We don't know yet."

"Did you call them or text them?"

"Yes." The fear on her face told Jocelyn there hadn't been answer.

"Don't cry," Georgie ordered. She pressed a tissue to Jocelyn's face. "Someone might see."

Jocelyn obeyed.

"There's a line of students coming out the side of the building. They might be there. We don't know anything for sure yet. We still need facts. And if it's bad news, we still need the facts. We owe that to them," Georgie said.

"Okay." Jocelyn gathered herself. Georgie was right. But despite all the torture she'd personally been through, she realized it was nothing compared to when it was someone you cared about. Another new lesson.

Locked at the elbow, she and Georgie worked their way along the packed sidewalk to get a view of the students evacuating the side entrance. Jocelyn closed her eyes and let her hearing wander and search through the layers in the building, peeling back one layer then another. She could hear an officer knocking on doors systematically, asking if they knew this person, then directing them one way or the next. She kept listening for Lena or Brittany, but nothing.

Her stomach hurt.

Then a skinny, white-blond figure appeared at the top of the steps, wearing a backpack and dragging a small roller bag of luggage.

"Lena!" Jocelyn pushed through. "Lena!"

Georgie hung onto her T-shirt, fighting the crowd behind her. Brittany popped out right after Lena, in jeans and bright banana-colored flowing shirt. She paused at the top of the steps, gazed out dramatically, and waved for the cameras. Jocelyn and Georgie began to scream. People finally cleared the way for the four girls to connect. This time Georgie cried as she held Brittany. "You jerk. Why didn't you answer my calls?"

"I just did! We literally just woke up and were being interrogated and locked in our rooms, then rushed out, then interrogated again."

"We were up until 3:00 a.m.," Lena said. "Our phones were on mute. I just tried to call you."

"We thought you were dead," Georgie said.

"They said one of the girls was Brittany!" Jocelyn explained.

Brittany nodded. "It was. There's like seven Brittanys in the building. The killer went to the one closest to the entrance. I don't know if it was coincidence, but I already identified him for the police. It was the guy who was here yesterday," she warned Jocelyn, "looking for you."

Lena interrupted. "We should talk later. There are a lot of people."

They agreed, leaning in for a long, group hug again.

When they separated Jocelyn saw Graeme on the sidewalk not too far away. He was bent over holding his side.

"Graeme!"

He straightened up and glared at Georgie. "Everybody's dead. Everybody's dead!"

"I didn't say that."

"That's what I heard!"

Georgie identified with the stressed expression on Graeme's face. She pulled the tight group forward. "Sorry," she said as they surrounded him in a long group hug. Finally, everyone took a breath.

Still upset, Graeme grabbed Jocelyn's shoulder. "I swear, I'm putting a tracking device on you. Why didn't you answer your phone?" He motioned to Georgie. "Georgie's been frantic."

Georgie nodded agreeably, deflecting the blame back to Jocelyn. "Frantic!"

"I didn't know you called." Jocelyn pulled the phone out of her pocket and he took it from her.

Hands shaking, he showed her. "'On' button."

"Oh."

The other girls looked down.

"It's not funny." Graeme wasn't going to let them off the hook yet. "Do you think it's funny, Georgie?"

"No. I thought you were all dead. I was worried sick." Georgie tried to get angry and failed.

Graeme handed back the phone. It started pinging with messages and missed calls. "You know how to operate how many top-secret weapons?"

Jocelyn cringed awkwardly. "A lot." She took his hand. "I'm sorry."

Graeme sighed, mostly giving in. He had it bad.

"Where were you last night?"

"With Seth."

"Oops." Brittany shook her head at Jocelyn. "Wrong answer."

Georgie saw that Jocelyn didn't have a clue. To make it worse, she tried to explain.

"We were up late. And Seth wanted…thought it was safer if I stayed with him."

"And where might that be?" Graeme stared at Jocelyn, his mind clearly boggled. Georgie gave him credit for keeping his cool and gathering information.

"A hotel," Jocelyn said, candid.

"With…one bed?" Graeme's expression didn't change.

Georgie intervened. "We should probably take this conversation to breakfast or something."

Lena and Brittany seemed not to hear as they watched the drama.

"Yes, but it's a big bed. Not like the mattresses in the hostels."

A pulse in Graeme's jaw beat, as if the pressure from his clenched teeth was too much. He stared silently at Jocelyn as she earnestly shared the details.

"And they give you little shampoos and soaps so I was able to wash and go to work. I left really early then went to get my stuff at the Chinatown hostel, but the police and FBI were there, and I thought they had found me. And I was really scared and regretted all these things I hadn't done yet."

"Wait." Graeme put up a hand. "These two locations are related to you?"

Jocelyn went silent. Like suddenly she had shared too much.

"Jocelyn?" Graeme's eyes flashed from anger to concern. Protection mode flipped on.

"The girl who shared my room was murdered. She was very sweet. She didn't deserve it. The Butcher cut her to pieces. The police said there was blood everywhere."

"The Butcher." Georgie felt her stomach flip. She locked her arm through Brittany's for comfort.

"That's who was here," Brittany said. "I identified him."

"Jocelyn?" Graeme asked urgently. "What do you have to do with the Butcher?"

Before she could answer, someone else called her name. Everyone jumped. Graeme stepped in front of Jocelyn while Lena grabbed her arm to pull her behind everyone.

Georgie saw the badge on the man's belt and inched in front of Graeme, increasing the barrier to Jocelyn. It's not that she was afraid of the police, but with everything they had going on between hacking the church, and hiding Jocelyn's identity, this tough-looking, no-nonsense, unsmiling cop put her on edge.

"You all look guilty of something. Care to confess?" the officer asked.

Graeme recognized the man. And as soon as he did, the pieces began to fall into place. With the help of a passing hiker, John Morrow had taken down the Butcher and his gang. He didn't need to guess now who that passing hiker was. *Hell.* He was proud of her and terrified at the same time. And now the Butcher was free, and apparently after her. But how?

Or did he really need to ask? If the Butcher had blue nails as Brittany noted, then there had to be a link to Holliwell. But why? They'd found Jocelyn easily enough. Did they want the Butcher to kill her instead of the government? He got a sour taste in his mouth at the thought. Suddenly he was very glad she was with Seth last night. It made him like Seth even less.

John Morrow surveyed them. A soft smile touched his lips, but his eyes missed nothing as he searched out Jocelyn.

"It's okay," Jocelyn said, coming forward. "This is Lieutenant Morrow." Jocelyn introduced everyone.

"Lieutenant, this is Georgie Washington."

"Georgie, huh?" He gave Jocelyn a knowing look. Graeme guessed there was another story there.

"The Fabulous Brittany Walsh. The brilliant Lena Bell. And this is Graeme." Jocelyn hesitated a fraction. "My friend."

Graeme sighed at that less than effusive description and reached out his hand.

"Rochester, right?" Morrow said.

He nodded. Graeme let him know he recognized him as well. "You should have killed him."

"I know."

Jocelyn defended the cop. "He followed the law."

"Ohmigosh. You're the one who put the Butcher away," Lena said. She connected the pieces. "Jocelyn? You're connected?"

Jocelyn lifted her shoulders. "Sort of."

Brittany shook her head. "I don't even want to know. Okay, I want to know, but really how do these things happen? He should be behind bars for like…forever."

Morrow took a card out of his pocket and handed it to Jocelyn. "My personal cellphone, and Kymber's information on the back. I'll tell her to expect you."

"Yes, sir."

"When?"

"Um. After lunch?"

Morrow typed into his cellphone. "Done. She's expecting you." He looked at the group, then Jocelyn. "I'm guessing you don't want police protection?"

"No, sir." Jocelyn looked down.

"Of course not. Can I get you to text or call me each morning so I know you're okay?"

"Um. I'll try."

"Call me too," Georgie said.

"Put me on that list," Graeme said.

Jocelyn gave Morrow a long-suffering sigh to indicate what he started.

Morrow smiled, unaffected. "Sorry about the wig."

"What happened to the wig?" Brittany asked.

"I left it at the hostel."

"What? The Butcher likes to play dress up? Why weren't you wearing it?"

"I needed a disguise."

"Trust me," Morrow said. "I've got a dozen reports of a blond with a beanie saving someone." He winked at her. "Time for a new disguise."

Graeme turned. "Jocelyn?"

"That's what I was telling you. I don't sleep much in bed."

"And…we're back." Brittany laughed.

Graeme studied Jocelyn. "My sister was admitted to the hospital last night." Everyone turned to him concerned and curious. Jocelyn maybe a little less curious?

"Is she okay?" Jocelyn stared at her feet.

"An allergic reaction. She'll be fine. She's coming home this afternoon."

"Did her face swell up and did she get giant boils all over her body?" Brittany asked.

"No."

"Oh." Brittany put some lipstick on. "Too bad."

"Brittany!" Georgie chastised.

"Fortunately, someone recognized the reaction and got her to the hospital." Graeme turned to Jocelyn.

Jocelyn shuffled her feet, silent.

"They're getting us the footage today to see if we can recognize the person?" Graeme added.

"A Good Samaritan?" Morrow questioned.

Jocelyn bit her thumbnail. "What's a Samaritan?" she asked.

"A Good Samaritan. I'll explain over lunch," Graeme said.

"I was with Seth," she reminded him.

"Impossible to forget," Graeme noted.

"It's the truth. And I'm meeting him for lunch."

"I might have to crush him."

Jocelyn panicked. "Don't do that." She looked to Morrow for help.

He held up his hands. "Too complicated for me."

Lena intervened. "Jocelyn, we should go and handle our chores."

"Brittany," Morrow said. "Take advantage of the police escort to and from classes until this is over." He touched Jocelyn's shoulder. "Today with Kymber and call me in the morning."

John Morrow seemed reluctant to leave them. He was worried. So was Graeme. He didn't know what the story was with Seth, but the Butcher was on the loose and on the hunt.

And his prey was Jocelyn.

CHAPTER NINETEEN

The morning flew by with talk all over the city about the Butcher and the murders. Everyone said it would be a miracle if the man wasn't caught—his face was on every channel. Jocelyn was less sure about that. He hadn't just shown up. He'd shown up where she had been staying. And he had backup—whether it was Cashus or someone else from Holliwell.

Brittany had to stay near school and Georgie had classes she needed to attend. The girls parted reluctantly. Jocelyn and Lena kept their appointment and Jocelyn got a copy of her birth certificate. Since she was under eighteen, changing her name was a little more complicated than planned. The only good thing—she could request to have the records sealed and avoid any public announcement if she got legal help. Lena had someone, but it was $2800 for the whole process plus expenses. Lena negotiated to have Jocelyn do translations for the lawyer in exchange. She hugged Lena gratefully, waved her off at the train, then hurried to meet Seth.

Jocelyn clutched her shoulder bag again, nearly neurotic as she checked everything. It contained her life's belongings, most important of which were the seven days of meds she'd retrieved, two sets of "peel and apply" fingertips from Lena and Brittany, her baptismal certificate, and now her birth certificate. Socks, a pair of sneakers, and a few toiletries rounded it out.

She'd be starting over with her wardrobe, as sparse as it was, but for now everything was okay.

With all the drama, she was surprised Graeme still wanted to see her. She refused to meet without new hair—mostly because she didn't want his or her family to see her with the nasty blond wig again.

Brittany gave her the address for the shop and promised she would cover the first wig as part of her advertising budget for the dress. It was $950. Jocelyn nearly had a heart attack. She needed her hair to grow back ASAP! Her total life savings was $87.11. And the store wouldn't let her get a wig without putting a credit card on file. And of course she didn't have a credit card.

Discouraged, she trudged on to meet Seth. It was hot, her old blond wig itched badly, and the beanie didn't help. She put the beanie in her bag and fixed her wig in the window of a store. August in New York was muggy. And it would probably rain this afternoon. She scratched her head again, this time violent enough to mess up the wig.

Spying a trash bin ahead, she ripped off the wig and tossed it. Passersby turned, as if shocked. She didn't care. She was burning up. Then she saw herself in a shop window and rushed back to the trash bin.

Too late. The wig was covered in coffee and fries.

She pulled out her beanie. She didn't put it on. Instead she walked to Bryant Park and found a spot in the shade. People glanced at her but only in passing. Bald people were common enough. She put her head in her hands and rested. She didn't know what she was doing. Three people were dead. She felt bad, guilty, but really grateful to be alive and that her friends were alive.

Death was very final—like Lieutenant Morrow said. And she had so much she still wanted to do.

"I thought that was you. Too hot for hair?" Seth took a seat next to her, his tan cowboy hat shading his eyes, and his ever-carefree expression on display, completely oblivious to the day's events.

She caught him up on everything related to the Butcher.

"You're definitely staying with me." He squeezed her against him. "And I'll get you a wig so you can see your family."

"They're expensive."

"We're livin' in the moment. I've got three grand and I can make more."

Jocelyn felt a breath of relief followed by concern. "Exactly how do you make money?"

He winked. "Lucky in cards."

"That doesn't sound reliable, but okay. As long as it's not illegal and no one comes after you. You don't cheat, do you?"

"I don't need to. Don't worry. I've got crazy math skills."

"You do?" She pretended shock and received a shove. She'd needed the boost and Seth never failed. She smiled and finally put on the beanie. "I'll buy lunch."

They walked the rest of the way to the pizza joint they had picked. Seth loved pizza. They ordered a large with everything on it. Seth served her a piece. "There's something we should talk about."

"What?" Jocelyn could tell it wasn't good.

"This thing you have with helping people."

She froze with pizza midway to her mouth. "You're kidding, right?"

"Uh-uh." He already had a mouthful. "It's bringing you too much attention from people and from *them*."

"But if I hear or see or sense trouble, should I just let bad things happen?"

"It's none of your business."

"What's wrong with being a Good Samaritan?" Lena had explained the expression to her.

"This is the real world. You need to look out for yourself. No one else is going to do it. Everyone else has their own lives. I know you think everyone is your friend, but they're not. They will revert to protecting themselves and what's theirs. *Every-one*," he emphasized.

Jocelyn wasn't sure she agreed, but she knew there was no point in arguing.

"I can't leave you knowing you're not even trying to be safe."

Her stomach flipped. "You're leaving soon?" She didn't really want him to leave now.

"Not right away, but it's inevitable. I need a sandy beach and sunshine."

She smiled. "Okay. I'll work on it. They're tracking me even now. I can feel it. There's nothing I can really do until they make their move. They want the Butcher to kill me. Then it all wraps up nicely without the government being involved. But it's not going to be nice. Not at all. I can tell you that."

"Yeah, well. The other thing you should know. When your drugs run out in a week, you're not going to be able to get more. I had a hard time and I wasn't on stuff nearly as long as you. It's going to be a shitstorm."

Jocelyn contemplated what a shitstorm might feel like. Then she decided it would be okay. "Kymber will help me if I need it."

"No one can help you, Jocelyn. That's what I keep telling you. You're alone. And after I'm gone you're really going to be alone." His voice got angrier. "And you being *really* stupid stresses me out."

"Okay. I'm sorry. You're ruining my pizza." She changed the subject. "Can we sightsee tomorrow? I want to go to the Top of the Rock. The view is supposed to be the best. Students get discount tickets." She held up the fake student ID that Lena had made her.

"Changing the subject. I can respect that. Yeah. Let's be tourists. It helps to get the lay of the land."

"See. Work and play. It's like we're real people."

Seth just shook his head. "And that's why I worry about you."

Georgie's phone had been blowing up all morning with calls and texts. It made focusing on class really hard. Okay, everything was making it hard. College and New York were a lot more exciting than she'd planned. She needed to find a way to balance—or put things in the right boxes. Brittany and Lena had no problem jumping right back into schoolwork after nearly being butchered.

Of course making a bulletproof corset was slightly more compelling than History 101 lectures, added to the fact that Brittany now had a moneymaking business driving her schedule. Lena had some kind of crazy programming disease that allowed her to type feverishly at any given moment. She really liked coding and hacking. Actually she loved the hacking. Only it hadn't gotten them any closer to the truth they sought about Jocelyn or Holliwell or the death of Brittany's aunt.

Georgie crossed the street toward the Harlem Windows installation and typed back to her cousin, Alastair. *When are you arriving?*

Al responded. *Here.*

What?! Where?

Times Square.

Georgie went to the Times Square side of the art installation and directed her cousin to do the same. Suddenly, she saw Richie in an MLK "I have a dream" T-shirt, pointing her way in the video. Richie looked scrawny next to Al, but he was mostly wiry muscle. They both still had haircuts that reflected their time in the military, but other than that they could be tourists—not an engineering genius and a gruff commando. She jumped up and down, waving. Other people noticed and turned. They made room and Al walked to the display, towering over everyone else, but smiling. Georgie met him on the other side and bumped his fist.

"Cool," she saw him say.

Richie ran his hand across the panel, a grin breaking out. Then she saw Graeme join them. Richie pointed to Graeme and indicated they had to go. Graeme saw her too and waved in surprise, then said something to the guys. Richie pantomimed beer mugs clinking in salute and waved goodbye. Al pretended to be helpless and forced to go along—as if anyone could make his two hundred and twenty pounds of attitude do anything against his will. He pointed to her and opened his hands like a book indicating she best go study.

Georgie typed into her phone. *You were supposed to come see me first!*

He texted back. *Important. Man stuff.*

You suck! she texted back.

Glad you're not dead. Dinner later. ☺

The three waved bye.

Interesting. What were they up to?

Graeme tossed Al and Richie some waters and welcomed them at the entrance of his future home.

It had been a fun and interesting afternoon after a stressful start to the week. Richie Dubois, his mechanic, who was also some kind of mechanical and software engineering genius, finally arrived with the 1965 Porsche 911 that Jocelyn had sent flying off a mountain road—in her own defense of course.

The car looked better than ever, but he suspected the only thing true to the original model was the shape and the cobalt blue color. Everything else had been discreetly modified from the fingerprint-identifiable steering wheel and bulletproof windows, to the computerized weapons system and voice recognition communications software.

And yet, Nellie, as Richie called his automotive love, was still leather and tactile on the inside, her brilliance expertly hidden.

And she drove like an angel on fire. Smooth. Sharp. Confident.

He understood why Richie had not wanted to bring her home.

Graeme toured the guys around his new purchase. They explored the gray, cavernous entrance hall with high ceilings, poked at rotted wood in the walls revealed through peeling wallpaper, and climbed what might have been a grand staircase in its day. The place was old by American standards, but as solid as they came.

"Phew. I can honestly say, G." Richie started sneezing from the dust. "It's a dump."

Al drank his water and nodded. "Definitely. Hope you got a deal."

"Thanks." Graeme smiled proudly. He showed them the space where he would temporarily set up office.

"Zombie Master 2?" Richie hoped.

"Yeah, and number three will be ready shortly after. I'm using the other space for my personal projects."

Graeme took them around the rest of the house without giving away the building's secrets. The ancient manor was once intended to be the first city hall, then was taken over by a railroad industrialist, then given to the military during World War II, then to one of the local unions before it fell to decay and people left the neighborhood. Graeme had always had his eye on it. Now it was his.

Richie sneezed again. "After that quality tour, I can honestly say"—he slapped Graeme's back—"it's a *big* dump." He wiped his nose. "But I trust your vision."

"It's going to take a while," Graeme admitted. "Come on. I have a cooler downstairs."

"Now we're talkin'," Al said.

They sat in foldout beach chairs in front of a massive marble fireplace. He already had cleaning people working on the first set of rooms, and some of his team arrived to unload stuff from their other office.

Graeme showed them the material they'd been working on for Benny's updated exoskeleton.

Richie fingered it thoughtfully. "The challenge is not developing this, it's going to be getting his brain to communicate with it."

"Exactly," Graeme said. "I need serious help there."

Richie nodded. "There are torture devices the government has that could help."

Not sure if he was serious, Graeme turned to Al for guidance on how to respond to that. Al sipped his beer offering no comment.

"How would they help?" he finally asked.

"The skin is an amazing organ," Richie began. "The brain doesn't talk to it directly but through several other functions, like most organs. You just need the language of translation between this"—he held the material then put it to the back of his head—"the skin, and everything between the brain." Richie stopped and thought again. "You need to study a map and find the quickest route that requires the fewest turns…you know, the fewest translations." His eyes glazed over in thought. "But it's possible without being invasive. I'm pretty sure of that."

"That makes sense." Graeme felt the excitement of possibility. "I can work with that. Thank you."

"Sure," Richie said. "I can help if you like."

"Are you kidding? Yes!" Graeme would bank money on Richie any day. The guy had serious skills.

"After our sightseeing," Al said.

"Of course," Graeme agreed.

Al reached for another beer and gave the two of them what seemed to be the resigned look of a much older and experienced man. "So what's going on with Jocelyn?"

There was something in his voice Graeme didn't like. "You don't like her?"

Al sighed. Then thought about what he would say. "It's not that. The government spent a lot of resources trying to stop her from escaping. It doesn't make sense that they'll let her walk around for long. And that means anyone in the way is a target too. So I'm worried about my cousin and Brittany. And Lena.

Your family might not even be safe. What's your security like? Are you going to put them all at risk by having her around?"

Richie breathed heavily. "Whew, Al. Bringing us down."

"I'm not going to abandon her," Graeme said.

"Noble," Al said. "Do you even know anything about her?"

"I know enough."

Al shook his head. "I'm just warning you, man. She's badass, don't get me wrong. But she might also be really messed up inside. And a girl like that has secrets. When they come out…you might not like what you learn."

Al seemed to know something. It irked Graeme. "Like what?"

Al shrugged, not revealing anything. "You seem like a nice guy. That's all."

"I know most of what I'm dealing with." Graeme decided to keep it light. "But there's this guy, Seth. You think you could make him disappear?"

"Yeah?" Al smiled curious.

"Cocky, Texas cowboy type."

"Oh." Richie pursed his lips and shook his head in warning. "Girls love that shit. Keep him away."

"Annoying." Graeme agreed. "Did you ever meet him?"

"Is he Holliwell?" Al asked.

"That's my guess," Graeme said.

Al shook his head. "Then you don't want to mess with him. Might be capable of anything."

"Great." Graeme busted open some pretzels and offered them before munching down. "He's a friend of Jocelyn's." The crunching of pretzels seemed to echo in the giant room. "I just want to punch him every time I see him. Or hear him." Graeme grabbed another handful of pretzels. "Or look at him."

Graeme liked Al, even though the guy was reserved and suspicious. He kind of respected that, especially under the circumstances. Al was close with Georgie and Brittany and didn't like them being mixed up in anything dangerous. They had that in common. But it also meant cutting Jocelyn from all their lives.

That's why his new place was timely. He needed to keep a safe distance from his family.

He wasn't willing to give up Jocelyn—with or without her secrets.

CHAPTER TWENTY

*J*ocelyn waited in a small patient examination room at the hospital where Kymber worked. The familiar smell of cleaning solution and the hard standard furniture weren't far from a room at Holliwell.

She shivered, restless—and more than a little nervous.

There were no windows. The only way in and out was the door. She should have told Kymber she would wait outside or in the cafeteria. This could be a trap. She stood up and debated whether the lieutenant and his wife had called the government. Maybe they wanted to collect the reward. Or they believed she posed a threat?

She decided not to wait and find out. Her hand reached for the door just as it opened. Kymber blinked in surprise.

"Everything okay?"

Jocelyn didn't see anyone else around. Hugging her stomach, she finally responded. "Yes."

She stepped back inside as Kymber efficiently rolled a portable tray table over to a chair and pulled another chair around for herself. She emptied the mix of drugs onto the tray from a plastic pill container and sat down.

"It's okay. Sit down."

Jocelyn finally sat.

"Show me again, the order that you took these throughout the day."

Jocelyn separated the pills into five sections, then pointed to each for time of day. "7:00 a.m. 10:00 a.m. 2:00 p.m. 6:00 p.m. 11:00 p.m."

Kymber pulled out a small pad of paper from her pocket with a pen. "Okay. I think I've got this worked out. The good news is that most of these are just vitamins. Everyone takes them. You can get them in a store."

Jocelyn breathed a sigh of relief. Maybe Cashus wasn't trying to kill her. Had she misjudged him?

Kymber continued, pointing out all the vitamins in each group and separating them from the others. Five remained.

"Do you know what these others are?"

Kymber nodded. "This is the pill. You've been taking it at the same time every day, which is correct. Are you sexually active?"

Jocelyn stared at her blankly. "What do you mean?"

Kymber gave an assessing look. Jocelyn worried.

"Are you sleeping with anyone?"

Jocelyn continued staring, trying to put the context together. Kymber didn't mean sleeping.

"Naked?" Jocelyn asked.

Kymber smiled.

"What kind of pill is it?" Jocelyn asked.

"Oh." Kymber rephrased. "This is a birth control pill. It's usually taken to prevent conception of a child. It's commonly referred to as 'the pill.'"

"Oh." Jocelyn blinked, intrigued. "Is there any other reason why someone might take one?"

"Yes, but…how long have you been taking it?"

"Since I was twelve or thirteen."

"Since menstruation?"

Jocelyn eyed her again, thinking about the question. She didn't know what exactly that meant.

"Have you had your period before?"

Jocelyn felt more confused. "I don't know what you mean." She'd watched a lot of videos about pop culture to get better informed, but this hadn't been covered. And Seth had never said anything about it.

Kymber frowned. "Okay. I'll give you some material. I think it might be a good idea to stop taking it and let your body recover. Starting very young can prevent your ovaries from developing and cause other problems so you should understand the risks. Unless you're having sex."

"I'm not having sex. You have to have sex to have a baby, right?" She knew that much. "So I don't need this pill." She slid it to the side and would research it later.

"All right. Here's where it gets complicated."

"Baby pills are already confusing." Jocelyn frowned at what else might be happening with her body.

"Well, I checked with another pharmacist, and quite frankly she was surprised you were still alive after taking these other ones for so long."

Jocelyn tensed, waiting as Kymber went through the remaining four.

"This is a muscle relaxer, and these two work as sleeping aids which might explain why they were at six and eleven in the evening."

"I still had to do homework before bed." She thought back. "But they put a sleep aid in my cocoa and that was usually around 7:00 p.m."

"It seems like you might have a high tolerance. Possibly built up over time. I'm surprised you have the energy you do."

It sounded like a question, but Jocelyn didn't have any answers so she kept quiet.

Kymber slid the final pill in front of her. "This one is perhaps the most worrisome. I couldn't identify it and it took some research. It's not available on the market, not even in experimental circles—at least not approved circles. It's a memory suppressant."

Jocelyn gripped her chair under her thighs, her thoughts going in a million directions.

"Doctors give things like this to soldiers to help with stress when they return from combat, but this is very different, and very advanced—at least according to my colleague."

Jocelyn thought back to when she'd first been given those. Resentment filled her. Her hands burned from controlling the anger. Then fear came. What if those memories were lost forever? There had been different dosages over the four years. Once she had asked about her parents. Another time, she'd wanted to take music classes. Cashus had not allowed much music in her life. Were those signs of memories coming up or him just wanting control?

"I don't need those." She put her finger on the memory pill and crushed it to dust on the table. "Do you think it erased my memories permanently? Will they come back?"

Kymber blinked, staring at the little pile of dust. "Uh. I don't know. But going cold turkey from them might be dangerous. At the very least painful. Headaches, nausea, mood changes." She wiped the dust of the destroyed pill into a small baggie. "I'll save this for now."

Jocelyn swallowed hard. With all the things Cashus had done, taking her few family memories might be the cruelest of all.

Kymber reached a hand across the table and put it over hers. "Jocelyn, I'm not sure why you were given these drugs, but very likely it was illegal. There are lawyers that could help you."

Jocelyn shook her head before Kymber could go on. "They're too powerful. My guardian works for the government. They run everything. If you go against them, they'll kill you." She felt utterly despondent.

Kymber didn't look like she believed her, but it didn't matter.

Silence.

Finally Kymber squeezed her hand and released. "All right. Let's make a plan for getting you through your detox period. The next two weeks are going to be unpleasant, but it will get better after that."

"Two weeks?" Yikes. She had things to do. "Can I still work?"

"Um."

Kymber's expression wasn't encouraging.

"Maybe for some of it…you'll have to be the judge, but we should plan that you take two weeks off."

"I'm not even 'on' yet." Jocelyn calculated the money in her head. "Just pick-up work while I get my ID processed." She could talk to Seth and see if he could help.

"You'll stay with us, of course."

Jocelyn froze.

"At our house," Kymber continued. "We have a basement room. My parents are staying with us, and there's also police protection. You'll be safe there."

Jocelyn bit her lip. It was tempting. The police protection made her nervous, but they seemed different than the government. She trusted John. And the thought of being in one place…and a home…

"It's really generous but—"

"Settled then." Kymber efficiently packed up the pills and took out a pen and notepad from her pocket. "Here are our address and cell phone numbers. If you want you can meet me here and we can go together the first time."

"I'll find it." She couldn't go, but what if this detox thing was really bad? The girls had college and work and scholarships to maintain. And she couldn't go to Graeme.

"You'll start feeling the effects in a few days. For the sleeping pills we can lower the dosage slowly to reduce the effects. I'll work that out on my end. You might need to see a doctor."

Jocelyn snapped to attention. "No doctors." She hugged her stomach again. "No hospitals."

Kymber soothed. "Okay. I'll take care of it. How about I meet you—"

"I have to think about everything. Can I call you?"

"Of course."

Kymber gave her a quick hug before she left. It felt good. Another temptation. Only Jocelyn didn't want to be responsible for another person dying because of her—so she didn't hug back.

John could tell Kymber wanted to talk about her meeting with Jocelyn. She'd been chatty since he got home—nervous about something. She hurried the kids off with her parents to eat popcorn and watch a movie in the den, then pulled out the crumb cake she saved for company or special occasions, cutting a big square piece for him to have with his coffee. Fork and napkin were at the ready. She sat down with just her coffee since she never cut cake for herself.

"So?" He waited.

She took a deep breath. "John, I don't know where she was or what they did, but she should be dead or comatose from the drugs." Kymber reached across the table, took his fork off the napkin, and began waving it to accent her point. "And one is a super high-end, experimental, memory suppressant drug." She took a small piece of cake from the corner of John's plate. "You have to wonder what they want her to forget, right?" Kymber shuddered. "I'm sitting there, looking at her, and she's very innocent about a lot of things. Didn't even know what the pill was."

John froze mid-sip on his coffee. "She's on the pill?"

"Yeah. And not for sex. I gave her some literature."

He held up a hand. "I don't need to know."

Kymber smiled and dug into his coffee cake, this time taking a bigger piece, continuing her story. "So I'm sitting there, thinking it's like she's a top-secret experiment or something. The government has been experimenting with drugs for years, right? What if they gave her some? She's really strong, right? She carried your pack and Max for miles and that was after fighting those murderers."

"She's definitely strong, fast, and trained."

"But none of the drugs were for strength or were steroids or anything, so she already has that from something else. Even training can't make someone that strong, can it?"

"Soldiers can learn to ignore pain. She might have a strong will and years of athletic training." John believed in sticking to the reasonable.

"Okay. Maybe." Kymber thought about it while chewing more cake. "I talked to her about the drugs. She wants to get off them, and she only has a short supply. I told her it would take about two weeks at least, to get through the hard part."

"She's been staying in various youth hostels."

"Oh." Kymber let that hang. "She was worried about not being able to work. She said it was just pick-up jobs and they pay cash under the table. She's working on getting her New York ID, but I still didn't get her last name. Did you?"

"No. But—"

"What?" Kymber's eyes zeroed in on him like a bullseye target.

"I didn't tell you this before so you would have plausible deniability."

"Tell me."

"She's supposedly 'missing' and there's a five hundred-thousand-dollar reward for anyone with information."

Kymber gasped, eyes wide. He told her the details from Special Agent Newell, and the notice that went out. Then he conveyed his conversation with Jocelyn.

Kymber's mouth finally closed. "So, she has the Butcher *and* the government after her?"

"Seems like."

"Shoot. That's scary." Kymber left one bite of cake on his plate and sipped her coffee thoughtfully.

"Yeah." He wanted to make sure his wife understood the situation and possible dangers.

"Do you think she's dangerous?"

"I think the circumstances around her are very dangerous."

"We don't even know what they are."

"Even more dangerous," John stated firmly. "But—"

Kymber sipped her coffee trying not to look too invested in Jocelyn's situation. He knew his wife well enough to know where she was going.

"I met some of her friends. Watched them together for a while. Then did background checks."

"Of course."

"They're all solid students. Scholarships. In top schools. Not slackers. I could tell they cared about each other. Girls who are real friends, you know. The kind I would want for Maddie. I think that says something about her. And—"

He smiled, preparing for Kymber's next reaction.

"What?" Kymber put her hands on the table. "What?"

"One of those friends I met was Graeme Rochester."

Kymber's eyes went wide. "The governor's son?"

He nodded. "And he's definitely got a thing for Jocelyn."

"I'd expect he'd go for models or something."

"That's the older son."

"Oh, yeah. Got that socialite pregnant, had a baby and is still partying—if you believe everything you read in gossip magazines." She smiled. "Surely the Rochesters have checked her out. They would be extra safe."

"They would. Or, they may not know or think there's anything to check out." John got up and refilled his coffee. "But all these kids live in dorms. Rochester lives at home. He just graduated. Good handshake. Maintains eye contact. Too old for her though."

"Maybe right now."

"Regardless, if Jocelyn has two weeks of misery ahead I don't know where she can stay. The hostels aren't safe. The Butcher has proven that." He put his coffee on the table and sat down again. "I'd say she could stay here, but my first priority is protecting our family."

"I know." Kymber sat quietly before finally speaking her thoughts. "John, our family wouldn't be here now, if not for her."

"I know." But that didn't mean they could take in a stranger.

A longer silence followed. "Are you going to finish that last bite?"

"No, go ahead." He pushed his plate toward her.

Kymber finished the cake, then put down her fork carefully. She gave him a fierce, determined look. "What if she had decided to not get involved? It would be better for her now. She wouldn't have the Butcher after her. I worry that she's not safe. Here we have police protection." She got up and took the plate over to the sink, then turned with hands on hips. "Too many people turn their heads the other way because it's safer. I want to protect our family too."

"I know you do. And with the complexities around Jocelyn that we suspect with the little information that we have, we don't know what it could mean. Going against the government in any way can cost us our jobs and a lot more."

"We're already living on borrowed time," she countered.

"We had a lucky break and we shouldn't waste it," he said.

Kymber took a breath. He could see her rethinking her approach.

"What if we are meant to help her? Isn't it better for her to have positive adults in her life? She saved us, John. God watched over us and sent her to us. I just think if we don't help her, who will? And who could be trusted?"

"You already invited her, didn't you?"

"Yes," Kymber said, unapologetic, meeting his gaze.

He sipped his coffee to hide a smile. Their home was modest, but they could make room. "That's why I love you."

"You thought all the same things too," Kymber accused.

"Yes," John admitted. "But you and the kids come first. We'll get her through this rough spot."

Kymber smiled back. "That's why *I* love *you*."

Medina flipped off the listening device along with Newell, Cashus, and the surveillance technician.

"Sounds easy enough," Cashus said. "We wait until she goes there, then send in Butch."

Newell was more careful. "There are four to six armed policemen around the house at any given time. The Butcher is not that discreet."

Cashus looked to Medina. "You're a super spy. That should be easy for you."

Medina nodded agreement. Easy kills. Only they were innocent. That made it less easy. But still within their collateral damage limit.

Newell didn't look like he liked it much either, but he wasn't an ally.

"I'll work up a plan and run it by the boss. Let's see if he still wants to do it this way," Newell said.

Medina already knew the answer. This was just entertainment for the SOI. Something about Project Sunday intrigued him. In fact, he wasn't convinced the SOI really wanted her dead. She was a unique piece of science that was still valuable whether they kept her or traded her to another government or organization.

Sure, she had caused havoc and destroyed hundreds of millions in top-secret equipment during her escape, but she wasn't a threat. At least not yet. If pushed—she could become one. That's what Cashus and Newell didn't understand. Did the SOI understand? Was he testing her? Was this a game to see if he could remake her into his image—a cold heartless killer?

They had done it before. Medina had seen it.

And now they were doing it to him.

He leaned against the technician's control board and knocked over his coffee. In seconds the team threw paper towels at the guy and Medina jumped away. He slipped the small audio scrambler in his pocket, uncertain it would work against the monitoring system implanted in his inner ear.

Jocelyn was his last hope. Not for salvation. It was too late for that. But for escape. Only getting her to help was going to take a high degree of force. Even then, he knew her well enough to know she might not be reliable.

"I have an idea about how to get her alone," Medina offered. He explained the opportunity. It would spare the family a little longer, even if it meant his death sooner.

CHAPTER TWENTY-ONE

$\mathcal{G}$raeme took over a booth at Cravings, working on his laptop and having a late breakfast. He needed a real business plan for the game company and had a full day of work filling out paperwork for some new patents related to Benny's flexible exo-skeleton. The material he was using had micro-transistors and he had an idea about how to get Benny's brain to talk to the computers in the wearable material. With Richie's help they could build and test it much faster than he originally thought. And it would help Benny beyond what they used now—when things really got bad.

His dad still waited to hear from Sergei Baratashvili. They'd put their hopes in Sergei having something that would lead to a breakthrough, but Graeme had given up on that. The answer to Benny's cure seemed unreachable. Not even Sabrina had been able to piece the clues together to figure out the leap Benny's mom, Illeana, had made that led to the cure.

The solution died with her and Grayson.

He stopped typing. His thoughts had turned unproductive.

As if to annoy him further, a swaggering figure in a cowboy hat sauntered in. Seth took off his hat and winked at Allie, a female server. Graeme couldn't believe that act worked on New York girls, but sure enough she gave him a sly smile and pointed him to her section. Seth went to order then took his seat. Allie brought him some water and chatted a bit.

Graeme was one of the silent partners in Cravings so he knew everyone. The owner, Josh, was a buddy from college who had started the restaurant a couple years prior. He considered banning Seth for a split second, just for fun, but it would hurt Jocelyn's feelings. Which would take all the fun out of it.

Was Jocelyn meeting him for breakfast? Seth noticed him, gave a nod, then picked up a newspaper left on the table. Huh. The guy could read?

Graeme decided to leave, just as Seth's food arrived. He pulled out a tip for the table, then turned to go. Seth stared at his food. For some reason Graeme turned back. Seth still stared at his food, only now he seemed to grip his fork unnaturally.

Not right.

He kept an eye on him, but Seth didn't move or look up, even when Graeme stood right by the table.

"You okay?"

His voice must have alerted him, because Seth tried to get out of the booth. Shaking, Seth pressed a button on his watch and said, "Jus' need five."

Yeah. Not right at all.

Seth pushed, or really fell, past Graeme and stumbled toward the back of the restaurant. Where was he going? The restrooms? The office? The alley?

The guy made a grasping sound for air, then collapsed in the narrow corridor. His body seized, limbs went rigid, and muscles contracted until every vein on his face and body seemed ready to explode.

"Josh!" Graeme called to his buddy in the kitchen. "Call 911!"

Josh ran out and checked the scene. "Got it!" Then he came back with a square pillow, rolling pin, and wooden spoon. "Does he need to bite on something?"

Graeme didn't know. He took the spoon as Josh put the pillow under Seth's head.

"I don't know if he's breathing." He panicked. "Freakin' breathe, Seth!"

Seth's eyes connected for a microsecond with Graeme's before rolling back. It only took that instant to see the fear and plea for help.

The seizure had full control of Seth. They could only wait it out. Graeme spoke to him encouragingly since he didn't know what else to do. Josh brought a cold cloth and they blocked the view from other diners.

"Don't worry, it's going to end," Graeme said, willing it to end. "You'll get through this. Focus on your breath. If something happens to you, Jocelyn will probably cry. It will be hard, but I'll comfort her. I'd rather have you alive of course. Not some memory whose ass I can't kick anymore." He kept talking. And though it seemed like forever, Seth's veins slowly went to normal. His body slacked, and his heart still beat. They moved him to the floor of the office. At least there was a carpet in there.

Graeme waited. Ambulances took forever.

Finally Seth's eyes opened. Confusion first. Then something else. He touched his watch. A stopwatch.

"This has happened before," Graeme said.

"Where am I?" Seth's voice cracked.

"The back office of Cravings. Here's some water."

Seth slowly pushed himself up and moved to lean against the sofa. He took the glass, most of the water sloshing over the side as he tried to hold it. Graeme couldn't help the pity he felt. Seth saw it.

"Screw you." The younger guy lifted his chin, then closed his eyes tiredly.

"Glad you're feeling better." Graeme grinned. "An ambulance is on the way."

"No ambulance."

A siren sounded in the alley.

"Too late. They're here. Let them check you out."

Josh ushered a medic in despite Seth's protest. His lack of interest in medical help was duly noted, and after advising him to seek a doctor, the EMTs left.

Josh cooked him a new breakfast and brought it into the office. It was slow going, but Seth ate most of it, his color eventually returning but his movements sluggish.

"Don't you have s-somewhere to be?"

"Nope," Graeme said.

"You know I think you're an effin' p-privileged, trust fund, pretty-boy."

"Yep." Graeme was amused. "And you're a dumbass, shit-for-brains, hick who thinks a wink and an accent will get you everything you need."

Seth winked with effort. "It has."

"Yeah. Well, keep away from my sister."

"Can't help you with that." Seth saw his expression and added with a knowing smile, "She's got sh-shit taste in men."

Surprised, Graeme laughed. Damn. He didn't know if he wanted to hurt or help the poor bastard.

They sat in silence while Seth closed his eyes and continued to recover.

"Does Jocelyn know you have this…uh, condition?"

"No."

"You gonna tell her?" Graeme asked.

"No." Seth opened his eyes. His motor skills improved. "I hope to be gone before she finds out."

"You're leaving soon then?" Graeme encouraged more than asked, mostly just to irritate him. "Are you gonna tell her?"

Graeme sighed. "No, but likely she'll find out. How often does this happen? Every month, week?"

Seth checked his watch. "Every few days."

That's not healthy.

"They're getting closer together," Seth added.

"Do you have a doctor?"

"I know Jocelyn from Holliwell. Doctors are what started this."

Graeme nodded. Answer confirmed.

"I knew this was coming. All experiments have expiration dates. Even the successful ones."

"If you're what's considered successful, this country is in trouble."

"Thanks, man."

"Always here to state the obvious."

Seth gave a half smile. "Jocelyn told me you helped her escape. She said she almost died in the turbines at the dam."

"I have a feeling she would have figured it out."

Seth lifted his shoulders, giving him credit. "Maybe not."

"Where were you when she escaped?"

"I'd already been transported to another facility. I escaped en route. We were able to meet up after." Seth confessed then. "I never thought she'd get out." He looked straight at Graeme. "They did things to her. To everyone. But to her…the most."

"There are others?"

"All dead."

Graeme leaned onto his knees rather than grab at the pain in his stomach caused by another realization. "Is this going to happen to Jocelyn?"

"I don't know. She's different." Seth gave *him* an encouraging look this time. "Maybe not." He struggled to his feet and put a ten-dollar bill on the desk.

"It's on the house."

"It's Allie's tip." He put his wallet away. "I know you're having lunch with Jocelyn today. If you can't protect her, or don't think you're up for this, I'll take her with me. We have a better chance on the road. She's a sitting duck here."

Graeme disagreed. They had resources here. On the road they were alone. "I know someone who can help you."

Seth grinned. "I'm beyond help. You should know that." He slid his cowboy hat on and turned to go, stopping in the doorway for a moment, as if trying to decide something. His head tilted down with a slight turn back to Graeme, his face in the shadow. "I heard you earlier." A long pause. "It helped."

Graeme leaned back on the sofa and sat there long after Seth was gone. He finally rubbed his jaw, coming to a reluctant and irksome realization.

Helping Jocelyn meant helping that swaggering, irritating Texan as well.

CHAPTER TWENTY-TWO

*J*ocelyn had been off her meds since meeting with Kymber. Four days. It felt like four weeks. She ate less, she slept less, and she saved money. If not for staying busy, she might have gone a little crazy.

She fell back into her old Holliwell schedule to a degree, planning her day as fully as it had been previously planned for her. She worked, she ran, she exercised, she visualized, she read as much as possible—and she spied.

Today she snuggled behind a shelf in a leather chair pretending to read while nursing the iced coffee that cost more than one of her budgeted meals. It was not unlike many of her missions in the past. She got close and she listened. Only now she spied on family.

Java Junkies was the trendy two-story bookstore-coffee shop that Morgan frequented. A few people checked out the new artisan gifts and specialty tin containers that were mixed in on the shelves for sale. A frothing machine sounded over the chatter in the line. It pushed her four-day headache a notch past miserable. She closed her eyes for two deep breaths and focused again. Hopefully this was the worst of what Kymber had predicted.

Jocelyn didn't feel great about spying on her sister, but Morgan didn't seem to have half the sense that Benny did. Fortunately, the Rochesters were making her get a part-time job to pay for the "gray hairs she'd given them," and apparently they had cut off Morgan's allowance, which sounded like a big thing. To hear Morgan explain it to her friend Meghana, this might be the last time they *ever* had coffee here again.

Meghana smartly said she thought three months' allowance was fair and a job was something Morgan could add to her resume. It made Jocelyn smile.

"And," Morgan continued her rant, "Chandler hasn't called me or returned my texts."

Good. Jocelyn went on alert. Wait. Not good. She sounded hurt.

"He was probably upset, thinking you ditched him, then he got questioned by the police. And you are under eighteen, Morgan. Come on. It was stupid. Really stupid. When I heard I was really upset. I'm just glad they caught those guys."

"But he could at least return my texts."

"Morgan, he's kind of a jerk. He's probably sleeping with tons of college girls."

Morgan huffed. "You don't understand."

Jocelyn heard a chair scrape on the floor and turned to see Morgan grab her purse and storm off, but then she reluctantly waited for Meghana to follow. Jocelyn quickly turned her head away, not wanting another confrontation with Morgan under bad circumstances. She didn't have enough experience with real world teenagers to know what to do or how to advise. But she couldn't let her sister think Chandler was a good guy and piss off the one friend she had who seemed nice.

Ugh. Dreading it, Jocelyn carefully approached. *Never thought I wouldn't want to talk to you, Morgan.*

She called out as Morgan reached the door and said hi, walking out behind them. Meghana smiled and said hi back, watching to see if Morgan would do the same.

Morgan gave her quick scan—up, down and up—then shuddered. "Are you talking to me?"

Meghana's mouth dropped open in surprise, her expression apologetic.

Jocelyn felt her throat tighten painfully. She smiled—a very small smile. "I heard you were in the hospital. I'm glad you're…back to your old self."

They stood to the side of the coffee shop entrance. Morgan turned her body away from Jocelyn and searched for something in her purse.

Tentative, Jocelyn touched her shoulder lightly. "Morgan?"

Morgan swung around and knocked her arm. "Don't touch me. What's your problem? Why are you still here?"

"Why are you so mad at me?"

"You destroyed my mother's cello."

"Graeme took it to be restrung. It's not destroyed. It will sound even better."

"Do you think I care?" She found her sunglasses and put them on.

Jocelyn glanced at Meghana for help. The other girl grimaced helplessly behind Morgan.

"Are you still mad about being caught kissing in the closet?"

Morgan didn't answer, just stared at her from behind her glasses.

"You deserve better than a guy who hides you because he's conniving or trying to do something to hurt you."

"Chandler wouldn't hurt me! You don't even know him. It's none of your business. And based on how you dress, you're the one who should be hiding."

"Morgan!" Meghana shook her head. "I'm leaving."

Morgan shrugged without saying bye. Jocelyn took a slow breath. Okay. Her sister was childish and Jocelyn wanted to slap her. "You're very focused on what everyone wears. Maybe you should look a little deeper at people and what they really want."

Morgan lowered her glasses pointedly. "I'm pretty sure I'd find a money-hungry slut."

Jocelyn sucked air so hard it made a sound. She hadn't been ready for that one. She took a calming breath and hoisted her backpack over her shoulder.

"The only 'slut' is Chandler. And he's using you and trying to trap you and hurt you—for his own reasons. He doesn't care about you. You can see it in his eyes, his attitude, and his behavior. You just refuse to see the truth. And I'm pretty sure"—Jocelyn turned shoulder to shoulder with her sister, meeting her square in the eye, and getting her courage back—"I'm pretty sure that your *real* mother would be very disappointed…" She paused for impact and swirled her index finger in front of Morgan the way she'd seen Brittany do at things which were an abomination. "…in *this*."

Morgan gasped. "You have no right." She clutched her bag fiercely. "I'm going to tell my brother what a bitch you really are." Then she swung her hair dramatically and spun away.

Jocelyn kept an eye on her as she reached the light at the corner. *Great.* Her sister was even more emotional now. She heard the little hiccup as if she might cry. Jocelyn thought she was more upset at getting a taste of her own medicine, than because she cared about their mother. Then Morgan's hand came up and wiped under her big sunglasses.

Jocelyn braced herself against the guilt and emotion. Her sister was a bully. And bullies needed to be confronted.

She just wasn't sure what you did after that.

The afternoon turned out much better than the morning. A light breeze cleared out the smell of yesterday's trash collection, the temperature for the end of August seemed tolerable, and there were actual neighborhoods in New York that weren't deafening. Since cutting her medications, every sense felt assaulted.

At the moment—she didn't care.

Jocelyn walked with her hand in Graeme's after their lunch date. She liked lunch dates. Specifically, lunch dates with Graeme. They laughed a lot. The idea of having time for just talking and making each other laugh was one of the best things about being free.

They were interrupted by Morgan calling in tears with her story, but much to Jocelyn's surprise Graeme seemed very calm about it. She admitted to saying what Morgan accused her of but left out everything else. She didn't want to kick her sister when she was down, which technically she had sort of done, but Graeme seemed okay with them sorting it out in their own time for now.

He squeezed her hand briefly as if knowing her thoughts and she smiled up at him, more confident in her new wig—a shoulder-length bob that Graeme had liked—until she told him Seth had picked it out. Lesson learned.

It was hard to explain her relationship with Seth. But she knew when the chips were down he would be there. At least she hoped. Honestly, with Seth you never knew, but by now she knew he would be there if he could.

There was no doubt in her mind that Graeme was unfailing. She saw it in every relationship he had, especially with family. That's why he'd wanted to know why Georgie had called their home. It was the thing that triggered him to come to Charlottesville. If he hadn't needed to understand the connection, he might not have been there to help her at Holliwell. So she told him the truth—at least as much as she thought would be safe.

"I was hiding one time at Holliwell in a science building where I wasn't supposed to be. I was looking for Seth. Instead, I ended up overhearing some scientists talking. They were talking about the Albrechts and a lot of other stuff." Jocelyn swallowed hard at the memory of learning she would die young. "Anyway, they said their kids might hold some secrets." That was the truth, even if they primarily meant Jocelyn. "I asked Georgie to find them and make sure they were okay. I was able to pass her messages sometimes at the movie theater."

"Yeah. I figured you two were doing something like that."

"I'm glad your family is okay." She glanced up to see if he was satisfied with the answer. "The main scientist said everything died with their parents. I think they planned on experimenting with volunteers, not going after Morgan and Benny—but I thought: better safe then sorry. When Georgie found out they were well protected, we didn't worry about it. But I'm sorry it caused you the pain it did—especially the laser burns."

"If I hadn't investigated I would have never found you."

"And I would be fish food." She tried to lighten the mood.

He laughed a little and kissed the top of her head.

Warmth spread deliciously through her body. It happened when he touched her. As if knowing it, he squeezed her hand and a tingle of energy shot up her arm to her neck and around her skull, temporarily numbing the persistent headache.

"Are you sleeping okay?"

He hadn't brought it up at lunch, but she didn't have any makeup that could hide it. She hadn't slept more than a couple hours a day this week, and it was fitful rest.

"A little less than usual." She glanced at him, but he kept walking, waiting patiently for her to fill in details. He seemed to know she needed time before sharing too much. "It will pass."

She wouldn't complain. She cut the pills on her own. No more memory suppressants or female organ suppressants. She also cut her sleep aid in half, taking a little less each day. According to her limited research on the Internet and at the library, she would eventually sleep. She just needed to get most of the drugs out of her system before her body could adapt to its natural rhythms. Georgie gave her some tea to help. It wasn't helping yet, but she told her friend it did. She stayed with Seth for now. He would get her through it.

She didn't tell Graeme the details, but suspected he knew something was up. He'd already offered his home, money for a hotel, a friend's house, and other options. She didn't want those options. One—it wasn't safe for Graeme. Two—she wanted to be independent. She'd spent her life being controlled. Survival was hard, but it gave her purpose. The last reason was harder to explain. She wanted Graeme to like her just for her, and not feel obligated. She didn't want to use him. Well…she was using him to be near her family. That was bad enough. But she wanted to have a relationship based on things separate from her family, her past, her needs, and her troubles.

In those moments when it was just them, and all the other stuff faded away, she felt a happiness that made her think anything was possible. Seth said it was because she was young and stupid. With any luck, she could be young and stupid a lot longer.

"A lot has been going on," he said. "All of my offers still stand."

"I know. Thank you." She changed the subject. "What should I get your mom for her birthday?" She added sternly, "And don't say I don't need to get anything."

"I'll get something from both of us."

"No."

He relented. "She likes Russian poetry." He named her favorite poets. "She always waits for us to buy the most recent book since she knows she's impossible to shop for. Any of those authors will be a hit."

She nodded, relieved. That was doable. She leaned her head briefly against his shoulder in gratitude as they strolled.

"What are you going to do after you finish your next zombie game?"

"I'm not sure. The team has been talking about starting a more official game company. I'm not sure that's what we all really want to do. Everyone's just appreciating the money from the first game. We might split up eventually."

"What do *you* want to do?"

"That's the problem. I'm not sure anymore." He looked at her. "A lot has changed in the last year." They turned the corner onto Broadway where Benny and Poem would be getting out of Chinese language school. "I'd like to do a few trips with Benny while he's still mobile. This winter might be his last ski season."

Jocelyn's stomach clenched. The finality of Benny's disease was not acceptable.

"My dad is working on something, but I don't think—"

He stopped. Jocelyn followed the direction of his sudden frown. Henry had just arrived and walked around the car to the sidewalk to open the door for Benny. Kids were starting to come out the doors of the Chinese school.

"There's no guard." Graeme's steps picked up.

Jocelyn hurried with him, scanning the scene. A man walked toward them from the other side of the school entrance. He wore baggie pants and a hoodie pulled over his head. He strode confidently forward, his moves loose and easy.

She moved toward him trying to see his face.

He lifted his eyes. Stared back. Right at her. The face could have been anybody or nobody. It wasn't. Her instincts cued.

Medina.

What was he doing here? He strode toward Benny. She saw his arm move to his side and reach. Her instincts took over. She ran toward Benny, shouting.

"Get down!"

Confused, Benny turned to them.

"Henry!" Graeme shouted.

Henry already had his gun out, but too late.

Medina swiped Benny with one arm, lifting him like he was nothing, and with one continuous motion, shot Henry.

CHAPTER TWENTY-THREE

Screams filled the street. Kids and parents scattered. Medina shot Henry a second time, backed away, and aimed toward Jocelyn and Graeme.

She dashed ahead of Graeme and lifted her hand to protect him, sending a surge of energy while running forward and deflecting bullets aimed perfectly at her chest. Medina was nothing if not accurate.

He jumped into the open back of a nearby van with Benny and took off.

Jocelyn dropped to Henry. He'd been shot in the arm and the leg. Not lethal. What did that mean? She called for help as Graeme reached her side.

"Press here and here." She placed Graeme's hands where hers had been. To Sir Henry, "You're going to live." She got up.

"Right behind you," Graeme promised. "Go."

Jocelyn took off. The van had pulled away. It zoomed past cars in the bus lane of the one-way street. She raced full-out to catch it as other cars pulled behind and blocked her.

Unstoppable, she leapt. And landed on a black sedan. Then she leapt to the next car.

Her heart pumped and legs raced as she ran over the tops of the cars to reach the van before it turned the corner.

It ran the red light and swerved.

A semi-truck rolled through the intersection. Racing forward, she couldn't stop. She flew into the side of the semi with a loud thud and hung onto the passenger door. The driver turned, stunned, and yelled something, slowing down.

"Go, go, go!" she shouted. "Faster!"

She latched her hand on the side of the front windshield, tucked her left foot into the door latch, and pulled herself up and over the engine, balancing with one hand on the roof to get the view ahead. Traffic. The white van was forced to slow down. This was her chance.

She jumped from the front of the moving semi-truck onto the red roof of a newsstand, ran across it with three blistering strides, and launched.

Thirty feet of air passed under her quickly. She hit the top of the van hard and planted her feet. The driver braked sharply knocking her on her back. The van swerved and she rolled on her belly to grab hold. There was nothing to grab.

Gunshots exploded through the roof of the vehicle. Medina either warned or wanted her dead. Hastily, she pushed herself toward the front of van, gripping the sides of the roof, while dodging danger and trying not to roll off. Her feet slid down the windshield until one foot landed on top of a windshield wiper. She saw the driver. He looked nervous. A regular agent, no doubt.

She dug a finger into the closest bullet hole in the roof, and held, searching out another. She needed to get to the back of the van.

The driver braked again and swerved expertly, taking a corner and sending her lower body flying.

She didn't let go.

Her skin tore viciously as she dug into each bullet hole and crawled fiercely to the back of the van. She swung her legs around and landed on the bumper, grabbing the door handles simultaneously. She yanked one of the metal handles, twisting it free. The motion sent both doors open and she swung backward as Medina shot at her.

A flash of Benny curled into a tiny ball with his hands over his ears fueled her fury and determination.

Jocelyn hurled herself into the van, her energy block emanating protectively from every cell, until she could focus all her fury on Medina through the open palm of her hand.

She plastered him against the back of the driver's seat. His arms flailed and he tried to reach out and stop her. Instead, she grabbed one arm, braced her feet, and with all her might, threw Medina out the back of the van.

She didn't bother watching as his body sailed into oncoming traffic causing screeches, skids, horn blasts, and screams.

Benny lifted his head, his eyes going wide when he recognized her. She didn't have time to reassure him. They were still moving.

She wrapped the driver in a neck hold. He lifted his gun, but she easily grabbed it free and threw it to the floor. "Stop the van."

He sped up instead, swerving and sideswiping vehicles.

"Benny, hold on!" She wouldn't risk him rolling or getting flung out the swinging doors of the vehicle.

She tightened her grip on the driver and pressed her mouth a fraction from his ear. "I know you're doing your job. This child is innocent. Stop now, or I'm going to crush your larynx and let you slowly suffocate before anyone can save you."

She applied pressure to let him know she was serious.

The van screeched to a stop. She squeezed the man in a choke until he passed out, grabbed Benny, and kicked the back doors open again.

They were met with a small pile-up of cars. Further behind them people gathered on the sidewalks, and two lanes of cars were stopped. Horns honked insistently.

She watched from a distance as Medina sat up in the middle of the road and shook his head, pushing away a man who tried to help him. Then he got up.

That was *not* natural.

"Benny! Let's go." She jumped down with Benny, making sure he was unharmed.

Benny stared at Medina in shock and fear as the man stood unsteadily on his feet, getting oriented.

She clutched her little brother's hand protectively. "Benny!" She pulled him urgently. "Run."

Graeme pressed Henry's injuries. Two teachers were there to help. The children had been ushered back inside the building.

Despite being shot twice, Henry had seen Jocelyn take off into traffic after the van. No telling how he might interpret that. Henry activated their security while they attended him. Even now, their team would be tracking Benny's phone. Graeme couldn't wait for them to mobilize.

"Henry, I have to go."

Henry already knew. "Take my gun."

Graeme took the gun and was going to take the car until he saw a lavender-and-white polka-dotted Vespa. The owner stood frozen, holding a matching helmet, her cellphone still in the air. He took the phone from the stranger's frozen hand, deleted the video and handed it back to her.

"I need to borrow your bike. I'll pay for damages. Go see Henry." He pointed to Henry.

Vespa girl nodded wordlessly and motioned to the keys in the ignition.

A second later he raced down the sidewalk of Prince Street, passing the traffic until he reached the pile-up. The van was nowhere to be found. Neither were Jocelyn or Benny.

He swerved to a stop and shouted to a bystander. "Where did the white van go?"

"Straight."

He revved the bike.

"But a girl and kid went that way," an animated older lady said, gesturing down the street. "And the terminator went after them."

His gut clenched with fear. Benny was free, but a terminator? What the hell?

He jetted the little polka-dotted bike and took off.

Jocelyn and Benny covered two blocks in the space of seconds. Her brother huffed and she needed a moment. Her ongoing headache had exploded, threatening to crack her skull open, and her stomach did not feel right—at all.

She dragged Benny behind a large, metal Dumpster in a dead-end street, and slid down against the wall to the heels of her feet. She needed to recover. She pulled an arm around Benny protectively, hoping they were safe.

"Are you okay?" she asked.

His hushed voice was shaky but affirmative. "I never ran so fast in my life!"

She felt bile build in her throat. A really bad time to be sick. She shouldn't have stopped the meds.

"Are you okay? You're like blue and white. Are you going to—"

She spun and threw up before he could complete the sentence.

"Did you get punched in the stomach? Sometimes that makes people throw up."

She heaved again, trying to reply. "Sick," she gasped.

"Here." His fingers trembled as he unbuttoned his Hawaiian shirt. He had another T-shirt under his exoskeleton. "You can use this. It's a hundred percent cotton. Really soft."

She wiped her mouth gratefully, then with a clean spot, pressed the moisture around her eyes.

"You kicked ass for being sick. Like you stopped bullets and the van, and—"

Jocelyn put a finger over his mouth. Fast steps came their way, then stopped. Her senses overwhelmed with information. She could smell the sweat and the scent of their assailant. It was familiar after so many missions. Why was Medina after Benny? And what had Cashus done to him?

She felt the vomit surge again and tried to quell it.

The steps continued. Toward them. She stood and vomited again, keeping her eye on Medina as he approached. She wiped her mouth with the shirt one last time and tossed it, searching out a plan as Medina methodically walked forward, completely at ease. She'd seen him do this before, on missions—right before he incapacitated everyone in sight.

"Benny. The fire escape."

She lifted him on top of the Dumpster, jumped up behind him, and nearly threw Benny to the bottom rung of the ladder.

Medina gave the Dumpster a forceful kick that knocked her down and sent her flying off the Dumpster to the ground.

His power clued her in. Cashus had been experimenting—this time on Medina.

Outstanding.

In her current state, that definitely evened up the odds.

She saw Benny hesitate and hurried to her feet. "Benny! Go!"

Medina waited for her.

"Any chance we can do this another day?" She was tired and in the city there wasn't an inch of nature for her to pull energy from. Just air—street and traffic air. She breathed in and focused anyway. Then breathed in again. Now that the vomiting was over, she felt a small reprieve.

Medina destroyed her recovery with a running kick.

She snapped her head back to avoid it, grabbed hold of his foot, twisted, and slammed him down. "Okay. We're doing this."

Medina was by far a more experienced fighter than she was. In the past, she'd been the stronger of the two, but now he seemed as strong as her. And he had the benefit of technique. Best not to underestimate him. The better choice was escape. She looked to see how far Benny was. He'd stopped halfway.

She yelled again for him to go.

Medina swung and she countered. They threw fists in rapid-fire succession, countering and attacking like the sparring mates they'd once been. Only he'd been one of her teachers. And there were things he hadn't taught her yet. One of them sent her flying backward on her ass. It hurt—bad.

She looked up to see him holding her wig.

He stared at it, as surprised as she was to see him holding a fist full of expensive hair.

"Do not mess with my wig," she threatened, rolling to her feet.

He laughed and tossed her the wig. She caught it grate-fully, then looked up. Benny stared, mouth open. She stroked a hand over her barren scalp. Then she balled the wig up and called to Benny.

"Catch!" He did.

"Don't let anything happen to that. It's the most expensive thing I own."

Benny clutched the wig to his stomach, nodding silently.

She turned back to Medina. He'd been remarkably pa-tient, occupied with picking out a piece of wood from the trash pile.

Happy with the one he found, he faced her and attacked.

She ran up on the wall and twisted midair to escape his reach and avoid being trapped. Fortunately, she'd had other teachers besides him. Medina swung as she came down with a kick that shattered the wood.

He tossed the remains, deciding on a different approach. In perfect parkour moves he spun himself up to the bottom of the fire escape and hung there a moment with dramatic ele-gance. He gave her a smile then took off after Benny.

Benny's eyes popped and he scrambled higher, this time in earnest.

Jocelyn wasted no time. Three easy leaps put her in reach of Medina on the other side of the escape. They met in the middle, exchanging punches. His elbow finally connected and gave him the second he needed to reach the next ladder. She grabbed one leg and yanked him down, avoiding a kick, as she forced heat through her hand, searing his skin until he gave up on Benny and dropped back down to the landing.

They faced off.

Then, with no concern for himself, he attacked her full throttle and brought them both over the side of the rickety rail. She hit the ground first, with only a small amount of protective energy around her to alleviate the force of the fall. His hands strangled. She flipped him. He flipped her with him. They rolled until finally they were both in each other's lock with him on top putting pressure on her throat while she squeezed his neck with her legs.

Up close, she saw that his eyes were not his own. They frightened her. She stared into them.

"They can see you. They see everything through my eyes and ears," he said through gritted teeth. "There's an audio scrambler in my pocket. I'm not sure if it's working. They control what I can do and where I can go."

"Come with me."

"I can't. Their implants prevent that."

"We can have them removed."

He laughed and moved his head in denial. "You can reach my gun. Use it."

Her heart pierced, understanding. "No! Medina, please. No."

"If you don't, I'll be back. And I'll kill everyone that you care about." He grabbed her hand and forced it on the gun.

"You're good." She couldn't see any emotion in the eyes before her. "You're strong. You can survive."

"I'm asking you as a friend." He fought hard, pulling the gun out, pressing it against his body. "Do it."

"Medina," she begged, trying to push the gun away from his chest. Then she heard the voice from his internal communication device. "What's going on? Medina, we don't have audio. Connect us or withdraw."

"Bastards." Medina tried to force her finger over the trigger even as she applied pressure to his throat.

Cashus spoke to her, distracting her from the battle. "Yes, I see you, Sunday. Take a good look at my puppet. He saved you so I tortured him with all the wonderful plans I had for you. I know you can hear me. You're a childish fool. You'll never escape who you are. You're just a toy. My toy. Don't ever forget it."

"Still making grand speeches." Jocelyn released her left hand and used it to maneuver the gun's barrel away from Medina.

"Freeze, asshole!"

Jocelyn turned her head and saw white polka dots. Then she saw long legs and Graeme walking toward them, gun aimed at Medina.

"Don't shoot! Don't shoot," she begged.

"Shoot!" Medina shouted repeatedly, countering her cries.

Then his body collapsed. He released her and rolled off, the gun falling from his hands. She retrieved it.

"Please," she said softly. "Let us help you."

Medina stood, partially bent, his face contorted with pain. She took a step forward.

"Jocelyn! Get back!"

Jocelyn obeyed, moving closer to Graeme. She reached him and put her hand on his gun, pushing gently down. Medina took a step forward, then another. He writhed with pain. Because of her. Slowly he moved past her and Graeme. Blood dripped from his ear and nose.

"Medina." Compassion, sorrow, and anger filled her. She stepped forward. He held a hand out for her to stay back. Her eyes filled. A small group had gathered in the alley entrance, peeking in. He walked by them, and they stepped aside in curious horror.

Fury filled her. Medina had done more for the country than any of them. He was a hero. He was a super agent. He had saved her life a dozen times. And none of them knew or understood.

"Get away!" she shouted. "Go!" The group scattered and she lost sight of Medina as he stumbled down into a subway station. She couldn't follow. She had Benny to watch over.

She turned back to Graeme and he stared at her, angry and confused. "I should have blown his freakin' head off!"

"He wasn't here for Benny. He was here for me."

"He shot Henry."

"He didn't kill him."

"We'll debate this later." He went to where Benny climbed down. They pushed the Dumpster under the ladder and Graeme was able to reach Benny's legs and catch him.

They turned back to the entrance as two giant policemen in full body armor approached.

"We're okay," Graeme said.

"Hey, purty gurl."

The taunt made her blood run cold. Jocelyn froze. Graeme and Benny didn't move.

It had been a trap all along. She realized instantly that she hadn't been afraid of Medina. She'd barely touched him. But the Butcher—he scared her.

As if to show his dominance, the Butcher swung his shield over his shoulder, went to the lavender and polka-dotted scooter, and lifted it over his head with a loud roar.

"Ahhhhrrr!" A glint of silver shined from a tooth in his mouth.

Standing next to him, Rabbit grinned psychotically and beat his chest like an ape, releasing a hyena-type howl.

"Are they the good guys?" Benny asked hesitantly, grasping Jocelyn's hand.

"Ahhhhrrrrrrr!" the Butcher growled powerfully in response.

The man was a straight-up nut case. The scooter came flying through the air. Graeme shoved them to the wall for safety, covering them.

They looked back. The lavender scooter lay crushed, the back wheel rolling helplessly in circles until it stopped.

"For really?" Benny shivered in exasperated shock.

She pulled Benny behind her and raised Medina's gun as Graeme drew his. "Shoot!"

CHAPTER TWENTY-FOUR

Graeme didn't hesitate. He unloaded, trying to find a weak spot through the armor, and failed. They were screwed. The men continued to approach, shields up.

Out of bullets. This was going to get personal.

He pulled Benny away as Jocelyn stepped forward, aimed, and threw her gun at the slightly smaller giant with enough force to knock him over. It made the other man pause.

Graeme stared at Jocelyn with respect. To say she had a warrior's face was an understatement. Her eyes glowed ferociously. He could almost feel the energy building around her. She put her hands out, palms to the sky, and breathed deeply several times. By the third breath, a wind swirled the dust and trash around them. She drew another, preparing for battle.

"Graeme," she said, not taking her eyes off the enemy, "get Benny out of here."

Then she launched.

What? Shit. Shit! Holy shit!

She grabbed the downed man's shield and she went for the bigger one. Graeme guessed this was the Butcher. He'd seen his face on the news, and though he had protective bullet-proof headgear, there was no mistaking the nose. She swung at his head with the shield, but he ducked. Smaller and faster than him, she swiped at his feet, hooking behind his protective gear and tripping him. He was cumbersome with all of it—which he soon realized as he divested himself in between rolling, kicking, and getting to his feet.

He seemed able to take a hundred punches with no impact.

"Crush him, Jocelyn!" Benny shouted from somewhere behind him.

Graeme saw the other guy get up and head for Jocelyn. He ran between them. "Benny! Go! Get help!"

Benny calculated the gaps between the four adults and sneaked past the attacker who swung for him and missed, thanks to Graeme's foot in his mouth.

Graeme had his attention now.

"You shouldn't have done that," he said.

Jocelyn backed into Graeme. "That's Rabbit," she said. "The big guy is the Butcher."

"I thought as much." Graeme felt his blood surge. They'd set a trap for Jocelyn. They didn't count on him showing up.

Rabbit laughed. If you could call it a laugh. It was more of a high-pitched snort and snivel. *Freakish.*

Graeme met Jocelyn's questioning glance with one of unbelievable resignation before he shrugged and faced his opponent. He couldn't say Seth hadn't warned him. "Yeah, I got this."

They were the same height, but Rabbit was a lot broader and thicker. It also meant he moved slower. Graeme quickly found out—not that much slower. He was grateful for the last three months of training, but he was going to need a lot more.

A loud crash vibrated behind him and Graeme turned to see the Butcher stunned against a brick wall. He turned back just as Rabbit's fist connected with his jaw. Thankfully he was moving enough to minimize the impact.

Graeme heard sirens and shouts get closer while they continued to fight. The Butcher and Rabbit heard them as well. Rabbit called out. He wanted to run.

The Butcher roared and Graeme turned defensively at the sound to see Jocelyn fly high in the air. She kicked the Butcher hard in the face, the force slamming his head backward into the brick wall. Wobbly a moment, he fell forward and she ducked low under his belly, lifted him at the knees, and flipped him over her shoulder. He landed near the nervous Rabbit, who urgently tried to drag him away.

The first patrol car squealed to a stop.

Butcher got to his feet and joined Rabbit, running from the alley. Jocelyn and Graeme sprinted after them. Then Graeme stopped, coming to his senses. He pulled Jocelyn back. "Wait!"

The two men headed down the same subway station steps as the other guy. They could be ambushed below. And Jocelyn needed a doctor. Her hands were bleeding, her skin was white, and her eyes looked…an unnatural blue. The skin around her eyes and lips was also blue.

She took a breath, also coming to her senses, realizing they were safe. Then she looked at him in horror, touching her head.

He quickly pulled her into his arms, kissed her scalp, and held her until she put her arms around him. "Next time I'll take the big one."

She smiled up at him like he was a hero. His adrenaline still coursed but began to fade as the pulsing in his cheek and knuckles warned him of injuries. He was going to have a shiner. He flexed his fingers slowly. Nothing broken.

Two more police vehicles crowded up on the sidewalk. The men got out.

"The Butcher and another man went that way." Graeme pointed. "Be careful."

The men called for backup. Three men went down the subway and the fourth stayed with them. Graeme searched for Benny. He spotted two of the family security sedans. He pointed them out for Jocelyn. A window rolled down and Benny waved. The other sedan waited for him. Three men stood around the vehicles, guarding.

He motioned for them to go. The cop was holding traffic but needed help—cars still tried to get by. They should get Benny out of here. It wasn't secure yet.

The first sedan started to move, then stopped as the door flung open. Benny darted out and began crossing the street to them, oblivious to oncoming traffic.

A horn sounded frantically.

"Benny! No!" Graeme's heart stopped as oncoming traffic, completely unaware of the situation, barreled across the intersection right at his little brother.

Jocelyn saw the disaster the same instant as Graeme. She took a step, then another. Off the sidewalk. Across the intersection.

Still too far from Benny.

Cars screeched. She saw the point of impact before it happened.

Realizing his mistake, Benny turned and froze in the middle of the street. He held her wig and a bottle of water. The water fell from his hand and hit the ground.

Jocelyn leapt, throwing every ounce of power she had at the two front cars, her hands up, her body shielding as she landed between Benny and the skidding car coming at him.

The car stopped.

It stopped with such sudden force that the entire backend lifted up, as if to flip over. She stood straight as the car reached full vertical height, parallel to her and Benny, teetering high in the air, ready to tip over on top of them.

The entire street froze. A hush fell. She heard the gasp of breath from the driver. She felt the power of Benny's heartbeat racing behind her.

Hands still in the air, she didn't move. Control. Clarity. Focus. With a slow breath she stopped the danger and gentled the landing. The car's backend fell hard but safely down.

A collective sigh of relief sounded. The woman behind the wheel transitioned from shocked to relieved. A policeman went to help her.

The world filled with noise, chaos, and commotion again. Jocelyn fell to her knees in the middle of the street, exhausted. She felt Benny put his arms around her. She turned and hugged her little brother, with everything she had, knowing she would do anything for him.

Graeme joined them.

Yelling.

"Benny! Are you trying to kill yourself? What were you thinking?"

It was too much for Benny. His eyes filled.

Jocelyn looked at Graeme. His face was white.

Benny's voice shook as he lifted tangled hair in his hands. "I have Jocelyn's wig." He wiped his nose and turned to her. She thanked him for the wig and put it on. "And I brought water because you're sick." He found the bottle squashed under the wheel of the car that almost hit him. It was his breaking point.

The tears rolled down his cheeks and he buried his head in her shoulder.

Graeme took a knee and encircled them both with his arms. "Okay. I'm sorry I yelled. You scared the living—" He took a breath and rephrased. "I just lost ten years of my life."

Benny turned and hugged his brother tightly now that it was okay. "I'm sorry."

Graeme picked him up and pulled Jocelyn's hand to help her. They were in the middle of the street and needed to move.

People stared while they walked to the sedans. Then everyone began to talk. Traffic moved. More cops arrived. The alley was sectioned off. The subway was searched. All to no avail. Medina, the Butcher, and Rabbit had disappeared.

Benny recovered quickly. The Rochester security wanted to remove him immediately. Jocelyn told him everything would be okay. He was worried. About her, it seemed. She was worried about what he would tell people.

"Benny," she said, as she hugged him goodbye. "I know today was scary."

"But you were awesome. Like a super ninja-robot, using the force to stop bullets and cars." He put his hands up to demonstrate, making strange high-pitched sounds. "And—"

She put a finger over his lips for the second time that day.

"Benny. It would be better for me if not everyone thought that."

"But it's true. I saw it." He karate chopped and made some matching squeals.

She turned to Graeme for help.

"Benny, you'll have to tell the police everything that happened, but it would be better if people don't know exactly what happened. They might come after Jocelyn for explanations."

"Are you a robot?"

"What?" Jocelyn jaw dropped, sincerely stunned.

"She's not a robot," Graeme said.

"That would explain it." Benny seemed to come to his own conclusion. "Okay, I get it. You're old school."

Jocelyn was even more lost.

Benny whispered, explaining, "You're the secret superhero, not like the Ironman or Thor who just go around and collect glory. More like Spiderman and Batman. Only you don't have a disguise."

"I'm not a superhero. I just have martial arts training."

Benny ignored her. "I'll come up with a costume for you. Don't worry. Your secret is safe with me. I won't even tell Poem," he promised—then seemed to regret it. "But that will be hard."

"Thank you, Benny." Jocelyn didn't want to leave him. She wasn't going to be able to see him any time soon. Not while she was in a cat-and-mouse game with Cashus. "I'm not going to be around the next couple weeks, but I'll see you as soon as I can."

"What do you mean?" This time Graeme interjected.

"I have some things I need to take care of."

"What things?" he demanded.

"Private, medical things." She didn't want to talk about it with everyone around.

"I told you she was sick. She threw up."

"You threw up? When?"

Benny told him. "After jumping on the van and getting shot at and busting open the doors and tossing that bastard to the dirt and saving me."

"Don't swear," Graeme said. He grazed her cheek gently. "Is it related to the headache?"

"Yes." His touch made her want to close her eyes. "I need some time to take care of it."

"Come home with us."

Benny jumped to agreement, but Jocelyn was firm. She didn't know how bad it was going to get or what she might do if it did. If she fell apart, her family and Graeme were the last people she wanted to witness it.

Disappointed, Benny was sent off while Graeme and Jocelyn gave statements to the police. She gave as little information as possible, remarking that fear and adrenaline took over and she must have been insane.

The cop concurred and warned her to let the police handle things next time. She received a long lecture on all the things that could have happened to her. Graeme thanked the man for saving him from the task.

She gave him a dirty look that only succeeded in making him smile.

"Benny is home with my mom. My dad is at the hospital with Henry's wife. He just texted that they were in surgery and it will be a while, but he's stable and doing well. I can visit tomorrow."

"Will you tell him I send my regards? I'm not sure if it's safe to go."

"Yes. Where can I take you now?"

"I have some work I need to do. Seth and I have a temporary place. It's off the radar."

"Okay."

"Okay?"

He shrugged. "We have the car. Can I take you grocery shopping as a thank you for saving my brother, then drop you off?"

She smiled, grateful. "Yes. But you can only drop me off nearby. Secret entrance and all that."

"Of course." He straightened her wig, escorted her to the car, and they finally left the scene. Graeme was very understanding about all this. But today no one had died. The next time it might be different. Then what? Medina had compromised Benny's security to get to her. What else were her enemies willing to do?

She was at a disadvantage. She didn't have anyone in her life she was willing to sacrifice.

The SOI folded his hands on the table in front of him. He smiled at Cashus and Newell. "Well now. That was interesting."

Laurence gripped his hands on the table to prevent his own squirming. Newell didn't say a word.

"We successfully tested Medina. We were able to turn him off, literally with a switch."

"Really?"

"Yes, sir. Very successful."

"And what happened with Clarence and the Rabid Rabbit? They were stopped by Sunday and her boyfriend?" The SOI leaned back in his chair. "It boggles the mind."

Newell stepped in. "Butcher and Rabbit are used to planning their traps differently and in smaller spaces with more control."

"I see."

Silence.

Finally, the SOI spoke. "I'm very dissatisfied with our progress. Are you sure you can control Medina?"

Cashus hesitated. "Eighty percent sure. It depends on the circumstances."

"Okay," the SOI said. "Let's think about more effectively using Medina next time. He's always been an efficient killer. Bring in the Butcher and his friend. Let's give Rabbit an upgrade. We'll talk next week about the plan. For now, keep up surveillance, but stand down.

"Sir," Cashus hastened to add. "Project Sunday is out of meds. This next week she will be at her most vulnerable."

"Interesting." The SOI nodded in contemplation. "Hardly sporting. But I like how you're thinking, Cashus. Keep at it." He clicked off, and the two men were left staring at the emblem on the screen.

Newell turned to him. "Not sure I understand the 'hardly sporting' part?"

Cashus stood up to leave and gave the man a sympathetic look. "You will."

CHAPTER TWENTY-FIVE

Rachel and Ford sat silently until their security detail closed the doors behind them.

Ford put the photographs on the table in front of them. "Benny can't take this kind of excitement. It weakens him and he doesn't recover. Sergei isn't going to help us." He said it abruptly. "Ketevan said she didn't know why."

Rachel swallowed hard and didn't speak. This was a blow she did not expect. She put a hand over her husband's. "All right. We'll find another way."

"Rachel—"

She heard his frustration. And fear. Time was running out for Benny.

"Let's focus on this. One thing at a time." She picked up the picture of Benny held by a man with a gun, and the traffic photos of the three men entering the subway. "Do you think these are linked attacks?"

"It has to be, Rachel. Graeme said Jocelyn was the hiker who helped John Morrow capture the Butcher. It was a setup to get revenge."

"Then why isn't she here with us, where she would be safe?"

"She's proud. She doesn't want our help. She's independent. She thinks she's safer alone. I don't know. If I knew what went through the mind of a teenage girl, Morgan wouldn't be such a mess."

"She's not a mess," Rachel defended. *She's a mess and we're the worst parents.* "This is just a rough spot. She needs structure, love, and consistency."

Rachel picked up a photo of Jocelyn. The image caught her airborne, flying above a car, leaping toward the van. The local traffic cameras had captured most of the chase and their security had intercepted the images before the authorities could erase or edit. "That was some homeschooling."

"I'll say. How much have we been paying?" Ford smiled.

"She fights like a 'ninja-robot'," Rachel repeated Benny's words. "Benny's smitten."

"An attractive girl dodged bullets and kicked ass to save his life. Of course." Ford winked at her. "He takes after me. Graeme is pretty 'smitten' as well."

Rachel nodded. "I know we promised no background checks, but I think we should run one."

"No," Ford said.

"Ford!" Rachel thought he'd agree.

"She's educated, has nice friends, knows self-defense, and is a hard worker. What else do you need to know?"

"Everything! I'm running for Senate."

"No excuse to spy on your son."

She stood and paced. "All right, listen. I meant to tell you this last week. My intern compiled my mail and spam from the last few months and mixed in was an email from a psychologist at Camp Holliwell."

Ford froze.

"When I investigated, her office said it was fake and not from her, that they'd had a security leak."

"And?"

"It's just that…the email said, 'Jocelyn Albrecht is alive. I'm treating her at Camp Holliwell. They call her Sunday Cashus. Please help.'"

"Please help? But she didn't want help."

"No. The email was a fake. Like every other one. We have a long list, remember."

Ford scowled. "Cashus isn't common."

Rachel agreed. She got up and poured two vodkas over ice. She didn't drink much, but a little something seemed in order.

"I always hated that sniveling ass, but he brought us a death certificate."

"Signed by a doctor who's dead." Rachel handed him the drink.

"Hell."

"I know."

"That doesn't mean this Jocelyn is the same." Ford sipped the drink. "It's a popular name for that age. There's a girl in Morgan's class with that name."

"That's Josephine."

"What about the tennis girl?"

"Justine."

"The super-model?"

"Yes, but it concerns me that you know that." Rachel shuffled through some different pictures on her desk and pulled one from the pile. "Who does she look like?"

Ford looked and shook his head. "The super-model?"

"No! Look at those eyes, Ford."

Ford looked.

"She looks like Grayson. And Sabrina." Rachel worried. "What if we made a mistake?" They had negotiated and given little Jocelyn to Laurence Cashus. "What if I made a mistake?"

"Rachel, you're looking for a resemblance that's not there. She was on death's door. Nothing could have been done to save her. A doctor proclaimed her dead right after we turned her over for treatment. And you, of all people, know that the government is terrible at keeping secrets. After General Brody died I made inquiries. I was assured that she was dead."

Apparently Ford had thought all this through as well. "What about the other angle?"

"This is just a distraction from the campaign and elections?" Rachel stopped in front of her framed copies of the Declaration of Independence and the Constitution of the United States of America. She could recite both from memory. "It makes the most sense."

"Could be Morgan walked right into part of the trap as well."

"I know. We have to better equip them. It's going to get dirty."

"Are you sure you still want to do this?"

Rachel turned to him. "Yes! Ford, we have to. It's bigger than us." She was more resolute than ever. And her master plan had taken years to put into place. She just needed to make sure her children were safe. It seemed no security was good enough anymore. There were sleepers and spies everywhere. Even she had planted some. "What's the point of all this if we don't use it to stop what's happening?"

"We could lead quiet peaceful lives, and our children would be safe."

"No one is safe anymore." Rachel walked back to her husband and took his hand fervently. "If there was a better way, I'd do it."

Ford raised her hand to his lips. "As long as we're together."

"We are. And we will be."

He picked up a picture of Jocelyn holding Benny protectively. "The good news is that *this* Jocelyn seems to be on our side. And Graeme is the happiest I've seen him in months." Ford took her hand again. "No background checks."

"Just one."

"Rachel."

"She needs to get her house pass anyway." She tried not to smile at having a loophole. "We do that for everyone's friends. It's only fair."

"Now you sound like Morgan." Ford frowned picking up one of the pictures of Jocelyn leaving the van with Benny. "Just the standard background, Rachel. If anything strange shows up, then we can consider more." He put the picture down. "We should have her over for dinner. We owe her serious thanks."

"I know," Rachel agreed. "I'll talk to Graeme about it." Dinner would be perfect to interrogate the girl further. If anyone could get to the truth, she could.

Seth patted Jocelyn's face with a cold rag. She'd been able to work in Chinatown for one more day, determined to make more money, and get in as much translation time as possible for her lawyer before she got worse.

Now they faced the shitstorm.

Hell. He wasn't even sure if this would be the worst.

Jocelyn's cries tormented him. She vomited nearly twice an hour and didn't want food. He was sure the headache caused her to vomit rather than her stomach being upset, but regardless, he was having a hard time keeping her hydrated, and in the two days he'd been taking care of her she seemed to shrink in weight.

He held a bottle of water to her lips, begging her to drink. "If you don't drink, I'll have to take you to a hospital for an IV."

"No!" She shoved him with all her might, which was still strong despite her not eating anything.

The bottle went flying and he fell back whacking the only piece of furniture in the little studio apartment. He cursed and got up, grabbing an energy drink this time.

"How about orange-flavored juice?"

Wild eyes stared back at him, the whites streaked with veins of blue. They had shaved the little bits of random blue peach fuzz, and her scalp was smooth again. She looked like a cross between an alien and a crazed drug addict.

The orange drink appealed and she sat up. Sweat beaded on her scalp from the effort. She touched the bottle and he held the juice to her lips making sure she didn't drop it. Realizing she was thirsty, she drank almost six ounces. He relaxed a moment, grateful.

The moment ended minutes later when she ran to the bathroom and it came back up. She rested her head on the toilet seat, sobbing tearlessly and silently, her body heaving in pain.

He wet more towels with cold water and wiped her down. She wore only a tank top and underwear, and seeing her bones protrude already scared him. Her temperature ran warm normally, but he didn't think her hot dry skin was a good sign.

He was in over his head.

He knelt next to her and placed a cold towel he'd put in the small freezer over her back. She didn't move.

"Jocelyn, I need to get help."

She squeezed her eyes shut. "I'm not going to a hospital. Please don't do that."

"I won't. But what about that nurse you went to?"

"Kymber." Jocelyn lifted her head a little, hopeful. "Yes. She said she would help me. I have her number."

"Where? In your backpack?"

She nodded and rested her head back down.

Seth ran to the other room and searched hurriedly, panicking when he couldn't find it right away. Once found, he dialed trying not to be frantic. "Please answer."

A friendly female voice answered, "Hello."

"Hi. Is this Kymber?"

She confirmed.

"I'm a friend of Jocelyn's. I have her with me. We need help. She needs help. She's really bad off. I don't know what to do."

John pulled up in front of a dark alley and checked the address. Dark and empty. He got out of the borrowed patrol car, grabbed his flashlight, flipped it on, and surveyed the area.

"Seth?"

A tall figure stepped from a doorway and came forward carrying Jocelyn. He was a handsome kid with a worried expression. John checked on the girl. She was wrapped in a sheet and breathing fitfully. Quickly, he opened the back of the cruiser and the kid balked visibly, still six feet away.

"Is this a joke?"

John wasn't sure what that meant, but guessed he had trust issues with authority figures.

"I'm a lieutenant with NYPD. My wife Kymber is a nurse. We thought the fastest way to travel was this. And our vehicle is too small."

"If this is trap, I swear I'll find you and tear every limb from your body myself."

"Deal. No trap," he said. "How is she doing?"

"Turn off the light. She's extra sensitive."

John obeyed. Seth came closer. Jocelyn didn't have her wig on. With only the lights of the vehicle he couldn't see much, but he touched her head, which was burning, and swore silently. "We need—"

"No hospitals."

"You don't like cops or hospitals. Got it." He took Jocelyn in his arms so Seth could dump the three small backpacks on his shoulders into the backseat. "I'll hand her to you."

No sooner had they gotten in than the kid questioned, "Is your house clean?"

John glanced in the rearview mirror. He didn't mean clean. He meant swept for bugging devices. A chill went up his spine.

Seth didn't relent. "We have one audio scrambler, but if you're not secure—"

"I'll take care if it." He called his buddy who lived two doors down from him. "Tim. I need a favor. Yeah, now." Next he called Kymber to let her know Tim was coming over and that he was on the way. He gave Kymber the rundown. "She's breathing erratically, her body temperature feels sky high, dehydrated, and she's obviously lost weight."

"She has," Seth confirmed.

John hung up, flipped on the lights, but kept the siren off. It was 11:00 p.m. The streets weren't too busy in this area.

He heard mumbling in the back.

"I'm taking you to Kymber's house." Seth spoke quietly to Jocelyn. "Any of this feel familiar?"

Jocelyn whispered raggedly. John couldn't make it out. He thought she said, "I'd rather be shot again."

"It's going to be okay." Seth looked at him in the mirror and caught his eyes, this time with worry. He needed reassurance.

"It's going to be okay," John promised.

Twenty minutes later they put Jocelyn, still wrapped in the sheet, straight into the ice bath Kymber had prepared. Her screams woke up the household and the shattering glass and tile around the bathroom gave John the first sign that everything might not be okay.

CHAPTER TWENTY-SIX

*H*er body felt wrecked. All she wanted was sleep. The sharp throbbing in her head prevented any peace. She fell in and out of awareness. There was the car, then the sound of Kymber's voice, efficient and comforting.

Until it wasn't.

Ice water cut through her skin and senses, confusing her. She saw Seth's face, then Kymber's, and bright lights. White walls. She was in a hospital again. Panic filled her.

"Get me out." She could barely hear her voice and tried again. "Out!" She grasped the edge of the slippery tub. She had no weapons. No defense. They were trapping her. The room was small. Too small. Hands pushed her down in the water. More panic.

"We need to lower your temperature, Jocelyn. Hang on. I know this is hard, but just a little longer," said the efficient voice.

She followed the sound, grasping at air until she connected with an arm.

"No hos-pi-tals!" She shuddered, breathing hard, unable to inhale.

Another hand grabbed hers, trying to make her release the arm. "We're at Kymber and John's house, Jocelyn. It's safe. I checked everything. This is not a hospital. It's the bathroom in their house. Do you understand? This is a house."

Jocelyn stared in the direction of the familiar sound, looking for Seth's face. She saw a silhouette on her right. He came down next to her.

"Seth?"

"I'm here. It's safe. I promise."

"I'm c-cold."

"Just a couple minutes more. Your temperature is still high."

Something touched her scalp. She screamed. It hurt. Water dripped down her cheeks. Then more. Pain splintered in her head. Something flashed. A crack in a door opened. The world shattered loudly around her. A woman yelped in panic. Blue smoke filled the air. She felt like she was falling. Then every muscle in her body seemed to freeze and she was trapped.

She couldn't move. She watched as the man put a gun to her dad's head. His blood and brains shot out. His expression gone. She looked up and saw the man with the gun smile down at her. Green-rimmed glasses. He held a small metal case that looked like her mom's lab box. She stared at it, then at him. He aimed the gun at her. Then he was gone. Her mom knocked him sideways. He swung, hitting her head with the gun, then recovered, reached the door, and escaped. Her mom crawled to the door and stood. She pulled. They were locked in.

Her mother was bleeding. She struggled to get something and spoke to Jocelyn, but blue smoke had already started to fill the lab and she'd breathed too much. She lay on the floor feeling dizzy.

Her mom stabbed her. "It will save you." She removed the syringe still half full, then shoved it in a small metal case and put it in the hidden floor safe, dragging the carpet over it. "Get this later. For Benny. Promise, baby? I love you. I love you, Jocelyn."

"She's having a seizure!"

Jocelyn heard someone yell. Seth?

She was being pulled from the wetness. She needed air. Suddenly she had it.

Her chest expanded and she gasped, then wheezed as she sucked in.

White light surrounded her again, but a little softer.

"I got her," Seth said.

Towels wiped off the moisture. Another voice came into the room. She spoke Korean.

Kymber and the woman put dry clothes on her and then Seth was back, picking her up and taking her down some stairs. "You're going to be okay."

She gazed at him, spent, barely able to lift her head. She landed gently on a large bed.

"We'll get you a cot," Kymber said to Seth.

"The chair is fine."

Kymber pulled a syringe out of a small bag. Jocelyn registered her poking it in a bottle to suck something out. She pushed away rolling off the other side of the bed into an IV stand. Panic struck again.

"This is a vitamin B shot, Jocelyn. That's all. Then I'm giving you an IV. You're dehydrated. This is the quickest way for me to help you. I either give this to you, or we go to a hospital. The hydration will also help with the headaches."

She looked to Seth for help. He took her hand and reassured. Having no choice, she closed her eyes, pathetic. They might be trying to kill her or subdue her or capture her for the reward money.

Seth spoke softly. "I'm not sure what's getting through to you right now. You don't look so good, but everyone here is going to take care of you. This is a safe house, okay? You are safe here. Kymber said it might be three more days of rough times, but it will get better." He held a bottle of water with a straw in it. "Take a little sip. Your lips are all chapped and dry."

She sucked a little. Then closed her eyes, trying not to get sick.

"I have orange juice ice cubes upstairs," Kymber directed Seth. "Why don't you get some of those?"

Seth disappeared instantly.

"Where am I?" Jocelyn asked.

"You're in our basement. It's converted. There's a bathroom right in front of you. The stairs go up to the kitchen." Kymber took her pulse and blood pressure. "Your vitals are very high. Are you scared?"

She nodded. She felt defenseless.

"You are free to leave at any time, but you're going to have symptoms from the drugs. It will be a little easier if you let me help you."

Jocelyn didn't believe her. Why would anyone help her? She closed her eyes and turned her head away.

"Okay. I'll be back in a bit." She ran into John on the way down.

"I've got the orange ice cubes," John said. "Who's up for some goodness?"

Jocelyn looked at him, worried.

"Seth is eating pot roast and corn muffins. He's probably going to have seconds. Can I tempt you?" He held up a frozen orange cube by a plastic stick.

Jocelyn moved her free hand and he put it in her grip. Slowly she turned her head on the pillow and rested the ice cube on her lips. It felt okay. Tasted okay. She closed her eyes again and sucked on it for a while. She could feel her body getting warm again. She didn't want to do another ice bath, but she had a feeling there were a few more rounds of misery before things got better.

Seth woke up to the smell of bacon. His mouth watered. He checked the time. 6:00 a.m. He'd slept for ninety minutes. He leaned over Jocelyn. Her eyes were wide, staring at the ceiling. Her body shivered and he tucked a blanket around her. She was still attached to the IV. That was a positive.

"Hey?"

Jocelyn blinked that she heard.

"You made it to morning. Always a good sign."

She blinked acknowledgement.

Her skin had a yellow-green sickly tint, accented by the blue eyes with blue veins that had given Nurse Kymber and Lt. John a shock the night before. They really hadn't known what they were dealing with. But they'd done their best. And Jocelyn was still here.

"Hungry?"

She closed her eyes, indicating even the thought made her sick. He guessed the smells coming from above weren't nearly as attractive to her as to him. He gave her a sip of water from the straw. She swallowed painfully.

"If you drank more it wouldn't hurt so much."

She stared at the ceiling.

"Headache."

She blinked again, as if any other movement would make it worse. "Got it. I'm jumping in the shower. Want to join?"

She closed her eyes and turned her head away.

He'd dragged her into the icy shower two times since the ice bath.

"I'll take that as a no." He took a quick shower and put on fresh jeans. They had a washer and dryer. He'd ask if he could use it later and clean their clothes. He went back in the room and dug through his pack for a clean T-shirt. When he turned there was a young girl with straight dark hair and rounded dark eyes staring at him. Specifically, staring at his chest.

He put the T-shirt on and smiled. "You must be, Maddie." The girl nodded.

He walked to position himself between her and Jocelyn.

"Are you Seth?"

"Yes, ma'am."

She smiled. "You have an accent."

"I think you have an accent."

She shook her head confidently. "I don't. You do." Remembering her goal she said, "My mom said to tell you breakfast was ready. Is Jocelyn better?"

"She's getting there. She doesn't want anyone to see her right now. Really bad headache."

"Migraines can make you really sick. My friend's mom gets them and once she was in bed for three days."

"Yeah. They suck." Seth rubbed a hand through his hair. He regretted it when she stared at his bicep. Crap. That was not deliberate. He did not want a cop's daughter crushing on him.

"Shall we go up?"

She nodded and reluctantly turned away, trying to check on Jocelyn. In the kitchen he caught her silent "wow" to her mom and pretended in front of John that he hadn't noticed.

Kymber patted her husband's shoulder after Maddie went upstairs to get dressed. "Don't worry, honey. She discovered boys long before this."

"I leave for work at seven. You need a ride anywhere?"

"Yes, but—"

"I'm off today," Kymber said. "My mom and I can handle it."

"I can be back tonight."

She nodded. They synced their schedules.

Seth hurried downstairs and grabbed what he needed, including Jocelyn's phone. He hadn't thought about much all night except her seizure. He wondered if that's how he looked when having one. Jocelyn's had probably only been ten seconds, but it was a sign.

He texted Graeme on Jocelyn's phone, a little surprised the guy was awake and responded so quickly.

Is Jocelyn okay?

Yes. Thought about what you said. You know somebody who can help?

Yes.

He debated for only a split second. *Meet me at usual spot. 8 AM.*

There might not be a cure in time to save him, but maybe it would save Jocelyn.

CHAPTER TWENTY-SEVEN

Graeme took Seth to see Sabrina at the A & R Technologies location in Astoria. The lab there was set up for clinical trials and patient examinations. And Sabrina was the only doctor he trusted with the hard stuff. His dad said she'd be a brilliant researcher like her brother if she chose to go that route. He knew she was torn between trying to find a cure for Benny and trying to help people "hands-on."

Right now, Seth needed the hands-on.

"I told you bare bones staff and only straight guys," Graeme said.

"Jonathan is our best MRI tech."

"He's gay."

"So?"

Graeme sighed and shook his head at Sabrina while they watched Jonathan fawn over Seth and try to help him with his shirt. This was going to take longer than necessary.

Jonathan did the MRI of Seth's brain then left—reluctantly. Seth just shrugged when Graeme shook his head in disgust at the new fan.

"It's the hat," Seth said, referring to his slightly rugged cowboy hat as if he couldn't help the power that it held.

Sabrina stared at the MRI images silently. Graeme could tell she was upset about being sworn to secrecy now. Something was up.

"I'll need to send these out to a radiologist for confirmation. And I'd like some blood samples."

That didn't sound promising. She was buying time.

"What can you tell right now?" Seth asked.

Sabrina shrugged and made a note. "Hard to say."

"Really." Seth smiled at her with a wink. "I heard you were the best. You must have an opinion."

Sabrina studied Seth. Then Graeme. Graeme took the hint.

"Fine. I'll give you some privacy." Damn. He wanted to know. He left the MRI room and went to the waiting area with Jonathan. "She's giving him the verdict."

"Did Dr. Albrecht say what it was?"

Graeme shook his head.

Jonathan kept talking. "I've never seen anything like that. He's so hot! It's so unfair."

Graeme nodded. "I know, man. Like, what was that?"

The tech shook his head. "It looked like tumors, but a different consistency. Filling in and pressing against his brain. A mess. Have to see what a radiologist says."

Hell. Brain tumors? That was not good. Jocelyn needed to know.

The door opened and Seth came out holding a cotton ball to the bend of his arm. Sabrina wrote on some blood sample vials. "Let's set up some time for next week. I'll have a plan then."

"Thanks, Doc." Seth slid his cowboy hat on nonchalantly. Graeme detected only a split second of fear. Bravado was Seth's middle name. He tipped his hat to Jonathan, who blushed. Then he turned to Graeme. "Get me outta here."

John dumped the box of listening devices on the desk of his captain. "Any reason at all why you or the department would be bugging my house?"

The captain's eyes widened with genuine surprise. He tipped over the box for a look. Then he picked out something, curious. "This was in *your* house?"

"Yeah. You might want to have your house swept. Maybe even"—he looked around— "the office."

The captain stood, his posture defensive. Then he buzzed for the tech team.

"I will. Then we'll get to the bottom of this."

"Let me know when you do. In the meantime, I need to take a few days off."

"Of course. That's what I've been telling you."

John nodded. That much was true. And now with Jocelyn at his place, a strange young man in his home, and his wife feeling stressed that she might not be the right person to treat Jocelyn, he needed to be there to help. Whatever their story was, Jocelyn and Seth were uneasy with the authorities. It meant he really couldn't trust them yet and he didn't want to be taken by surprise.

Kymber's relief when he arrived home early said it all. She was downstairs changing the sheets on Jocelyn's bed. He heard Jocelyn in the bathroom throwing up.

He gave Kymber the update from the rest of the house. "Dad's playing with Max in the yard. Mom and Maddie are making sandwiches and cookies. How are things here?"

"She ripped her IV out stumbling to the bathroom. She keeps calling me mom. I think she's hallucinating. I don't know what to do or how long it will take. Maybe they gave her those drugs for a reason. Whatever she keeps reliving…" Kymber shook her head. "It's not good, John. I think we made a mistake."

Her eyes filled.

"You're tired. You need a nap." He helped her with the bed quickly and they turned as the door opened from the bathroom. With her bare scalp, blue-tinged skin, and bony frame, Jocelyn looked like a breeze would knock her over. Fortunately, he knew she was stronger. At least he hoped she still was. Right now she stared blankly into the room.

"Jocelyn?"

Her head turned toward his voice and her mouth opened. No sound came out. It was like she was trapped in a dream and couldn't scream. She spun quickly when Kymber touched her arm telling her to lie down. Then she fell to her knees. Her throat tightened dangerously.

John cursed. "Is she having another seizure?"

"I don't know."

Jocelyn's eyes widened in terror. Kymber kneeled, checking her pulse. "It's too fast." Jocelyn's throat muscles tightened sharply.

John stepped slowly in their direction not wanting to threaten Jocelyn. He didn't know what was going through her head, but he agreed with Kymber. It wasn't good. "Jocelyn. Take a breath. Everything's okay. Breathe."

"Dad." Her voice begged with a pained gasp.

Kymber looked at him.

He did what he needed to do. "Yes, honey. You're sick. I need you to take a breath. Can you do that?"

Jocelyn obeyed.

"Good. Another."

Her muscles relaxed a little. He picked her up and brought her to the bed. They tucked the sheets around her as she continued to stare blindly in his direction. Just when he thought she might be past whatever vision tormented her, she grabbed his forearm. Fiercely. Definitely still strong.

"They're coming to kill us."

The clarity in her eyes and certainty in her voice unnerved him. "Who, Jocelyn?"

"The man…" She struggled with the words, her muscles tensing dangerously again, her fingers digging into his arm with painful urgency. She sucked a breath like it was her last one. "…with green glasses."

He felt a pulse of heat shoot up his arm just before the lights in the basement shattered around them and they were plunged into darkness.

Graeme threw down the exo-thread, his new name for Benny's project, and paced restlessly. He checked the text from Richie and the photo of him and Al drinking beer at a pub on Broadway. They were covering a lot of ground on their visit. Graeme just wasn't in the mood for bars and crowds. Jocelyn was sick and there was nothing he could do. She didn't even want him around, according to Seth. The only thing that made him feel a little better was that she was with the Morrows. He had to thank Seth for that bit of info.

He heard Benny and Poem running down the hallway, caught up in a popular ghost-hunting game. Poem no doubt ran slow. The stress from Benny's kidnapping experience had taken a toll. He needed his special forearm crutches again. The exo-thread would need to compensate for a lot to be successful. He should be working on it now.

Instead he grabbed his jacket and the keys to his bike.

The evenings were finally a little cooler. He pulled up to the hospital and made his way to Henry's room, knocking softly on the open door.

"Graeme!" Henry put the e-reader down on his bedside table and reached for the bed remote with his good arm.

"Careful."

"Don't worry. Just had my evening drugs. Feeling good. You just missed the family."

"How are they?"

"Good. Good. Want me to retire early or drive for an old folks' home."

Graeme pulled up a chair. "Can't blame them. I'm sorry about what happened."

"Not your fault or anyone in the family."

"We think they were after Jocelyn and used Benny as a lure."

"Not her fault either. She left a card at reception for me." Henry pointed to it. "The world is full of bad people." He closed his eyes resting. "But I'm glad you're here. I wanted to talk with you privately. Pour me some water?"

Graeme jumped to comply.

"How is Miss Jocelyn?"

"She's sick right now. She was coming down with something already. Didn't want me around to see her at her worst."

"Too early in the relationship," Henry advised. "Don't let it bother you. Though—"

"What?"

"She moved mighty fast for someone coming down with something."

"Fighter instincts. She grew up on a military base. Her summer vacations were not normal."

"I believe that," Henry said. "She was protecting you."

"She saw the guy first."

"She was protecting you," Henry insisted again.

"Maybe." Graeme didn't understand what Henry was getting at.

"How well do you know Miss Jocelyn?"

Graeme shifted. "Well enough."

"She's fast. She didn't panic. She was worried. I saw that in her eyes, but she had confidence. You let her run off after some bad dudes while I lay there. Like you knew she could handle it."

"I only hoped she could. I didn't know."

"Umm-hmm. Guess now you know."

"The adrenaline and all. Neither of us was thinking straight."

"Don't bullshit me, Young Graeme." Henry's tone was harsh.

Graeme didn't say anything.

"Why are you here?" Henry finally asked.

"I missed you. I wanted to talk to you."

"Are you trying to silence me?"

"What?" Graeme sat up. "No! Silence you about what?"

Henry studied him hard. Then waved a finger. "Get my suit jacket. Hanging inside the closet."

Graeme got the jacket and brought it over. Henry struggled with his one arm to get what he wanted.

"When I grabbed these, they were still hot."

Curious, Graeme waited, staring at Henry's big, gnarled hand. He opened his fingers to reveal them. Three bullets. He looked at Henry, not understanding.

"I told myself I was hallucinating from the shock. But I wasn't. She dropped them in the gutter just before she came over to me." Graeme shook his head. "Jocelyn?"

"Bingo."

"That's impossible." His mouth went a little dry. Then he dismissed it. Super strength was one thing. This was literally not possible.

"I guess she has some secrets."

The comment struck a harsh chord after hearing Al say the same thing. Did Al know? Henry closed his fist and put the bullets back in his jacket.

"My souvenirs."

"Have you told anyone?"

"No one would believe me if I did."

"I'm not sure I do," Graeme said.

Henry nodded. "I really like her. She's a sweet girl. Very kind. Self-aware. Sees other people. I was proud of your choice."

"Was?"

"I'm worried. That's all. Don't want to see you hurt, or anyone else. The bullets were one thing. How many other secrets might she have? And are any of them dangerous?"

Graeme didn't know. He was even more unsettled than when he walked in. He wanted to give Jocelyn time. He was certain she would tell him everything when she was ready. But some secrets were dangerous. He had learned that the hard way. His body was still scarred from deadly lasers during her Holliwell escape, Henry was in the hospital, and Benny had deteriorated in just a couple days from the shock.

How much was he willing to risk for her?

CHAPTER TWENTY-EIGHT

*J*ocelyn woke with a start, sitting straight up.

The movement made her dizzy.

She focused on the light coming from the television. A movie played. A lot of death and destruction seemed to be taking place. A brick wall seemed familiar. Where was she? She turned at the sound of breathing and saw a man in a corner chair, his feet up, sleeping. For a split second she thought he was her dad and the last ten years had been a dream. The moment was long enough for her to feel the loss again. Her eyes burned but nothing came out. She unhooked the IV and tried to figure out where she was and how she got there. As she sat up, she saw a figure on the ground in a sleeping bag. Georgie.

"Hey," John Morrow called softly from the corner. "You're awake."

She didn't know what to say to that.

"At first we thought you'd never sleep, then we thought you'd never wake up." He rolled his chair to sitting position. "Do you remember who I am?"

She felt her heart breaking again. Her throat stung, dry and painful. She rasped, "I remember *everything*."

He stared at her for a long moment. "Okay." He pushed the footrest down on his recliner and stood. "The girls know where the food is. I'm going up. Kymber will be awake in a few hours and can check on you."

He went upstairs leaving Jocelyn to figure out the rest. Georgie stretched, then sat up, surprised to see her awake.

"Where's Seth?" Jocelyn croaked.

A voice sounded in the dark. "He's in Atlantic City." Jocelyn turned as a blond head popped up on the other side of the bed. "Said he needed some quick cash."

Another female groan came from the foot of the bed.

Georgie handed Jocelyn a bottled water. "Drink slow. Kymber said it would take a while before your stomach would accept anything."

Jocelyn sipped. "How long have you been here?"

"Two days on and off. Lena got here last night. You were still sleeping. She missed all the fun."

The groan at the foot of the bed became the cranky voice of Brittany. "By fun she means you vomiting on my overnight bag and screaming at me like I was solely responsible for ruining your life," she grumbled, her voice sounding tired. "It hurt my feelings."

Jocelyn crawled weakly to the foot of the bed and saw a giant pool of wild hair that she guessed was Brittany's head. "Sorry."

"I'll forgive you if you let me shoot you wearing my bulletproof corset."

Jocelyn flicked a little water at her friend. "Forgiveness is overrated."

Brittany turned her head on the pillow and smiled up at her. "You are back."

Georgie filled her in. "Kymber and John have been taking care of you for five days. Kymber's mom, and me and Seth helped. Seth left yesterday after Kymber said you seemed less combative."

"Combative?" That didn't sound good.

"Yeah. You destroyed the bathroom upstairs and a few things down here. Maddie was crying one time because she thought you were a druggie and going to die. Her grandparents got into a fight in Korean, which I would have loved to understand, but I think it was about the kimchi not you. Oh, and you gave Kymber a black eye—totally by accident."

"Oh. Wow." Jocelyn swallowed.

"Yeah. It's been a drama," Georgie said.

"I don't remember any of *that*."

"No one remembers their dark side," Brittany said. She snuggled back into her sleeping bag.

"They're really good people. You lucked out. Especially with Kymber being a nurse. The rest of us were pretty freaked out."

Lena crawled up on the sofa bed and rolled onto the mattress still in her flowered sleeping bag that looked to be Maddie's. "What *do* you remember? Your past?"

Jocelyn nodded. She still had to sort through it all. So many things had assaulted her senses in the last days. Her mother's cooking, her father's voice, Morgan's laugh, Benny's gargles. She didn't know if she was grateful for the memories, even though this was what she wanted. The memories of the past also came with memories of her parents' deaths. She swallowed hard.

Not death—murder.

She could see the man with the gun. He'd shot her father, then left them for dead while the lab burned around them.

But one important thing stuck in her memory. "Jocelyn?" Georgie prompted her.

"My mom had a cure for Benny. I think that's why they were killed."

Brittany sat up. Georgie sat down. Lena curled into a ball. All waited to hear.

"She wanted me to give it to him."

But how? And where was it now?

Jerry changed the passcodes on his safe. He did it twice a week, more from habit than concern. He had a lot of aces up his sleeve to access before he'd ever need to use the contents of the safe.

Mercer called on his line. He answered.

"Sir, I'm patching through the president."

"Mr. President."

"Jerry, you said she was dead. Dead, Jerry!"

Jerry knew who he meant right away. "I said Project Sunday had been taken care of." He plugged the phone into his home system and pressed speaker and record. "Project Sunday was shut down. It's over."

"By over, I thought terminated. Everyone involved."

Jerry took a relaxed breath and leaned back in his chair. He loved the worn leather chair in the home office of his colonial estate.

"Mr. President." He repeated the salutation for the tape. "We took three stripes off the general, demoted the lead scientist, reprimanded the security head, and imprisoned the traitor. Many of these people are good, loyal servants and scientists, supporting the cause of freedom. They made some mistakes, but they learned from them, and still have value to add. I see no reason to just fire everyone."

Frustrated, the president's voice rose. "I mean kill, not fire. Terminate the freaks! All of them! That girl is running around New York City free. I read it in the *New York Times*!" He nearly screamed. "She's helping people. You think I'm so stupid and I don't know who this mysterious Good Samaritan is? What happens when they call her a superhero or something? I want her dead. And anyone who helps her."

Jerry paused a long moment. "Mr. President, I hear your concern, but—we are the leaders of the free world. We don't go around killing private citizens."

The president guffawed like he'd just made a joke. "Tell that to the Federal Reserve."

"Sir, I…"

"Whatever. Just take care of it, Jerry. And make sure we don't lose the Senate either."

The line cut off.

"Yes, sir." He waited. "Sir?" Then he hung up and stopped the recording, a satisfied smile on his face. This was one for the safe.

Sometimes things just all came together.

Jocelyn sipped on chicken broth at the kitchen table of the Morrow house while Maddie and Max chatted away. John went back to work, her friends were back at classes, and Seth was still missing, supposedly in Atlantic City gambling. She didn't feel good about that.

Physically, she felt okay, considering.

Her headache seemed gone. She hadn't vomited in twenty-four hours. Kymber took the IV out of her hand vein. She was hungry but couldn't hold solid food just yet. And the grandparents seemed to think she was okay despite a pretty horrific introduction—probably because she was helping Maddie and Max practice Korean with them.

She was through the worst.

Max got up from his chair and reached for a cookie on the plate next to the coffee pot. He dragged the plate precariously close to the edge of the counter and no one noticed that it was about to fall off.

"Max, careful." Jocelyn's warning had the effect of startling the six-year-old. He leaned forward intending to push the plate away and instead tipped it.

Jocelyn's hand went up instinctively to stop it. The plate teetered in an instant and landed on Max's foot, the cookies hitting the floor all around him. His face turned sorrowfully to his mom.

"It's okay. The cookies are still good, Max. How's your toe?"

He nodded. "Hurts." He had a cookie in his mouth already.

"Jocelyn?" Kymber gave her a quick look. "You okay? You look more startled than Max."

Jocelyn's hands shook. She *was* startled. "I'm fine."

She rubbed the skin on her arms to ward off a chill. Something was very different about her. She was not okay.

She was normal.

CHAPTER TWENTY-NINE

Jocelyn watched Seth work his way through a large plate of bacon. They met at Cravings for her first trip to the city in nearly two weeks.

"You're not normal. Trust me." He attempted to reassure her. "Even without powers you'd be the least normal person on the planet."

"That sounds insulting."

He smiled and let her decide.

Jocelyn rubbed her back against the back of the booth, trying to subdue an itch. Satisfied, she sipped on a mango smoothie. They were waiting for Graeme. It made her stomach get flip-floppy again, only not from drugs. Seth said Graeme had wanted to come and help, but Jocelyn and Seth had agreed it wouldn't be a good idea for secrecy and security reasons. Mostly, Jocelyn didn't want the guy she liked seeing her as a sweaty, vomiting, psychotic mess. She had enough things against her. She bent and scratched her leg.

"Look, it wasn't the meds that gave you powers. PTSD drugs don't cause people to levitate objects. And the energy came through your skin." He touched her skin. "It's warm. Not as crazy warm as before, but you're still undernourished. I think it's like when people fast and cleanse their body they have to build up again. Going off the drugs wouldn't change a major organ overnight." He lifted his fork. "Would it?"

"I don't know." She scratched where he had touched. "It's bad timing. Now that I'm recovering, I thought…" She needed to find Medina and help him before it was too late.

"Thought what?" Graeme slid into the booth next to her.

Her temperature shot up a few degrees and her cheeks warmed when he pressed his lips to her forehead. She felt excitement, relief, contentment, and safety all at once. She'd desperately wanted a hug from him. Not just a hug. To be held. His arms around her made her feel like everything might work out.

"Hey, man." Graeme nodded to Seth before examining her. "So. You've been sick." He studied her a long while before finally deciding she passed. "I hope you don't have what he has."

Jocelyn blinked, confused.

"You know," Graeme explained. "Batshit crazy."

She smiled.

Seth drank his orange juice. "Thanks, buddy. I see your mom still dresses you."

"Yeah, she has great taste." Graeme stroked his chest over the pressed shirt.

Jocelyn tried to assess the back and forth. Their expressions weren't angry. Was this a new level of communication? She rubbed her head, causing Seth's fork to freeze.

"I'm okay," she reassured. "I was just trying to figure men out."

"We're simple creatures," they said it in unison.

She laughed. So did they. Okay. She had missed something.

The bell of the café door chimed and a familiar click of heels made its way across the polished concrete floor. She didn't need to look to know who was coming. She took a breath. Definitely not recovered enough for this.

"Hey," Morgan said.

Seth turned to her and smiled. "Hey, beautiful. What brings you down here with the mortals?"

Morgan laughed, relaxing a little. She wore jeans, a pretty red blouse that showed off her cleavage, and three-inch-heeled sandals. In a moment she would turn and see the same outfit Jocelyn had worn at their last encounter. Her wig looked good, but she knew she didn't look great. Her sister looked beautiful and perfect—at least when she smiled.

"I'm just bringing in my application. Looking for a part-time job."

Seth's eyes widened. Surprisingly, he didn't say what she expected. "Cool. If you work here, I'll get to see you more." He winked. "And Jocelyn's doing a night shift. Maybe you'll get to work together." He smiled at Jocelyn, knowingly. "That'll be fun."

Jocelyn shrank into the booth. "It's not for a few weeks," she explained to Graeme, guessing from his expression that Josh hadn't told him yet. "When I'm better and my ID arrives."

Seth took a breath. "Okay. Don't want to hold you ladies up. Don't you have to go to Little Russia?" He cued Jocelyn, then turned to Morgan. "Good luck with the job hunt." He slid from the booth and told Graeme, "I'm gonna use your office for a private call. Back in a few."

Jocelyn felt Graeme's body tense next to her.

"Sure," he said.

Morgan left them, and Graeme leaned down to kiss her on the forehead again. "Are you really okay? Seth didn't give me very good details, but Georgie said you had the 'flu of all flus.' I'm guessing it wasn't exactly that."

"I'm better." She scratched her arm again. "Just really dry skin. Thank you for not coming."

"I would take care of you," Graeme insisted.

"It's better if you don't. At least not right now. I'd like you to remember how I looked at the ball, not when I look like a spewing green alien."

"That bad?"

He glanced down toward the office door. Something about it put her on alert. She instantly tuned into Seth to hear if he was okay. He wasn't on the phone.

She pushed Graeme out. "Something's wrong."

She heard a straining sound. "Seth!" She ran to the office door and burst in. Seth lay on the floor by the sofa. His body strained, rigid. She felt his pulse race. His eyes rolled back.

"Graeme! Help!"

Graeme was already there. He put a cushion under Seth's head.

Jocelyn's voice shook. "Seth. Oh, my god." She took his hand.

"Get a cool rag."

Jocelyn jumped up and obeyed. Graeme knew she needed to do something. She came back and began to wipe Seth's face.

"He's having a seizure. There's nothing you can do except talk to him. He can hear your voice. It might help him get through."

Jocelyn held one of Seth's stiff hands against her and pressed the cloth to his head. Her voice cracked and he heard the tears. "Seth, it's me. Come back. You're scaring me. You promised not to do that." She sniffed. "If you can hear me, think about the ocean. You're supposed to be in Zihuatanejo, remember. The Pacific. The water is colder there. Not sure you'll like it other than the big waves, great sand, and pretty girls."

Morgan walked in and stared at them. "Get some waters." The last thing they needed was his sister freaking out.

She didn't freak. "Should I call 911?"

He shook his head, then put his finger to his lips, indicating he would explain later.

For once she obeyed and came back with a tray of waters. She also dropped a box of tissues on the floor. Presumably for Jocelyn. Reluctantly she left, closing the door behind her.

He and Jocelyn stayed with Seth until he became coherent, at which point Jocelyn fell onto him, hugging him tightly on the floor, her voice shuddering for control.

"It's okay, baby." Seth lifted a hand slowly to her hair.

Graeme swallowed. It was hard to watch. It was hard to see how much Jocelyn clearly loved him.

"It's not okay. I thought you were going to die." She wiped her face before turning to Graeme. "You knew about this?"

That sounded like an accusation. Graeme stuttered for one of the first times in his life. She was the one with secrets! He was definitely throwing Seth under the bus first. "I convinced him to see a doctor. We're going for the follow-up this morning." He turned to Seth. "You haven't told her yet?"

"You s-suck."

Graeme helped him onto the sofa. "Yep."

"This is what happened at the hospital, isn't it? I thought you'd been drinking," Jocelyn confessed.

Graeme could see she was putting puzzle pieces in place. She took Seth's hand firmly, getting a little angry now. "How long?"

Seth shrugged, giving her nothing. It didn't matter. She added the clues in her head and came to her own conclusions.

Her eyes filled again, this time he saw the bluish moisture before she swiped them away. Softly she asked, "Is this why you came to New York?"

"Yes."

She nodded. "Okay."

Graeme missed what was going on until Jocelyn looked at him. Then he understood. The pain in her eyes was resignation. The same way his dad looked when they talked about Benny.

Seth was going to die. And they both knew it.

He hated it. He hated the sadness in Jocelyn's eyes and the fear in Seth's. He hated not having any control over it, and not understanding why it was happening. He called for their car. "You're not dying today. Let's give the doctors a shot." They stared at him. "Let's go."

Jocelyn put Seth's arm around her shoulders, and as weak as Graeme knew the guy was, Seth still had the nerve to kiss her head and wink at him like he'd just won a point. Nice to see he felt better. Graeme would punch him later.

Once Seth was in the car, he came around to say bye to Jocelyn. His sister exited at the same time, preventing the kiss he wanted to give her. Jocelyn hugged him tightly. "Thank you." She leaned back and made purposeful eye contact, squeezing his arms. "Thank you."

Gratitude. *Great.*

Not the moment for the kiss. Better anyway to keep taking it slow.

He gently pushed her away, his body tense. "You're going to the bookstore then straight back to the Morrows, right?"

She nodded. Morgan lifted Jocelyn's backpack, holding it up by two fingers as if it was too disgusting to touch.

"You forgot this."

Jocelyn thanked her and Morgan stayed put, as if to make sure nothing happened. She raised a brow when he put several bills in Jocelyn's jeans pocket. "Take a taxi and text me when you're there. I'll let you know how it goes with the Seth."

She agreed.

He hopped in the car and watched the girls part ways in the side view mirror. His stomach tensed when Jocelyn went in the complete opposite direction of the Russian bookstore.

Jocelyn pulled her baseball cap low over her face. She had a stop to make before the bookstore.

She zipped her hoodie and slipped down into the subway station where she'd last seen Medina. A cellist played music with her case open to collect donations. The acoustics in the hollow space made the instrument sound even more powerful, the music evoking feelings of loneliness and loss that seemed to be inevitable.

She liked people—and being around them. But after what she'd just put everyone through, she wasn't sure if it was good for other people to be around her. At least not until she stopped the Butcher and saved Medina.

She walked toward the platform. Unable to exercise or run, she'd been meditating extra hours. It helped her control sensory overload. Now, in the bowels of the city, she allowed herself to be open for the purpose of her investigation. A mix of body odor, dirt, cologne, urine, and metal assaulted her. It made her skin itch even more.

She assessed the jump across the track. Medina could make it even without his new strength. Rabbit not so much. Had they caught a train, or was there something else here?

It was a smaller station with not many places to go—just down the dark tunnel into an oncoming train.

She walked slowly toward the dark tunnel where the train would come. A couple people in the station noticed her, then went about their business. She went to the very edge, then down a few feet into the tunnel.

"Hey, lady! That's not safe," a man warned from the waiting area.

"Okay. Just looking." She could hear a subway car move along the track. But it wasn't on the track in front of her. Was there another track? She gazed into the darkness, then lifted her phone to shine a light on it. Yes! There was a parallel train rail.

She went back to the waiting area near the man. He shook his head at her.

"It looked like there was another track in the tunnel."

The man lifted his head and nodded. "Old maintenance track."

"Oh." Interesting. "Does anyone ever use it anymore?"

He smiled a little. "Maintenance workers. They can travel up and down the line with their tools. Used to make things easier and safer. Then it got too expensive. Only the B line still has it."

"Oh. That's really interesting." She went to look at the map on the wall to see where the orange B line went. It was a long distance. All the way to Harlem. Nearly the length of the city. Medina could be anywhere. She walked back up to street level and her phone vibrated.

The bookstore is the other direction.

Jocelyn smiled. Graeme must have seen her leave. She texted back and headed toward her original destination. As soon as she was a little better, she knew where to start looking.

CHAPTER THIRTY

*R*achel entered the room where her family awaited. Ford served Rex and Sabrina a cocktail while Graeme checked his watch and phone anxiously. Benny sat patiently in a chair near Sabrina while Morgan was nowhere to be found.

They'd invited Jocelyn. Rachel and Ford wanted to thank her for saving Benny. And Graeme had indicated this wasn't just any girl in his life. Otherwise, she wouldn't have her come to her birthday dinner. She was protective of her family time.

"I'm sure she'll be here soon. Did we send a car?" Ford asked.

"No. She wanted to come on her own." His frustration was evident. "Some independence thing. I reserved a car to take her home."

"Well, that's not a bad trait," Rachel noted. "But tardiness is."

"I know, Mom," Graeme snapped then apologized. "Sorry. Happy birthday." He came over and gave her a kiss on the cheek.

Morgan breezed in and did the same. "I got a job."

"What?" Rex's eyes popped wide. "Who would hire you?"

She wrinkled her nose at him. "Cravings. I'll be a cashier and learn how to serve." She corrected herself quickly. "To be a server."

"Oh, a family job. Okay. Don't blow it," he teased.

Rachel studied her daughter, hopeful. "It's honorable 'to serve,' Morgan."

"Uh-huh."

"Shall we go in?" Ford suggested.

Graeme checked his phone.

"No, let's take our time." Rachel joined Ford near the bar. "I'll have a little something."

"That's my woman." Ford winked and made her a drink.

With any luck Jocelyn would be here soon. She delayed for Graeme's sake, not the girl's. He wanted Jocelyn to make a good impression. As a street fighter, Rachel had no qualms. As her son's true love, that remained to be seen.

Jocelyn stood in the center of the subway car, holding the pole while the train bounded through the tunnel, rocking side to side as they made their way into Manhattan. It was a full car, and she held Mrs. Rochester's gift against her small shoulder purse, heeding Kymber's warning to be alert while in the city.

The humidity combined with the body odor of "end of the day" people made her slightly nauseous and unsteady. She still had bouts of queasiness, but they were less and less. Unfortunately, her itchy skin remained and she had begun to get a little pink with spots of redness. She tried not to be vain about it. It was probably like Seth said. Her body needed to recalibrate.

She closed her eyes as a wave of dizziness assaulted her.

He's going to love it.

Her eyes opened. What?

She stared at a teenage girl about her age, sitting down with two younger girls on either side of her.

'Personal gifts are the best,' the teenager explained.

'Can I see it again, Aunt Sabrina?' the youngest girl asked.

'No, it's all wrapped. You have to wait until your dad opens it.'

'But I wanna see it!'

'Of course you do. You always want what you want.' She smiled at Jocelyn and winked.

Jocelyn blinked and cleared her eyes, returning to the present moment. She took a breath. *Another memory.* The woman sitting before her was definitely not Sabrina. But Jocelyn remembered that birthday gift. A photo of her and Morgan for her dad. Where was it now?

She inhaled slowly, trying to calm the turmoil in her stomach. That's when she saw a figure in a hoodie move between some other guys by the subway car's connecting door. He lifted his gaze to her. Lights flickered.

Her stomach clenched for a split second. *Medina?*

Lights flickered again and the subway slowed to a stop. She searched the faces. Had it been her imagination?

An announcement came over the intercom letting them know there was an incident on the line and it would be shut down the rest of the evening.

What! Ugh. She checked her phone for the time. She needed to hurry.

Someone jostled her and she spun defensively. It was an old man. She wiped her brow. *Get a grip.*

People began to move. As soon as she could, she raced up the steps out onto the street and took a deep breath, texting Graeme to let him know she was close.

She wiped a hand down her ice blue, cotton dress. It was a simple sheath that fell straight to the top of her knees and had a modest white collar. Only fifteen dollars. Kymber and Maddie had helped her dress it up with a faux pearl necklace and faux pearl stud earrings. She wore simple ballet slipper shoes she'd miraculously found in her size when at a thrift store in the city recently and had felt good about her outfit when Kymber dropped her at the station. Now she felt a little worn. She patted down her wig to make sure her hair was still in place.

Once on the street, she assessed. It was dusk. An occasional breeze relieved the warmth and humidity and she began to feel better. The Rochester home was still one subway stop away. She hurried, her stomach flipping with excitement and anxiety. Dinner with Graeme and her family!

Her mood began to lighten the closer she got. She made good time. One more block. Her stride picked up. Checking the time on her phone, she didn't see the older woman until she nearly knocked her down.

"Oh!" A little blue-haired lady wobbled and Jocelyn caught her.

"I'm so sorry."

"Can you help me? I've lost Mr. Katzman!" Matching blue eyes pleaded with her.

"I'm sorry," Jocelyn said again, confused. "Your…husband?"

"No, no dear. Not anymore. My cat."

"Oh."

"But I found him. He's up there." She pointed.

Jocelyn searched the large tree. She heard the meow and spotted the yellow-green eyes staring down. It was pretty much the only tree in the city and the cat had found it.

"There you go, dear. Go get him." The woman reached for her gift.

"What?" This could be a ploy to rob her. Only she didn't have much to take.

"Well, *I* can't go up there. I'm old and I can't hardly see and I'm wearing Gucci." She gave Jocelyn the once over. "Your shoes are okay."

"I—"

The woman's eyes filled with tears. "Please. You have to save him. He's all I have. I can't bear to lose him again."

A big tear rolled down her cheek. "I'll be all alone."

Jocelyn hesitated, gazing up into the dark branches. There didn't seem to be anyone else around who would help. She gave Mrs. Katzman her gift and purse, then with a jump, clasped the bottom branch and pulled herself up.

She knew immediately it was a mistake.

The bark caught and snagged her dress every which way and pine needles poked her, making her already sensitive skin so itchy she wanted to rub against the tree. She stopped and did exactly that for her itchy leg. Relieved, she got her footing and climbed up. To her dismay, Mr. Katzman did the same. He didn't want to be rescued.

"Come on, Mr. Katzman," she begged.

The large but scrawny cat glared at her unblinking.

She tested a smaller branch above her. "These are the choices we make," she mumbled, a little irritated with herself. Slowly, she went higher, finally getting in arm's reach of the stubborn feline. Her plan was to grab its collar.

The cat hissed.

Outstanding.

"I'm trying to help you!"

Impatient, she reached, hooked the collar with one finger, and pulled the cat to her. Its claws came out and attached to the front of her dress, surprising her.

"Ouch!"

She leaned back instinctively, her foot slipped, and she grasped the one branch she had, wrapping her bare arm around it, and dangled a split second in the air trying to find her footing. It was long enough for her weight to snap the small branch and she skidded downward, her right thigh hitting the branch before she was pitched forward into more bark and pine needles.

Mr. Katzman screeched, clawed at her throat, snapped her pearl necklace free, and climbed over her head then down her back trying to escape. A claw got tangled in her wig and they fought to see who would keep it.

He won.

She felt it being torn off and caught a glimpse of it being dragged by his back paw as he leapt down from the tree.

Furious, she gave chase.

Rachel finished her martini and twirled the stem of the glass. Graeme checked his phone again.

"She's probably with Seth and forgot," Morgan said.

Graeme glared at her.

"Maybe she got sick again," Benny offered helpfully.

"Who's Seth?" Rex asked.

"Her boyfriend," Morgan offered. "And roommate. And who knows what else?"

Rachel turned to her son in surprise. "Graeme?"

"It's not like that. And I thought you liked Seth. You act all dumb around him."

Morgan flushed angrily, but before she could speak Sabrina spoke.

"Seth knows Jocelyn?" she asked Graeme, curious.

"Yeah. That's how I met him. Through her."

"They were"—Morgan held up her fingers to make quotes— "homeschooled together."

"They were?" Sabrina's wine glass froze in midair. Her attention focused.

Rachel saw something working out in the young woman's head. "How do you know Seth?" she asked Sabrina.

Sabrina opened her mouth. Then closed it. Then turned to Graeme. "Graeme introduced us in passing."

She changed the subject to Benny and Morgan's school schedules and events and the mood switched, but Rachel couldn't help feeling that whatever that moment had been with Sabrina had been important. Jocelyn was fast becoming a focal point of conversation…and concern.

Jocelyn jumped down and landed at the bottom of the tree. She was missing her wig and one shoe. Mr. Katzman was in Mrs. Katzman's arms, still wide-eyed with terror. Her wig hung from his paw down to the little woman's leg. Jocelyn pulled it off the cat, trying to detangle the mess. Mrs. Katzman lifted her head from her dear pet to see what Jocelyn was doing, took one look at her hairless head, and began to scream. It was enough to scare Mr. Katzman again and he took off down the street. His owner ran after him and they entered a large brownstone home.

Jocelyn fixed her wig on her head, her hand touching something sticky.

Sap! On the back of her wig. Really?

Her chest tightened. What time was it? She looked around for her gift and thankfully it was still at the bottom of the tree with her purse—no thanks to Mrs. Katzman. Right above, dangling from a branch was her other shoe. She jumped and grabbed it. Checking her phone she saw multiple messages from Graeme. *Coming!* Pulling herself together, she ran as fast as possible.

She raced through security not appreciating the guard's worried expression. Okay, she needed to clean up.

She stepped into a lit area in front of the giant double doors and gasped. Her dress had noticeable marks down the front left by Mr. Katzman's unwanted hug. Her legs and arms were scratched, and she had a feeling there was dirt or something on her face. Her hand was sticky with sap, and there was a tear in the side of her dress.

The butler opened the door and greeted her without expression. Then he got a better look. The barest flicker of concern showed in his eyes.

"Miss Jocelyn?"

"Yes. Am I terribly late?"

He hesitated. "No, the family is still having drinks."

"Do you think I could, um, freshen up somewhere?" She handed him Mrs. Rochester's gift.

"Of course." He hurried her in, taking sympathy. "This way."

This way ended up being the wrong way. They ran smack into the entire family about to exit a room. Graeme called out to her, sounding relieved.

She and the butler froze, staring at each other in panic. Recovering, he dutifully presented her, despite her less than grand appearance.

Reluctantly she stepped into the room, close to the door and ready to run for cover.

She lifted her embarrassed gaze to Graeme. He blinked.
Surprise!

"Oh. My. God." Morgan laughed out loud.

Sabrina's hand went to her mouth silently. The men smiled pleasantly as if she looked perfectly normal, and Mrs. Rochester broke the silence.

"Jocelyn, what happened?"

"I'm so sorry I'm late. I had a near deadly encounter with a cat."

"Not Mr. Katzman, I hope?" Ford Rochester asked. He came forward and took her hand in welcome.

Surprised, she nodded.

"Oh, no," Graeme said.

Rex laughed.

Mrs. Rochester put a hand over her heart. "Oh, I'm so sorry."

Jocelyn brushed her dress self-consciously, attempting to joke. "The cat won."

Graeme joined her, took her hand, and picked a pine needle from her dress. "Or the tree."

"Two against one is hardly fair," Rachel added with a smile.

Benny shook his head sympathetically, hurrying to give her a strong hug. He used crutches but moved easily. She hugged him back, inhaling his freshly shampooed hair with a smile.

"Did Mrs. Katzman give you the, 'if something happens, I'll be all alone' line?" Ford asked.

She nodded, surprised again. Dang it. She'd been played!

Rex added, "And the big tear down the cheek?" He made a sad face and drew a finger down his cheek.

They laughed, causing Sabrina to jump in defensively. "It was a noble effort, Jocelyn."

"Don't feel bad, Jocelyn." Ford Rochester smiled. "I did the same thing thirty years ago. She's perfected her act since. You're part of a time-honored club now."

"Mr. Katzman is thirty?" Jocelyn exclaimed.

"This is the fourth Mr. Katzman," Graeme said. "Unless you count the original."

"A nice man," Ford said. "Ironically, didn't like cats."

"Not a cats man," Jocelyn deadpanned. "Noted."

Graeme's dad shook his head to confirm.

"I'll take you to get cleaned up," Sabrina offered. "Give us ten minutes," she told the group. "We'll meet you in the dining room."

"You could take forever," Morgan muttered. "Won't help."

Her mother gave her a stink eye.

Jocelyn glanced at Graeme and he nodded for her to go. Nobody seemed upset with her, and she took her first easy breath, relaxing a little.

Sabrina led her to a large and luxurious room that could have been a bedroom, not a bathroom. She began pulling out supplies.

"Are there scissors?" Jocelyn asked. "I have a lump of sap in my hair."

"You poor thing."

"I feel so stupid."

"Don't," she assured. "Ford, Rex, and Graeme have all been in that tree. No shame in compassion and kindness." Sabrina smiled.

That was comforting. "It's like the only tree in New York," Jocelyn exaggerated.

"It's taken down a lot of men." Sabrina pulled out scissors and a sewing kit. She held them up. "Don't worry. I took surgery and suturing."

They went to work. Sabrina angled her bob in the back to get rid of the biggest chunk of sap and they washed the rest out.

Jocelyn took off her dress and Sabrina quickly stitched the gaping hole in the side while Jocelyn readjusted her wig and cleaned her limbs and face. Sabrina hadn't said anything about her wig, just acted like it was normal to move your hair around.

"There's some ointment in there—" Sabrina paused. "What happened to your back?"

Jocelyn saw Sabrina's face in the mirror. A doctor's expression. Her aunt examined her back, but Jocelyn quickly turned. It had gotten worse. Her skin was bright red. Her arms and legs were starting to get the same.

"It's an allergic reaction," she said immediately. "It's going away. What did you get Rachel for her birthday?"

Sabrina accepted the change in subject. "She's impossible to shop for. I opted for a framed photo of our ski trip last year."

"Personal gifts are always the best," Jocelyn said.

"I think so." Sabrina smiled at her through the large mirror.

They finished their work, which included a little makeup freshening. Finally, Jocelyn faced the mirror, side by side with her aunt. They looked alike. Other than the color of their hair, the family resemblance was strong. She met the other woman's eyes, willing Sabrina to recognize her.

Sabrina stared at her, frowning a little. Whatever it was, she shook it off and kept their schedule. "Come on. It's been fourteen minutes. But that was the fastest recovery on record. You look lovely. Nothing we can do about the marks on the dress, but the lighting is low in the dining room so no one will notice."

Impulsively, Jocelyn grabbed Sabrina's arm and leaned into her. "Thank you. Best fourteen minutes ever."

Sabrina squeezed back.

Smiling and bonded over their efforts, they joined the others. Jocelyn caught Mrs. Rochester's curious glance at them when they entered, but Graeme's mom was very cordial. Jocelyn sat next to Graeme and he reached to give her hand a squeeze. His smile and eye contact told her everything was okay.

Benny chatted easily and pulled her into the conversation. The meal began, and despite an itchy, scraped-up body, she enjoyed herself. Morgan was the only exception to her moment of happiness. She did not like Jocelyn being there.

Her sister's childhood report card flashed through her thoughts. *Has trouble sharing.*

The family took a short break before cake and presents, and Jocelyn excused herself to use the restroom. She pressed a cold cloth to her face and neck. She felt a little bit off again. Something was happening to her body, and not knowing made her anxious. She could be dying and not even know it. Her cheeks were bright red. She gave thanks for dim lighting. So far no one had noticed. Or they were just trained not to notice? She could walk around with a cat on her head and Mr. Rochester would smile politely, albeit with a twinkle in his eye.

Morgan showed up as she left the room.

"My mom said I should get you a sweater for the garden in case you want fresh air. Do you want to pick one out?"

Jocelyn dried her cheeks. "Um. Okay."

She followed Morgan to her room. Jocelyn already had good and bad memories here. "How is Chandler?" she asked.

"Fine," Morgan said.

"I might have been wrong about him," Jocelyn lied. "I saw him helping a girl to a cab the other night when Seth and I were out walking. She was really out of it. Couldn't even stand up. But he and his friend took care of it."

She let that hang there. Put two and two together, sister. She walked toward a wall she hadn't had time to look at last time—it had lots of photos on it. She quickly searched. Her heart skipped a beat with excitement. Morgan had a picture of their parents. They were young.

"Are these your parents?"

"Yes."

"You look like your mom. She was really beautiful."

Morgan pushed her way between Jocelyn and the photo, shoving a pink sweater at her. "I know what you're trying to do."

Jocelyn tensed at the cold tone.

"You don't have anyone, so you're trying to make up for it with my family. Stay away," Morgan warned. "*My* mom. *My* dad. *My* brothers. Get your own life."

"I'm just here for dinner."

"It was a polite invitation. No one expected you to actually show up."

"They didn't?" The question was out before she could stop it. She'd been taken aback.

"Of course not. This is a family event. You're not family. Then you show up late looking your usual common self, blaming a cat. Graeme was totally embarrassed."

She thought maybe he had been but he didn't show it. She started to analyze everyone's behavior. They'd been very nice and polite. But she didn't know how they felt. Except for

Graeme. She knew he cared. Right? A crack of doubt entered.

"Graeme likes smart women with college degrees and good families. You're like a stray dog. He feels sorry for you and wants to fix you. I can tell he's already over it. He was out partying with some buddies the other night and didn't come home until the next morning."

Put two and two together, sister.

"That doesn't mean anything. And that's between us."

"He didn't call you his girlfriend. I'm just telling you so you don't embarrass yourself. He doesn't think of you like that."

Jocelyn's mind whizzed through every interaction with Graeme in race mode. Oh, God. Was Morgan right?

"I'm right, aren't I?" Morgan pushed her point. "You couldn't see it because you're so needy. I've read how orphans try to replace what they lost with others, but it never works out. You'll never fit in here. You have nothing to offer my brother, and he knows it. Family is everything to him. Good family," Morgan said. "You have nothing. No connections. No people. No family. My parents would never accept you. But," Morgan ended, "if you want to keep humiliating yourself go at it. It's the most entertainment we've had in ages."

Jocelyn couldn't move. She felt like the air had been sucked from her lungs. Morgan was mean, but she wasn't wrong. Jocelyn didn't have anything, and the fantasy she'd had of being reunited with her family was still just that—a fantasy. They didn't need her or want her. Seth had warned her of this. Why hadn't she listened?

Morgan stood in the doorway of her room. "Are you coming?"

Jocelyn put the sweater on Morgan's bed and forced herself to move. "I think I should go."

Morgan agreed sympathetically. "Probably for the best. I'll let everyone know. FYI—your face is really red. If you're sick it's not safe to be around Benny."

Dazed, Jocelyn followed Morgan downstairs to the entrance. The doors closed resolutely behind her, their vibration of finality sending a shudder through her body. Her family had moved on—without her. She had no place here.

She hurried past the guard gate ignoring the man's concerned call to her. She just wanted to get away.

She'd been a fool this whole time.

Jocelyn hit the street and took off at a run, her only goal to get away.

Morgan was right. She had no family.

At this rate, she never would.

CHAPTER THIRTY-ONE

*R*achel returned to the dining room with Ford. The kids were already seated and ready for cake—except for Graeme and Jocelyn.

Graeme hurried in. "I can't find Jocelyn. Morgan, did she follow you downstairs?"

Rachel turned to her daughter. Uh-oh. She knew instantly from Morgan's look that something had happened. So did Graeme.

"Morgan?" he repeated.

"She left," Morgan said. "Didn't she tell you?"

"What!" Graeme's voice rose.

Rachel saw her husband tense. Sabrina's mouth dropped open in concern.

Graeme grabbed his sister's chair and jerked it out, but Morgan doubled down. "She wasn't feeling well."

Ford's voice was low, and Rachel recognized his rare temper simmering. "Did you call the car for her?"

"She didn't want it. She ran out before I could help her."

"What did you say to her?" Graeme shouted.

"Nothing. Why does anyone care?" She dared to face her brother. "She's not good enough for you. She's a nobody."

Ford stood abruptly, his expression deadly. You could take the man off the street, but you couldn't take the street out of the man. For all his urbane charm, her husband still had an edge from growing up poor in Hell's Kitchen.

"She saved Benny's life. That's good enough for me," Ford stated, hands flat on the table as he leaned forward.

Morgan withered under his gaze, whispering defiantly, "If it weren't for her Benny wouldn't have been in trouble. I heard you. They were after her, not Benny."

"We don't know that, and it doesn't matter," Rachel said. "The government is in the wrong. Not Jocelyn. Citizens must stick together."

"Morgan's right in that we don't know much about her," Rex said.

"I know what I need to know. And we don't send young women out in the dark alone." Ford laid down the law. "Graeme, do you have her number or know where she would go?"

Graeme called her. A phone rang near Rachel's presents. She went and found it, pulling the phone out of the bag. "This is hers?"

Graeme took the phone, swearing under his breath. "Morgan, what did you do?"

Morgan squirmed. "Nothing! I don't know why you even like her. She's nothing special. And she doesn't belong here."

"That's stupid, Morgan." Benny spoke up, angry as well. "And mean. Jocelyn is really nice. And she's a hero!"

Graeme stood over his sister looking ready to throw her across the table. Rachel had never seen her son so angry. Not like this. Outraged fury made the muscles in his throat and chest contract.

"I like her, Morgan, because she is kind, and smart, and funny, and incredibly brave. Because she would help a stranger even if it put her at risk."

Morgan shrugged and looked away, but Graeme yanked her chair for attention.

"I like her because she thinks the world can be really wonderful despite having met some really bad people and suffered a lot in her life already." Graeme didn't wax poetic; rather he drove home to Morgan a litany of Jocelyn's virtues that would make any woman insecure. "I know she's a loyal friend, she fights for what is right, and she works really hard. She's curious and interested in the world, and with all she can do, the things that are most important to her are simple—family, friends, and integrity."

He put Jocelyn's phone in his pocket. "In short, Morgan. I like her because she is *nothing like you.*"

"Graeme," Rachel stood. This was enough.

Ever polite, Rex stood as well and Benny hurriedly scrambled to his feet.

"Sit boys," she motioned. When they didn't move, she sat down. The men followed, including her husband. Graeme remained on his feet, unrelenting.

"Yeah. Cheap shot," Graeme said. "How does it feel, Morgan? Because that's how you make everyone else feel."

Rachel turned to her husband for help, but Ford put a hand up to let them hash it out. Rachel knew he was right, but it was hard to endure. This had been a long time coming with Morgan. Graeme was just the first to fight back.

Morgan's eyes filled up. "I'm sorry. I'm just trying to protect you."

"Please don't. Protect yourself! 'Cause I, for one, am really tired of worrying about what *you're* going to get up to next."

Graeme looked to his parents. "I need to go. I think she'll go back to the Morrows."

"Call me when you get there so we can apologize," Ford said.

Graeme rushed out.

Morgan wiped her cheek surreptitiously. Sabrina shook her head at her niece in disappointment.

Everyone was silent. The festive mood had taken a serious nose-dive.

"Let's open presents," Rex suggested. "Mine first because it's the best." He brought the presents over and kissed her on the cheek.

Grateful for the change of topic, Rachel made her way through the myriad of gifts, ending with Jocelyn's. It was wrapped in newspaper with a black bow.

"Old school," Ford noted.

Rachel opened it and found a book of poetry signed by the Russian author. She shook her head in disbelief. It was his new work, not yet in America to her knowledge.

"What is it?" Ford asked.

"A book of poetry by Nicolai Petrovsky. Signed by the author to me. *Rachel, you must be a true fan to go to such lengths. Perhaps one day I will read for you in person. Until then, Nicolai.*" Rachel stared at it and shook her head. "I don't know how she got this."

"The author's signature? Maybe he was in town signing," Ford said.

"He's been in prison in Siberia for fifteen years."

Rex leaned back in his chair. "Dang. Definitely beats my personalized golf balls."

"She's a hero *and* she gives good gifts," Benny said, mostly for his sister.

Rachel sighed—her daughter still sulked.

"May I please be excused now?" Morgan asked.

Rachel allowed it.

Rex and Sabrina glanced at each other for support. Rex finally stood. "Sabrina, how about a walk around the garden?"

She jumped eagerly.

"Can I go too?" Benny asked.

"Sure," Rachel said. Sabrina gave her a kiss on the cheek and the kids left. Rachel moved to a chair next to her husband and brought her cake, plopping it between them.

"Happy birthday to me."

Ford leaned over and kissed her. "All part of my grand scheme to get you alone."

"Yeah?" She smiled. "For your birthday, we're going out of town."

John heard someone jangling the front door. He grabbed his gun, then put it away when he heard Jocelyn's voice.

"You're home early." He opened the door and swallowed a surge of concern. "What happened?"

She shook her head, not speaking, and pushed past him.

"Jocelyn!" Kymber spotted the teen. "What—? Oh, my gosh. Let me help you." Kymber rushed to Jocelyn and followed her into the guest bathroom. "Oh, no. Oh, dear."

John heard a controlled hiccup. Then he noticed the floor. Blood tracks.

He knocked on the bathroom door. "Kymber, check her feet!"

"Oh!"

He heard his wife's concern. Maddie pushed her way into the bathroom. "What happened?"

Jocelyn still didn't speak. She just shook her head.

"It's okay. Take your time," Kymber said. "I need to get your feet clean. Maddie, get me your pedicure bin and fill it with water."

Maddie rushed to do it. Max stood outside the bathroom.

"Go away," Jocelyn said loudly.

John sent Max back into the living room with his in-laws. "Go watch some TV." The cop in him prepared to interrogate. "Did someone hurt you?"

Jocelyn shook her head.

"I left. They didn't really want me there."

Kymber gasped and shook her head. John saw her temper rise, but they didn't have any facts yet. So he kept asking.

"How do you know this?"

"M-Morgan."

"Who's Morgan?"

"Graeme's s-sister." Jocelyn squeezed her eyes shut. "She said I was a nobody because…" A tear squeezed from under her lid and left a track on her reddened face. "Because I have no family."

"That's ridiculous! And you have family," Kymber stated. "You have us."

John saw Kymber's hands tremble with fury and her eyes light up with fire. He took over the questioning. "Where was Graeme in all this?"

"They were on the patio." Jocelyn pulled her feet away when Kymber scrubbed too hard.

"Sorry," Kymber's said.

"How did you get…um, in this shape?" John continued.

Jocelyn wiped her eyes with a wet towel. "The train broke down, and Mr. Katzman attacked me."

"Someone attacked you on the subway?" Kymber's worry grew.

"No, in a tree. Mr. Katzman is a cat." She explained about Mrs. Katzman. "The train is still down so I ran here."

"All the way from Manhattan?" Kymber voice rose.

She nodded.

"When were you in the tree?" John asked.

"That was before dinner," She covered her face with the cloth and hid behind it, her shoulders shaking with silent sobs. "I don't want to talk about it anymore."

Kymber scowled at him like it was all his fault.

He lifted his hands. "What?"

Kymber examined the teen. "Your skin is pink everywhere and extra red on your back. I'll put something on after you shower and we'll do antiseptic on your feet and scratches. Are you hurt anywhere else?"

"I don't think so. I fell on my leg but it's okay."

Kymber nodded, then gave Maddie instructions. She grabbed her purse and car keys.

"Where are you going?" John asked.

"To give those people a piece of my mind!"

John opened his mouth to say something then thought better of it. If this was what awaited him with Maddie's teenage years, he needed to start cleaning his guns.

CHAPTER THIRTY-TWO

*J*ocelyn put on the sweatpants and T-shirt that Kymber left for her. Maddie put cucumber aloe on Jocelyn's red back and face, and Jocelyn covered the rest of her body with spray-on antiseptic. Her skin burned more than itched now and she was bright pink.

She shook out her wig from the little bits of stuff that still remained from her visit with the tree and hung it over the standing mirror on the counter.

Jocelyn sniffled and wiped her nose again. "The worst part is that I think maybe Graeme was just being nice to me all along, like Morgan said. I'm so embarrassed. And stupid."

Maddie gave her a light hug so as not to hurt her tender skin. "She probably doesn't know anything. Has he kissed you?"

Jocelyn shook her head.

"Oh." Maddie's expression changed.

Her stomach sank. "What?"

"He might not be into you."

Jocelyn sniffed again and sat on the toilet, pressing another cold rag to her face. She felt so humiliated.

"I'll get you more water," Maddie said sympathetically, closing the bathroom door softly behind her.

The doorbell rang. Jocelyn heard Maddie's grandpa answer then say go away in Korean.

"I need to see her."

Graeme!

She looked in the mirror and panicked.

She couldn't let him see her like this. Her entire body was red, her wig needed an overhaul, and her eyes were puffy from crying. Not to mention she had aloe over most of her body, her feet were in white bandages, and her outfit looked like a fashion abomination. *Now he shows up!* She almost started crying again.

Maddie knocked urgently, whispering loudly, "Jocelyn? *He's* here!"

"Jocelyn?" Graeme's voice was outside the door. "I'm so sorry. Morgan is an idiot. My parents send their apologies too. My mom texted me that she loves the book. She wanted me to tell you. She was in shock. She said it was the best present ever."

"She saved that stupid cat!" Maddie told him.

"And then the blue-hair screamed at her for being bald!" Max piped up nearby.

"I know," Graeme said to them. "Well, I didn't know about the screaming."

"And you sent her away," Maddie continued. "And the subway line is down, and her feet were bleeding all over the carpet and the floor. What kind of people are you?"

Maddie sounded like Kymber. Jocelyn smiled a little. It seemed Maddie had made herself a human barrier between Graeme and the door.

"I know," Graeme agreed with her. "It was wrong. My sister made a really big mistake. It was cruel."

"I'm sorry she's your sister," Maddie said with sass, not sympathy.

"It's not easy, trust me. Do you think Jocelyn will ever forgive me?"

It was silent.

Jocelyn leaned against the door. "It's okay. I forgive you. You can go now."

"Let me see you. I need to know you're okay."

"No. Please just go."

"Jocelyn," Graeme sighed. It was silent. "Jocelyn," he said softer. "Let me talk to you face-to-face."

"No. I look like a…" Jocelyn looked in the mirror and shook her head, tears building up again. She hiccupped. "Like a tomato monster."

"I like tomatoes. I love them." He knocked softly. "I'm not here because of what you look like. I'm here because I care about you. I adore you. No matter what. You could have green skin and it wouldn't matter."

Jocelyn thought it over. He probably wasn't going to go away easily. "Maddie, can you come in?" She opened the door a crack for Maddie to squeeze in then locked it.

Maddie advised Jocelyn in hushed tones. "Okay." She lifted two hands to stay calm. "He is like—" She closed her eyes and took a breath. "Wow." Maddie wiped her own cheeks with the wet cloth on the counter. "Really cute."

"I know," Jocelyn said. "And he's nice, right?"

"I think so. He seems really sorry. And I was wrong. He *is* into you." Maddie added, "And my dad is cleaning his guns and he's still here. So, I think you should give him a chance."

Jocelyn sat on the closed toilet seat undecided. "Can you help me?"

Maddie nodded vigorously.

"I need a bandana or something for my head. My skin hurts too much for the wig. And some mascara? And I have jeans downstairs."

Maddie hurried out.

"We need a few minutes," Maddie told Graeme.

"Thank you, Maddie."

Maddie returned with supplies and they quickly did the best they could. The bright scarf wrapping her head helped a lot. Her jeans felt painful against her skin, but they looked better than the sweats and she could tuck in her T-shirt. Mascara only helped a little. Her face was getting pinker by the minute.

Maddie finally opened the door. "Okay. You can go in."

Jocelyn did a double take when Graeme came into the bathroom. He looked sexier and handsomer than ever. The room instantly felt crowded and dinky compared to the bathroom she'd shared with Sabrina. And the temperature shot up exponentially. She heard his heart beat faster. It seemed to match hers. He had changed into a black T-shirt, jeans, and black biker boots. And he smelled so good she wanted to curl into him. Instead she stared at his boots.

"As soon as I heard what happened I took one of the bikes here. Faster."

She nodded.

"Let me see you."

She lifted her face, worried at what he would think, but his eyes were gentle and so was his smile.

"You look beautiful."

"I don't have hair, and my face is red, and—"

He put a finger over her lips, causing them to tingle magically.

"I don't care. And whatever Morgan said to you, it's not true. Please don't disappear like that. It's very stressful."

Her stomach hurt. "I'm sorry."

"It's okay." He moved back as much as he could in the cramped space to get a better look at her. "How are your feet?"

"Okay. Better when I'm sitting." She didn't want to sit. She wanted to lean into him. She could tuck her head into his shoulders very comfortably and be happy for a very long time. Instead, she said what was in her heart. "Morgan said you didn't really want me to come tonight and your parents thought I would know that it was a courtesy invite, not a real one."

"That's bullshit."

She felt the tension in his body change and knew it was true.

He pushed back a flop of brown hair. "We all wanted you there."

"To thank me?"

Graeme didn't answer right away. "What do you mean? Yes, to thank you. We owe you everything. But we could thank you a million ways. This was because I wanted you there. I want my family to get to know you better because you're important to me."

"Oh."

"Are you just getting that?"

"I wasn't sure."

"How can you not be sure?" He stared at her long and hard. He seemed a little upset. She looked away. This had to be the smallest bathroom on the planet.

Graeme took her hands. "I try to take every spare minute you allow. I should have ignored you about tonight and sent a car, but I'm trying to give you space."

She nodded, silent.

"What? Talk to me." One of his fingers caressed the line of her jaw. "You have too many secrets. Let me in on one."

"Well…" She was too embarrassed to say the truth. And it's not like she looked like The Fabulous Brittany Walsh had dressed her. He might not want to kiss her right now. She felt her skin get hotter and took a fortifying breath. "You've never kissed me."

His lips slowly curved into a smile.

Oh, God. He thought it was funny. Her skin sizzled with embarrassment. A drop of sweat trickled down her back.

"I kiss you all the time." He leaned down and kissed the top of her head, then her forehead. "I kiss you here. And here." He softly touched the curve between her neck and shoulder. "Your skin is on fire."

"I know." She felt breathless with anticipation.

He straightened up. "We've been interrupted a few times. Like after the ball."

"I know! I'm sorry."

"And we never seem to be alone for long." He pulled her into his chest. "Does this hurt?"

"No." It felt so good. Her body could feel the strength and hardness of his. She smiled a little. She would never admit that she felt dizzy from the heat they were generating in the small space or that her jeans were a new form of torture against her skin.

"Jocelyn?"

"Um-hmm."

She could hear his smile. "I'm almost twenty-two. You're seventeen. Things need to move slowly with us."

There was an *us*? That sounded nice. "You smell yummy."

"You smell like cucumber."

"It's the cucumber-aloe. It's all over me."

There was a rap on the door. "Everything okay?" John asked.

"See what I mean?" He laughed and pulled back. "Wait here."

She sat back down on the toilet seat, dizzy but happy. "I'll wait here."

"Ma'am! Please wait here." Their butler's voice sounded outside the door.

Rachel and Ford stood when Kymber Morrow entered the dining room, head high.

Rachel had already checked out the Morrows and knew a little about them. Mrs. Morrow stood only about five foot two in her pink sneakers but carried the power of a personality much bigger.

Ford motioned to Jeffrey and he closed the door behind him.

Rachel recognized the motherly outrage as well as the distinctly uncomfortable feeling of someone who just walked in underdressed to a party. Mrs. Morrow's spine straightened. She had to respect that.

"I'm sorry to interrupt your dinner, but I've come to let you know that Jocelyn is not a 'nobody'! My husband is a well-respected lieutenant in the NYPD and I'm a staff nurse at New York Presbyterian. She has family and friends who love her. She was nearly killed falling from a tree saving a crazy cat and all she cared about was getting here on time and making a good impression. As far as I'm concerned, you're the ones who need to make the good impression. The subway is down and her feet were bleeding when she got home. You sent a kid away like that—into the night?"

Rachel's stomach clenched. "I'm so sorry. We didn't know."

"Well, if money causes oblivion, you should think about downsizing."

The woman took a breath, then apologized. "I'm sorry, that part was rude."

Rachel could do nothing but agree. They needed to deal with Morgan head-on. "Mrs. Morrow, you're absolutely right. Is Jocelyn okay? We were worried when we learned what happened. Graeme left right away to find her. Jocelyn is staying at your house?"

"Yes. And who the hell is Mr. Katzman?"

"The product of an evil genius," Ford said. "He was just trying to make a break."

Rachel offered her hand. "I'm Rachel." The woman took it reluctantly. "My husband, Ford."

"Kymber," the woman allowed.

"Our daughter, Morgan, is going through what I pray is the worst of her teenage years. She made a very big mistake. The entire family was upset and can't apologize enough. We are so sorry. Jocelyn is a delightful young woman. I'm just relieved she made it home."

"We had a car for her tonight. I don't like young women out alone," Ford added. "I spoke to your husband just moments ago and apologized. Graeme is there now pleading outside your guestroom bath."

Kymber took a calming breath. "Your daughter needs a brain transplant."

"Know any good surgeons? We're in the market." Ford held a chair. "Please, join us. We have too much cake."

"And the children abandoned us," Rachel added, cutting a piece of cake and passing a fork. "It's coconut." She considered having Morgan come apologize but wanted to interrogate Kymber first.

Kymber contemplated the cake for a moment and finally sat. "I love coconut." She tried it and approved. "Very good. Happy birthday."

Rachel accepted the gesture and poured some coffee, surreptitiously sliding cream and sugar closer to the Korean-American tiger-mama. "Morgan's parents died when she was just six and she has never liked change. I think she feels threatened by Jocelyn. But that's no excuse for her behavior."

Kymber's expression turned sympathetic. "I didn't know that."

"Benny was a baby, so he doesn't know anything different. But Morgan still has nightmares occasionally." She changed the subject. "Graeme told us Jocelyn was with you when you were attacked hiking."

Kymber nodded. "It was frightening." She didn't say more.

"I can't imagine. How long have you known, Jocelyn?"

Kymber put down her fork, a challenging expression took over. Ford sat at the head of the table between them, a reluctant referee.

"It seems like forever. We're sort of her godparents."

"Oh. I didn't realize."

"Her parents died in a house fire."

Rachel took that in. Jocelyn wasn't homeless, though she might be trying to be more independent since their security said she stayed in mostly hostels and other temporary locations.

Ford asked questions about her husband, their life in New York, and their children. Kymber asked about Graeme and their children. They did the mutual exchange of parents assessing parents. Kymber also explained that Jocelyn did a lot of translations on the side and had made a lot of friends doing it. Thus, the book of poetry.

Kymber answered a lot of questions, and at the end Rachel had a large portion of cake wrapped for her to take home. A cop and a nurse were always useful friends to have.

She hated to admit, but she'd probably overreacted a little. Jocelyn Marques was a martial arts expert and had an inordinate amount of courage, but according to Kymber, Jocelyn got sick, she had jobs, and she was legitimately building a life like any other ordinary girl. And she certainly wasn't immune to surly cats. Not exactly a ninja-robot.

She called the security office before she and Ford joined Rex and Sabrina in the garden. "Lee? I want to stop the background check on Jocelyn Marques."

"The whole thing?"

"Yes. And make sure no one finds out I requested it. My son will kill me," she joked.

"No worries, ma'am. I'll put it to bed."

It seemed silly now that she'd thought this same girl could have been someone else. Jocelyn Albrecht was dead. She had the death certificate to prove it.

CHAPTER THIRTY-THREE

Graeme didn't waste time. He put Max on guard at the bathroom door. Grandma put a towel on the back lawn and cut some flowers to arrange around it. Grandpa found the portable Bluetooth speaker for Graeme to play music from his phone, and the lieutenant helped him quickly string white Christmas lights. Just enough to create a romantic ambiance.

"I can't believe I'm doing this," John muttered.

"I'm not having our first kiss next to a toilet seat," Graeme insisted.

"I should have just shot you."

"I appreciate that you didn't," Graeme said. John had still been cleaning his guns on the kitchen table when he came out from the bathroom. Message sent loud and clear.

Graeme gave Max the cue to let Jocelyn out. She was warm and rosy-cheeked when he reached out to her. "Put your arm around my shoulders." She did and he scooped her up, enjoying Maddie's and Max's gasps of delight. Her feet were bandaged so he didn't want her walking too much. Maddie held open the kitchen door and he brought her into the softly lit yard. Stars were out and it had cooled just enough.

Gently, he let her down until her feet touched the towel. "Does that feel okay?"

"Yes." She smiled, her face half lit by twinkling Christmas lights.

His heart raced again in anticipation, while his brain told him to maintain control.

She started to talk. "I like the—"

He swooped down before she could finish. Their lips touched and his tingled at the connection, warmth shooting through his body. He sucked in a sharp breath, heart pounding, and met her wide eyes. Then she sighed and her lips curved softly with contentment. He took his time. He wanted her to remember this moment.

He carefully folded her into him, wondering what had taken him so long.

Jocelyn vaguely heard Maddie's "Ohmigosh" and Max's giggle—the downside of having exceptional hearing. Then her mind went blank. All she could do was feel. They were sensations she'd never felt before. His fingertips lightly caressed her face before cradling it for his kiss. When their lips met, it felt like she had finally reached her destination after a long journey. Then her body came alive and something very new began.

His skin seemed as hot as hers, and when their tongues touched she sunk into his body, willing to take what he had to give. One of his hands took hers and put it around his neck. She didn't need help with the other.

They took a breath, hers gasping, then found each other again. His hands grazed down her sides lightly to her hip, exploring. It made her skin come alive. She felt her body tingle head to toe with a zip of energy.

Graeme stepped back suddenly.

Her hand went to his chest for balance. "What?" Their hearts pounded in sync, fast and hard, making her light-headed.

Graeme shook his head. "Nothing. Must have been the Christmas lights on your cucumber skin." He grinned. "I thought you glowed for a second."

"I am glowing." She smiled. "On the inside."

He leaned back down to brush her lips. His groan made her tremble as his hand crept down over her jeans. Just as he pulled her flush with him, the lights on the porch started flickering on and off.

"Okay," John said. "Time for a break."

Jocelyn stared at Maddie, Seth, and the Morrows watching from under the patio cover.

Kymber stood next to John, holding a dish. "I have cake."

"I think he's had his cake," Seth said, arms folded across his chest.

"Come on." Graeme put her hand around his shoulder. "Gig's up." He carried her past the group and into the kitchen. Her skin burned even hotter.

"Graeme texted me. I came to make sure you were okay," Seth said. "I see you're in…hands. Not sure if they're good hands."

"They're good hands," Jocelyn affirmed without thinking.

Max giggled and Maddie put a hand over her forehead and tucked her face as if too embarrassed by the conversation.

"Thanks, babe." Graeme leaned over and brushed her flushed cheeks with a kiss.

Kymber's mom cut cake, smiling, while Kymber examined Graeme then Jocelyn. She touched Jocelyn's cheeks and forehead. "You're redder and hotter."

"I have that effect," Graeme offered.

Seth lifted his fork threatening. "Don't rub it in, man."

"Let me see your back," Kymber demanded.

Jocelyn stood and lifted her shirt part way for Kymber.

"What is it?" John asked.

"It's red and the skin is hardening a little." Kymber got Jocelyn a large glass of ice water and put three aspirin on the table next to it. "Are you feeling okay?"

"Yes, just hot and my stomach is sort of funny."

John looked at Graeme, then at his wife, as if to indicate that was the source.

"Thanks." Jocelyn smiled, not taking the aspirin.

Kymber stood next to her and didn't move. "It's just aspirin. Everyone takes them. It will help the inflammation."

Seth nodded approval and Jocelyn reluctantly swallowed the pills. The water went down easily and she had a couple glasses more.

When she started on the fourth glass, Kymber gave her analysis. "I think it's going to get worse before it gets better. Then you're going to peel."

Great. She would be a red, shedding, tomato monster. She looked at Graeme. He seemed to read her thoughts.

"Don't worry. I'm not going anywhere."

She nodded, reassured. She didn't want to tell anyone what her skin really felt like. Something strange was happening all over her body. She only knew that Kymber was right. It was going to get worse before it got better.

Newell observed Dr. Cashus and the technician that seemed to follow him around lately. Cashus put his e-pad and phone down on the table, parallel and squared to the corners before hitting the button on the wall to reveal the observation room below.

Newell leaned forward and touched the phone, pushing it off the squared alignment. "That the new model?"

Cashus observed the change and adjusted the phone again. "Yes."

"Nice," Newell said, smiling. The psychiatrist was OCD. Interesting.

Without further response they proceeded to watch Rabbit in the room below. The latest test subject played with his new-found strength by throwing heavy bags and boxing equipment, raging, and occasionally pumping his arms in ape-like displays.

After a time, when he settled, they allowed the Butcher to join him. The two pushed each other then posed dominantly. Finally, the Butcher slammed his fist on his chest in a primitive alpha display. Rabbit took it as an invitation to attack and approached with a swing before getting completely laid out by the Butcher. The scientists had given both men equal parts of the new solution, but the Butcher was still naturally bigger and stronger than Rabbit.

Rabbit got up and started throwing things again. The Butcher, fed up, walked over and knocked him out with one punch. Then he pressed the exit button on the wall and went back to his room.

They watched for a while as Rabbit slowly came to.

"Are you sure those two are ready for primetime?" Newell asked.

"In another day," Cashus said, "the more aggressive symptoms will wear off. Then it will be their natural aggression, hopefully tempered with our controls."

"We can barely control Medina. I have less faith in these two."

"Medina is strong-willed. These two will be a cinch," Cashus assured. "They don't have the years of discipline and habit that give a person the endurance and self-control to overcome pain, torture, or even extended discomfort."

Newell thought about that as Rabbit started knocking things over again in frustration. "Medina does."

"Yes. But he'll do what it takes to survive. He always has. It's a different motivation."

"And yet, he was the one who helped Project Sunday escape."

Cashus nodded. "That was a mistake. Probably unplanned."

"He's been pushing the limits of the GPS control every assignment. What makes you believe you can control him?"

The scientist gave him a closed-mouth smile that irked Newell further.

"For the obvious reasons."

Newell didn't think he'd ever warm up to this asshole. "Care to share?"

"The same reason we can control most of the population." Cashus tilted his head, condescending. "Because suicide is not in his profile."

Jocelyn and Maddie curled up against a pile of pillows on Maddie's bed two nights after "the first kiss" watching Maddie's favorite movie. It was about two sisters. And since there was a lot of snow, Maddie thought it would help Jocelyn stay cool.

Jocelyn's skin had hardened around most of her body but at least her temperature had come down. She was varying degrees of red and purple. Until her appearance normalized, she didn't want to be seen in public. Her muscles ached, but Kymber said as the swelling went down that would improve. Her feet had healed the quickest. Other than that, her strength continued to return, but not her ability to control energy. It might never. Maybe the drugs had some strange combination that had enabled her powers?

Maddie leaned into her as they watched the movie where a main character literally imprisoned herself in ice. Her sister, meanwhile, was freezing inside and turning to ice. In her last heroic moment she saved her sister. Jocelyn sniffled and wiped her eyes, surprised by the emotion.

"Don't worry. It's not over. Watch," Maddie said.

She did. It had a happy ending. It made Jocelyn's tears flow even worse.

"What is it?" Maddie asked.

Jocelyn shook her head. "My sister would never do that for me."

Maddie gasped. Then she put her arms around Jocelyn and hugged her. "I would. I would give my life for you."

Surprised and touched, Jocelyn hugged her back. "Thank you, Maddie." She released her and smiled. "I hope you never have to!"

"Me too. But I would!"

Jocelyn smiled and wiped her face. "I'm going to head down and shower. I need to cool off again."

"Okay. Maybe we can watch another movie. I can stay up late on weekends."

Jocelyn agreed. "But maybe something about animals. Seth said he was coming by. We can let him pick."

"He is?" Maddie looked at her purple-flower-patterned pajamas. "I should put something else on." Suddenly she was rushing through her packed closet, mumbling, "Ohmigosh. I have nothing to wear."

Jocelyn laughed and headed to the basement. September was as hot as August. It was a little cooler down below. She hopped in the shower and put it on cold, standing under the spray for at least fifteen minutes, not wanting to move. She thought she heard a door slam. She listened. Nothing. Finally, she cut the water. Her scalp peeled and her face shone bright red against the white T-shirt. She put her bandana back in place and slid on some light, cotton pants.

She stepped out of the bathroom and paused.

The television was on in the living room, but it was strangely quiet. She stepped toward the stairs. The door to the kitchen was closed. It was usually open and attached to a hook on the wall.

A hushed sound made her skin tingle with fear. Her senses went on alert. Something was *very* wrong.

CHAPTER THIRTY-FOUR

She stared at the door. Had Kymber been warning her? She assessed the small window to the yard and decided better safe than sorry.

She crawled out and ended up close to the kitchen door.

"Not a word." A high-pitched male voice snorted with humor.

Rabbit! Fear shot through her body. That meant the Butcher was here too. As if to confirm, Maddie began screaming from upstairs and was muffled.

Oh, God. Jocelyn peeked through the screen door toward the living room. Rabbit paced with a gun in his hand. That meant the Butcher had Maddie. Where was Max? He'd been sleeping already? Was he safe?

Something touched her leg. She looked down. It was Max curled in a ball, his eyes wide like saucers, remnants of a crushed cookie in one hand. His other hand clamped on her ankle, terrified.

She held her finger for silence, picked him up, and brought him to the far side of the yard.

"Can you make it to Tim's house to get help?"

He nodded. She lifted him over the fence and the child ran into the darkness.

At least one was safe.

She tamped down the fear. It served no use in battle. She needed to be clear. She took a calming breath, calculating. She had to get inside without alerting them…or not. She considered the distance to the cast iron skillet on the stove.

She opened the door and ran for the stove.

"Who's there?" Rabbit yelled. He rushed into the kitchen. "Is it Sunnie?"

Jocelyn swung the skillet upward with maximum force toward Rabbit's face. He fell back and she struck again from the side, sending him into the wall. He turned angrily, nose spewing blood, and she swung again. This time he reached for the pan. She twisted under his arm and spun low to the kneecap then up between his legs. Rabbit bent over in agony. She cracked the top of his head.

He finally fell. She pushed the table quickly out of the way to prevent the blood from getting on Kymber's new tablecloth and let Rabbit fall to the linoleum.

She grabbed a knife and ran to the others, leaving the pan on Grandma Lim's lap. She cut Kymber free first and left her the knife before vaulting back to the stairs and to Maddie.

She met the Butcher in the narrow hallway coming from Maddie's room. He must have heard the noise.

The Butcher quickly reversed back into the room. She ran hard, her voice sounding with a battle cry. No way was he going to grab Maddie as a hostage.

The door slammed. She leapt and kicked it down, feet first, sending it off the hinges.

Maddie was gagged, her hands zip-tied in front of her.

Seeing Jocelyn, she rolled off the bed and onto the floor, as if to escape. The Butcher turned and sent his hatchet flying at Jocelyn. Her senses had recovered better than she realized. She moved her head slightly and it landed in the wall.

She reached for it. The Butcher dove, slamming her against the wall, a hand to her throat, his other on her wrist, powerfully forcing her to release the weapon.

She was close to blacking out. Her right hand reached for anything that would help. She saw Maddie's prized wand on the nearby shelf and stretched her arm to grab it while the Butcher stared at his big knife, waiting for her to give in.

She grabbed the plastic stick, let her body go limp, and when he turned his head, she drove the wand through his eye.

His roar shook the house. He fell back and reached for something else. A gun. He pulled the trigger just as Maddie came flying between them.

John got off the train and headed home. The night was clear after another afternoon storm. He checked his watch. Almost nine. They could still make popcorn and watch a movie.

He approached the first patrol car in the neighborhood and gave a knock on the back window. The guys didn't move.

Shit!

He went to the passenger side and put his finger on the pulse of the cop. He still had one. But they were both out. He ran to the next patrol. Same thing.

Terror struck his core like lightning. He heard a shot sound. He pulled his gun, taking off when something struck him on the back of the head. He fell to his knees blindly, a sharp kick on his wrist jostling his weapon free.

Then he was being dragged forward and down the street to his home.

Jocelyn saw the bullet. They were in close range. Too close. Too close to beat a bullet.

It flew directly at Maddie. And Maddie wasn't bulletproof.

Jocelyn reached for the girl and spun, her hand up to redirect the force coming at them. It was as instinctive as breathing. The energy around them swished like a tornado, sending the bullet and everything else in the room into a furious spin.

She felt energy from her back burst free.

Jocelyn shoved Maddie into the hallway toward Kymber who approached with a shotgun, then spun back to the Butcher, her adrenaline pumping. A fierce, electric energy fired through her entire body like a flame ignited. She gasped from the power that surged through her as her arms and body transformed, glistening light shooting out her fingertips toward the Butcher and his gun.

Temporarily confused, and blinded in one eye, the Butcher tried to regain balance. She grabbed his arm with two hands and, with strength that surprised even her, swung him out the window of the second story. Most of the wall followed behind.

She jumped to the roof and leapt to the street below where he rolled to his knees, getting up.

Jocelyn went on attack.

She was back.

She pulled energy through her body intending to send the Butcher as far as possible. Only nothing happened.

She cursed, tried again, and sent nearby trashcans flying into the neighbor's front yard. Her direction and force were off. A lot.

Okay, sort of back.

Hand-to-hand combat still worked. She kicked the Butcher in the head before he could get to his feet. His face dripped blood and fluid, and it was enough to frighten her into kicking him again.

He caught sight of something the same time she did. His gun. They sprinted for it, but she got there first.

He froze when it was aimed at him. Then he smiled and shrugged. Something else had his attention. She turned her head partially and saw.

Medina dragged John Morrow down the street until they were just far enough away and out of the streetlights to make seeing them difficult for the average person. But not for her.

John's head lolled and he sort of shook it dazedly.

"Drop the gun," Medina said.

Jocelyn didn't think that was a good idea. The Butcher gave a sick lopsided smile, made more sinister by his missing eye.

Jocelyn saw Tim and some neighbors freeze behind them in the street. Kymber and Maddie ran out on the lawn.

Medina pulled John into the light so everyone could see his gun on him.

"Clarence," Medina called to the Butcher, disdain sounding in his voice. "Get out of here."

Jocelyn heard Tim curse behind her. The Butcher got up slowly and backed away from her. She thought he would disobey, but then he ran past Medina and into the darkness.

Jocelyn still held the gun. Only now she aimed it at Medina.

"Let him go."

Medina shoved the gun into John's head. Maddie cried out as Kymber pulled her back.

"Medina, please. It doesn't have to be like this." Fear trickled down Jocelyn's spine. She released one hand from the gun to try to stop Medina with energy, not bullets. But her energy betrayed her and nothing happened. She tried again, demanding her brain obey while doubt and fear began to swallow her.

She grabbed the gun with both hands again. Her throat constricted, her muscles tightened, her hands shook. She couldn't do it.

"Someone has to pay, Jocelyn. He's as good as anyone."

"No! This is not you. Please. Fight it, Medina." Her senses tuned into his ear comm device. She could hear Cashus.

"Medina, we picked up Clarence. Get out when you're able."

"You can go," Jocelyn encouraged.

"You know I can't." Medina looked right at her. "Do what you need to do. Do what I told you to do. Or he's a dead man." Medina turned back to John and yanked his head against his gun.

Jocelyn felt her mind separate from her senses. She could feel heartbeats racing around her. She could hear the prayers on Kymber's lips as she watched in terror. She could smell the scent of fear—even her own.

The only one calm was Medina. His heart beat as if it was at rest. Steady. As steady as when he would take a difficult shot on a mission.

Then he whispered something that only she heard.

"Please."

Medina put his finger on the trigger. His palm pressed while his finger pulled.

Her heartbeat stopped as the bullet exploded.

From her gun.

And his.

Medina crumpled instantly.

The bullet went through his head…his brain. Just like her father. Unforgettable. One moment he was there.

Then he wasn't.

John fell forward. Kymber and Maddie cried out, running for him. Max broke free from Tim's partner but was caught by Tim who finally let him go when John appeared alive. Tim went and freed John from the zip ties on his hands and the family huddled, weeping gratefully. Tim cautiously approached her, and when she didn't move he took the gun from her hands and went into the Morrows' house where Kymber's parents guarded Rabbit.

Jocelyn couldn't move. Her body felt heavy, like an unknown force pressed down on her.

She took a slow step—then another—dragging herself forward, reaching Medina, willing him to move with everything in her. She fell to her knees at his fallen life, her hands grabbing him and shaking, desolate—devastated.

Medina.

She heard the lamenting cries echoing in the dark.

But she didn't know they were her own.

Seth curled the money in his pocket. He was going to do something fun this weekend.

He stepped off the platform, dreaming of food and hoping for some of Kymber's leftovers. All that changed when he heard Jocelyn's shattered cries. He didn't stop to think. He ran flat out to the Morrows' house.

Neighbors were in the front. People rushed to help John. Everyone looked to be alive except one.

Hell.

Jocelyn huddled in the street screaming over a single body. He slid to his knees across from her, a sick feeling coming over him as he recognized what had once been Medina.

Death was frightening and unnatural.

"Jocelyn. You need to get away."

She shook her head, rocking. "I killed him. I killed him."

"Oh, God. Jocelyn." He grabbed one of her hands, comforting but trying to wake her from her daze. "I'm sorry."

Then something else got through to him. Another voice.

"Do you hear that? Is that Cashus?"

Jocelyn blinked, then listened. Sure enough. It was Cashus. Still talking in Medina's ear. They both heard him. "I hope you enjoyed tonight's performance. You two are next."

Seth balked from the body. *Creepy.*

But he also understood Medina. Jocelyn did too. She just didn't want to. Hearing Cashus's voice reminded him of what he needed to do.

He stood and assessed the chaos. Then he went to the Morrows' garage and hunted around. He returned with his supplies.

"Get back."

Jocelyn stared at him, confused. Then she smelled the gasoline and threw herself over Medina's body.

"Get away," Seth said. He meant it. He started to pour the gasoline on Medina's legs. She cried at him in frustration to stop.

"No! You stop. Stop being naïve. This is what he wanted. He begged you. Now get the hell away." His harsh words jolted her. He felt bad, but this had to be done. "Jocelyn, you know I'm right. They'll take his body and make him an experiment even after death. We have to free him completely."

"I can't."

"You have to. What about me? Will you let them take me? If you do, you are not my friend. When I die, you sure as *hell* better finish it! Do you hear me?"

He didn't want the government or scientists chatting over his body and putting his brain in a jar. She didn't respond and he got right up in her face. "Do you hear me?" he yelled again.

They faced off over Medina's body, both trembling with emotion—him anger, her sorrow.

Anger won.

She pulled herself away and he covered the rest of the body in gasoline. Sirens sounded in the night and rushed down the block as he flicked the match, setting fire to the man who had once been their trainer, Jocelyn's handler, and even her salvation.

Seth knew the things that people would say about Medina now. They would describe him as evil, as a mercenary, maybe even a killer.

But in his heart, the man was a hero.

Agent Newell listened with Cashus and the team to the operation. And to the cries of Sunday Cashus aka Jocelyn.

They weren't the cries of a killer.

They were heartbreaking cries. Even the technician looked uncomfortable. Medina was dead. And sure, he was by all accounts a foot soldier in this affair, but she knew him.

They tracked Rabbit's communication and life stats. Someone shot him shortly after Medina. Newell didn't feel so bad about that one. Medina had honor. Rabbit was just crazy. And the Butcher was still in play. They prepped the operating room for him now. A new eye would be inserted, but there was no doubt deeper damage. Newell wouldn't feel too bad about that either. No one would cry over the Butcher and his men.

But he wondered more about Medina now.

And Project Sunday.

She wasn't just a science experiment anymore.

She was a person.

CHAPTER THIRTY-FIVE

Graeme reached New York Presbyterian Hospital and found a waiting room filled with strangers. It took only a second to find Jocelyn in the corner with Maddie, Max, their grandparents, and Georgie. Brittany walked the room with a box of coffee and a bag of donuts.

He spotted Kymber coming down the hall. She called to Maddie and Max and they jumped to follow her. John was fine. Just a concussion from the massive lump on his head and some skid marks where the bullet burned its path. They were keeping him overnight for observation.

Graeme's main concern was Jocelyn. She wore black sweats, a T-shirt, sneakers, and had a beanie pulled around her face. She looked withdrawn, almost catatonic. He knelt in front of her, worried by the slight shake of the head Georgie gave him.

He took her hand and immediately noticed her skin was different. The burned skin was gone. She looked normal again, except that her spirit was somewhere else.

Seth had texted him the briefest of details.

"Jocelyn? Hey. How are you doing?"

She regarded him silently then shook her head before closing her eyes and turning away. She pulled her hand free from his, blocking him out.

He felt the wind get knocked out of him. What was going through her brain? Georgie's eyes were sympathetic.

"Jocelyn, talk to me." He spoke gently, trying to reach her.

She finally opened her eyes and whispered hoarsely, "It's dangerous for you. You should go. You must understand."

She was telling him that she was dangerous. Shit. He needed to talk with her privately.

Kymber came back into the room. "Jocelyn? John wants to see you."

She nodded and got up. Graeme made room for her, then fell into the seat next to Georgie.

"What happened?"

"I don't know exactly," Georgie said. "Three men came to the house. Tied everyone up. She fought the Butcher and he got away. One of the neighbors killed Rabbit. Jocelyn shot and killed another man who was about to shoot John."

Graeme swallowed hard, a bad feeling coming over him.

"He didn't leave her any choice. Tim called it 'suicide by cop.' He wanted to die. The bullet grazed the back of John's head, but he's totally okay. Might have a scar. The other patrol cops guarding the house were all drugged."

"And?"

Georgie leaned over and whispered in his ear, "I think she was friends with the man she killed."

Graeme remembered the alley and the look on Jocelyn's face when she wanted to help the attacker that led her to the ambush. Her past kept coming for her. This time she stopped it. He was glad she did. John would be dead and the kids fatherless otherwise. He was damn sure everyone here felt the same way.

But that was the logic of people who didn't know the whole story, or everything Jocelyn had been through. He tried to imagine what she might be feeling. Sad, angered, manipulated, helpless?

Vengeful?

"Where's Seth?" Graeme asked.

"He took off. Didn't want to be questioned. He only arrived after the shooting. He said he would come by tomorrow to help clean up."

Brittany handed them both coffees and took a seat next to him. "The house is likely going to be a mess from evidence collecting. Cops have no mercy with that stuff—according to Tim. And there's a big hole in Maddie's room where the Butcher got his ass handed to him."

"I saw the news footage. I can help with that," Graeme said.

Kymber came back out with the kids and they began letting in key neighbors who were there for support—just a quick visit before leaving for the evening. The waiting room slowly emptied out. Graeme, Georgie, and Brittany waited for Jocelyn. He wanted to bring her home with him and lock her in a guest room. At least she would be safe for one night. Eventually the last neighbor trickled out. The Lims were going to stay the night at Tim's house, while Kymber and the kids stayed with John. They didn't want to be apart. Graeme didn't blame them.

"Is Jocelyn still in with John?" Georgie asked Kymber.

Kymber panicked. "No. She left the room a while ago. I thought she was out here."

"I'll check the restroom," Brittany said.

Graeme rushed down the halls toward the patient rooms. There were elevators. He turned the corner and spotted a stairwell. She would have taken the stairs. He ran down, calling her name. He called her phone, but no one answered.

Please don't go rogue.

The stairs were empty all the way down. He burst out the doors to the back side of the hospital and an emergency entrance.

"Jocelyn!" He ran to the dark street. People walked, crossed, checked their phones. She was nowhere to be found.

He raked his hair, nearly pulling a clump of it out. Then he texted her, begging for a response.

Droplets of water began to fall, thunder sounded, followed by a flash of lighting over the buildings. It was late in the summer to have a storm. But another was on its way.

Jocelyn ducked down into the subway system and pulled on a hoodie. She had the bare minimum supplies in her pack. John looked good. His family would be okay, as long as she wasn't there to draw attention to them.

She took two more connections, got off, and walked through the rain until she reached a metal door near a parking garage. Lightning flashed as she buzzed the bell and said the code.

Four flights up and three hallway turns later, Seth opened a door and let her in. The room was smaller than the last place but clean. The furniture looked new. There was a syringe on the table with bottled waters and a plate of sandwiches still wrapped in paper from the deli.

Seth locked the door behind her but didn't bother with a hug. She didn't want one. He understood. He ignored her, giving her some space, then picked up the syringe.

"Is it working?" she asked.

Seth gave himself the shot, then looked up. "Don't know. This is only the second dose." He tossed the device in the trash. "But it hasn't gotten worse."

Jocelyn walked to the window and looked out. She smiled faintly at the view. It was her old neighborhood. The building across the street was now owned by Sabrina, rebuilt after the lab accident. The lights of an all-night café next to the building revealed a guitar player by the window. She closed her eyes and listened to the melancholy song of love against the patter of rain, trying not to think about Graeme. The music of the city could lift her spirit or crush it with longing. Graeme had to understand. First her roommate at the hostel, then the other girls in Brittany's dorm, then Benny, and now the Morrows. Trouble found her no matter what she did. Until she had some ability to fix the situation she was afraid to be around anyone.

Seth came up behind. "I thought you'd like this spot."

She nodded, forcing her thoughts from Graeme. Her old home and neighborhood had been calling to her. She had more memories, and new ones seemed to come back every day. Not in a way memories should work. But then her brain wasn't the same as anyone else's.

She could remember sounds and smells and words from deep in her childhood. Tonight she remembered walking in the rain with just her mom. The feel of her soft but firm hand holding hers as they crossed the street from the cupcake shop, and the smell of chocolate and rain when her mom lifted the umbrella and touched her belly. *He's a kicker.* She let Jocelyn feel and she had jumped backward into a puddle at the shocking kick of Benny still in the womb. They had laughed and hurried home.

These were the memories she wanted. But the harder memories remained and she didn't know what new surprises they would bring.

A light went on in the building next to the restaurant. Sabrina walked across a room then another light went on. Her aunt was in the kitchen getting something to drink. Fourteen minutes alone with her had not been enough.

"What's she—" Jocelyn caught herself. She shouldn't get too interested in anyone. Her future was short, and now that she understood what she was up against, she needed to be more focused.

"What's Sabrina like?" He gave her a glance then tossed the cotton he'd been pressing to his arm.

"That's okay, forget it."

"She's really nice. Very 'doctorly' and professional with me, but you can tell she's a good, solid person. Gentle bedside manner."

Yes, that's what Jocelyn had thought.

He unwrapped the sandwiches and pulled out some paper towels, putting a half sandwich on each. "Have a seat. Night-time snack."

She washed her hands, then sat at the table and didn't stop him when he shared more about her aunt. She hated to admit how hungry she was for information on her family. It was her weakness.

"She's torn about research and practicing medicine. I think I'm giving her the best of both worlds. She has a small lab at A & R Technologies and she said a giant office at corporate headquarters because she's one of the board members. She said there was a Russian doctor who could help me."

"Sergei. He's actually Georgian. They're more hospitable. His wife was Russian."

"Yeah, whatever."

"Medina and I blew up his hospital so he won't help Benny."

"I gathered." Seth bit into a sandwich and chewed. He pushed the other half toward her. "You did save the kids, and his family, and get his freedom. So, it's kinda bogus."

She shrugged.

"Do you want to talk about it?"

Her eyes burned a little. He meant Medina. She shook her head and took a drink of water. She had to force herself to eat but chewing meant she didn't have to talk. After gathering her emotions she questioned him.

"Does Sabrina think she can help you?"

"Well…she doesn't know what caused this, so that's part of the problem. Not sure how much to tell her without making her a target."

Jocelyn thought about the risk. "This is all about Benny. My mom had a cure for him. I think when others found out, they wanted the formula. I remember two people at our house, but only one face is clear. This man with green glasses." She took a pained breath. "He shot my dad and took the medicine meant for Benny. Before she died, my mom gave me a dose. But there were other gases released. Probably from other things in the lab. Whatever she gave me somehow saved me. She knew it would."

"Maybe the formula wouldn't work on Benny. It was never tested."

She tensed at his assumption. "They were bringing Benny to a hospital that week. I heard all the planning. They believed it would work."

Seth reached for another half sandwich and didn't argue, but she could see he doubted.

"Ever since, they've been taking my blood and extracting elements to test on others," she said. "You weren't the first experiment."

"I know."

"There were hundreds."

"I know."

"And there will be hundreds more."

"I know!" He slammed the sandwich down making meat, cheese, and tomato squirt out. "So what are you going to do about it?"

It upset Seth as much as it upset her, even if he didn't like to show it.

"I have a plan." She bit into the sandwich again. She was going to need all her strength and she needed to harness her powers again. Her skin felt sensitive and alive, but different. Hopefully it wouldn't take long to find her control.

Seth waited for more information.

She wasn't ready to give him details, but she needed to give him something.

"I have to get back into fighting shape."

"Okay." He thought about it and smiled evilly. "I can stand on your back while you do push-ups."

"And I'm going to need all your money."

Seth froze. "That hurts."

"Seriously. All of it."

"Yeah. I heard you the first time. And I get what?" Seth wanted to negotiate. It lightened the mood.

"You'll get what I give you." She crushed her sandwich wrapper into a ball and tossed it into the basket across the room.

"You're the worst negotiator."

She smirked a little. "Or the best." She went to the small double bed in the corner and grabbed a pillow. The mattress was lumpy but not the worst she'd slept on. She curled up on her side, her back to him. "You can share the bed."

"Finally!" He bounced on the bed excitedly like a kid, jumping up and down, then snuggled up behind her, making a big deal about spooning her and sighing heavily.

She slapped his hand away when it crept up her leg.

"Just teasing," he said, as she sensed his smile.

Pulling his hand around to hers, she checked his pulse, reassured by the steady rhythm. Then they lay quietly for a long time.

"I spoke with John," she told him.

"And?"

John had said a lot but in a few words. She had a feeling it was a conversation she would remember for the rest of her life. And probably important for Seth too.

"He said in life there are defining moments." She would never forget the image of Medina falling lifeless, or the knowledge that she was the one who did it. "But you don't realize them until you see the action afterward. He said, killing someone doesn't mean your life has to become all about that. It can do just the opposite."

"And?" he said again.

"That was all."

Seth sighed and pulled her closer. "A cop philosopher. Great. I'll have to think about that one."

"Me too." She had a feeling that avenging Medina and finding the cure for Benny and Seth would put her in situations where she might need to kill someone else. And if she only had three to four years left, and Seth even less, they both needed to decide what they were willing to risk—and what they were willing to do. In Jocelyn's case, it was more about whom she was willing to risk. Graeme didn't know the whole story. She wasn't being fair to him. And that could get him killed. But how much of the truth could she share? And would he believe her?

The rain eventually stopped and the guitarist across the street slipped into another song about love. She'd been so hopeful when she came to New York. Now, a reunion with her family seemed even further from her reach. And with all that she and Seth had done to survive, maybe they weren't the type of people who got happiness—or deserved it. She tuned her body to the music, blocking out the world. Eventually she fell asleep, promising herself that these were the last of her tears.

CHAPTER THIRTY-SIX

*J*ohn sat on the front lawn of his house in a camping chair next to Tim, his feet resting on a cooler of drinks. He'd been released that morning. He felt fine. He wasn't staying in a hospital when he was needed here. In the twelve hours he'd been gone, their house had been searched and wrecked. Now it was time to put it all back together again.

He watched the activity of neighbors and friends bringing food, setting up worktables, and discussing how to fix the gaping hole in the second floor of his house. There were still police barricades in place when a black sedan, classic Porsche, and a rental car grabbed his attention. He stood to meet them.

Graeme waved from the Porsche and called to him.

"My family wanted to come and help."

John looked at the elegant couple in the sedan behind the Porsche. An automatic window lowered and Governor Rachel Winslow Rochester reached out a hand. "John? I'm Rachel. Graeme's mom."

Yeah. That's the most natural thing in the world. He accepted the hand before touching the bullet skid marks on the back of his head to make sure he was awake. Kymber was going to freak. She liked a neat home. Said home was currently smeared with black fingerprint dust and broken furniture.

"Welcome, Governor. Thank you for coming."

"Please, just Rachel. Our kids are dating," she added. "This is Ford. Our daughter, Morgan. Our youngest, Benny."

John took a closer look at the infamous Morgan. She didn't look too comfortable—whether it was because she didn't like Queens or she had a guilty conscience, he didn't know.

Graeme parked and joined him, introducing two African-American men. "Al, here, is Georgie's cousin visiting from Virginia, and Richie is our team genius." The guys shook hands with him. The bigger guy, Al, had a steady gaze and warrior's bearing. His smaller, wiry friend, Richie, bobbed his head repetitively in some kind of self-comfort tic and shuffled from foot to foot, clearly needing something to occupy his mind.

John filled them in. "Georgie and Brittany are in the house helping to clean. There's a contractor upstairs assessing."

"I can help with that," Al said. "Construction background."

"Okay," John said. "Uh, introduce yourself on the way up." His wife was on edge today with everyone coming through the house, even though it was to help.

Everyone mobilized and John remained in the same spot, a little dazed. Ford brought some beer and sodas over to him and Tim. Rachel and Morgan unloaded trays of food from the trunk. And Benny got out of the vehicle with crutches.

Benny grinned up at him. "I just point and tell people what to do. You have kids too, right?"

John pointed and Benny made his way to the house, introducing himself to everyone on the way. Morgan made a detour to John and gave him a humble apology for the trouble she caused then asked if his wife was inside. He suspected Kymber would get an apology too. Too bad Jocelyn wasn't here.

Graeme pulled John aside to see if he had heard from Jocelyn. He hadn't.

"What did you say to her?" Graeme frowned, frustrated and worried.

"I don't know." John sighed. "We talked through what she thought her options were in that moment. I *think* she's glad I'm alive."

They walked into the house. The living room was better already. Georgie and Brittany seemed to understand Grandma Lim's orders and the three made a good team. The guy named Richie looked about suspiciously while everyone cleaned around him. John saw Rachel give Kymber a hug in the kitchen. Morgan was introduced to Maddie, and his daughter stood taller, about to open her mouth.

"Maddie!" John called out.

Her stubborn expression showed real struggle. Damn, he loved her for that.

Benny saved the moment. "I know. She's sorry. Wanna go outside?"

Maddie seemed unable to be mean to Benny and agreed.

The two left and Max remained. He just stared at Morgan, smiling. Geez. Kid crush. Morgan seemed okay for now. Probably a good experience to witness how the other half lived.

Just when he thought it couldn't get weirder, Seth appeared in the kitchen door.

"I came through the back. Too many cops out there," he said to John. "Your friends?" Seth took off his cowboy hat and assessed. "Hey, Morgan. Graeme." He picked up Max and gave him a big squeeze. "Hey, buddy." He gave Max a tickle, then put him down.

"Is Jocelyn with you?" Graeme asked.

"No."

"Did you see her?" Kymber asked.

Seth hesitated. "Yes." When no one spoke, he added, "She was gone before I woke this morning. And she took all my money." He shifted and added a smile. "I mean, she told me she was going to take all my money, but I thought she'd leave ten bucks or something." He shrugged. "She said she'd be in touch."

Kymber turned to John. "What did you say to her?" Her voice accused. It did nothing for his mood.

He lifted his hands helplessly, everyone watching him.

Seth turned to Rachel Rochester.

Graeme introduced his mom.

"Ma'am." Seth presented himself respectfully. "Mighty nice ya'll came out." To John. "I thought I could help with upstairs."

John motioned for him to go. Graeme followed. John thought he should keep Graeme downstairs considering the look on his face, but then Richie distracted him with a handful of bugging devices and surveillance technology.

"Are you kidding me?" John nearly cursed in front of the women. There had been NYPD and FBI at his house all night. This was definitely the FBI. "Tim!"

Richie held a finger to his lips. "I'll clean it up, sir."

Kymber saw his temper and put a hand on his arm. "Go outside. Ford, would you mind getting him out of here? He's still recovering from a concussion."

John turned to find Tim and Ford behind him and his in-laws behind them in the living room. He motioned for Tim to follow Richie. He took Ford outside and plopped back in the camping chairs. His father-in-law joined them. The construction worker directed the guys up in Maddie's room. Brittany stuck her head out and waved, then told everyone below to watch out.

He sat back as Seth proceeded to take out the entire exterior wall of Maddie's room with a sledgehammer.

"A lot of pent-up anger after last night," John explained.

Ford nodded. Then called out to the younger man. "Hey, you missed a spot."

Graeme pointed and Seth swung one last time and cleared the spot. The big guy, Al, and the two girls all stood surveying the work. Then the contractor started giving directions, mobilizing the team.

He rubbed his skid marks again. Shoot. What had he said to Jocelyn?

They worked a good portion of the afternoon, quickly getting the frame, window, and insulation done. Graeme kept texting Jocelyn regularly, letting her know what was happening, but nothing elicited a response.

Frustrated, he took it out on Seth.

"You seriously don't know where she is?"

"No." Seth hadn't given more than one-word responses to his questions.

"Did she leave the state?"

Seth lifted his hands, clueless.

"Well, what was her mindset?"

Seth finally spun on him angrily, hammer in hand. He threw it down. "She shot the brains out of a man that she cared about, who literally saved her life more than once! There's no effin' mindset for that. She's somewhere between punishing herself and plotting revenge. That's where she is."

"Glad to hear you give a shit." Graeme let the sarcasm hang.

Seth's face filled with outrage. He lifted his fist, just as Graeme intended. Graeme jumped forward his own fist ready. Georgie jumped between, hands out, face squeezed in anticipation of being hit.

Al pulled Graeme back. "Everyone chill." He separated them further for safety. "This family has had enough. We're supposed to be helping."

"For reals," Georgie added. "And all Maddie's personal, precious belongings are under these tarps, so have a little respect."

John called to them from down below. "Everything all right?"

Brittany waved a rag out the window to reassure. "All's well. Just hungry men!"

"Come down and eat."

Al stopped them, blocking the door. "Y'all need to shake."

"Screw that." Seth tried to push past, but Al stood firm. "Don't mess with me," Al said. "I'm hungry. I'm on vacation. And I have a splinter in my finger." He held up his middle finger to show them. "Seriously."

"Fine. I deliberately tried to piss you off." Graeme offered a hand. He still wanted to punch him.

"Whatever. You suck." Seth took the hand and squeezed until Graeme thought he might break a bone. Thankfully, Georgie got Seth to release before that happened.

Brittany shook her head at all of them, pulling tweezers from her bag of tricks. "Al, give me your finger."

Everyone headed downstairs to the folding tables and the food set up in the backyard. They passed Morgan and Max in the kitchen, putting the kids' artwork back up on the refrigerator and bulletin board.

"Coming?" Graeme asked.

"Yes, almost done." She held another drawing for Max to stick magnets on.

Graeme was at the door when he heard something strange in Morgan's voice.

"Max," Morgan asked. "Did you do this?"

Graeme turned back at the door, to see what had her attention. His sister knelt in front of the refrigerator, holding a crayon drawing. Max proudly answered that it was his.

"Who's this?"

"That's Jocelyn. When she saved us."

Graeme walked over to them, concerned. "Food's going to be gone."

Morgan pointed to the figure. "Why is her hair yellow?"

"'Cuz she used to have blond hair."

"Oh." Morgan didn't seem to understand that answer. She kept staring at the stick figure with yellow hair and what Graeme recognized as her dark beanie. He looked back at his sister to see if she made the connection. After a long moment, she put the art on the fridge with a magnet. "How's that?"

"Perfect," Max said. He rested his little arm around her shoulders where she knelt.

"I see you have a fan," Graeme said. "Max, save us a seat."

Max ran out and Morgan straightened up. They hadn't talked to each other since the night of their mom's birthday.

"You doing okay?" he asked.

Morgan nodded. "Not so horrible as far as Mom and Dad's lessons go. Were you and Seth fighting?"

"We have a love-hate relationship. And I'm hungry."

"Have you heard from Jocelyn?"

"No."

"It sounds like it was pretty bad. She probably has to process. I'm sure she's okay."

Graeme cut his sister some slack. She was trying to be comforting. He put an arm around her shoulders like Max had and led her to the kitchen door.

"I'm sorry about what I did." She stopped him at the door. "I mean it, Graeme. I don't know if I'll ever like her, but I know what I did was wrong. And it hurt a lot of other people who are really nice. I just—" She shrugged wryly. "I like how things are. And I like being the only girl in the family. I know that's stupid."

Graeme squeezed her shoulder and pulled her in for a side hug. "You'll always be *special*. That's for sure," he teased.

They walked outside and his mom gave him a smile as she continued to pour ice tea before taking a seat between Brittany and his dad. He heard Brittany pitch his mom a bulletproof wig, and his mom, taking invention very serious, wanted to make sure there was skull cushioning for impact. Brittany made the note.

Morgan sat near his family, away from Seth and the gang, but she checked the Texan out regularly. Maddie and Benny were still talking. Maddie had a more relaxed expression on her face. His mom had said other kids might be a good thing. Kids can express themselves better to each other than to parents sometimes.

John said a prayer over the food, a simple moment of gratitude for life, family, friends and healing.

It should have been a perfect afternoon after the tragedy last night. But one person was missing.

The bowels of the city had a life of their own—one that reminded her of solitary confinement—black, musky, and filled with strange sounds that tortured you. Jocelyn had to fight her own instincts and memories to do reconnaissance down here. She craved sunshine. Looking for clues was tedious, but she had a process and she was thorough.

Swallowing hard, she committed to her job, lightly following the pipe on the wall into the side tunnel where the maintenance track led. The occasional scurrying of a rat warned her when a train was coming. The rats were incredibly in tune to the vibrations. More so than even her.

Today she didn't find a train car. She found new tracks that went directly into a wall. Strange.

She pulled her hoodie tighter and bent over more, limping slightly like the homeless person she'd passed earlier on the street. Medina had always been a master of disguise. She used all his tips now. If this wall led somewhere, then there were cameras watching, even now. She took out a little baggie from her pocket and ate apple slices—slowly. Then she limped away toward the main line and hunkered down at her post. She'd explored every passage in the area, and the ones below. The tunnels all led nowhere around this central area. She would bet that these beautifully disguised walls moved somehow.

Yesterday there were trucks driving below, but they too disappeared before she could track them. She mapped their routes and waited. Eventually she would catch them and find a way in. But she also needed a way out.

Determination fed her. She was going to find the Butcher and bring him to justice.

Then she would decide what to do about Cashus.

CHAPTER THIRTY-SEVEN

It had been a few days with no word from Jocelyn, other than a text that she was okay and she'd be in touch. Not very satisfying, but Graeme put his energy into plans for his new place.

"Geez!" Rex's expression was one of horror. "It's a dump!"

"It has potential."

"I hope your games continue to be successful, 'cuz this is a money pit."

Graeme sighed. There were no believers anymore. "The floors are perfect and worth a mint. They just need to be cleaned. The roof is intact. There's never been mold. A building like this can withstand anything. And look…" He led his brother through the large hall and showed him the ceiling with crisscrossing brickwork.

"Is that the Grimaldi recipe?"

"Yep. Lifetime guarantee for the past one hundred and seventy-five years, and they are still in business. The family already came over and said they would replace any bricks that were damaged—if I could find any."

"Well, at least you can make it a historic monument if all else fails."

"Anyway."

"Yeah, anyway. Have you heard from your girlfriend?"

"Yes," Graeme said. He didn't elaborate that all he got was a text that said, *I'm okay. I'll be in touch.* She probably thought that was a huge concession. "She's taking some time."

"Are you guys okay?"

"We sort of never got to a 'you guys' but I think we're okay."

"I finally recognized her."

"You did?" Graeme was surprised.

"Yeah, she's the one you were stalking in Charlottesville, right?"

"Uh, yeah. We finally met at the movie theater."

"Okay. Cool. It was just bothering me. Glad you two connected after all the chaos." His brother didn't seem to have any other motives, so he said thanks.

They walked through the mansion toward a bunch of folding tables where Graeme had set up a space for Richie. Al was Richie's guinea pig for the day and wore the mockup of the exo-thread from the base of his skull to the bottom of his spine and along the length of his right arm. In his hand was a giant weight.

"Okay, try now." Richie turned to Al and waited.

Al tried to lift the object and barely budged it. And Al was strong.

"Hmm." Richie typed some more. "Hold on. Okay now."

Al moved a little and the massive weight went flying from his swinging hand. They all stared in shock as it landed in a wall, stuck, then fell with a thud.

Rex glanced at him. "Do you have homeowners insurance yet?"

Graeme gave Richie the thumbs up while Al ripped the thread from his body, done being the guinea pig.

Graeme's secure cellphone rang and he answered with urgency and hope. "Jocelyn!"

"Hi, it's Lena."

"Hey, Lena. Why are you calling on this line?" The guys listened as he put her on speakerphone, making the introductions.

"Hey," Richie said. "Is that Lena, like in Lena Horne?" He and Lena said "Lena Horne" at the same time and laughed.

"Yes, my mom loved her music," Lena said.

"I do too!" Richie started talking about music, and Graeme waited patiently. Rex smiled. His brother understood a little about dealing with high-functioning minds. Sabrina could turn down another direction just as quickly as these two.

"Um, Graeme?" Lena questioned him. "I was wondering if you knew what security protocol would work best if I was trying to live stream video to a phone that only worked inside a highly limited network."

Graeme thought about the question. "What's this for?"

"Uh, um. It's a theory I'm working on for a project."

His phone screen flickered oddly for less than a half second, but he saw it. He picked up the phone and went to his security settings and entered the coding screen, scrolling to check it.

"I mean did you use SRX protocols for this phone?"

"No. I wrote my own."

"You did?"

"Your surprise hurts my feelings."

"Uh. Sorry. So how's things?"

Graeme heard rapid-fire typing on her side and saw the code suddenly change on his phone.

"Lena? Why are you hacking my phone right now?"

Silence.

"Lena?"

"Uh, sorry. We're breaking up." She coughed badly. "I forgot I'm late to class." Cough. "Bye, everyone! Bye, Richie! Hope to meet you soon." Click.

Richie took his phone and checked out the code before smiling. "I like her."

Graeme scowled.

"Don't worry," Richie said. "We can see what she sees." Richie started typing into the phone, then went to his computer. It took a few minutes, then the camera screen showed streaming video. He recognized it immediately. The Windows on the World camera system. Lena was manipulating three of the Times Square cameras.

He turned to Rex. "College prank. You know how competitive computer nerds are."

Rex shook his head. "No kidding. Give me stable molecules any day."

"I'll let you know when I actually move in." Time to get Rex out. "It'll be a while." He escorted his brother hastily.

"Uh-huh. Here's your hat, what's your hurry?" Rex mumbled with a suspicious eye toward Richie and Al.

"We're close to a breakthrough, that's all." He nudged Rex out the giant front doors and locked them, running back to the room.

"What is it?" Al asked.

"Jocelyn. She's up to something. Richie, will you record the video whenever it's set for these coordinates?" He looked at the iconic building in the middle of Times Square. A camera zoomed on a yogurt shop up front and two other cameras covered the alley and street views on each side. Millions of tourists passed by it every day. What did you find, Jocelyn? And what's going on in that building?

Jocelyn picked up Lena's call. "Yes, that works brilliantly, Lena."

"Good. But…uh. I think Graeme suspected. When are you reporting in?"

"Soon, I just need a little more information." Jocelyn needed a second way into the building. One of those yogurt people would do the trick. "Talk later."

"Uh."

Jocelyn paused. Something was wrong. "What is it?"

"Um. You know how you were kinda concerned about Morgan?"

"Yes."

"Well, I made friends with her on Zombie Master. She's pretty good, by the way. And anyway, we're on a team together, but don't worry. She doesn't know it's me."

"Okay." Jocelyn ducked into a deli on the corner and walked out the other side to avoid the street camera coming up. She wasn't sure what Lena was getting at, but she usually got to something.

"So, Zombie Master, it's one of those games—you know Graeme made it, right?"

"Yes, with some college friends."

"Oh, good. So it's one of those games that includes GPS tracking to see where your friends are, and I did it so I could see where Morgan was in case you needed to know."

"Lena, that's great. Thank you."

"Um, yeah. So right now, she's on NYU Campus in Washington Square. And that's where that guy Chandler goes to college, and I thought maybe you would want to know."

Lena stopped talking and it was silent except for the sounds on the street and tourists asking for directions.

Jocelyn's brain went into speed mode. How fast could she get to Washington Square? "Lena, I think I can be there within ten minutes. Can you track her in detail? I'm going to hop on the subway and I'll contact you when I'm above ground."

"Yes, it's not perfect, but she's still walking. I'll text the addresses as she goes by, okay?"

"Thank you, Lena."

Jocelyn shoved the phone deep in her pocket. She should call Graeme, but she didn't know where exactly to tell him to meet her. She had to do something.

Can you meet?

The reply was instant. *Where?*

Washington Square. I'll send details when I get there.

Jocelyn ran down into the subway station. For once, a train pulled up quickly. She switched out her ball cap for a vintage felt hat and sunglasses. When she surfaced at West Fourth Street she looked like a Bohemian student.

Texts came in from Lena. The last text tracked Morgan to a building. Jocelyn hurried, checking the addresses, and found it. The entrance had a courtyard with a fountain. A bunch of students sat around the fountain, some of them playing guitar and working out tunes, others reading, eating, or staring at their phones. On the other side of the fountain and plaza was a student café. She sent Graeme the location.

Students walked into the building and she followed. It was a pretty nice apartment building for college housing—at least compared to Brittany's and Georgie's places. She looked for Chandler's name on the mailboxes.

Lena texted her. *She's still there. Not moving. Did you find her?*

Jocelyn took a breath. She tuned her hearing trying to pick up Morgan's voice. Got it. She ran up four flights of stairs, down a hall, and stopped before turning left. She peeked around the corner.

Morgan was outside Chandler's apartment.

"It doesn't mean we can't see each other anymore," she said.

"I have a lot going on." Chandler stood in front of his door, holding the knob protectively.

"Yeah. I get it." Morgan seemed to finally give up. Chandler reached down to kiss her when suddenly Morgan moved sideways and kicked open the door, surprising Chandler *and* Jocelyn.

"Oh my—" Morgan's shock was apparent.

Chandler grabbed her and dragged her inside. Jocelyn ran to the door but it fell open on its own. Inside, a girl lay unconscious on the bed, not moving. A blanket covered her. Chandler was on the ground getting his ass beaten by her sister.

"You bastard!" Kick. "Sicko." Kick in the face.

Jocelyn approved. That would leave a mark.

Chandler crawled to his feet and grabbed a trophy in defense, making for the door. Morgan charged him. And he was twice her size! Jocelyn pushed the door open enough for them to fall into the hallway. Chandler fell against a wall, regained his balance then scrambled to his feet, taking off at a run.

Morgan ran after him.

A girl and a guy poked their heads out of a door.

"Call 911," Jocelyn said. "I think the girl in there has been drugged. You need to get an ambulance."

"I knew it," the girl said. "Dirtbag."

"Guard the door but don't touch anything."

"Evidence," the guy said knowingly.

Jocelyn ran toward the window. There was a fire escape. She leapt downward quickly and circled the building in time to see Chandler race across the plaza and Morgan yell for someone to stop him. She aimed for Chandler's feet, her directional skills still a little off. The guitarist was going to feel this.

Graeme checked out the café, but no Jocelyn. He waited on the corner, hoping to spot her.

Instead, of all people, he spotted his sister. Yelling. And running at top speed in high-heeled boots. She shot her hand out at the target and he tripped.

What? Did his sister just do that in public?

A guitar fell from the sky nearby and shattered, shocking the students and the guy who'd been playing it moments earlier. Graeme stopped, confused then ran toward his sister.

He recognized Chandler and didn't need explanations. "Morgan!"

She jumped on Chandler and slapped the guy's hands away.

"Morgan! Let me." He pushed his sister away, grabbed Chandler by the collar and punched the asshole twice before flipping him over on his stomach and locking his arm in a hold.

"I should break it!" His sister let out a colorful stream of curses and threats that impressed. She breathed hard, hair flying loose from the formerly perfect braid, her hands shaking, the knuckles already showing signs of redness. She looked up, eyes glazed as if only just recognizing him.

"Graeme! Thank God, you're here." She reached for his arm as if to ground herself. "I think I—"

He stopped her before she could say anything dangerous. "I saw. We need the police."

A siren sounded.

Morgan recovered a little. "I have to go back. There's a girl inside. Send the cops and an ambulance. Unit 455."

"Got it," Graeme said.

Then she leaned across Chandler's prone body, pressing one knee hard into the pervert's back, and hugged Graeme fiercely. He pulled her close with his free arm.

"I love you," she said.

"I know. I'm proud of you, Morgan." He smiled at his wild-eyed sister. "You rock the heels like a track star."

She laughed and got up, pressing hard one more time into Chandler's kidneys, trembling from the fight, but fierce. He really was proud of her. And sorry she had to experience this again. But she'd saved another girl, and likely many more.

"Hey, Morgan!" he called to her.

She turned back.

"You're a hero!"

She shook her head, but he saw her smile as she strutted back to deal with the trouble inside. She walked a little taller—until her heel broke, then she walked tall with a limp.

An officer came his way, and just before he released Chandler, his eye caught the figure of a student on the corner as she turned.

He received the text moments later.

Too many cops. See you later.

CHAPTER THIRTY-EIGHT

Brittany closed the door of her dorm room and gave Jocelyn a long, tight hug. "Are you sure you're okay?"

It had been over a week since she'd shot Medina. But she didn't want to talk about that.

"Yes," Jocelyn said. "My strength is back. I'm running every day. I have excellent focus." She was mostly in perfect order.

"Umm-hmmm." Brittany didn't act like those were the answers she wanted.

To demonstrate her health, Jocelyn held out her palm and called the bulletproof corset from the table where it rested and into her hands.

Brittany blinked, then swallowed. "There's probably some useful purpose for that. Did your skin just glisten or did I imagine that?"

"It does that now and then." She sent the corset floating upward then back in her hand while examining her arm. "Now nothing. I think there are surges now and then. I'm still getting certain powers back and they haven't settled yet." She had stronger power surges than ever before, and it was an effort learning how to control them at this level. She might be rushing her plans, but she didn't want to miss her opportunity.

"I also wanted to see if you'd be okay with Seth giving Sabrina the files from your aunt." Brittany's aunt had died getting

DNA reports on Holliwell patients, but they didn't know what they proved or how they could use them yet. "It might help her save Seth. I don't honestly know. There are risks, but she's a board member at A & R, so she can keep her work the most secure."

"It's fine," Brittany said. "Really, the more people who have them, the better. Science should be public. What's wrong with Seth?"

"He has seizures. He's going to die."

Brittany froze. She came to stand in front of her.

"He's an experiment," Jocelyn explained. "All experiments die. They take my blood. They give it to people, and people die. No one has ever lived. That's why they want me back. I'm the source of evil." She felt relieved saying it out loud.

Brittany stared, jaw hardened. "You are *so* not okay."

Jocelyn lifted the navy and white striped undergarment. "Show me how to put this on."

Brittany pulled the bulletproof corset around Jocelyn and began lacing it. "Your bullet scar is gone."

"Yeah. Weird," Jocelyn said. "My skin completely regenerated."

"Well, good news for my future fashions." Brittany pulled the ends of the corset together. It overlapped in the front. "The front closure is important so a woman can do it herself. Is John going to put it on a mannequin?"

"Uh…" She hadn't exactly said John would be shooting it. "Probably a wood stump."

"That's so awesome. Save the bullets and shells so I can use them in my display. Can he use his Glock *and* his shotgun? Or two to three different gun types?" Brittany asked. "It helps with proof of concept."

"I'll ask." Jocelyn tried to breathe as Brittany tightened the laces. "It's pretty. You definitely sit up straight wearing it."

"I know. I went for a more classic look, but for safety covered the breasts and I'm going to add something to give it a distinctly modern feel, I just haven't figured that out yet. How's it fit?"

"Tight."

"Perfect. Text me any notes. Graeme gave us all secure phones, so you can reach me and Georgie and Lena directly."

Jocelyn swallowed. Graeme was thoughtful that way.

"I texted you earlier but didn't hear back. Did it work?"

"Yes," Jocelyn admitted.

Silence. Brittany didn't make eye contact. She was either mad at her or focused on her art. Brittany untied the front to adjust the folds better, then gave the fibrous threads a strong yank, causing Jocelyn to gasp for air. *Definitely mad at her.*

"He's worried about you." Brittany tied the fibers.

Jocelyn exhaled her agreement once her ribs recovered.

"Seth is a person. Not an experiment. So are you." She pulled out some different colored pieces of material. "I made you some bandanas for your head since you keep messing up your wigs."

"Thank you."

"And even if a person is going to die, you shouldn't do anything to hasten death. Like take unnecessary risks."

"I'm not."

"Right." She shoved the bandanas at Jocelyn, hitting her in the front of the corset with a thump.

Brittany went to her sewing kit and pulled out a USB stick from her collection. "I keep multiple copies everywhere. You can give this to Sabrina."

"Seth is doing it, so I'm not involved."

"Good." Brittany pulled some other stuff out and began shoving it in a plastic bag. I got you some things in the fashion district. Super cheap. Just basics. And a pair of cute, baby blue walking shoes. Try not to melt them in one day."

She shoved the bag at Jocelyn, hitting the corset again with a thump. Then she stopped and hit it again. And again. *Thump. Thump.*

"Evil is the man who came in here and cut the skin off a sweet girl named Brittany, then left her in pieces for her parents to mourn over. If you ever"—Brittany took a breath from her punching—"ever call yourself a 'source of evil' again…" She heaved. "I can't believe how out of shape I am." She took a breath. "I swear, Jocelyn. I'll take my needle and thread, and I'll sew your lips together."

"It's—"

Brittany thumped her in the gut again. "I swear." She reached to her desk and grabbed a needle, holding it right between Jocelyn's eyes with a threat. "Don't forget what this looks like."

Jocelyn felt her throat tighten. She couldn't let emotion control her. She had a job to do. She needed to leave before she wanted to stay. "Okay. Thank you for the supplies. I owe you."

"Yes, you do. And I want my project full of bullets—unless of course they bounce off, which would be even more awesome, but get video."

Jocelyn smiled and escaped, feeling a little guilty about not actually planning on shooting at the corset, and for causing Brittany to be more worried than when she arrived. She didn't need anyone to worry about her.

She was doing what she did best—what Medina and the government had trained her to do. She adjusted the corset above her hips. Now she had a way into the building to get the rest of the information she needed. She just needed to make sure she had a way out.

Seth walked into the mini-studio to find Jocelyn putting something in a small manila envelope. There was a corset on the bed next to her backpack. He looked at the rubber band and syringe on the table.

"What are you doing?"

"You should sit down," she said.

That pissed him off. "Don't tell me to sit down after you've been MIA for a week with no word."

"I left a note."

"That's bullshit." He threw his pack on the floor and dumped a bag of what smelled like Chinese on the table.

"I brought Chinese," she said.

"So did I." He sat down and ignored her. "I suppose you were going to leave before I got here."

She didn't respond.

"Yeah, that's what I thought. How are the Wongs?"

"Well. They're letting me stay in the storeroom in case you really do need me this week. How are the seizures?"

He dug into the food with a plastic knife. She got some bowls from the cabinet and brought him a real fork, putting it on a napkin.

"They're not every day anymore. I went seventy-two hours without one. And it was shorter."

Jocelyn looked relieved. "That's great news."

"It buys me time."

She sat down and slid the envelope to him. "I'm not sure if it will help Sabrina, but the files in there have DNA sequencing from other…victims. A woman died getting them out of Holliwell. There might be a clue."

"And?"

"My blood sample in a lab vial with anticoagulant. That's where it all started—essentially. You asked what I was going to do. I'm going to make sure there's a cure for you."

Seth smiled wryly. "And?" She was clueless. He gave her a hint. "And you're sorry? For not coming back at night, or contacting me, and leaving me alone?"

"I'm sorry." She said it very softly. "You left me before. Don't be mad."

"That's low." But true. "Graeme's out of his mind. I almost had to beat him up."

"What?"

He kept eating, remorseless. Graeme could give her a lot. And he really cared about her. She wouldn't need to live hideout to hideout. But Seth wasn't willing to let her go yet.

"I don't want to be alone." Dying scared the shit out of him. Dying alone, with no one who knew him, scared him the most. He would be forgotten by everyone but Jocelyn.

She looked up from the noodles. "I'll be there."

"What if I had needed you this week and you weren't there? You didn't even respond right away."

She shrugged.

Her nonchalance got to him. If it weren't for the mess, he'd flip the table over. "You not being you, is not who I want holding me on my death bed."

"We'll be at the beach in the sand, not a bed. And you're not dead yet. Sabrina has already helped, and this is going to help more. Bring it to her tomorrow." She got up and cleaned the table, putting the leftovers in the mini-fridge.

Seth came up behind her and she turned into his chest, wrapping her arms around him. He felt the heat she sent into his core and smiled into her bandana-covered head. It was her way of apologizing. And it let him know she was getting better too.

She mumbled into chest. "I promise to be safe if you promise to keep fighting to live."

"Deal. For now." He held her for as long as she allowed; then they went to sleep and he held her longer.

When he woke in the morning, she was gone.

And she took all his money again.

Jocelyn hugged the trench coat around her, glancing up through the wild-haired gray wig and carrying a bag of mostly trash. There were plenty of homeless people underground, and they were clearly becoming a nuisance for the guards. Earlier this week, two had been removed from this very spot, right before a truck mysteriously exited from the wall designed to lower like a ramp. She'd been fake napping and eating in that spot for more than eight hours. Her patience finally paid off.

"Hey!"

She looked toward the voice. The man had come out of a hidden side door. She saw it clearly now. She stumbled toward him.

"Get out of here. This is private property."

"Whaa? Dis is public," Jocelyn said, acting like a belligerent drunk she'd been studying for the last week.

He pulled his gun and came closer. "Move on."

She continued her approach. "I don't need to nothin'." She mumbled incoherently for a while, until she was close enough to see inside the door. "You city workers are real jerks."

"All right. You asked for it."

The tranquilizer dart hit her square in the chest. She wrapped her fist around it with a grunt then fell to the ground.

A voice on the guard's comm device said to drag her to the main track and leave her. Jocelyn slumped forward while the guard dragged her under the arms down to the main track and around the corner, off camera. She pulled the tranquilizer from her bulletproof corset and stabbed the man in the arm, forcing the medicine into him, and silencing him before he could call for help. In seconds she removed his pants and shirt, covered him with her coat and nasty wig, then donned his hat over her barren scalp. Sometimes it paid off to be bald.

She grabbed the backpack and hurried to the security door before they could get a good look at her.

"Another bum?" the second guard asked.

Jocelyn shut the door and grunted.

"Wait! Who—"

She stabbed him with the remainder of the tranquilizer then pulled out a gag and zip ties. Once he was in the closet she made a quick survey of the camera system and began taking pictures of all views with her phone. She looked for a building map and photographed that, noting the exits, and finding what she suspected. Security cells. The Butcher would be in one of these.

She clicked through until she found the monitor view of the cells. There were twenty-four large, nicely furnished cells and half of them were full! What were they doing here? Were they controlling or causing other crime in the city? She photographed each just in case, and found the Butcher in number ten, second row.

She tested to see if she could open his cell. A light flashed red that said "Clearance Required from Command." She would need to get control of Command. *Outstanding.* That meant she would need help.

She kept both guard badges and grabbed a third in a drawer that had a woman's picture on it.

Then she walked out the guard post, down the hall, and straight into the offices filled with security people.

Seth waited patiently while the MRI finished thumping. Then he got up and chatted with Jonathan until Sabrina dismissed the young technician.

"No change, but it's too early to tell," she said. "Right now the drugs are stopping the excessive electrical activity of the nerves that are causing the seizures, which seems to be preventing further damage. Every seizure you have is causing more nerves to weaken. It's not a cure, it just gives us time to find one."

Seth nodded.

"We have a lot of talent here, Seth. We *will* find a way to help you."

Seth smiled. Optimism ran in the family. But at least she didn't lie and say she'd find a cure. "I know you have resources. Science is like the weapon of the future, isn't it?"

"Well, anything can be a weapon if misused. But there's a lot of competition."

"Hold this." He gave her his new audio-video scrambler. "Can't take any chances. What kind of security do you have?"

She stared at the scrambler, offended. "The best."

Seth nodded again. "I doubt it. But you're going to need it."

Sabrina glanced at him, wary. "What do you mean?"

He opened his backpack and pulled out the manila envelope. "There are items in here that might give you clues. But if I give them to you, your life could be in danger."

She raised a brow.

"I'm not kidding. And no one can know I gave these to you. I have enough problems and so do the people who gave me these. And Graeme doesn't know anything about this, so don't ask him. You'll just get him into trouble too. He's too investigative."

Sabrina stared at the envelope thoughtfully. She didn't laugh or smile or look doubtful. She looked worried and hopeful. "I could arrange for a more secure lab space. What is it?"

"The USB has files of patients who were genetically altered. They're all dead. So what they were given was not successful. But it gave them certain enhancements. The woman who got these files out is dead too. We believe murdered via a car accident."

Sabrina nodded, understanding, but paled a little. It seemed like she might know a lot more than she'd previously let on.

"Don't ask me where, but know she got this from the government. That's why this is not safe. I can keep this if it's too much." Seth didn't want anything to happen to Sabrina. She was good and kind and smart. And she wouldn't suspect the evil people could really do.

Her jaw tightened a little, as if knowing what he thought, and her bright blue eyes turned directly on his. "I'm in."

He smiled. "Then get ready. The other item is a blood sample."

"From?"

"The prototype, and to answer your question, yes—still alive."

Sabrina swallowed hard. "What do you mean the prototype?"

"I mean the person everyone is trying to replicate. The person the government wants back. The person who holds the key to my cure and maybe several others. The prototype." He took a breath and handed her the envelope, taking the scrambler from her stiff hand. "Or as the government likes to say—the black swan."

CHAPTER THIRTY-NINE

*J*ocelyn used a discreet blast of energy to shoot out a camera in the stairwell then made her way up. The first floors of Holliwell-New York were beautiful open spaces filled with sofas, tables, booths, bean bags, coffee stands, and food spots. Most notable, they were filled with young people who could have been the same age as any of her friends—maybe more like Graeme and Al. They worked on laptops and in groups, talking about projects. She walked through each floor, as if doing her guard rounds. She nodded to people and grabbed a free coffee as she strolled. She guessed she had about ten minutes before a guard went to check on her sleeping buddies. As much as twenty if she got them at the right time in their shift.

Every conversation she listened in on worried her. These young people were like Lena—passionately doing their work, but with no idea as to what end.

She logged the building in her head. Transport and security were where she came in. Cold storage right below. She didn't need to guess what they stored. Likely their morgue. Maintenance and laundry were above transport. The ground floor was alias school. The new recruits had to learn a trade and work with the public. Every one of the storefronts was fake.

It got interesting after that. Technology and security solutions were on the second floor with the free café. Chemical projects and cafeteria were on the third. Genetic tech was on the fourth with a cozy library and auditorium.

She bumped into a girl and palmed her badge, smiling as she kept her coffee from spilling and letting the girl apologize before she carried on.

The fifth floor was locked. She went further up. Also locked.

New plan.

She emerged back on the second floor in jeans, a T-shirt and her backpack slung over one shoulder like some of the other young employees. Her shoulder-length brown wig had long bangs, and the pink glasses further changed her look. She ordered two coffees, a chamomile tea, cookies, and brownies. Then she joined a group in the elevator.

From the back of the crowd, she asked someone to hit surgery. They definitely had a surgery center here. They would have needed it for Medina and to fix the Butcher's eye.

"Which floor?"

"Oh. I'm new. How many floors of surgery are there?"

"Six."

Six! What are they doing here? How many patients are there?

"Shoot. They just finished eye surgery. I think it's one with a viewing area."

"Thirty-seventh. Surgery D has theater seating."

"Thank you! Saves me a trip back down."

Someone tapped their badge and pressed thirty-seven. The young people were off by the sixth floor. As they went up, the hallways on the upper floors looked like labs in Cell Block C at Camp Holliwell. The tea spilled a little as she stifled a shiver at the memory. An older man got off and held the door for her on thirty-seven. She thanked him with a serious nod.

When he turned right she went back to the elevators and entered a new elevator going up. A short man with dark hair was the only passenger. She looked down and saw an FBI badge on his belt.

He noticed her look.

"On snack duty?" he asked.

"Yes, sir. The life of an intern." She smiled slightly staring at the elevator buttons.

"Who's it for?"

"The tea is for Dr. Cashus. Chamomile." She shook her head with distaste.

"I know," the agent said. "Never trust a man who drinks chamomile."

She smiled.

"Want me to take it? I'm heading to his office."

"Really? That would be so great. I still have to drop these others off." The doors opened and she handed him the tea, watching as he headed down a hallway on the fortieth floor. *Now I know where you are.* The doors closed. She went up one floor, entered the stairwell, blew out a camera, and added a white T-shirt over her blue one, then switched to long blond hair in a ponytail, ditching the glasses.

The forty-third floor was jackpot. Definitely the surveillance center for the building. A big stern woman sat at the reception.

"Wow." Jocelyn laid the coffee tray on the counter. "They didn't show us this on the tour."

She smiled only slightly. "We're not on the tour."

Jocelyn nodded. "This is for, umm…" She looked in her pocket at a napkin. "Jones? Jonas?" Her scribble was mostly unintelligible. She showed the woman.

"Johnston," she said.

"Sorry. I was in the middle of calculations when I was recruited."

The woman nodded.

"The cookies and brownies were extra if you want one."

The woman eyed the tray. Then reached for a brownie.

"Is he down the hall?"

"Yes. I'll buzz him for you. You can leave it."

Shoot. "Can I bring it? I love this tech stuff. I'll just take a peek?" She held up her fingers to show it would just be a little peek. The woman relented. "All right. Bring it through and come right back." She pointed the way. It was a short distance.

"Yes, ma'am!"

Down the aisle, in the corner section of the floor, a copper-colored heavy door opened and a man came out.

"Not sure you have the right person," he said, taking the tray.

"If not, I'll be back." She smiled. "I seem to have gotten snack duty today."

He laughed.

She took a quick survey of the room behind him. It had an elaborate control panel manned by four people including Johnston. One of the guards called for clearance of the security elevator.

"Enjoy," she whispered as he went back inside and the giant door buzzed to a close.

Jocelyn returned to the reception desk, waved to the woman, pushed the elevator button, and headed down. It stopped on the fortieth floor. She was smiling until she saw the same man—the FBI man. She quickly pulled out her phone and typed on it intensely. He faced forward. They went down another floor and two people joined them. That's when she felt him looking at her. She had the same backpack. Shoot. Did he recognize her? Act confident.

She got to the fourth floor and walked off, saying hi to the first young person she saw, hoping to make it look like she fit in. She heard the elevator doors close behind her.

"Hey! Wait!"

Shoot. She didn't turn. In another second she would be in the library. She hustled in the most casual way, found a restroom, whipped off her top two shirts down to a pink tank top, lost her hair, donned a beanie, then went and joined three youths around a table, sticking her head in with theirs.

"You are not going to believe what I just heard."

The all looked at her with varying degrees of confusion, curiosity, and interest. One guy raised a brow and gave her a shot. "I give, what?"

"Dr. Cashus, this professor on the high floors, has a serum that makes people super strong, right?"

"Uh."

They looked at her and she went on. The FBI agent circled the room then stood at the entrance before spotting a stairwell exit. He went through it.

"Right, well, he does." These people should know whom they were working for. "But it's killing people, so not perfected yet. Anyway, a guard said they gave it to the Butcher."

"The—"

Jocelyn put a hand up for silence. The girl looked disbelieving and confused. "The Butcher is being kept in the building. Cell 10B. But you didn't hear it from me."

"That's in the basement," the other young man said. "If it's true. It would be totally illegal, but kind of cool."

"He's been on the loose killing people," the girl whispered.

"And we're all behind it," Jocelyn said. "It's a big experiment. For the good of mankind." Then she added the motto of Camp Holliwell, trying to keep the bitterness from her voice. "Science, Technology, Service…and all that. Anyway, I'm going to find out the truth. Just thought others should know."

"Thanks." They nodded. One of them got up and went to another table. She heard the rumor spread as she crossed the fourth floor to the elevator and went down. On the ground floor she entered an open office space and saw a sign that said learning center. Arrows pointed to the various businesses. She went to the pub hoping for a crowd. The security door opened easily going outward. The hallway had signs for the manager, storage, uniforms, break room, etc. She opened a storage room and found beer kegs. Hoisting one up on her shoulder, she made her way forward hoping to get to the bar unnoticed.

It worked. A few servers cleared the way. She dropped the keg behind the bar and started serving water in customers' glasses on the other side of the counter as she casually made her way to the other side of the bar. She spotted the public restroom on her left and entered. Secure in an empty stall, she stripped down to the bulletproof corset and a miniskirt, snapped heels on her reversible shoes, adjusted a bright pink wig on her head, put her security badges in a black purse and shoved the backpack and extra clothes deep into the metal trash bin.

She sauntered through the pub with confidence in her new tights and mini-skirt, casually adding some sunglasses on her way out the front door. She stepped into the sunshine and moved to the side as the FBI agent ran out into the street. He whirled his head back and forth. She kept texting gibberish on her phone then pretended to answer it.

Finally she made her way over to the Windows on the World installation. A new game started. She joined in, breathing slowly to gain her composure.

She did it!

She grinned at the person in the Harlem location. He smiled then suddenly looked past her.

She turned too late.

A strong hand ensnared hers, pressing it deeper into the textured haptic screen. Another arm encircled her, powerful, the surge of energy surprising and trapping her. Her pulse quickened at the threat.

"Got you."

Georgie joined Graeme and Richie in the tiny office where the Windows on the World servers were kept just off Times Square. Two of the surveillance cameras were aimed at the building with a yogurt shop and Irish bar.

"What do you think is in there?" Georgie asked.

Graeme spun in his chair, frowning at her. "Don't know. The lobby of the building says it's offices for an image archive and various small businesses, lawyers, etc."

"Weird."

"More weird, we tried to call a bunch of them and got sent to voice mail no matter what we did."

"Tight," Richie said. "Different voices and messages."

"It's a front?" Georgie couldn't comprehend it.

"Yep," Richie typed into a laptop.

She looked at the building again. People walked out of the yogurt shop with yogurt. That wasn't fake. "Where's Al?"

"Getting lunch," Graeme said.

"Okay, well. I might have some information." Both guys turned to her. "Jocelyn borrowed Brittany's new project." They waited for her to explain. "It's a bulletproof corset."

Richie's eyes widened with approval.

Graeme scowled more deeply. "What the hell is she up to?"

"And why didn't she come to us!" Georgie added.

"Heh, heh, heh." Richie laughed.

"What?" Georgie got furious. She could have protected Jocelyn, or talked to her, made her come to her senses. Something!

Graeme answered for Richie. "We would've seen through her. And stopped her."

"Of course!" She sighed. Okay, Richie had a point. "She should trust us more."

Richie typed away on the laptop again. "Trust issues."

This time Graeme sighed. "Have a seat. She'll show up sooner or later. And when she does, we can make contact. Hopefully prevent her from going in. At least alone."

Georgie agreed and put the envelope she'd just received in the mail down on the desk. "I think this is Joss's documents. I thought she'd need them right away."

Richie pulled out some exo-thread. "Here. Try this upgrade." Richie attached the one-inch wide strip to the base of Graeme's skull and tucked it under Graeme's T-shirt, pressing it to his spine. They put another down his arm.

Richie adjusted the electrical pulses. "Okay, lift something."

Graeme looked around and tried to lift Georgie in her chair. "Nothing,"

Richie adjusted something.

"Wow, I can feel the pulse. Is that safe?"

Richie shrugged.

"Graeme, I don't think this is safe," Georgie said.

Graeme lifted Georgie in her chair with one hand, getting her a foot off the ground before dropping her.

Georgie gripped her chair. She stared at Richie. So did Graeme.

"Heh, heh, heh." Richie smiled. "You might need it to help your crazy girlfriend." He nodded to the monitors. "She just walked out of the Irish pub."

Georgie and Graeme stared at the pub monitor. A girl with short pink hair, a mini-skirt, and striped leggings stood casually in front of the pub checking her phone. A shorter man zoomed out the doors behind her, searching, before running off toward them. She adjusted her sunglasses and strolled the other way.

Georgie swallowed. "Geez. I really *do not* know her some-times."

"No kidding." Graeme grabbed the envelope and ran out the door.

Richie smiled as he continued to type. "True love."

Georgie stared at the action in Times Square, her stom-ach tightening with worry. Trouble would always find Jocelyn, but now her friend *looked* for it. How far would she go?

And how far were they all willing to follow?

CHAPTER FORTY

Graeme released his hand from Jocelyn's and felt sorry for half a second when he sensed Jocelyn's fear. She turned, put a hand on his chest to push him back then lowered her sunglasses to the tip of her nose.

She didn't say anything. But she kept her hand on his chest. The other pushed her glasses back up.

"Nothing?" he asked. "Really?"

"Hello?" she offered.

"That outfit's pretty hot. You trying to pick up old men?"

Her cheeks flushed. She took her hand from his chest and pulled away.

He regretted being a jerk. "I'm kidding. Pink hair suits you. I don't suppose you ever got to wear mini-skirts and cute tights back at Holliwell."

She shook her head. He released his arm from around her and put it over her shoulders to firmly lead her to a quieter spot. The crowds were heavy, but a block off the main hub the noise dimmed substantially leaving just the occasional train rumbling under them.

He pulled her into one of the many Irish pubs on the block and ordered some water and sodas. "So what have you been doing?"

She took a stool and pushed against the bar to spin it back and forth. "Just stuff."

"What's in the building? We've called every office listed and got all fake messages."

She stopped spinning and turned to him, surprised. "Did Lena tell you?"

"No, but when I realized what she was doing Richie helped me hack your line to duplicate your phone. You've been watching the building a lot. I was surprised to see you walk right out. I was waiting for you to walk in."

"I was in the pub."

"Uh-huh." The server brought them drinks and he put cash on the counter for their tab. "So let's start over. This time the truth."

She touched his arm where the exo-thread was attached and traced it to his elbow. "Is this the new skeleton for Benny?"

Her touch distracted. "Yeah." He swallowed hard. "It works. Not sure if it's safe, but based on the first trials, it shows promise."

She nodded, approving.

"So—the pub?" He tried not to look down at her lean legs, or the way her hot corset plumped up her cleavage. *Focus.*

"I was in the pub." She smiled. "After I was in the build-ing."

"And?" He turned his stool to face her and their knees intertwined. His temperature shot up again.

"It was productive. I found the Butcher. I just need to capture him and hand him over to the police. Piece of cake."

Graeme leaned in with a smile and twirled a strand of pink hair near her cheek. "You're so cute when you're optimis-tic." His hand trailed down her throat. A delicate pulse raced under his touch. It gave her away. She hadn't completely shut him out. But the cool demeanor let him know there was another side that was all business—a side that wanted to eradicate emotion. He couldn't let that side win.

He slid the envelope across the bar to her. "Georgie brought that."

She picked it up, wondering, and carefully opened it. Her whole expression changed. With hushed wonder she read the letter from her lawyer and pressed the enclosed government document to her heart. "My papers went through." She stared at a small card, swallowing hard. "I have an identification card." Then more softly, "I'm a person." After a long moment, she showed him the card.

His throat tightened at the hope and quiet awe in her voice. He received the card with two hands, holding it like a precious gift. She deserved to celebrate this.

"Good picture," he said. "You are now a resident of the great state of New York."

The real Jocelyn appeared for a moment, grinning wide. "Isn't that outstanding!" Her excitement was palpable.

"I think we should have champagne."

She laughed, taking back the card and staring at it again. "I wanted this so much." Her laughter went away. "But now…"

"Now you have it. It's the beginning of a new life for you, Jocelyn." He wanted to be part of that life. "Don't give it up."

She put the ID and papers into her little black bag, and the Jocelyn he adored seemed to disappear with it.

"I have a plan," she said.

"You'll need help."

"Yes," she admitted.

Agreement. He thought he'd be fighting her on this.

She drank the glass of water in one breath then sipped the soda a little before rolling the stool away from the bar and sliding her long legs to the floor. "Text me a secure location and assemble the team for tomorrow, 0900."

"0900?" He repeated the military time with foreboding.

"Thank you for the drinks. And this." She patted her purse meaningfully before slipping out the door and disappearing down the street.

She looked anything but thankful. She looked resigned. He was losing her.

He needed to figure out how to reach her. Before it was too late.

John walked into his office at the end of the day to find Tim talking with someone. His late shift was wrapping up and he wanted to be home. It had been a hellish week. What now?

Tim got up with a wink to him. "I'm trying to recruit her."

John saw Jocelyn in his chair, wearing jeans, a T-shirt, and a bandana over her head. She twirled the seat to and fro, holding a police academy brochure. Some of the weight lifted from his chest. *She was safe.*

"I'll give you some privacy." Tim closed the door behind him.

John took a breath. "So." How did you scold and embrace a teen that you had no responsibility or control over?

She sighed, sinking into the chair a little. "Are you mad at me too?"

Okay, he couldn't take that tack. "Is everyone mad at you?"

"It seems like it." She put the brochure down and picked up a pen on his desk to twiddle.

"Why do you think that is?"

She shrugged.

"Hmm. I think I can help with that." He dialed Kymber. "I found her. Yeah, she's here." He held out the phone. "It's for you."

Jocelyn stared at the phone before reluctantly taking it. "Hi."

John heard the loud rant and smiled a little when Jocelyn pulled the phone away from her ear. Kymber could be the bad cop tonight.

"We've been worried sick. You can't keep disappearing without telling us where you are and if you're okay. The children can barely sleep worrying and having nightmares that something happened to you."

John sat on the edge of the desk, satisfied, as Jocelyn apologized in response—several times. It didn't stop his wife. Then Jocelyn had the bad sense to say she "didn't know" and he heard Kymber go off again about how could she not know they cared about her and she was part of the family. Kymber went into detail about taking care of her when she was sick and laid on the guilt with a final, "and not so much as a goodbye!"

Jocelyn stared silently at the floor.

"So you're coming to dinner on Saturday?"

"Um. I can't this week. I have to do some things. Okay. Next week." She handed him the phone. "She wants to talk to you."

John made a few comments of agreement then hung up. "I guess you heard that?"

Jocelyn nodded. "She's *really* mad."

"It's called worry. That's what happens when you care about someone and you don't know if they're safe."

She stared at him, uncertain.

"I'm sensing a 'does not compute' thing going on in your head."

"Is that a cop thing?"

"Yeah. And a dad thing."

She smiled at that. "I understand it. Intellectually. I worry about people. I just…I just can't believe they worry about me."

"Well, they do. Your friends do as well. And when you show up like nothing happened, they get angry because it seems like you don't care about them as much as they care about you."

"Oh." She sunk into the chair, not looking at him, silence stretching the moment. "That makes sense now." Finally she spoke. "Tim's a nice guy."

"Yeah."

"He killed Rabbit in your kitchen," she said.

"I know." *What was going on in her head?*

"Are you mad about that?"

"Are we here to talk about Tim?"

She started twiddling the pen again. The speed created a butterfly-shaped blur. "I'm just trying to figure out the rules of life. And just life."

"You're at a tough age. That's understandable."

"It is?" She put down the pen.

He took a seat on the other side of the desk and waited. She was in confession mode. All he needed to do was wait it out.

"I got my New York ID today. Wanna see?"

"Absolutely." He took the card from her hand and examined it with care. "It's the real deal. Cops know." She smiled at him. "Good picture too. Jocelyn Marques. Solid name." *Real name?*

"Thank you." She took the card back and put it in her purse with the police brochure.

"I found the Butcher. I was going to bring him to justice, but I think I might kill him. I might have to kill him." She looked at him as if to assess his reaction to her next words. "I might *want* to kill him. Not sure how it's all going to go down."

John swallowed. *Hell.* Not the things you wanted to hear from a kid. Especially one that you knew could do it. He cupped his chin in his hands and rested his elbows on the desk. She mirrored his pose and they looked at each other while she gathered her thoughts. Jocelyn was a unique human being. He couldn't rush this.

"I know you want to know where he is, but even if I told you, the police couldn't get him, and they would move him before you ever got in. But he's in the city. And I saw an FBI guy in the building, so it's military, and government, and whatever the FBI really is."

"What do you want from me?"

She shrugged. "I just—" Her eyes suddenly filled, making them bluer. "I just wanted to see you before." She scrubbed her cheeks. "And tell you thank you for everything you did for me. Would you tell Kymber and Maddie and Max too?"

John's stomach tensed with emotion. The stupid kid. He got up. "Come home and tell them yourself."

"I can't." She looked past him and her entire demeanor changed. "Uh-oh." She rubbed her cheeks again, composing herself.

"What?"

"That's the FBI agent from today. But I was in disguise."

John turned his head. "Crap." Newell. "I know this guy. Just be cool," he told her. "Follow my lead."

Newell pushed his way through the rows of desks. Tim caught sight of his aggressive demeanor and followed the agent into the office. The three men stood alert in front of his desk. Jocelyn sat frozen, staring up at them.

She finally stood and broke the silence, walking past the agent. "I'll leave you men to talk."

Newell flashed his badge at her, grabbing her arm. "You're coming with me."

She balked, surprised, then turned to John. "Uncle John?"

Damn, the kid was good.

"Special Agent Newell, this is my goddaughter, Jocelyn. Is there something we can help you with?"

"You can stop with the BS," Newell said. He pulled open his government-issue digital pad and showed the Missing Poster.

Jocelyn leaned over to look, surprising Newell when she touched the pad to tilt it toward her. "Wow! That's a lot of money. I'd turn myself in!"

Tim laughed. "She does look a little like you, but different cheek bones. And a lot younger."

John nodded agreement. Tim went back out into the main room and motioned to some others.

"You were in our building today. That's trespassing."

"What building is that?" John asked. He really wanted to know.

"Classified, Lieutenant."

"A classified building?" John smiled, stepping closer to Newell and crowding the shorter man. "How could she possibly get into a classified building?"

Newell scrolled and showed some pictures of girls caught on a surveillance camera. Each had a different look, but most had the same backpack. Could be common enough.

"Did you get fingerprints?" Jocelyn asked. "Then you'd be able to see if all those people really are the same person."

"I know they are," Newell insisted.

"I think it's a case of mistaken identity, Special Agent." John spoke with calming reassurance. "Jocelyn, show him your ID."

Jocelyn nodded and pulled it out. Her photo might look like the missing girl, but Newell couldn't deny that this Jocelyn was not missing.

"And there's no resemblance?" Newell scowled at him.

"Oh, no. We agree there's a resemblance," John said, plucking Jocelyn's ID from the agent's hand and returning it to her. "We get mistaken identities all the time."

"I'm taking her in anyway on suspicion of trespassing, and we'll let the FBI decide."

"I don't think so," John said. This time his hands went to his hips. He nodded to the door. "I think you should go now."

Tim held open the door, and fifteen other officers stood in the room, at the ready.

"It was nice to meet you, Mr. Newell. Good luck with your search." Jocelyn said it with all seriousness, but clearly concerned.

He turned to her, angry. "This is not over. And Cashus will have no mercy when he gets you. It would be better to come freely. Don't say I didn't warn you."

"That sounds like a threat, Agent Newell." John spoke loud and stern. *The damn midget bully.*

"This isn't over."

Tim shook his head at Newell. "I can't believe people really say things like that. Let me guess. 'You'll be back.'" The men on the floor chuckled but remained standing until the agent left.

He felt Jocelyn grab his hand and squeeze it briefly but there was fear in her eyes where a moment ago there had been confidence. Who the hell was Cashus?

"That's why I can't come home."

"Jocelyn? You define your life. Not others."

She smiled enigmatically and patted his shoulder.

Her world-weary look did nothing to alleviate his concern. And his gut told him she wanted to kill this Cashus man too.

CHAPTER FORTY-ONE

*J*ocelyn stayed out of sight as she studied the old building. She'd passed this spot in her many walks of the city and still wasn't sure if it had been a mansion or a museum, but the stone exterior was impressive. The windows were boarded up on all the top floors and it had a dome in the back where she guessed a finial once stood proudly. Maybe a church?

She measured about fourteen feet of space between the entrance and the curb, which would be valuable extra real estate in New York—if the area weren't so rundown. There were no street or traffic lights in the vicinity. It was as if the neighborhood had been forgotten.

She approached cautiously, taking the side door from the alley. It was locked. She checked the time—0900 hours. She rang the bell and waved into the moving camera. A stranger opened the door and sent her down the hall. She passed two rooms filled with people, tables and computers. Graeme waited for her at the end. She went to him but kept her distance. Contact with him threw her off balance. She needed to be clear.

He led her to the main hall, where one would normally enter. It was fantastic. She couldn't resist an appreciative smile. "It's outstanding. Even bigger on the inside. That staircase must have been grand in its time." She tilted her head to the ceilings.

"And I recognize that brickwork. It's in a bunch of churches."

"It's done by the Grimaldi family. Secret recipe. Made to stand the test of time."

Graeme finally relaxed a little. "I'm glad you like it. I bought it."

"You did! This is the place you decided on?" She knew he had been looking. "It's big." It drove reality home for her. He was rich, had resources, good work, great family and nice friends. She was the one who kept messing it all up for him.

"Come on. The guys helped me set up a secure room."

Graeme led her across the hall where Georgie, Brittany, Al, and Richie waited. She shook Richie's hand, curious to finally meet him. He was a wiry man with super short curly hair and lots of nervous energy.

"I'm here too," Lena said over the phone.

"Great." She unloaded her pack. Georgie and Brittany didn't say much. In fact they kept their distance. After talking with John she understood why they were a little mad at her, and in some ways that was good. Maybe when this was done they would rethink being her friend. It would make it easier for her if they turned away. She didn't think she could.

Pushing unwanted details aside, Jocelyn launched into the mission planning. "If anyone is not up for this just say so. The goal is to break into the Times Square headquarters for Holliwell, acquire Clarence Cooke, aka the Butcher, and—" She paused.

"And bring him to justice," Georgie filled in, giving her an assessing look.

"Yes." She agreed for now, laying her drawings on the table. She'd figure out the killing part later.

Graeme ran a hand over the papers. "These are good. Drafting part of spy school?"

"Yes," she responded without thinking, then looked up realizing he'd been making a joke. "You don't always have tech to back you up. How do you say—old school?"

He rubbed his jaw. "Right."

Jocelyn continued. "Lena already put the recon into a 3D model."

"I downloaded it," Richie said. "We're adding the rest in."

"Great. Most of the action will take place below ground level where they have the security cells. The Butcher is super strong. They gave him a drug that enhances strength and other senses so he needs to be kept where there is double-reinforced concrete. And we want him heavily drugged when we transport him. There's a whole labyrinth of tunnels that they are using to bring supplies in out of the building—things that are not regular supplies. That's where we will exit. The biggest challenge is that the cells require security clearance in two locations before they can be unlocked. That means someone has to get here." She pointed to the forty-third floor. "This is where all the controls are for the building. Lena, I was thinking that might be you."

"Sure thing," Lena said over the phone.

"Sure thing?" Brittany glared at the phone, then at her. "Milk is not going in there alone. Are you crazy Milk?"

They all stared at the intercom. Lena finally spoke. "I'm the one who can most quickly figure out how it all works. It just makes sense."

Brittany's mouth opened to contradict, but instead she waved a hand to continue.

Al rubbed his jaw. Jocelyn continued.

"There are several exit options, depending on where you are in the building. There are four underground on the transportation floor, any of the businesses on the main floor, and an alley exit next to the neighboring building, but you'd need to get over the construction fence. It looks like they are going to connect the two buildings for expansion. Most of the bottom floors of the new building look inhabited, but they don't have the elevator system installed. It's all open cables and guts on the outside."

"Brittany"—she handed her phone to the speechless diva—"there's image reference for the yogurt shop uniforms and guard uniforms. We'll need several of both. And we need badges that look like these." She pulled out the three she had and laid them on the table, along with Agent Newell's badge that she had snatched when he threatened her. She added the bag with the bulletproof corset. "I didn't get to test this for bullets, but it works against tranquilizer guns."

Graeme picked up the FBI badge and studied it before shaking his head at her. "Who *are* you?"

The surprise in his voice hit an emotional trigger.

She spun on him angrily. He didn't know her. Now he would. Energy shot through her body causing her skin to shimmer with the briefest flash—enough to make Richie step away.

"I'm a genetically enhanced military asset. I completed four summers of Ranger Training, seventy missions before I was fifteen, I know how to operate nine classified vehicles, and for the record"—she reminded him of their earlier conversation—"*seventeen* top-secret weapons." She wanted to hurt somebody. The dust on the floors whooshed away from her feet, but Graeme didn't back away. "*That's* who I am."

She felt power surge from her being—from anger, regret, and fear that she had already lost everything she wanted.

Instead of stepping back, he stepped forward. "You're wrong." His voice was soft. Soothing. He smiled gently.

It disarmed her. She backed away.

He took another step forward.

"You're wrong," he repeated, keeping eye contact. "You're more than that." He reached out a hand to her. "To all of us."

Jocelyn felt the crack in her armor split. He must have sensed it because he enfolded her in his arms. Georgie came behind her and hugged, repeating his words, "To all of us, Joss."

Brittany joined.

"Wait," Lena called out. "Are you having a group hug? You can't have group hugs without me. That should be a rule or something."

"I got you, Lena." Richie picked up the cordless speakerphone and joined the hug. "Umm. It's really nice."

Jocelyn closed her eyes finally, resting her head on Graeme's chest. He was steady and grounded, someone she could trust. The uncomfortable squeezing of the others caused her insides to melt before they finally released her. She couldn't look at Graeme, so she stared at the table.

"You guys mean a lot to me, too." She didn't know the words to use, but those seemed to work.

"Well," Brittany said, saving her, "you have a poor way of showing it." She held up the corset. "Seriously? Not a single bullet."

The group laughed. Everyone but Al.

"No offense," he said. "But am I the only one here who thinks this whole plan is insane?"

Georgie nodded her head to agree with him. "It is insane. That's why we need to work together."

Graeme put a hand over Jocelyn's on the table. "We're stronger together."

Jocelyn finally chanced a look into his green eyes and thought he might be talking about more than just the mission, but she couldn't plan that far. She didn't truly know what was in her heart or what she was capable of. She wanted to stop the Butcher, but she also wanted to stop Cashus. And when she figured out who killed her parents and took the serum that could have saved Benny—she'd want to stop them too.

But one problem at a time.

"Let me get this straight." Jerry Ramstein leaned back into his big leather chair, an amused smile on his face. "Project Sunday, whom we've been tracking, observing, sabotaging, and recently marked for termination—walked into the building and just *hung out*?"

Special Agent Newell felt sick. Laurence Cashus sat next to him with an equally frustrated expression.

The SOI lifted the report on his desk, reading it. "She delivered tea and snacks?"

"Yes, sir. We're not sure of her intent."

"Well, clearly to deliver tea and snacks," the SOI said, laughing. "I tell ya. She just tickles me. Cashus, can we turn her? She's just too good to let go."

"Sir, with techniques similar to those used on Medina and deep hypnosis, I'm sure we could."

The SOI waved a hand. "That was an abysmal failure. Free will is a bitch. We'll have agents killing themselves right and left. Do you know with all the work we've done, willing agents who believe in the cause are seventy-three percent more successful, and live longer, than the ones we've manipulated?" He shook his head. "We need a different approach. Where's Sunday now?"

"Sir, she's been extra careful," Newell admitted.

"Probably because you tried to take her in at a Police Station, Newell!" Ramstein leaned in, furious. "Go to Code Red security there. Hopefully she didn't plant a bomb or something. You should probably check." He pressed a button and the screen went to the logo of the office of the President.

Newell wiped his brow.

"Careful you don't get on his bad side, Newell. Scientists have value. FBI are a dime a dozen."

Cashus left without a goodbye, but Newell took the warning for what it was.

Truth.

Georgie was excited, nervous, and impressed. They'd made incredible progress in four days and their plan was coming together. Having Richie and his extra tech was the one thing that made her feel better about it all. There wouldn't be enough exo-thread for everyone, so they had to prioritize, but their communications system was stellar, and the plan, on the surface, very simple—unlock the Butcher's cell, drug him, load him in a truck, and leave him outside police headquarters. Piece of cake.

Brittany stretched her back, then bent back over her sewing machine again, working on the guard uniforms. She'd printed adhesive fingerprints for the biometric scan and had made some perfect-looking badges with all their photos and fake names.

Lena and Richie had their heads together as usual, the two were inseparable since Lena arrived, occasionally giggling like kids over some uber-genius plans they were developing.

Georgie had a table for each of them set up with uniforms, badges, outfit changes, technology, and tools—including two plastic laser guns compliments of Richie. She checked off each item as it was ready. Today Graeme had brought the drugs they needed from A & R Technologies. He didn't say how he'd gotten them, just that they'd be effective. She unpacked them extra carefully and prepped syringes. The baking products they would make the day before.

Al, Jocelyn, and Graeme worked on logistics and timing, talking through the 3D model and Jocelyn's sketches. Al still encouraged them not to try this, but his military background helped in the planning. He and Jocelyn had that in common, sometimes switching to "mission" chat unconsciously until Graeme snapped his fingers in front of them to remind that he didn't know what their LBRs, OMGs, and ABCs meant.

Jocelyn kept Georgie from playing a key role and didn't want her in the building. She was hiding something from Georgie—and the others. It was the one thing that put Georgie on edge. Georgie wanted justice. Badly. But within the law. She wasn't sure what Jocelyn's version of justice looked like.

Seth caught her attention, and Jocelyn's, when he entered the room carrying several bags from Cravings. The aroma made her stomach growl.

Jocelyn turned angrily, blocking Seth's entrance. "Who invited him?"

Graeme interceded and took a bag from Seth, standing next to him. "I did. He's in."

"No." Jocelyn's voice was adamant.

The others waited watching the test of wills.

"I'm strong. You need me," Seth said.

"I'm not going to risk you going"—Jocelyn stiffened her body and straightened her arms in a fake seizure—"and putting someone in danger."

"Ow." Brittany cringed. "That was harsh, girlfriend."

"Reality." Jocelyn took a bag of food from him.

"She's right," Graeme agreed, reluctantly. "Too risky. You're out."

"I could drive the Porsche," Seth offered.

"We're *not* taking the Porsche," Graeme said.

"But—"

"Sorry, man." Al slapped his back. "Look at it this way. You won't have to wear the yogurt hat." He plopped the dorky white hat on his head to demonstrate.

"I brought you a mango slushie," Seth said, trying to bribe.

"Thank you." Jocelyn dug the drink out of a bag.

Seth sighed. "Brittany, need a break?"

"You can sew?" Her sarcasm dripped.

"I used to work in a sweat shop. Take a break."

She did. And he did—sew. Rather confidently. The girls all smiled at each other, impressed.

"Huh. Good work," Brittany praised.

"That's right, Graeme. I'm good with my hands, too." Seth didn't look up from his work, but a wry smile lifted his cheeks.

Brittany studied Richie and Lena and looked to Georgie with a frown.

Richie nodded approvingly at Lena. "I see what you did there. Heh, heh, heh. Smart."

Lena's cheeks turned bright red from the compliment. Brittany held up her hands to Georgie, shaking her head.

Georgie shrugged. Lena had a crush on Richie.

"Milk, come join us for food," Brittany said.

"Uh," she looked up, then at Richie.

"Come on. A little girlfriend break. It will be okay," Brittany added.

Richie nodded and she joined them. Brittany scooped her some chicken quesadillas and salad, and sat Lena down across from her at the folding table.

"That's enough," Lena said. "I have to get back. Richie's showing me how to program lasers with his code. He's like the most brilliant person I've ever met when it comes to writing code for physical applications. Like the exo-thread! OMG." She pushed her glasses up on her nose. "I'm just—" She shook her open hand over her head frenetically and shoved two bites of quesadilla in her mouth. "Mind b'wown."

"You've had too much caffeine."

"I know." Lena swallowed the giant amount of food in her mouth. "But I feel great!"

"You realize you two have nothing in common," Brittany said.

Georgie kicked her under the table.

Lena's cheeks turned pink again. "What do you mean?" She got up with her plate, informing her tartly, "We're both engineers."

Lena left, but Georgie sensed her feelings had been hurt. "Geez, Brit."

"What? Does he not have PTSD? I don't want Milk with a guy who could go psycho on her in the wrong circumstances."

"Al said he's been getting better. Actually, ever since he started working with Graeme. He's more grounded. It's not an incurable thing."

"Fine. But she's an albino and he's black as night. They look like they should be on a dinner table."

"Really?" Georgie passed her the salad, waiting. Something was up.

Brittany sighed. "Okay. I sort of liked it when it was just the girls."

Al walked in still wearing the yogurt hat. He leaned over Brittany to reach for a burger. "You mean when it was just the girls and *me*." He sat down and joined them, pulling a pamphlet from his pocket to read—a police academy brochure.

"Are you staying?" Georgie got excited.

"Naw, just curious. Think I could get in?"

"Of course!" She paused. "You'd have to be honest about your past and all. But I bet John would help."

He shrugged. "Gotta get home." But he kept reading.

Georgie took her food back into the other room. A lot was changing. She smiled. Mostly for the better. As long as everyone was alive and not in jail by Sunday afternoon, there might be hope for their little super unit.

CHAPTER FORTY-TWO

Graeme watched with curiosity as Seth glanced over at the clothing pattern, then masterfully ran the material through the machine. Geez, he probably did work in a sweatshop.

"Don't stare," Seth said. "Sucks my magic."

Graeme approached Jocelyn. She focused intently on studying the plans.

"We need to let him in," Graeme said.

"I know." Jocelyn put the papers down.

The sewing machine paused. Seth looked up, hopeful.

"The badges I took have likely been changed in the system by now." She flicked through her phone to some photos and showed one to Seth. "Do you think you could make contact with her? She opens on Sunday mornings. Very meticulous. Keeps her badge in the side zipper of her purse. Unless she gets a new purse, then you might have to hunt around. Get her badge, replace it with the fake, pass the original to Richie, then keep her occupied for an hour."

Graeme doubted. "Not sure that will work. New York girls aren't that easy."

"It'll work," Lena, Brittany, and Georgie said in unison.

"Heh, heh, heh." Richie laughed. "No accounting, G."

"But, no cowboy hat," Jocelyn said.

"What?" Seth grabbed his hat from the table and hugged it. "It's the source of my powers!"

"No hat," Jocelyn said. "And take it easy on the accent." The girls agreed.

"Wow. Okay, throwing down a challenge. I can appreciate that. I'll rely on my intelligence." He stretched his arms out as if taking a break from the sewing then bent them, flexing his biceps. "And my other obvious attributes."

Graeme walked behind Seth and tilted his chair back, startling him. "Yeah. That'll work."

Seth smiled and put on his hat before bending back over the machine.

Graeme understood Seth enough to know he wanted to belong. It was human nature, even if the guy didn't like it about himself. And he understood Jocelyn better too. She was preparing herself emotionally to be separated. Which meant she planned on killing the Butcher, not bringing him to justice.

On Sunday they were going to need every kind of backup possible. Their plan was easy. But you didn't know what you didn't know, until you knew. Holliwell was on alert. Anything could happen.

The last Sunday in September promised more record highs. The kids were sound asleep, the house peaceful, and only the click of a fresh magazine chambered broke the morning peace. John clicked the safety and checked his other gun.

"Something's happening today, isn't it?" Kymber stood on the stairs in her pajamas.

"Not sure."

"You've been worried all week. You didn't sleep much last night."

He put on his shoulder holster, not sure what to say.

"We did what we could. She has to make her own decisions."

"And?"

"And we do what we do on Sunday mornings. We go to church."

"And pray?" He didn't mean for his tone to sound so cynical.

She pressed her lips and went back up the stairs. "Exactly."

Richie and Graeme took up mission control in the server room of the Windows project office. The team was dressed, prepped and ready.

After a discussion on whether or not they should bail, Jocelyn gave everyone a pep talk. "If at any moment you don't feel okay, for whatever reason, just get out. Otherwise, the most useful thing you can do is act as if you are the person you are supposed to be. Own your character and their life like it's yours. Be confident, even when confronted…which likely won't happen since the building is mostly empty today. We are the weekend crew."

Seth was up first, laying the charm on an unsuspecting, but junior Holliwell spy on her subway ride to work. He was disgustingly successful and negotiated walking with her to her job. She went through an employee entrance, then came out and opened the front of the yogurt shop. Seth entered and took a stool chatting her up.

The first customer of the day, Richie, purchased some yogurt, and Seth, being helpful, handed him the spoon and napkins on his way out. Pass completed.

Richie passed the badge to Al, who entered the same employee door with Lena. They pressed their fake thumbprints on the pad and cleared security, then donned their disposable gloves to guard against leaving real fingerprints. They entered the yogurt shop from the back, joining Seth and the other "customers."

Seth was trying to get the girl to just take an hour for a coffee or soda. Georgie and Brittany, student customers, encouraged her, saying no one was up yet anyway.

"I should check with the manager on duty."

Seth pulled his cowboy hat out from his bag and tipped it over his eyes. "I don't want to cause trouble. Just following my heart." He glanced up beseeching at the girl from under the brim of his hat. "I'll let you get to work." He turned to go.

"Wait!"

Success.

"That's disgusting," Graeme said over the comm as Seth offered his arm to the girl and they scooted off.

Georgie and Brittany quickly went behind the counter, put on their yogurt shop uniforms, and emptied their bags of goodies. They arranged the food on trays and prepped a collection of yogurt flavors, thoroughly mixing in the sedative.

Stocked up, Brittany and Lena headed for the forty-third floor and security headquarters, while Georgie and Al manned the shop. Richie returned to mission control, and Graeme left to join Jocelyn.

Brittany started shaking the closer they got to their destination. Lena tapped Richie's electrical scanner to the elevator and pressed forty-three. It worked. Lena was perky as could be, even greeting the random scientist who got on with bleary eyes and wanted coffee. She gave him a cup!

The poor man would be out in minutes. Hopefully he had an office nearby.

The entire affair made Brittany both more terrified and more confident. *Time to pretend.*

The man at the lobby desk on the forty-third didn't look too scary. Brittany put on a brave smile.

"Hi," Lena said brightly. "Our manager sent us up with some Sunday goodness." She held out the coffee and snacks. "Or you can try some of our new yogurt flavors. Do you like peach? It's pretty nice."

Brittany held out the tray. He took a coffee and a peach yogurt and blueberry muffin. No problem. "Only one person at a time in the Security HQ." He buzzed the team to let them know.

"Sure thing." Then Lena proceeded to chat about the weather until the guard's eyes fluttered closed. "More coffee?" she offered.

He drank the coffee and Brittany scooped it up just before his head hit the desk. She scooted around the desk and propped up his elbows, Lena held his head, then they balanced it, arranging a magazine in front of him.

The offices all seemed to be empty, which was a good thing, and they made their way to the security room on schedule.

A camera spun on them outside the large metal door entrance. They waved. It opened with an electronic swish.

Lena brought in one tray and Brittany marveled at her composure.

"Bob, the lobby guy said only one person at a time, so I'll set this all up for you and come back later to clean up." She offered coffees, put down the tray, then came back with the yogurt. "We have yogurt specials. Original tart, chocolate, coconut, strawberry, peach, hazelnut, and pistachio. Something for everyone!" She walked to each station and offered frozen yogurt to the two men and two women who watched the monitors.

Brittany simply smiled with amazement and said good morning when they looked at her. Lena came back for the muffins and again brought the tray around before setting it up on the counter, arranging it nicely.

"This coffee is really bitter," one woman said.

"Guaranteed to keep you lively," Lena said as their eyes fought to stay open.

"Who are you?" one of the guards asked suspiciously, his speech slurring. He reached for a red button.

Lena interceded. "Careful! You almost knocked your coffee over!"

"Oh…thank…" Head thump.

"Wow, those were loaded," Brittany whispered. Lena dragged Brittany inside and closed the metal door. The guards were securely passed out in their chairs. Moving quickly, Brittany and Lena rolled the sleeping security team to the side and out of the way.

Lena quickly took the controls, looking around. "We're in. I'm turning off the cameras and I want to wipe the last twenty minutes before we get started. Need to be safe. Over."

"Copy," Richie said. "While it's erasing, plug in my remote access so I can see what you've got. Over."

Lena whipped off her thick bracelet and stretched it out on the control panel, opening once to extend the length. It was a mini-computer with keyboard. She connected it to one of the computers, then began to explore.

"And here I thought you finally got some style," Brittany said.

"It's style and functionality," Lena answered.

"Hmm." Brittany checked out the device. "I think I can improve this."

Lena nodded agreement, already absorbed, pressing buttons and exploring. She shoved her glasses further up her nose and grinned suddenly at Brittany. "This is fun, right?"

"No." Brittany shook her head. "You need to get out more."

Lena just smiled bigger, speaking through the team communication device. "Jocelyn, Graeme. I just unlocked the east security door. You should be able to enter." She turned to Brittany. "Don't worry. We'll be in and out."

"Famous last words." They were cursed for sure.

Graeme joined Jocelyn in the subway station. She seemed as relaxed as someone taking a stroll on a Sunday morning. A train left the station, and after casually flashing a metro worker ID at some random people she led him down the wall path that quickly became a ledge and told him to jump. He jumped. She definitely knew her way around down here.

"Careful," she warned, holding his hand from behind until they reached the maintenance turn. She walked to the hidden door and pulled the piping made to look like part of the wall. It opened.

"Wow," Graeme whispered. "Dangerously cool."

Now they just had to pass as guards.

They had on guard uniforms with matching hats. Jocelyn had an army green backpack and utility belt, and Graeme had a green puffy jacket over his somber guard uniform, plus a few key pieces of tech he'd selected—hopefully none would be needed.

"Hey, where'd you two come from?" the guard inside asked.

"Homeless duty," Graeme said.

"That's what happens when you pull the night shift," Jocelyn added. She stretched a hand to the guy. "We haven't met."

He smiled. "Bryan. Nice to meet you."

"Is your shift short?" Jocelyn asked.

"Naw. Keith just went to get coffee."

"Good, Sundays are always a little tedious. You'll have company."

"That's a generous description of Keith," Bryan joked.

They made to leave, and as Bryan turned in his chair, Graeme watched Jocelyn stab him with a syringe from her utility belt. The guard's head fell back in the chair and she adjusted him, putting his hand on the panel and turning him toward the furthest monitor. She was precise and efficient.

"Damn. Is it wrong that I find that hot?"

"You're on the comm," Brittany noted.

"Sorry," Graeme said.

Jocelyn chastised but with a smile. "Stay focused."

"Trust me, I am so focused right now it's insane. Keith is out that way." He pointed down the hall. "We'll have to wait for him."

As if on cue, the door behind them buzzed and a big old gruff guy walked in with a paper plate and two muffins.

"I hope one's for Bryan," Graeme said. "He was complaining you never share."

The man grunted. They laughed.

"You guys take it easy," Jocelyn said as Keith put his food and coffee on the table in front of the prison cell panel. "We're just heading out."

"Okay. Be good," Keith said. He turned to Bryan to say something, and with another syringe, Jocelyn silenced him as well.

"They seem nice," she said. "It makes me feel bad that not everyone knows they are contributing to evil."

Graeme touched her arm and gave a quick squeeze. "You'd be surprised at how much people really know. They just don't want to admit the truth because it would inconvenience their lives."

She sighed. "Yeah. I sort of get that."

They pushed the two chairs aside, and Jocelyn pressed "Prison View." She scanned quickly for 10B then froze.

"What?" Graeme asked.

She pointed. "It's empty."

CHAPTER FORTY-THREE

ocelyn took a breath. She was not aborting this mission.

Graeme shook his head. "Houston, we have a problem."

"I heard," Lena said over the comm. "One minute." They waited. "Okay, I've got something. Zooming in. Uh…yeah. That's him. Fortieth Floor. It looks like a hypnosis session. There's a guard outside with a wheelchair."

Jocelyn tensed. Cashus's lab. Two of them in one spot. Fate.

"Straight out the elevator, down the hall and to the right."

"I'm familiar," Jocelyn said. "I'll pick him up and transport him in the wheelchair. Easy peasy, safe and breezy." She used to say that to Medina. When things were about to go wrong.

"I'll go with you," Graeme said.

She didn't want him with her. She definitely didn't want him to see her kill in cold blood. "You need to stay here. Make sure no one discovers Bryan and Keith. We'll exit the garage ramp as planned. Pick a vehicle."

"Jocelyn—" Graeme looked worried.

"There's a security elevator in the northeast corner," Lena said. "That's how they move them without people seeing. You can bring him down that way. It's right between the cell block and transport ramp."

"It's a plan." Jocelyn checked her utility belt, grabbed Bryan's badge, then unhooked Bryan's holster and gun, strapping it on. "Just in case," she told Graeme. She leaned up and kissed his cheek.

"Jocelyn." He grabbed her arms to hold her still and gazed straight into her eyes.

"I can't not be who I am," she said.

"I know. I'm just asking you to *be* that person. This is one day in our lives. Let's get out unnoticed." He squeezed her arms. "Please."

She nodded and took the security elevator up, checking the gun. Seth's voice broke through the comm. "Honey, I'm not thinking that's a good idea."

"Are you talking to me or your girlfriend?"

"Uh-huh."

"Richie mute his comm," Jocelyn asked. "Too distracting."

"I'm with Seth," Georgie added. "Whose office is it? Jocelyn? Hold off."

"I'm almost there," she told them. "Don't worry." The elevator dinged open and she started down the long hallway.

"Uh-oh," Lena said over the comm. "The office is assigned to Dr. Laurence Cashus."

"Jocelyn, don't go," Georgie said. "Please. This is not a good idea."

"Don't worry. I have a loaded gun."

"I'm coming up," Graeme said.

"Secure the truck! Everyone stick to the plan," Jocelyn insisted.

"This wasn't in the plan," Graeme reminded.

"Jocelyn!" Georgie beseeched.

"That's why you're scooping yogurt. Graeme get the truck. Muting now." Jocelyn continued to walk down the hall. The guard looked up and she waved, finally reaching him. "Keith told me to come up and give you a break."

"Already? That's great." He got up from the wheelchair he'd been using to sit in. "Fifteen?"

"Sounds good." She sat in the wheelchair and watched him leave. Probably should have tranq'd him. After he was out of sight she got up and cracked the lock of the door with one strong turn. She walked in, absorbing Cashus's surprised face and the back of the Butcher's head. He didn't recognize her. Not at first. She took off her hat and tossed it, revealing midnight blue hair beginning to surface on her scalp.

A slow sinister smile stretched across his evil face. "I wondered when you'd show up."

She lifted her hand to the corner of the room and the camera exploded, causing him to flinch slightly. "Yeah. I figured you'd be waiting." She pulled out her gun.

"I lost visual. Lena?" Richie asked what was up.

"Me too," Lena said.

Brittany jumped in, "She did it. She blew out the cameras."

"Jocelyn, I know you can hear us. Think this through," Georgie said. "Yes, that will be five ninety-five. Thank you."

Jocelyn ignored the voices in her head. She moved carefully to observe the Butcher. He sat calmly in the chair, his expression catatonic. He was under hypnosis. "Don't speak, Laurence. Or I'll aim for your mouth. Just nod yes or no. Do you understand?"

He nodded yes, sneering at her.

"I know why my parents were murdered. Do you?"

He nodded yes.

"Do you have the serum?"

He smiled.

She shot his hand on the desk and drew blood. "My directions were simple."

"Ah!" Frightened, he shook his head. "No!"

"Do you know who does?" She glanced at the Butcher. He sat perfectly still. One eye still covered where he had surgery.

Cashus shook his head no but reached for something.

She shot his arm then she shot the gun he pulled, blasting it out of his hand causing him to whimper. "I have five bullets left."

"How is little Benny doing?"

She moved in and shot his ear. Just the tip. He had big ears.

It did nothing to alleviate her rage or disappointment. He'd been her hope. But it meant she could kill him and not be concerned.

"Bitch!"

She shot his opposite arm. Just grazed it.

His knowledge of her brother filled her with rage. He'd known all along Benny and Morgan were alive. Her blood seared hot, and objects in the room rattled around them.

"Shame your mother couldn't save him."

She leapt his desk and swung hard at his jaw with the gun, knocking him off his seat. He crawled to the wall and she unloaded the gun with the remaining bullets, creating a halo in the wall around his head.

She tossed the empty weapon.

Beating him with her fist felt better than anything. Definitely more personal. She pulled him to his feet and hit him three more times before sending him across the desk and head first into the Butcher's lap, knocking the prisoner backward in the chair.

"Clarence!"

The Butcher's eye opened, but he remained still, lying on his back in the chair as Cashus crawled across the floor to get away.

She raised her hand and sent him rolling into the wall, anger flowing freely. She focused in on his throat and kept her energy steady. She squeezed a little, thinking about what it would feel like.

Satisfying. She took a breath. *Oh, God. Very, very satisfying.* Time slowed between heartbeats and she could hear Medina's heartbeat again in her head, as if it were her own. Steady. Calm. Peaceful.

He had deserved so much more. So did Benny and Seth. She took another long inhale and the room settled down.

So did she.

Slowly, she lowered her hand, releasing the pressure. "I'm not going to kill you."

He put his bloodied hands to his throat, massaging it while assessing her.

"I don't want to be linked to you for the rest of my life. You're too despicable for that." She motioned to the Butcher. "Tell him to go sit in the wheelchair outside."

"Clarence. Get up," he croaked. "Walk to the door. Outside is a wheelchair. Sit in it."

Jocelyn watched, unnerved when the monster of a man obeyed. "I see your brainwashing skills have improved." She and Cashus were still in the office. She pulled a tranq from her utility belt. She'd leave him here.

Cashus held up his hand, palm down, waiting.

She froze.

He smiled.

Her heart raced in panic. The old routine felt ingrained in her being. She clutched the tranquilizer desperately. He did not have control over her anymore.

So why did her feet move inexorably closer to him?

He raised his hand higher and the visual gripped her. She rolled her shoulders fighting it off as another step brought them closer. She knew what his hand would feel like, smell like—soft and plain with a strong scent of lemon sanitizer that he used religiously. And when her lips touched the top of his hand, gray hairs would brush her mouth, the thought of which caused her immense nausea.

But still she took another step.

He would want the words too. Words that she hated. *I love you, Uncle Laurence.* Her memories caused sweat to form on her temples as she fought the propelling motion of his demand. She hated him.

She took his hand. Bloodied from a bullet, she raised it to her lips. "I—"

Brittany stared at the control board. Not good. She was alone. She watched the cameras as Lena ran down six flights of stairs.

"Al, I think you should get up here."

"I'm in the elevator. It's stuck." Al had taken off his yogurt outfit and had a guard uniform underneath.

"Wait, I need to give you permission. It's one of these buttons." She watched as the two-sided elevator opened on the wrong side."

"Not that way." Al backed away. "Literally no building. Press up."

"I'm pressing up."

Richie jumped in. "Show me the panel, Brit."

She connected her phone.

"Heh, heh. Okay, wrong panel. Go to the right. Identical switchboard. Easy mistake. Flip the unlock switch."

She did.

"It's working," Al said.

"Where's Lena?" Richie asked.

An explosion on one of the screens caused Brittany and Richie to exclaim loudly.

"Jocelyn!" Brittany screamed.

"We've got visual," Richie cried out. "We've got visual. Oh-my—"

Jocelyn bent over Cashus's hand. His hubris was unmatched. There was a reason for that. He wasn't a complete idiot.

She clutched the syringe in her hand.

And she wasn't a complete innocent anymore.

She lifted her head before her skin could touch his and stabbed him hard in the center of his hand, sending the needle straight through his palm.

He squealed in outrage, trying to yank it away.

She pulled the needle back out and this time stabbed his arm, releasing the drug.

Fury filled his eyes. "Clarence! *Interfectus!*" He called out in Latin while falling backward against the wall. Then he desperately reached in his pocket and took something out. A pill. What was that for?

Jocelyn turned to the door. The Butcher stood angrily, awake and alert.

He recognized her. Not good.

She thrust out her palm, sending a force of energy that shot him into the hallway wall. Cashus slid to a rest on the floor, a freakish smile on his face.

"Now Clarence," Jocelyn soothed, inching her way out of the office. "I think we should talk this over. I don't want to hurt you."

Much.

He roared angrily just as Lena turned the corner. Her friend froze, staring at Jocelyn and the giant behind her.

"Elevator! Elevator!" Jocelyn yelled, running to her. "Go."

Lena moved, frantically pressing the elevator button. "Brittany, unlock!"

"I'm trying!" Brittany cried out.

Jocelyn turned back at the sound of a crashing noise and saw the Butcher smashing something in the wall. "What the—" A weapons cabinet. He pulled out a big black, hollow-piped machine.

She recognized it. Power blower. Very strong. Could flip large vehicles. Number seven of weapons she was trained on.

"Lena! Get back!" She tried to call out directions. "Secure yourself!"

She faced the weapon and directed her energy, but to no avail.

The powerful blast filled the hall and sent her backward, airborne through the long hall toward the elevators, her arms grasping for something to hold onto. Miraculously the elevators opened before impact. Then opened again out the other side—to the nothingness of construction.

She grasped for an edge, partially hit the elevator, and spun like a starfish to the ground, sliding on the ledge.

Her fingers grasped desperately against the velocity.

Then she slid off.

CHAPTER FORTY-FOUR

*G*raeme grabbed his badge and locked the prison surveillance area with Keith and Bryan resting at their posts. He put his anger on tap for now. He'd lecture Jocelyn later—if she survived her stupidity, and rashness, and vengeance.

Okay, anger still there. He took a cooling breath. He needed to make sure they had their transportation ready to go.

A couple guards watched a game in the break area. A third looked at him and approached. "Hey, can you help unload a truck that just came in?"

Graeme smiled. *Not good.* "Sure."

He looked at the back of the truck and two more delivery guys helped roll out the bikes. "Wow!"

"Right." The guard winked at him. "Tunnel duty just got better."

"No doubt." The black, military-styled motorcycle assault vehicles looked like something out of a futuristic war movie. The two deliverymen pushed them out, and he took one, rolling it behind the other guard to their underground garage. They moved the other two bikes, and the delivery guys took off into the tunnels.

What else was going on down here?

"Do you want the keys to stay in the ignition or collect 'em?"

"You can leave 'em. I need to log them in first."

A light on his utility belt buzzed and her pressed it. A voice called out urgently. "Security! Fortieth Floor. The Butcher is loose! Something went wrong. Need backup! ASAP! And a medic."

The man met his eyes with panic.

"I heard," Graeme said. "I'll alert medical."

The guard called to the other two watching the game and the three ran to the security elevator. He grimaced. Jocelyn wouldn't be coming down that way.

"Brittany," Graeme spoke into the comm. "Three guards are in the security elevator. Stop the elevator. Shut it down."

"Okay, got it." Brittany called out. "Richie? Help!"

Graeme heard Richie's directions to Brittany and watched as the elevator stopped somewhere between the tenth and eleventh floors. He breathed with relief and ran back into the prison control center to see if they had outside surveillance views.

He flicked some switches then froze when he came upon something. The new building—it looked like a penitentiary— with people in it. He changed the view for more detail of the other building. "Holy—" Not good. "Richie, do you have this?"

"What is that?" Richie asked.

"The prisoners in the building next door. Some of them have been haunting the city this summer. Impossible to catch. I don't understand."

"I told you, G. Bad people."

"Team?" A sense of urgency surged through him. "We need to abort. Everyone get out." This was a lot bigger than any of them could have imagined.

"Who has eyes on Jocelyn?" Graeme asked.

Richie muted Brittany and spoke directly. "G? Lena has Jocelyn. Channel 17 in the exterior surveillance mode. Stay calm. Al is near."

Graeme felt his tension rise at being told to stay calm. His hand shook as he pressed a button to view the exterior surveillance. Then he spotted her.

His pulse rocketed and his stomach dropped. *Not. Good.*

Jocelyn dropped.

Lena jumped.

Her friend's glasses jolted off her face and fell to the abyss of forty floors, but she had the fire hose around her waist and she had Jocelyn's left wrist in both her hands. Jocelyn reached and grabbed her forearm. Lena's face exploded with purple as she strained to hold.

"Sorry," Jocelyn said.

"'Kay." Lena gasped.

They could both hear Brittany's hysterical screams and the Butcher's heavy stride as he jogged toward them, vibrating the entire floor. They dangled over the edge with only Lena's toes touching the platform as they swung, their lives dependent on the strength of the hose not ripping out of the wall.

"Her gun!" Richie cried. Then tried to be calm. "Joss, your right, Lena's left hip. I gave her a laser gun. Can you reach it?"

Jocelyn carefully stretched, while Lena acrobatically attempted bending her body sideways for her to reach it.

"This plastic thing?" Jocelyn snatched it and shot immediately, testing.

"Easier to pass security," Richie defended.

She heard Al's voice calling to them. He was about to intersect with the Butcher. "Close the elevator, Brit." Jocelyn instructed. "When Al is inside."

It closed, pulling on the fire hose. Al banged for it to open again.

"The other side!" Everyone yelled.

Jocelyn searched for something to anchor to besides Lena. She heard Al's curse when the Butcher joined him in the elevator.

The other side closed.

He was trapped.

Seth couldn't take it. The shouting in his ear, Jocelyn going off alone, the plan gone to shit. He should be in the middle of it. He hadn't been there to help her last time.

"I have to go." He stood up abruptly.

"Wha-what?" The Holliwell girl blinked, confused.

He pulled out Special Agent Newell's badge that he procured from the tech table—in case they needed backup. "I'm with the FBI. We're raiding the building today. Everything you think you know is a lie. I didn't want to see you get arrested and questioned. The group in the building is doing scientific testing on people. Very seedy. Very illegal." He flipped the badge closed and dropped a twenty on the table. "Sorry about our date. Stay out of trouble, okay?"

She nodded wordlessly and he took off.

Running to the frozen yogurt shop, he bumped into a girl before excusing himself, and realized it was Morgan and her friend. "Oh, wow. Sorry. Running too fast. New job. Gotta go!" He waved bye, then dodged across the street to the yogurt shop.

Georgie patiently tried to get rid of a picky child and mom.

"Fire in the main building. Everyone out!" He held the door. "Come on, yogurt's free. Get to safety. Thank you."

"Here!" Georgie tossed some keys and he locked the front door. "Brittany! Stop screaming."

Seth and Georgie stared at each other.

"What now?" Seth asked.

"I'll get the building evacuated, everyone can get out. Check on Graeme. He's been quiet."

"Plan." Seth gave her a last second hug, some sixth sense warning him. "Be extra careful. I have a bad feeling."

She nodded, and he watched her go off alone, not sure if separating was a good idea.

~ ~ ~

The next half-minute was perhaps the least productive for everyone. Brittany's panicked yelps and screams were all anyone heard. Lena winced and Jocelyn wasn't sure if it was the struggle to hang on or the noise in her ear.

She felt the pounding in the elevator between Al and the Butcher. Based on Lena's timed blinks of pain, she felt it too. Richie called the match, cheering when Al got a good hit in.

"That's right! Feel that exo-thread, asshole!" Richie said.

Finally Brittany managed to open the elevator doors again.

Lena and Jocelyn dropped sharply a few inches. Then a little more. The Butcher roared—always a sign of something about to get worse.

He leaned over the edge of the platform, lifted the firehouse with them on it, yanked it hard above his head raising them into the air, and swung them like a toy above the abyss.

Jocelyn fired the laser. He dropped one hand. She got him again, continuing until he dropped their life rope and them with it. Lena gasped. They jolted hard, causing Lena to release. Jocelyn's grip slid down her skinny arm but Lena grabbed her again, just in time. Lena's hands were weakening. She couldn't hold on much longer.

Jocelyn shot the laser again, simply trying to distract the Butcher from grabbing the fire hose.

Irritated, and seemingly a little confused, the Butcher forgot about them. Escape took precedent and he saw the opportunity. He did a short run and leaped forcefully across the divide. She shot him in the air, spinning herself and Lena on the fire hose as the green laser burned into the criminal's skin.

He landed, roared threateningly again, beat his chest like a madman, then got blasted through a wall of the other building. She spun and saw Al above them holding the power blower.

Lena and Jocelyn were slowly pulled to the ledge and safety—by Al, and with the help of exo-thread. He breathed hard, sitting against the wall, nose bloodied and eye reddened.

"You white sisters have serious thrill issues."

They hugged him and each other. Jocelyn checked to make sure Lena didn't have a broken rib or dislocated shoulder. She would never underestimate her ninety-five-pound friend again. Taking a breath, she picked up the big power blower, set it to recharge, and gave it back to him.

"There's a maximum setting," Al said.

"Good call." Jocelyn grinned for the first time that day. She stood and helped Lena, who promptly walked into a wall and banged her head.

She rubbed her forehead, eyes dilated. "I lost my glasses."

Al turned her shoulders and redirected her into the elevator. The office side opened.

There stood Special Agent Newell, gun at the ready, looking none too happy. He aimed his weapon at Jocelyn. "Not so fast."

Al sighed heavily while Lena turned blindly toward the threatening voice.

"Hey, Agent Newell. You keep showing up," Jocelyn said.

"You can count on it," he answered.

"I've got her." Al took Jocelyn by the arm, playing the guard, intending to take her away. "Dr. Whitey," he nudged Lena. "You're welcome to return to your lab."

Lena turned to go and bumped into the elevator wall, just missing the opening. "I lost my glasses," she explained, putting out her hands. "Agent Newell, can you escort me?"

Newell hesitated half a second. "No. All three of you. In the elevator."

"Wait!" A cry from down the hallway made them turn. Cashus wobbled into a wall trying to get balance, making his way to them. That pill he took must have been an antidote to the tranquilizer. As he stumbled forward another call came from their left. The guard ran over.

"Where's Cooke?" he asked Cashus.

"Loose. But he'll be back. It's part of my hypnosis."

"I don't think so, Laurence," Jocelyn said.

Newell turned to her. She explained. "*Interfectus.* It means kill, or destroy, depending on the context. Cashus woke him from his trance with that order and he went on a rampage before jumping over to that building."

Newell and the guard paled.

"What's over there?" Al asked.

"Three floors of murdering criminals," Richie said in their earpiece.

"OMG." Lena clenched her gut.

"You have more felons on that side?" Jocelyn's voice rose in outrage. "Have they been experimented on, like Clarence?"

"I don't know. Some have had different enhancements."

"Some!" Lena shouted. She lifted her finger at Newell but was off. Al turned her to adjust direction. "That's highly illegal. You're putting everyone in the city at risk."

"It's not me. I'm just a visitor," Newell said.

Jocelyn studied the exposed guts of the building and open elevator shaft across the alley. "Can he get out of that building?"

"Only the way he got in," the guard said. "And from the basement transport bays. It's very secure otherwise."

Cashus, still groggy, but recovering, leaned on the guard. Jocelyn saw his move too late. He took the guard's gun.

"Sir, now give that back. You're not yourself. You need medical help."

"More than you know," Jocelyn said. She lifted her hand and shot power toward the weapon, flinging it safely away from everyone. The guard jumped back in shock. Newell stared at her in surprise.

Cashus lunged at her.

Jocelyn, alert, stepped backward in the elevator and Cashus stumbled into Newell sending the two of them tumbling over the ledge. She grabbed Cashus quickly and pulled him back.

There was no one to save Newell.

Except her.

So she did.

She vaguely heard Al's roar of shock echoing in the vast chamber between buildings when she jumped and dove.

CHAPTER FORTY-FIVE

"No!" Graeme saw her one moment then she was gone. "No!" His heartbeat exploded as he searched empty screens. Then he turned, gagging violently from the adrenaline rush.

Nothing came out. The adrenaline slowed but lingered, his heart still racing. Tension made his stomach hurt. Taking a second, he whizzed through options in his brain.

Locking the control room, he ran down the hall, opened the transport bay, hit the lights on one of the new bikes and revved it into action.

Images of Jocelyn broken in a deserted alley made him shake. But if Henry was right about her stopping bullets then he prayed she had a few other tricks up her sleeve she hadn't shared yet.

The darkness of the underground crowded him. He remembered the 3D model and called up to Brittany. "Richie? Brittany? I'm in the tunnels. Open the parking structure under 1540 Broadway. I'm surfacing in about thirty seconds.

He approached the wall at full speed, depending on trust. Thankfully, it moved. Behind it was a ramp into the building's parking lot. He went up, further and faster until the regular parking garage signs led him to the exit and daylight.

He shot out of the garage, catching air, landing, and spinning sideways on the bike to avoid tourists posing with an Elvis impersonator. The king gave him a 'thumbs up' and he righted the bike, turning directly into two shoppers—his sister and Meghana.

"Hey." Morgan's face registered shock followed by concern.

"Hey," Graeme replied, equally surprised. "Uh, trying a new bike. Gotta go."

He raced across the intersection and burst through the chain link construction fence.

Jocelyn had a vague plan when she dove off the side of the building. She knew it would not feel good, but at least it was a plan. She just needed to reach Newell before he hit the bottom.

Her energy was strongest when aimed outward. Pulling things to her was much more difficult, especially at high speeds. But the cables of the other building were loose and reachable. She compelled them to her with her right hand while stretching her left in the dive to grasp one of Newell's flailing limbs.

Their eyes locked. His were wide with shock. Then he reached.

She caught his wrist just past halfway, and they fell together. She focused all her sources on one cable. It moved toward her, but not enough.

A millisecond of panic was not allowed. She used every cell in her skin to send her body closer, her hand reaching, the cable moving two feet outward.

Almost…

Then catch!

They jolted with a swing, hit the wall with brain jarring force, and she screamed as their combined weight and velocity dragged them down, her hand sliding around the cable—hot, burning, blistering, cutting through her skin. The agony made her cry out with fury and determination. She willed herself to hold on, desperately trying to slow their descent. Down they went until her fingers grew crippled, worn, and she nearly let go.

But they slowed.

Then stopped.

Her grip released.

He thumped, hitting the ground first. She fell to her knees, whimpering as she carefully released the cable, sticky with her blood and skin. She clenched the hand to her stomach and closed her eyes a moment to get the pain under control.

Newell lay in silent, gasping shock until he slowly realized what just happened and rolled to one knee. He yelped at his shoulder.

She opened her eyes, breathing hard, eyes tearing.

"Your whites have blue," he said looking at her.

"Your shoulder is dislocated." She stood with effort. "Lie down, give me your arm." Fortunately, his bad shoulder was opposite her good arm. She pressed her foot firmly. "On three. One—" She yanked and heard the pop.

"Ahhh." He screamed like a woman. "Better. Thanks." He slowly stood, holding his stomach, shaking, and clearly not sure if he would be sick. He sat back down and put his head between his knees.

She looked around for his gun and found it, moving it across the concrete with her foot, still gripping her hand to her stomach. She needed recovery time too.

Newell took the gun when she kicked it to him and stood. It seemed to confuse him more. They stared cautiously at each other, two adversaries, really seeing the other for the first time.

"Why did you save me?"

"Because I could."

He didn't understand.

She tilted her head up to see Al kneeling over the edge, holding his chest. "Get out!" She shouted the order.

He nodded.

"You're wanted for murder," Newell told her.

Jocelyn spun, surprised. "What?"

"Megan Oakridge. Your old trainer."

It took Jocelyn a moment. "What happened to her?"

"Shot in cold blood."

Jocelyn reeled. "It's a lie."

"True." He added, "That she was shot. You're the one being blamed."

She closed her eyes a moment. "They'll never let me go?"

Newell didn't respond. He didn't have a chance. A black, hyper-military motorcycle shot through the fence, knocking it flat before spinning to a stop.

Graeme jumped off and ran to her, pulling her away from Newell who still held his gun. Newell holstered it.

"You're bleeding."

"Just my hand. It's okay."

"Show me."

"I can't," she said. "Can't move it yet."

"What happened?"

Newell explained. "Cashus knocked me over the side. She jumped and saved me."

"Of course she did." Graeme grunted like the guy was an idiot. "That's who she is."

Jocelyn smiled at him. "How did you know?"

"I just know these things." He shook his head, trying to pull her hand free from her body. "Geez, and now you're bleeding to death."

"Graeme?" They all turned and saw Morgan standing on the sidewalk. "What's going on?"

"Morgan." Graeme hesitated, stepping in front of Jocelyn to block her.

It was too late. Morgan walked around him and stared at Jocelyn, her shirt red with blood, hand clutched against her stomach protectively, and spikes of blue-black hair finally surfacing. Jocelyn waited for her reaction. Instead Morgan was silent.

"Give me your scarf," Graeme said.

"What?" Morgan knew what he intended. "It's Hermes." She took it off anyway.

"And versatile." Graeme took Jocelyn's hand, gently peeling each finger open and cursing when she revealed the damage—nearly down to the bone.

Newell watched, expression grim. "Thank you is not enough."

"No shit," Graeme muttered under his breath

"Wait." Morgan dug in her purse and pulled out a water bottle. "Rinse."

Graeme did so. Jocelyn sucked air. Then he quickly wrapped her palm, thumb, and knuckles bringing the leftover scarf around her wrist with a bow.

"Thank you."

He cupped her face gently in his hands and kissed her. Deeply. In front of Morgan and Newell. Her heart pounded and her body bent into his. She felt her skin tingle with rejuvenation all over. She gasped for equilibrium when he lifted his head up an inch.

"We have to go now," she said.

"Promise me you won't jump off any more buildings today."

"I promise."

"What's going on?" Morgan asked. "I can help."

"You already did," Graeme said. "Just keep this to yourself, okay?"

Jocelyn saw Morgan's indecision. She could help them. Jocelyn pulled out her phone from a zippered pocket and handed it to Morgan. "The code is Benny. Call John Morrow in the contacts. Give him this address and tell him he'll need backup."

"A lot of backup," Newell said coming forward.

"Then?"

"Then get out of here and wait for us at the pie shop on Forty-Seventh." Jocelyn went to the bike and hopped on.

"Uh, I was driving," Graeme said.

"I know the underground better than you. It's safer."

"But your hand."

"You fixed it. And I heal fast. Get on."

He got on, albeit with a disappointed expression. "What about him?"

Newell answered. "I'll go to the guard entrance on the other side. Warn everyone."

Jocelyn took off, watching Morgan on her phone in her rearview mirror before she turned into the garage and down into the catacombs of the city.

Georgie told everyone on the lower floors there was a security breach in the neighboring building and they needed all guards on deck. The place cleared out quickly. The few staffers worriedly picked up their things and left. Apparently a lot of people knew what was going on here. There were some young people working, but it was mostly empty. They should get everyone out. No telling where the Butcher would show up. She called Brittany to see if there was an intercom for the building. There was.

"Attention, everyone in the building." Brittany sounded almost calm and professional. "This morning, at approximately, uh, ten minutes ago, we had a severe security breach of our prison population. We are asking all scientists and civilians to immediately evacuate until this can be resolved. Please use standard evacuation procedures. And enjoy your day."

"Nice, Brit." She pressed her comm. "I think everyone is mostly out. Where's Lena and Al?"

"They just walked in. Cashus ran off with the guard after pushing Newell. We have cleanup to do, then we'll be down. Al is on his way to the guard level to make sure Seth is okay and they'll meet us at the rendezvous."

"Okay, I'll wait for you by the elevator."

The comm went eerily silent and Georgie studied the empty space designed to brainwash a new generation of Holliwell employees. What they did today might expose some of the corruption, maybe even save some of the trainees, but it was a long way from stopping Holliwell or the forces determined to keep power in their hands. That job was an impossible task. And too many lives would be sacrificed pursuing it. But somehow there needed to be justice.

The elevator lights blinked nearby and she waited.

Today, she could only be grateful that everyone was safe.

Seth searched the guard area. It was quiet. Like right before a zombie attack. The bay door was open. He studied the other building wondering where the opening would be. Slowly a wall began to move on the far side of the tunnel. He stared, curious. It lowered forward like a ramp. And there were people on the other side.

Angry-looking people.

He hit his comm. "Uh, anybody there? Anyone! I'm in the guard and transport bay and I need backup!"

A loud roar, like a prison raid gone wild rumbled, creating a frightening echo in the dark tunnels.

Seth stepped back as an elevator dinged.

"Get down!" Al shouted from behind him. He aimed a giant gun at the crowd just as they surged forward. A loud blast sent them backward like a wall of dominoes.

"Brittany!" Al shouted. "Send those guards down in the security elevator! Now!"

"Okay, okay," Brittany shouted.

"Do it again!" Seth encouraged Al.

"It has to charge," he yelled back.

"Oh, shit." Seth watched the temporarily stunned men slowly get to their feet. "This is gonna get ugly."

"No kidding."

Another elevator dinged. The three guards came out, clueless and relieved to be free.

"It's a prison break!" Seth shouted to them. "Over there! And they're coming here!" The men mobilized unlocking a closet and passing out large shotguns.

"Load up!" one of them ordered, throwing him a gun. He obeyed, filling the barrel. "Tranqs only. These are expensive experiments. Don't let any of them get away."

Something turned inside Seth. He saw the men differently. They were as scary as the prisoners. But who was the victim? Al grabbed a gun.

He didn't have time to decide. Forty men came at the five of them.

"It's like Zombie Master!" Al said, shooting bodies left and right.

The wave finally stopped, with a few men getting within feet of them before falling unconscious. Seth shook off the shiver that ran down his spine. He was creeped out. They sort of had been like zombies.

Then one man appeared, both hands loaded with weapons.

The Butcher.

"Take cover!" a guard called out.

Seth dove as the blast of energy scattered everything in sight. The Butcher jogged over. Shot at the scattered guards with another gun, then hopped on a bike, and took off. Seth would have gone after him, but something else got his attention. A group of boys, younger than him, huddled together and looking out to see if it was safe.

A recovering guard got to his feet and took aim.

So did Seth—but at the guard.

CHAPTER FORTY-SIX

*L*ena bent her head low over the keyboard, her hair swinging back and forth from her furious typing. "We can't let them get away with this. People deserve the truth!"

"Are you sure you know what you're doing?"

"Yes. I'm nearsighted, not stupid."

"That's not what I meant, Milk."

"Sorry." She typed more then leaned over to press her face two inches from the monitor, reading to make sure it was correct.

"Ohmigosh." Brittany got a little nauseous.

"It's the truth!" Lena defended.

"I know, but—we're not going to make any friends."

Lena pressed her lips, clearly not caring. "Richie, I just linked the Holliwell system to broadcast on the Windows on the World system. Please do not interfere." She pressed a button then unplugged her wrist computer from the Holliwell system.

"Um, okay. Do I get a preview?" he asked.

"It might be better if you get all our stuff out of there and meet us at the rendezvous. They'll likely try to shut it down there first. Lock the door on your way out."

"Gotcha, boss girl. The eagle is shedding the nest."

Lena finished, wrapped the mini-computer around her wrist then checked the room. "Do we have everything?"

"Yes, all packed. Back away." Brittany sprayed down the room. "Don't worry. It won't bother these folks, just clean up any accidental prints and biohazards. They will be very clean."

Lena turned and bumped her head in the doorway, cursing.

Brittany grabbed her and led them to the elevator. "We're getting you Lasik surgery."

When the first guard fell, the others stared in shock.

Seth took the other two down just as quickly. Al gave him a questioning look but didn't say anything. Seth walked over the bodies to get closer to the remaining prisoners. A light whizzed down the tunnel illuminating the prisoners on the ground.

Jocelyn braked a badass motorcycle inches from the bodies. Graeme sat behind her and surveyed the mess.

"The Butcher went that way," he instructed.

"You got this?" she asked.

"Yeah."

She took off.

Seth called to the kids. "It's safe."

"What the hell?" Al said.

They didn't move. They were clearly *very* suspicious.

"Can any of you drive?" he asked.

No response. Finally, one kid raised his hand and stepped forward. "I can."

"Come on," Seth walked toward the transport area. "Take this truck. It might have a tracker, so abandon it as soon as you are out of the city, or by dusk. Go straight, take the first left then immediate right into an open garage. It will take you up through a parking lot, through Times Square. Follow any signs west. Don't look back."

"Thank you."

"Al, how much do you have on you?"

Al pulled out some cash. "Two hundred."

"Here. Two-seventy-five." He handed the kid the cash and pulled a pen from the glove compartment of the truck. "If you can make it to this address in Texas, you'll be safe." He wrote the address on the boy's arm. "Tell the lady, Seth sent you."

"Got it."

"Do you have implanted trackers?"

"Yes."

Seth pulled out his pocketknife and gave it to him. "Cut them out once you are out of the city and toss 'em. They're only good if someone has you within a mile distance, so you can make it for now. Do what I say. Lay low. Don't be stupid."

"We won't." The boy sounded more confident but began to tremble with relief. He called to the guys. "Let's go." They ran into the truck and after a bumpy start took off in the right direction.

"What the hell?" Al touched his shoulder. "The world is not as it appears."

"Not at all."

"Do you think the guards over there are okay?"

Seth shrugged and left the scene. "I no longer care."

Graeme leaned right with Jocelyn and they raced through the tunnels catching sight of the Butcher. He wasn't sure what they would do if they caught him. But he did have a gun.

"Can anyone hear us?" Graeme spoke over the comm.

Nothing. They were too deep in the transportation catacombs.

Jocelyn took another turn at a blood-tingling speed. His arms wrapped tighter around her. Motorcycle chase. No drones. And this time he had the laser weapons. He should feel confident.

They made a sharp left.

Man, did she drive with intent.

The lights of the other bike were in sight. Their speed increased until they were just behind. The Butcher swung a weapon backward and before he could shoot, she lifted her hand. Graeme felt a surge of heat and tingling around his hands. Then the Butcher went wobbling and sliding out of control. The light on his bike went off.

Jocelyn turned their light off as well, stopping the bike. "Shhh."

Her arm glistened in the dark as she held up her hand, moving it lightly in the air as if feeling out the space. She took a breath.

"He's coming this way. Get ready." He heard the other bike rev as she backed up, turning and swinging around a corner for safety just as the Butcher came back at them. An explosion of gunfire lit up the tunnel, sounds reverberating and echoing around them. A whish of wind swirled around their bike and he felt them encircled in heat as Jocelyn directed her palm outward, keeping it on the Butcher until he was gone. The elements seemed to calm as she took a breath then checked on him.

He took a breath. "This might not be the best time to ask, but are you bulletproof?"

"No."

"Bummer." So, she had blasting, energy field protection? Something to ask about over dinner maybe? The bike roared back to life and they took off after the Butcher.

They caught up to him, but Jocelyn cursed, slowing down. "What?"

"Rat way. Not safe. Seriously scary."

They crept deeper, watching and waiting. The Butcher switched on a high beam light. Graeme pulled out the gun he'd taken from the guard and aimed.

He hit the Butcher's back wheel spot on, causing the bike to skid and allowing Graeme a second shot at the front wheel. The gun exploded a third time and blew up the gas tank, sending fire and sparks in the confined space.

The Butcher roared as he slid and hit a wall in the tunnel. He got to his feet, lifted his arms and roared again. "Arrrrrrrh!"

"I hate it when he does that," Jocelyn said.

The Butcher's face glowed menacingly in the fire of the burning gas tank. He roared again, but this time it got cut short. His bike mysteriously flew forward and hit his knees hard, tripping him.

Graeme noted Jocelyn put her hand down and took a breath. *Interesting.*

The Butcher's shirt caught on fire and he scrambled to get it off, rolling on the ground. Then he got to his feet, let out a frustrated grunt and ran down the rat-infested tunnel.

The fire died a little, and as it did, something else became noticeable.

Thousands of red, beady eyes.

"Jocelyn?"

"Ohmigosh."

A cold shiver ran up his arms. "Turn around. Now."

She obeyed, their bike skidding a little so that his leg went down. The sound of scurrying made his skin crawl. As they righted the vehicle, the swarm of rats grew, encircling them on the walls like a tidal wave.

"Gas it!" he shouted as rats leaped on them in attack.

They both yelled in horror. He ripped one out of his hair, one clung to his back stubbornly and he reached for his laser, shooting it over the shoulder. They were on their legs, causing them both to kick wildly. He lasered them with no remorse. Finally, they outdistanced the rat wave and Jocelyn pulled to a stop.

She took a breath. Her voice hitched. "Graeme?"

On the handlebars clung a giant rat bigger than any cat he had ever seen. It opened its mouth making a rat snarl of attack.

He blasted it to kingdom come.

"That was the most disgusting thing I ever experienced," she said.

"New York rats can eat through concrete and glass," Graeme said. "The Butcher won't survive."

"I don't think so." She headed back for the surface, parked outside the yogurt shop, and checked in. Richie, Seth, and Al were all out.

"Where are the girls?" she asked.

Graeme tapped her shoulder. They both stared at the screens of the Windows on the World project. It broadcasted all over the city. "I'm going to hear about this."

He watched, grudging admiration taking over.

This is your government. Here in the building are more than forty of the state's most dangerous criminals. The cells and names of criminals played behind the text. *They are being experimented on, tested, and let loose to observe…or in some cases, directed to destroy.* Lena had pulled up the image of the Morrow's home. *If you work here, you too are a criminal. Surrender and cooperate with the police, or you will be brought to justice the hard way.*

The message repeated, but the names of the criminals were the most effective. They'd been terrorizing New York, New Jersey, and several other nearby states. Crowds stared.

Richie came up behind him. "Heh, heh, heh. The truth will set you free. Heh, heh, heh."

He and Richie hugged. City police asked them to move along behind the barricade. He turned to Jocelyn.

She was gone.

Jocelyn broke through the yogurt shop, into the open training area, and froze. Her heart skipped a beat. "Dammit, Georgie. I kept you down here for a reason."

"Sorry," she whispered. Her hands were cuffed in front of her, likely by the guard helping Cashus.

Jocelyn kicked herself. She should have tranq'd him. The guard, for his part, shook with nerves, waving his gun.

"Go over there." The guard pointed to Jocelyn's right where Lena and Brittany were against the wall.

Cashus had a syringe of blue serum pressed to Georgie's neck. "Certain death for your friend," he promised.

"And?" She kept walking, making the guard more nervous.

Brittany inched her way closer to Georgie while Lena pressed her hands to the wall, following the sounds of voices like a blind woman.

Jocelyn hugged her right hand to her stomach. She would not be transmitting energy again until her skin healed. With her left she could get either Cashus or the guard. Or she could do a power blast and send them all flying. But that wasn't safe either. She could leap and kick at Cashus and blast the guard. That seemed like an option. She walked closer until she was halfway across the long room, past Lena, and almost to Brittany.

Georgie seemed to read her mind. Her hands reached in front of her, inside the long white yogurt shop lab coat. She had a dart gun. That might work.

"How about I take the guard and you take the doctor," Georgie suggested.

Cashus stepped back and the guard blinked from one to the other suspiciously.

"Done," Jocelyn said.

Jocelyn aimed hard at the syringe and shot it backward, whiplashing Cashus's head against the wall, while Georgie spun forward and nailed the guard with her dart gun in the chest.

He in turn froze, stunned, then pointed his gun at her and shot three times.

"Nooo!"

Everyone was slow to move except Brittany. And then Jocelyn was blocked. Brittany seemed to know the guard's intent before it happened.

She leaped in front of the guard and her body flew back from the force of the first shot in her chest. The second shot sent her arms flailing like a rag doll, and the third sent her with finality into Georgie's arms, both of them falling against the wall then sliding to the floor.

Georgie cried out in shock.

The guard looked as shocked as them. "I didn't mean it."

Jocelyn slammed the man through the air into the corner. She swung back at Cashus and made sure he was down for the count. She sucked in air.

Then she ran to Brittany.

Lena cried out in confusion, crawling to them. Georgie wailed, holding her friend, unable to move. "Brittany! Brittany! Oh, God!"

Lena reached them, and took Brittany's still hand, silent tears forming. "Brittany?"

Brittany's free hand touched Georgie's. Her eyes were wide in shock. Her breath came in a light gasp, struggling for air as she tried to say something. "I-I—"

Georgie sobbed, shaking, her eyes blinded with tears. "I'm sorry I haven't been around enough. You know you're my best friend. I love you. You're my sister." She held her friend closer. "You're my family. Forever. I love you. Hold on."

Filled with a shockwave of emotion, Jocelyn's own tears formed. Nobody moved. Finally, she knelt down to take Brittany from Georgie's protective hold and lay her on the floor. Brittany stared at her desperately, pain taking hold. She closed her eyes.

Georgie took her friend's hand, her entire body weeping silently.

Finally, Brittany opened her eyes again, attempting to speak.

Jocelyn touched Georgie's arm, alerting her. "I think she's trying to say something."

"It's okay, Brittany," Georgie comforted.

Brittany gasped for each word. "I'm so…" She inhaled, a pained breath. "Going to…" She exhaled. "Get an 'A' on this project."

Georgie blinked in confusion and Jocelyn ripped open Brittany's yogurt coat to loosen the ties of her bulletproof corset. Jocelyn smiled, waiting for Georgie to realize.

"What!" Georgie screamed with outrage and relief. "You crazy—" She stopped herself. "What if this hadn't worked? It's never even been tested."

"Works," Brittany wheezed.

Lena reached blindly and touched Brittany's face with two hands, poking her in the eye. "You're alive?"

"Yes," Georgie confirmed, happily.

Jocelyn stood and they helped Brittany to her feet.

"You're welcome," Brittany said.

"She saved your life, Georgie." Jocelyn couldn't stop smiling. They'd never hear the end of it. Jocelyn got the keys from the guard and uncuffed Georgie. Georgie hugged Brittany properly before scolding again, then led her out of the building.

Jocelyn didn't want to leave Cashus. She plopped him in the wheelchair the guard had used and wheeled him out. He needed serious medical attention. She guided Lena to the wheelchair, and they made their exit via the yogurt shop.

A cheer went up from some bystanders when they came out. John Morrow was the first person to approach them.

"Are you girls okay?"

"Yeah, but there's a lot of dead people inside," Jocelyn said.

He didn't say anything.

"Sleeping," she said. "Just sleeping." She saw a hint of relief in his eyes.

They brought Cashus to an ambulance and the EMTs helped lay him on a gurney. Jocelyn used the restraints and bound him over chest, arms and legs. "He's a violent psychotic delusional," she told the crew. Newell walked over and stood on the other side of the gurney. He lifted a brow while she insisted, "He needs to be in the most secure psychiatric facility you have. *Do not* engage in conversation with him."

They looked uncertain and didn't do anything.

"You heard her," Newell said. "She knows. Now move it." They moved.

She smiled at the agent. He gave her a slow nod then walked away. Government agencies were filling up the sides of the roads. He went to direct them.

Jocelyn joined the girls in the middle of Times Square. They were about to leave when a noise behind them got her attention. She turned. The manhole cover moved.

"Get back!" she shouted.

The manhole cover lifted and slid powerfully down the road, stopping at the feet of John and Tim. Smoke and dust billowed out. Jocelyn pushed the girls back protectively with her arms.

"I can't see!" Lena panicked.

"None of us can," Brit explained. "It's smoke or dust. Ugh. And it stinks."

The smoke cleared and towering before them stood the unstoppable Butcher.

"Seriously," Georgie said. "I mean, seriously?"

Jocelyn didn't move.

The Butcher did. He put his hands up in victory and roared. People gasped and took cover. He was covered in rats. They clung to his legs, his arms, his chest. He started to grab them and throw them at the crowd causing more havoc as the rats rolled and scurried about.

With the last rat removed, he took a breath then about to roar again, choked instead. His head went back in agonized strain; his face seized up and contorted horrifically. She thought he would have a seizure. Then he completely relaxed, shrugged and fell forward.

A rat still on his back looked up, blinked in frightened surprise, and ran off. Two more rats peeked out from the manhole, crawled up and over the Butcher, and followed. Tourists screamed in terror and ran.

Tim and Newell went to the body, weapons at the ready.

Newell checked his pulse. "Dead."

Tim holstered his gun. "Too bad."

Jocelyn closed her eyes. It was over for now. John motioned for her to leave. She didn't need to be urged. Just past the SWAT, the ambulances, FEMA, and the FBI, stood four really great guys who parted the way and applauded as the girls walked by.

Holding hands, Jocelyn, Georgie, Brittany, and Lena walked up to the pie shop.

Smiling like heroes.

EPILOGUE

Sabrina walked into Ford's office in the A & R Towers wearing the dress and lab coat she'd had on Friday.

"Thanks for coming." She clutched a folder in her hands. "Ford…I've got something."

He took in her drawn eyes, shaking hands, and determined face. "When did you last sleep?"

"I don't know. What's today?"

"You need rest."

"Ford." Sabrina stopped him. "I've *got* something."

Ford understood. *Benny.*

"I can't tell you where the information came from so don't ask."

"If it's the government, it's a trap," Ford warned.

"It's not. They're maybe running from the government. I'm not sure." She pulled a single paper from the file and handed it to him. "The blood sample I have is astonishing. The DNA is not just self-healing, it has markers that search and replace bad DNA with seemingly organic efficiency." She pulled out some more papers—a list. "This is everything I need. Lab, staff, supplies. I want Margaret Little as well. She worked closest with Illeana. She might remember something. Sabrina began shaking again. "And we'll need extra security. The best. Everyone needs to have deep background checks done."

"What are you saying?"

"I'm saying…" Sabrina bit her lip, uncertain. "This work was Illeana's. I'm sure of it. It has all the hallmarks." She took a breath. "I'm saying, I don't think their death was an accident."

Ford took the list, nodding as he scanned. Then he told her the truth. "I never thought it was."

Rex slid the picture a few inches on the bar to his old Army buddy.

His friend glanced down. "Yeah. That's her."

"What can you tell me?"

"Not much. We picked up her and another agent from a mission. I don't know what happened after, but word was she was some kind of special government asset. They were known as a kickass team, to be honest. You wouldn't believe it to meet her. Seems normal and sweet, but killer instincts."

"Great." Rex didn't like any of that. "What do you think she wants with my family?"

His buddy shrugged. "She might be spying, or they want an imbed in the family. Maybe she's supposed to get to your mom. Could be anything. The leaders of Holliwell don't necessarily have a moral compass. They do what they think they need to do—to keep their power or get more. Sometimes it's good for the country too." He slid the photo back, taking a drink of his beer. "Don't mess with Holliwell, brother. Nothing good can come from it."

"Yeah," Rex said. Except now his family was involved. And whoever this girl really was, she wanted something.

But what? And who was she working for?

The SOI closed the door of the NSA office behind him. "What do you mean we lost all communication?"

"Video, audio, everything," the NSA agent said.

"The backup system?" Jerry asked.

"That too."

"Did the hacker leave a signature?"

"Hehehehehehheh," the agent said.

"Are you laughing?"

"No, sir. That's the signature."

Jerry leaned back in the chair. He had that one coming to him. "What's the street view?"

"The same. Until we get here. Then this happens."

They watched as Project Sunday walked to the center of the intersection and stared up at the camera—for a long time.

"It's as if she knows we're watching," the agent said.

"She knows," Jerry said.

Satisfied, Project Sunday planted one foot over the other and spun her body, a single arm out. The connection was lost.

"All the cameras and traffic lights malfunctioned in a ten-block radius," the agent said.

"Interesting."

The NSA agent turned to him and Mercer. "Do you want to bring her in?"

"Bring her in?" Jerry repeated. "No. No. She's well connected now. Her boyfriend's mother is going to be elected senator. There's value in that. It's about to get interesting."

"Yes, sir. Shall we keep watching her?"

"Oh, yes. Keep an eye. Let me know if she leaves the city or does anything suspicious. But leave her alone. Let her get comfortable."

"But, sir."

Jerry turned and raised a brow in question.

"Don't you think she was sending a message?"

"She blasted out the camera and electrical grid in a ten-block radius. Yes, I would call that a message." Jerry explained further. "She's here to stay. So watch out."

Seth grandly held the door of the pie shop for the girls. They divested themselves of their disguises and tossed them in the trash as they walked in. Jocelyn's guard shirt was filthy, and there was blood on her white shirt that seeped through from the outer one. She still had her utility belt. She pulled the wig from her pouch and pulled the used brown hair over her head. They made their way to the counter and took four stools. The guys took a booth and gave them some time.

They put in their pie requests and Jocelyn went to the restroom to clean up. She washed her left hand and wiped the dirt streaks from her face, then gave it a scrub. She finally appeared less like a soldier of war and more like a human. She stared a moment, then pulled off the wig and tossed it in the trash. She touched the soft bits that finally came up evenly around her head.

Growing.

The others smiled at her when she returned. Her friends. Real friends. It was still hard to take in.

The server behind the counter studied their appearance curiously, delivering their pie. "Coconut cream, apple, cherry, and two chocolate cream."

"Thank you," they said.

Lena bent over, nearly putting her nose in the coconut cream looking for her spoon. Georgie put a spoon in her hand.

Richie came up behind Lena and surprised her with glasses. "I found your extra pair with our supplies."

"Thank you!" Lena turned quickly and blindly, her head knocking his chin. They both apologized profusely. She grabbed his chest reaching for her glasses and he put them in her hand. Her brilliant grin seemed to make him nervous and he patted his hair self-consciously, suddenly aware, before hurrying back to the booth.

Brittany laughed. Georgie kicked Brittany. Jocelyn thought it was cute.

Lena put her glasses on and checked things out. "I can see!" She dove into her coconut cream with gusto.

"So, I have to ask," the server said, leaning over the counter. "You all came from the chaos down the street. What have you been up to this morning?"

Lena's sass came back with the helping of sugar. "Just servin' up a little truth."

"And justice," Georgie added.

Brittany released her bulletproof corset so she could eat. "And the American way."

Jocelyn looked down her row of friends and finished it. "Together." They smiled at her. Yeah, together sounded really nice.

Meghana and Morgan were at a table behind them. "I want to be like them when I grow up," Meghana said.

Jocelyn heard and turned to them with a smile and a beckoning hand. Meghana came over right away and Brittany chatted her up.

Jocelyn pushed her extra pie to the empty seat on her right. When nothing happened, she took a spoon from the jar of utensils on the counter and slid it next to the pie. She kept her focus on her own pie when Morgan casually took the stool, putting her designer bag on the hook underneath.

"Heroes get pie."

"I didn't do anything," Morgan said.

Jocelyn turned her head. "I heard about you. You saved that girl."

Morgan smiled a little, picking up the spoon. "Chocolate cream is my favorite."

I remember.

"My mom used to make it," they said in unison. They turned to each other, questioning. Jocelyn smiled. Morgan shook it off and dug into the pie.

"Thanks for the scarf." Jocelyn held up her hand. The scarf had done the trick.

"You can keep it. Or throw it out. It's ruined."

"I can clean it," Brittany said. "Then we can give it to a grandma." She shuddered as if she couldn't believe Morgan would wear such an old lady accessory.

Morgan gasped.

"And we're back," Georgie said.

The bell of the shop rang, and recognizing the heavy cadence, Jocelyn turned in time to hear her name boomed across the tile. It was John. "Jocelyn Marques?"

She stayed still, uncertain if she was in trouble. "Yes?"

He crossed his arms over his chest and checked out the place, nodding approval to the group. "We're expecting you for dinner next Saturday. And brunch. So you should probably spend the night. Kymber will make you go to church but then we're going to barbeque." It wasn't an invitation. It was an order. "Family day."

"Okay." *They were expecting her.* She swallowed hard. *For family day.*

His hands went to his hips. "Are you too embarrassed to give your old man a hug in front of your friends?"

Her throat tightened more. She shoved off the stool and ran the few steps needed.

He squeezed her hard. She squeezed back. Then he ruffled the top of her blue-black fuzz and told her to be there by five. "You can bring your friends if you want. They're growin' on me."

He walked outside and stopped in front of Seth who had just pulled the outlet cap off a fire hydrant. Seth looked up guiltily then sat on the hydrant, wiping his brow. "Sure is hot today."

"I'm going to pretend I don't see what's about to happen. Have a good day."

"Later, LT."

Seth pulled the cap, water burst out and he used his strength to direct it straight into the air. Kids came running around excitedly, cooling off and dodging the water.

Graeme got up and tugged her hand. "Come on. Let's play."

They went out and laughed at the giant spray. Jocelyn hadn't really moved water before. She circled it slowly, gaining momentum. The water twisted upward and spread wide at the top, like an umbrella. The others joined and kids followed her as she ran around in a circle.

When everyone came underneath and looked up at the magical water fountain, she stopped, wrapped her arms around

Graeme for cover, and let the glistening, cold water collapse downward, garnering squeals of laughter and delight. She lifted her face in happiness.

They were the sounds of her most cherished memories.

Family.

THE END

…for now.

Dear Reader,

If you liked *Glisten*, I would love to have you leave a review on your favorite social media and book review spots. Your positive review really makes a difference to indie authors. And please check out *Shimmer*! The next installment is action-packed!

I hope you will also keep in touch on social media or through my newsletter where I run monthly contests and share early news on books as well things that inspire my daily dreams and schemes. Please visit my website: www.triciacerrone.com to sign up. You can find me on social media as @triciacerrone.

Happy Reading!
Tricia Cerrone

BOOKS BY TRICIA CERRONE

The Black Swan Files
001: Glimmer
002: Glisten
003: Shimmer

BOOKS BY TRICIA CERRONE
WRITING AS TRISH ALBRIGHT

Keepers of the Legacy
Siren's Song
Siren's Secret

The Time Keeper